Winter

By
Allan Martin

Dedication

As always, to Vivien

Table of Contents

Prologue

No-one noticed the odd hump in the centre of the wide forecourt in front of the main entrance to the castle until it began to get light. But, it being almost the last day of November, that didn't happen till around half past seven. And the snow helped to cover it up too; two inches had fallen during the night. The staff had been up for a good while, but it was only when Old Jaak started sweeping the snow away from the paving in front of the open porch that he caught sight of it. His first assumption was of an animal, perhaps a deer. Then he saw the glint and realised there was something sticking up out of it into the chill morning air.

He went back to the outbuilding where he kept his tools and fetched an electric torch. Now he recognised the projection from the snowy hump as the point of a cavalry sabre. He called his wife Eda from the kitchen, where she was getting ready to prepare the general's breakfast. He liked to have breakfast in the dining-room promptly at eight. She put on her boots while Jaak fetched the wooden snow shovel. Then she held the torch while Jaak cleared the snow from around the hump. But she sensed he was avoiding the hump itself.

"What's the matter?" she asked impatiently.

"I know what this is," he said, "I saw enough in the war."

"A body?" She wasn't stupid.

"Aye. But the sword gives me a bad feeling. That's the bit that isn't right. If it's a body, that is. A cavalryman wouldn't leave his sword sticking through his latest victim."

"So we'd better see what it is, then," said Eda briskly, "You hold the torch and I'll use the brush."

Her first sweep at the top of the hump revealed a dark coloured leather coat. They both recognised it.

"*Kurat!*" cursed Jaak. "Quickly, uncover the head."

The man lay on his side, his arms and legs drawn up to his chest and his head on the ground. "I can't use the brush on him, not on his face." She brushed a little of the snow from the face with her hand.

"Holy Spirit help us!" she muttered.

1

Friday, 29th November, 1935

At 7.45 a.m. *Ülemkomissar* Jüri Hallmets and his wife
Kirsti came out of Tallinn's Baltic Railway Station
through the archway in the main building, and paused at
the top of the steps. They exchanged a swift kiss and a
squeeze of hands, before Kirsti turned to the left to make
for the Technical Institute. The chief inspector crossed the
road and set off along Nunne Street, entering the Old
Town area at the spot where the Nun's Gate used to be. It
had snowed during the night, but the feet of others before
him had already cleared a slushy path along the pavement.
The sky was a leaden grey, with a puffiness suggesting
more snow might be on the way. Arriving at the top of
Pikk Street, he turned left, and walked on down until he
reached Police Headquarters, near the bottom, just before
you got to St. Olav's Church. He took the lift to the third
floor, and arrived at his office just before eight.

As usual, he spent the first half hour digesting the
morning papers, with a cup of coffee to keep him alert.
The coffee was necessary because much of the content of
the printed media was rather bland. Under the censorship
introduced earlier that year, the only political or world
news which could be printed was that issued by the NPS,
the National Propaganda Service. In one way, that was
very positive: no bad news was printed, so that everything
in the world seemed very rosy, unless it was far away and
not at all relevant to Estonia. But if you wanted to know

what was really happening in the world, even in your own country, you had to turn to the wireless, and tune into Helsinki.

The main headline in *Pealinna Uudised* (Capital City News), was a speech by the President, Konstantin Päts, congratulating those who had participated so far in the campaign to replace foreign surnames with Estonian ones. Hallmets could see the merit in this. When surnames had been required by the Russian imperial bureaucracy back in the nineteenth century, the German barons who owned most of the land had given many of their peasants German surnames. And native Estonians who wanted to get on in the world also found it useful to have a German name; then you could be perceived as part of the ruling class. But now that Estonia was finally free, after seven centuries of rule by German barons – even if the ultimate overlord was the Teutonic Order, or the King of Sweden, or the Tsar of All the Russias – it seemed sensible to replace the names acquired in the past with ones which proclaimed your own heritage. Hallmets himself didn't need to change his name; Hallmets was Estonian enough (it meant 'grey forest').

But he also knew there were things happening, both in Estonia and in the world, that people were not being told about. That included crime. If a murder was committed, nothing would appear in the papers until after it had been solved and the trial held. He knew from occasional meetings with *Pealinna Uudised's* crime reporter Jaan Kallas how frustrating this could be. Kallas had, before the censorship, loved to speculate about any crime as yet unsolved, often at great length. Now he was reduced to reporting yet another success for the police in apprehending a lawbreaker or enemy of the state.

4

There was plenty of safe news inside the paper, about social events, concerts, plans to erect Christmas Trees in town centres, and, especially, sport. And of course, speeches and parades. Indeed, every week there seemed to be a parade by one or other of the official organisations permitted under the dictatorship. Political parties had been banned the previous year, shortly after Päts had assumed full powers. He had done that simply by, as Acting President, declaring a state of emergency. Päts was not foolish, and had acted in concert with General Johan Laidoner, the nation's military hero, who had immediately been appointed army commander-in-chief. Now the newly-formed Fatherland Union was the only permitted political organisation.

Hallmets had finished the papers in twenty-five minutes, and was just wondering what to do next when the phone rang. It was his secretary Marta, telling him that Colonel Reinart at the Interior Ministry was on the line. Hallmets allowed some moments to pass before picking up the instrument on his desk. His relationship with Colonel Reinart was fairly cordial, but never casual. Reinart always phoned for a reason.

"*Tere hommikust, Kolonel!* What can I do for you?"

"Good morning to you too, Chief Inspector. How are you?" The colonel's voice was as suave as his person.

"I'm fine, Colonel. Yourself?"

"Yes, I'm also well. Thank you for asking. There's something I'd like you to look into."

"Please, tell me more."

"This is very sensitive, and we need it sorted out as quickly as possible. It's General Madrus. You know him?"

"He was in Supplies during the war, wasn't he? I met him a couple of times then. But that was a long time ago. I noticed he retired a few years back. What's he been up to?"

"I'd rather not go into that on the phone, if you don't mind."

"Is it relevant to us?" Hallmets was head of the National Special Crimes Unit, set up two years previously, in 1933, after he and his team had successfully dealt with the murder of a senior policeman in Tallinn. The Unit was called in to deal with crimes which required a national, as opposed to the local, police force to address. Sometimes local police were obliged, reluctantly, to involve the unit, when they had run out of ideas on a case. On other occasions, when there was a national or even international dimension, the unit's involvement was ordered from the Interior Ministry. So Hallmets' question was purely formal. But he asked it in order to remind the colonel that he was his own man, that if he judged it not to be appropriate he would not take it. He had no intention of doing the regime's dirty work. The political police existed for that. Maybe also agencies even he didn't know about.

After a pause, Colonel Reinart replied. "I think you'll agree that it is, Chief Inspector. Look, how soon could you get over here."

"Five minutes do?"

Since the Interior Ministry was next door to Police Headquarters, Hallmets did not have far to go. The colonel's office was on the third floor, at the side, with a view across the lane between the two buildings.

He accepted the offer of coffee. Reinart always managed to get hold of the best quality, whatever it was he was looking for. The colonel was his usual immaculately presented self, his uniform pressed, his boots gleaming, his hair neatly oiled and combed back, his moustache perfectly trimmed, his expression urbane and his manner courteous. In short, a perfect actor.

He waved Hallmets to a leather upholstered chair opposite his desk of polished oak. The coffee was delivered in minutes by Reinart's secretary, a slim woman with long plaited ginger hair and a neutral expression.

"Thank you, Roosa," murmured the colonel. The woman merely nodded, and silently left.

"Nice coffee," began Hallmets, "Tell me about General Madrus."

"He's dead."

"I rather suspected that might be the case. How?"

"It looks as if he's killed himself!"

"Looks as if?"

"No, he probably has. The thing is, we need to know why."

"It's always helpful to know why someone killed themselves. But what's your interest in it?"

"We'd like to know whether there's a political dimension."

"Another enemy of the state?"

Reinart smiled faintly. "Let me give you bit more background. As you said, the general retired from the army; that was five years ago, in June 1930. He retired to an estate near Viljandi. Rauakivi, it's called. It was awarded to him by the government in 1922, as a reward for his services during the war. More than either of us got, I should add."

"Don't tell me. He got bored being a landowner. Too few people to order about. Started betting on the horses. Lost big-time. Took to drink. Shot himself."

"If only. Unfortunately, as far as we know, only the first

bit's right. Maybe he did get bored, or maybe he was always political, and just kept it quiet, as was the correct thing for a serving officer. Anyway, we've picked up a rumour that he was involved with the League of Veterans."

"Vaps? Are we still allowed to mention them?"

"In this room, we can talk about anything. There are no microphones or hidden cameras. You'll know that Vaps was founded to further the interests of veterans of the War of Independence. Its initial focus was on making sure veterans were given land and support to farm it. That was fine."

"Then it got political."

"Quite. That was Artur Sirk's doing. He encouraged people who weren't veterans to join, and moved the organisation politically towards the far right. They even began to adopt some the trappings of the fascist parties."

"Black berets, the 'Roman salute,' the *führerprinzip*."

"Exactly. Anyway, as everyone knows, it looked as though they were going to stage a *coup d'état* once they'd won the presidential election last year, and that's why our current President stepped in to take emergency power."

"Some folk might say he was the one who staged the coup."

"They would be very unwise to do so."

"The evidence at their trial was very unconvincing. Now most of the Vaps people are already out of prison. Someone even let Sirk escape from the Patarei Prison."

"Take it from me, we knew more than was said at the trial."

"Yes, Colonel, I'm sure you had bulging files of rumour and innuendo. Anyone can make up what they want, and anyone can choose to believe it. But that's not evidence.

What's your point?"

"The point is, and this is just within these four walls, that we think they're planning another coup. Sirk is just across the water in Finland, and we've been keeping a close eye on him, as have the Finns, since he's been meeting with elements of the Lapua Movement."

"Now they were a nasty bunch. Kidnap and murder aren't the usual tools of political organisations. Except maybe in Germany. But wasn't Lapua banned there a few years ago"

"Yes, 1932, after they kidnapped ex-president Ståhlberg and his wife. But since then they formed a new party, IKL, The People's Patriotic Movement. Our fear is that Sirk's going to bring them over here to help Vaps stage the coup that was pe-empted last year."

"And you think General Madrus might be involved?"

"We don't know. We've no hard evidence to suggest he's been involved in politics since his retirement. But we've heard whispers that the coup attempt will happen soon. And that Madrus was involved. It's only rumour, and, like you, I take it with a pinch of salt. But unlike you, I can't ignore it, since there might just be something there. If they stage a coup, and prominent generals who fought in the War come out in favour, they might just succeed."

"And that wouldn't be good for servants of the present regime. Like yourself."

"And you too, don't forget that, chief inspector."

"Point taken. Anyway, that's all speculation. Tell me about his death."

"All we know at this moment is that General Madrus was found dead this morning, on the forecourt of his mansion. It looks like he fell on his sword."

"Like the Romans used to do?"

"This might be nothing to do with Vaps, and if that were the case I'd be very happy. Maybe a scandal involving him with a Turkish belly-dancer will break next week. But, coming at this time, there could be a link, and we'd like to be sure one way or the other."

"Don't you have your own people to do that?"

"The political police are good at what they do. But that's not investigation. At least, not this kind. We need a good investigator to get to the bottom of it. And preferably someone patently apolitical."

"Thanks for the compliment, but I'm not apolitical."

"That may be even better. We know you don't agree with the emergency rule. What better person to discover whether Madrus was involved in a plot against democracy."

"What democracy?"

"Come, come, Hallmets. Don't be too rhetorical. What we have now I agree is rather limited. But compare it to the sort of regime Sirk and his creatures will set up. It's there to see already in Italy and Germany. In that sort of regime we'd both be dead men."

"You seem to have got wind of the event very quickly. News of suspicious deaths usually come to us via the county police headquarters, when they've got to the point that they need help."

"There are a number of people in the country that the political police like to keep an eye on. Since the emergency was declared, that number has obviously increased, and retired generals were added to the list. The local police have orders to report any incident involving any of these people directly to us here, so that if necessary we can take immediate action. I've already told the police in Viljandi that you're coming. Oh, and one other thing.

No statements to the press. Once we have a good idea of what happened, and can decide exactly what information can be released, we'll do that through the NPS. Good luck, and do keep me informed of any developments."

2

Back in his office, Hallmets glanced at his watch. 9.15 am. The team would meet at ten. The Madrus case would be the main business. The colonel, as usual, focused on possible political aspects. But an old soldier falling on his sword, a long time after the war, was an unusual occurrence, even if there were no political angle. After all, if the man wanted to kill himself, why not just use his old army revolver. He probably kept it in the top drawer of his desk, or at the foot of his wardrobe. And do it in the comfort of his lounge or his study.

He asked Marta to call the police station in Viljandi, in the south of Estonia. Two minutes later he was connected to the duty sergeant. Hallmets introduced himself.

"Good morning, sir," said the sergeant, "I'm Sergeant Lauk. It was me who phoned the Interior Ministry to let them know what had happened. Someone from the Ministry phoned back later and said your unit had been alerted. How can we help you?"

"Tell me, sergeant, who's in charge of the case at the moment?"

"That would be Inspector Einmann."

The name did not ring a bell with Hallmets. That was unusual. "Is the inspector available? I'd like a word with him."

"No, sir, he's over at the castle, that is, er, was, the general's residence. Can I get a message to him for you? I'm afraid the telephone line to the castle has gone down because of the snow. It's quite thick here. But I can send someone on a motor-bike, who ought to be able to get through."

"Thank you. Yes, can you let him know that I'll come down with a couple of colleagues this morning. We'll go straight to the castle, if that's possible."

"How are you coming down, sir? I mean, on the train or in a car. If you're in a car, take care, the roads could be tricky. There's a lot of snow lying about, and it could start again any time."

"Thanks for the warning. We'll bear that in mind. I'll hope to see you later today."

Hallmets asked Marta to call Lembit, the unit's driver, and let him know they'd be heading off about eleven for Viljandi. He should bring his overnight bag. Then he got Marta to call off a couple of meetings, give his apologies for absence at another, and put other activities on hold. He wasn't sure how long they'd be down in Viljandi, but it was best to be on the safe side. Luckily they had no case on, and the plan had been to spend the week working on some training materials for new CID officers; that would have to wait. Besides, the prospect of a real investigation was a lot more inviting.

At ten his team gathered in the workroom next to Hallmets' office. Inspector Henno Lesser, Hallmets' number two; tall and thin, with receding brown hair, an experienced officer as sharp as his nose, who'd previously worked in Viljandi. Sergeant Eva Larsson, slim and athletic, her long blond hair twisted into a braid at the back; she came from one of the Swedish-speaking villages on the west coast. Officer Ilmar Hekk, short, plump and balding, sometimes called 'the Invisible Man,' could disappear in a small group of people. A man with a gift for being unnoticed was a valuable asset. Finally Officer Ants Kadakas, who'd joined the team after his police training. He'd worked with Hallmets, as had the others, before the unit had been set up. He'd been seconded from the army, but realised then that the military wasn't his cup of tea, and Hallmets had helped him make the transition. Tall and handsome with short fair hair, part of his emancipation from military discipline had been discovering how to think for himself. At her desk by the door of the workroom sat Marta Kukk, the unit's secretary, older, experienced and well-organised, and fazed by nothing. The only member absent was the unit's driver, Lembit Osav, a useful mechanic and extra pair of eyes when one was needed.

Hallmets explained that they'd been asked to investigate the death of General Madrus. The news of the general's death caused a certain amount of stir. Madrus hadn't been one of the well-known figures in the War of Independence, like General Põdder, who'd died a few years previously, or General Laidoner, who'd led Estonia's army in the fight for independence. But he was nevertheless remembered as one of the leaders of the military struggle, though few could have said what he actually did.

"Viljandi, that's your neck of the woods, Henno," said Hallmets to Lesser, "Do you know anything about Madrus?"

"Not a great deal. He lived in a big house not far from the town," said Lesser, "Rauakivi Castle, it's called."

"A real castle?" asked Larsson, "From the Middle Ages. Like the one in Põltsamaa? But it's just a ruin."

"No, no," replied Lesser, "A nineteenth-century manor house, it was just called a castle. It's quite impressive building, a big white building, with lots of turrets. Modelled on a romantic-era mansion in Scotland, so I was told."

"Interesting. Anything you can tell us about the general's life?"

"Well, we never saw very much of him in the town. He was away a lot when he was still in the army. Once he retired he was seen about a bit more, opening fetes, turning up at Independence Day parades, honorary president of this and that. But he didn't really get involved in the day-to-day life of the town. Kept to his estate. I heard he did a lot of hunting. There was a local taxidermist who did a lot of work for him. I only went out to the castle professionally once, when he had some shotguns stolen. He was really annoyed, he'd had them hand-made in England, said they were worth a fortune. We never found them, reckoned they'd left the country the same day they were stolen. Same day the taxidermist's apprentice vanished. We never found him either."

"Any rumours about him being involved in politics?"

"Not that I heard. And his speeches at events were always very bland."

"Any scandals?"

"Not a whiff. The impression we got was that he was just very dull."

"Okay, that's very helpful. It's going to be useful having you there, Henno, you'll still know some of the local cops. I was only over there on business a couple of times when I was based in Tartu. Anyway, we should get down there as soon as possible. We could go down and back by train every day, but it takes at least two hours each way, and that's a lot of time that could be better used."

"So when do we go, boss?" asked Hekk.

"Today, soon as we can. I called the local police, so they know we're coming. I'll try to take the car straight to the castle, though apparently the weather's not so good. I'll take Henno and Eva too. Ilmar, do you mind going down on the train? I'd like someone at the police station there as soon as possible."

"No problem," said Hekk.

"Good. Sergeant Lauk seems to be in charge at the moment. If you hang on there, I'll bring you up to date once we arrive from the castle."

"Lauk!" said Lesser, "Is he still there? He's all right, knows the place inside out."

Hallmets turned to Kadakas, who was about to ask a question, "Ants, I'm sorry, but I need someone to stay in Tallinn for the moment. We'll probably need information that's only accessible up here. Or people here to be interviewed. Can you do that?"

Kadakas looked disappointed, but put a brave face on it. "Yes, sir. You can count on me."

"Thank you, Ants. All right, it's 10.15 now. Let's meet up again at eleven, and then we can get off. That gives you time to make any calls you need and round up your travel bags."

"Actually," put in Lesser, "Do you mind if I stay with my cousin Greete? She lives in Viljandi – her husband's a lawyer, Aarne Kirss is his name."

"Of course," said Hallmets, "Thanks, Henno, you're saving the unit's budget a few kroons! And it's useful having people we know on the spot – they may have heard something useful."

"If I ring them now, they could probably suggest a good place for you to stay. Unless Marta's already got something arranged, that is."

They all looked towards Marta, who shook her head. "Not yet," she said, "A few suggestions would be useful."

16

"Till eleven, then," announced Hallmets, "Ants, can you hang on a moment."

The others filed out to fetch the overnight bags they kept in lockers in the store room along the corridor, phone anyone they needed to inform that they'd be away for a few days, and get something to eat.

Hallmets motioned Kadakas into his office, and offered him a seat. "I know it's disappointing to be stuck here, Ants, but you know that it's important we have someone here to hold the fort. Take note of the fact that I trust you to do it. The first thing I'd like you to do is get any information you can on General Madrus. Start off in our archives. I'll phone later in the afternoon to let you know what's going on."

"What about the newspapers? They'll have archives too."

"That's true. But stick with what you can find downstairs for today, till we've a better idea of what we might be looking for."

Kadakas set off for the archive room in the basement of the building. Marta popped her head round the office door ten minutes later. Lesser's cousin had suggested a place where her husband had clients from out of town to stay, and he knew to be modest but comfortable. Just right for people who wanted to keep a fairly low profile. She'd phoned them right away and mentioning the name of Dr Kirss the lawyer smoothed the way for bookings for Hallmets, Larsson, Hekk and Lembit.

At 10.35 a messenger brought a large brown envelope, closed with the seal of the Ministry of the Interior, bearing the instruction, "To be opened only by *Ülemkomissar* Hallmets." It contained several sheets of paper, all reports from the political police relating to General Madrus.

However, there was nothing in it which looked either secret or suspicious. If anything, it showed the general living a rather tedious and repetitive existence. As he closed the file, Hallmets shook his head, wondering again why so much money, which could be used fighting crime, was spent on a political police force.

For a moment he regretted having to go down in the car. The roads were not all metalled, and if the snow were to return, could be dangerous. The train would be a much smoother and probably quicker journey. However, having the car at their disposal down in Viljandi would be very useful.

He remembered with a jolt that he hadn't told Kirsti he wouldn't be home for a few days. He asked Marta to call the library at the Technical Institute of Tallinn, and ask for *Proua* Hallmets. A few minutes later he was speaking to his wife. She wasn't unduly surprised, as this wasn't the first time her husband had to be out of town at a moment's notice for a case. The unit had had to deal with odd cases all over Estonia in the two years since it had been set up, and even a few which required some investigation in Latvia or Finland.

Hallmets had met and married Kirsti when he'd been doing his police training in Scotland. She'd readily come back to Estonia with him, and learned the difficult Estonian language remarkably quickly, the benefits of immersion. She'd also changed the spelling of her name, replacing the 'y' at the end with an 'i' so that Estonians could pronounce it correctly. When they'd been living in Estonia's second city of Tartu, she'd worked in the University Library. And when they moved to Tallinn, thanks to her experience in Tartu and her excellent linguistic skills, she'd quickly found a post in the library

18

of the Technical Institute. Their daughter Liisa they'd left in Tartu, as she was a student at the University, but their son Juhan had moved with them to Tallinn, and now attended the gymnasium in Nõmme, the suburb where the family lived.

3

By eleven they were all back, with the exception of Kadakas. Hallmets kept his overnight bag in a cupboard in his office, so he was ready to go too. He made sure he also had his pistol – a Browning FN1910 – and slipped the material sent from the Ministry into his briefcase. Marta gave them the details of their accommodation in Viljandi – The Elk Tavern, on Tartu Street, not far from Town Hall Square – then they went down to the main door of the building and out onto Pikk Street. Hekk set off for the railway station. There was a train at twelve that should get him into Viljandi at half past two.

After a few moments a sleek black Volvo Pv652 sedan slid up to the entrance, and the uniformed driver leapt out and saluted Hallmets smartly, before opening the rear door for them.

"*Tere, Lembit!*" Hallmets greeted him, "I hope you brought your overnight stuff."

"No problems, boss. I'm always up for a trip. And the missus can get them novels read without me always talking to her. Viljandi, nice little town. Just leave your bags there and I'll stow them in the back. Make yourselves comfortable, folks, and we'll be off in a jiffy."

Inside, the smell of leather filled the car. It was indeed very comfortable, the envy of the other senior officers at Pikk Street. The car and its driver had been part of the deal to persuade Hallmets to take up leadership of the new unit two years previously, and to move up from Tartu to Tallinn. Both were very useful elements of the team. The car gave Hallmets a certain amount of status, and Lembit was an extra pair of eyes and ears who could, as simply a driver, talk to people who would have said nothing in the presence of a policeman.

Lembit steered the car smoothly into the traffic and headed up Pikk Street. It took a while to get through the slow-moving traffic in the streets of the Old Town, and reach the main road heading to the resort town of Pärnu, on the Gulf of Riga. The road had been tarmacked a few years previously and the going was smooth. Once out of the city, the traffic soon dwindled. However, that meant there was still a lot of snow lying on the road, so Lembit had to drive carefully, and they didn't make the speed they might have in the summer. The interior of the car was cold, despite the winter coats they were all wearing, and the blankets Lembit provided came in useful. The car had a heater, but Lembit didn't want to risk running down the battery, given that he might have to use the windscreen wipers and headlights if it started snowing.

At one o'clock they reached Pärnu, crossing the long bridge over the wide Pärnu river, and passing through the Old Town, which had been a fortress in the Middle Ages. They stopped briefly for lunch at a café on the road out of town: cabbage rolls and boiled potatoes, with coffee, something hot and filling to keep them going on a cold day.

The coastal road south from Pärnu would have taken them all the way to the Latvian capital Riga, but after a few kilometres Lembit swung the car to the left, onto a road signposted for Valga, on Estonia's southern border with Latvia, and thirty kilometres later, he turned left again onto the road to Viljandi. So far the snow had held off, but now it began, and soon they had slowed to a crawl with the wipers seeming hardly able to keep up with the snow mounting on the windscreen.

Lembit rapped with a knuckle on the glass screen separating the passengers from the driver. Hallmets leaned forward and slid the centre panel aside. "What's up?" he asked.

"Any of you know exactly where the castle is. I saw on the map that it's somewhere along this road, but I'm not sure I'll be able to spot the entrance."

"Don't worry," called Lesser, "I think I'd know it. On a sharp corner just after a stone bridge. I'll give you a shout when we're nearly there."

Twenty minutes later, Lesser leaned forward again. "Here's the bridge. Now it should be along here." And a few minutes later, "Those two round stone gateposts, that's it."

The car swung right between the gateposts onto a gravel track leading through trees. They could soon make out through the snow a grey stone wall, about two meters high, and now the car had to stop at an arched gate. The wrought-iron double gate was shut, guarded by a uniformed policeman, huddled into a wooden sentry box. The man was completely muffled up, in a long coat, a heavy muffler wrapped round his neck and the lower part of his face, a fur hat, and thick woollen mittens knitted in black and white in a traditional pattern. Lembit explained to the man who they were, and as he did so Lesser, who was sitting at the driver's side of the car, wound down his window and greeted the man, "*Tere, Ivo! Kuidas läheb?*"

The man gave Lesser a wave. "Good afternoon, inspector. I'm well, since you ask. Not seen you for a good while. How are you liking the big city, then?"

"Suits me fine," replied Lesser, "But it's nice to come back here now and then. How are the family?"

"Oh, they're good too, sir. Our youngest daughter got

married just last year, so we've only the one still at home. Anyway, I better let you through the gate, eh, otherwise you'll catch your death of cold." He pushed open first one of the gates, then the other, then waved them through.

Lembit followed what he thought was the line of the drive across the snow-covered forecourt and halted at the main door of the castle.

4

Lesser was right: 'castle' wasn't quite the right word. The building has been put up in the 1870s for a Baltic German baron who loved all things Scottish, and was designed in what he thought was an appropriate *hommage* to the country he so admired. A solid, low-lying whitewashed stone building with stepped gables and round towers lay before them. To their left a series of outbuildings disappeared into the swirling snow. In front of the house the wide forecourt was flanked by grey stone walls, converging on a gateway large enough for the entry and exit of horse-drawn vehicles. At the centre of the main building, an open porch supported by solid stone columns sheltered the main door.

Lembit exited the car smartly out and opened the passenger door on the side closest to the castle door, allowing the three passengers to get directly into the shelter of the porch. The iron handle of a bell-pull was visible by the heavy wooden door, and Lesser gave it a couple of good yanks. They could hear a bell jangling inside, and soon the door was opened by a uniformed officer.

"DCI Hallmets from Tallinn," said Hallmets.

The officer saluted and opened the door. "Come in, sir. If you'd like to wait here in the hall, I'll report your arrival to Inspector Einmann." He disappeared through a doorway on the left.

Larsson shut the main door behind them. The hall, panelled in dark wood, was smaller than Hallmets expected. To the right and left were doors, presumably leading into the main ground floor rooms. Further back on the left a staircase led to an upper floor. On the right was a large oak coat-stand. The rear wall of the hall contained two further doors

"We can hang our coats here," he said, taking off his hat and hanging it on a hook, before getting out of his coat. The others followed suit. They heard the car engine outside as Lembit moved the vehicle, hoping to find some shelter for it among the outbuildings.

"Are the garages at the back?" asked Larsson.

"No," answered Lesser, "The castle was built on the edge of a bluff, and there's a little lake in the valley below it. That area was designed as a picturesque garden, with walks around the lake, and one of the burns flowing into it was dammed higher up to create a natural-looking waterfall. You couldn't go there while the German family owned it, but when it was given to General Madrus, part of the deal was that the gardens had to be open to the public."

"So getting into the estate's an easy matter?" asked Hallmets.

"Absolutely. The main gates down at the road were removed at the same time, and just inside the estate there's a car park, so that sight-seers can come by car and walk around in the grounds. While I was stationed in Viljandi there was a plan for a bandstand and a cafe too. But the general wouldn't hear of it, and since the town council were rather in awe of him, they didn't take it forward. Pity."

"He was a local celebrity, then?"

"Yes. But if you asked anybody what he actually did during the War, they wouldn't be able to tell you. So people imagined all sorts of heroic deeds, and even attached to him stories that were in fact about other generals. It wouldn't surprise me if some people thought he'd led that charge of yours at Võnnu, chief."

Hallmets smiled. After the surrender of Germany to the British and their Allies in November 1918, freelance German *Landeswehr* forces, led by General von der Goltz, and backed by the Baltic German barons, tried to set up a Baltic German state covering the Russian provinces of Estonia, Latvia and Lithuania. The Germans were already in control of Latvia and parts of Lithuania when they came up against the Estonians, who had just seen off the Red Army at the other end of their country. Hallmets had been awarded a medal by the Latvian government for his part in the final victory over the Germans at Võnnu in June 1919.

"What *did* the general do in the War, then?" asked Larsson.

"I'm not sure I could tell you," said Lesser.

"I believe it was to do with supplies," added Hallmets.

"So he wasn't at the front line," said Larsson.

"No. But that doesn't mean he didn't play an important part in our victory. Somebody had to make sure the munitions were in the right place at the right time, and the troops were fed and clothed."

The door to the left opened again, and the officer who'd opened the main door reappeared. "Sorry to keep you waiting. Can you come this way." He held the door open to allow them to pass through into what seemed to be a lounge or sitting-room. Animal heads gazed at them from high on the panelled walls, including deer, elk and even a bear. A framed photograph showed an elderly gentleman, presumably the general, holding a large fish. Two leather-upholstered sofas flanked a wood fire in the large fireplace in the centre of the inner wall of the room. A low table sat between them. There was no other furniture. A door opposite the one they'd entered by no doubt led to another room.

"Do sit down," said the officer, "By the way, I'm Officer Juurup. Inspector Einmann will only be a minute. He's next door, in the general's study, writing up his initial report, and you'll understand he'd rather finish it before handing the case over to you. Can I order you some coffee?"

"Yes, thank you," said Hallmets. Juurup nodded, and left by the door leading into the hall. Hallmets understood what was happening. The local man was reluctant to hand over the case to the outsiders, and was making a small assertion of his power while he still had it.

"That's how the old man spent his time," said Lesser, indicating the stuffed heads. "Perhaps he didn't do enough shooting during the war and wanted to make up for it."

"Was he married?" asked Larsson.

"Yes," said Lesser, "But his wife died during the flu epidemic back in 1918. That was well before he came here. I never heard any talk of him remarrying."

"What about children?"

"I'm sure there were, but I never came across any of them whilst I was here. I guess they were grown up and off somewhere else."

"So it was just him living here," reflected Hallmets, "How did he occupy himself? Apart from shooting things, that is. We'll need to speak to the staff."

As if on cue, the door from the hall opened, and a girl of about twenty came in, bearing a tray. She was of average height, quite slim, with brown hair woven into two plaits, and a white apron over her brown dress. She put the tray on the table between the sofas. On it were three cups of coffee, a bowl of rough chunks of brown sugar, and a plate of plain oatmeal biscuits.

"Would you like anything else?" she asked.

Hallmets and Lesser had stood up when the girl came in. Hallmets now motioned to the spare place on the sofa next to Larsson. "Please, sit down for a moment." The girl, looking puzzled, sat down. Hallmets sat down again, Lesser too. "I'm Chief Inspector Hallmets," he explained, "This is Inspector Lesser, and sitting next to you is Sergeant Larsson. We're from the Special Crimes Unit in Tallinn, and we've been asked to investigate the general's death. Can I ask who you are?"

"I'm Anna, er, Anna Mäesalu. I'm the general's maidservant."

"How long have you worked for him?"

"Since I was sixteen, so that's four years now. I'll be twenty-one in February. I was going to leave his service next year, I'm getting married in June."

"Congratulations," said Larsson warmly, "That's lovely. Somebody local?"

"Yes, miss. Tõnis works in Böck's bakery in Viljandi."

"Böck's bread's the best you'll buy!" chanted Lesser.

"Yes, that's the one," said Anna, smiling, "One day he'll be a master, *Härra* Böck's very pleased with his progress. When he got raised from an apprentice to an assistant, that's when we decided to set the day."

"So what are your duties here, Anna?" asked Hallmets.

"Well, I clean the rooms, light the fires, make the general's bed and do his laundry, and help Eda when she needs it."

"And Eda is …"

"Oh, she's the cook and housekeeper. She keeps everything going. And Jaak, he's Eda's husband, I suppose you'd say he's the handyman. Any job that needs a man, he'll do it." She blushed. "I mean, practical things, joinery, digging, that sort of thing."

"Is that all of you? The staff, I mean."

"The only other one is Raud, he's the general's manservant, butler and driver. He used to be in the army with the general, I think he did the same sort of thing there, so Eda says. But he keeps himself to himself. He thinks we're just simple peasants. And his attitude to women is, well, I'd rather not say. But more than once he and Jaak have nearly come to blows over the way he treats Eda. He seems to pick on her more than me, I think that's because she controls the household budget, and he resents that."

"How does he treat you?" asked Larsson.

"Most of the time he behaves as if I don't exist. Even if I'm in the same room. If he thinks I've done something that's not up to scratch, he always tells Eda, and she passes it on to me. I think I'm better off that way."

"I'm sorry to ask this," said Larsson, "But have either the general or Raud, or even Jaak, tried anything on with you, you know what I mean."

The girl pursed her lips. "No, not really. The general, well, he's looked at me now and then, how can I say, a bit speculatively, if you get my meaning. Once, not long after I arrived, he put his hand on my, em, bottom, while I was serving his dinner. I had a bowl of soup in my hands and I tipped it onto his lap. He was furious, and I thought I was for the sack right away, but Eda rushed in. She sent me out immediately, and I didn't hear what she said to the general, but I never got fired, and the next day he even apologised, said he didn't know what had come over him. After that he never tried it again. Eda's been with him a long time, ever since he came here, and she knows how to handle him all right. And Jaak's okay too. He's never tried anything."

"What about Raud?"

"To be honest, he makes me a bit uncomfortable. Eda and Jaak don't like him at all. I won't repeat what Jaak calls him, it's far too rude for a respectable girl to say."

"Do you all live in?" asked Lesser,

"Oh yes. I sleep in a room in the attic here. Jaak and Eda live in the cottage that's just beside the castle. Next to it is a storage building, then the stables. The general's car's kept in there now. There's an apartment above the stable building, and that's where Raud lives."

"And are there any other staff. I mean people who don't live in and just come to the castle on a regular basis?"

"Well, there's a couple of men who come in now and then to work in the garden, but that's only when they're needed, and Jaak hires them. Then the doctor, he comes regularly, maybe once a month, to check on the general's heart and so on. And there's Villem, he's a sort of secretary. He comes in twice a week, on Tuesdays and Thursdays. He spends most of his time in the study – that's the room through that door there."

"What's his full name?"

"Villem Jonsson. He lives in the town, and comes in on his bicycle. I've always found him very pleasant."

"Was he here yesterday?"

"Yes. He arrived a little late, there was snow on the road. The general was quite irritated; punctuality is his number one virtue. Sorry, I mean, was."

"Just one more question, Anna," said Hallmets, "How did you find out about the general's death?"

"Well, I was up as usual at seven to light the fires, and

check the downstairs rooms were all in order before the general got up. He tends to get up about half past seven, then he's down for his breakfast at eight. Always the same every day. Routine is what makes a good soldier, he says. Once I'd done the fires I went to the kitchen to help Eda. Well, she wasn't there, and the kettle was steaming away on the range. So I took it off. It was then I noticed a light moving outside – it wasn't really daylight yet – and when I looked closer it was a torch, and Jaak and Eda were out there in the forecourt, just standing there looking down at something. So I put my clogs on and went out. They were just staring at the body on the ground. It was the general. He was dead, you could tell that right away. His eyes were staring, just like he was looking into the next world. And his sword, it was sticking right through him, I could see the handle sticking out here" – she pointed to her chest, just below her ribs – "and the pointed end, well, that was sticking right out his back. That was what Jaak saw first, he said, the sword blade glinting in the torchlight. Like in a film, I suppose. I saw this film once, I don't remember the title, it was about Napoleon. But this general, he'd lost a battle and Napoleon wasn't too pleased, anyway …"

At this point the handle of the door to the study turned with a squeak, and the door began to open. "Please come in, gentlemen," called a loud voice from the room.

Anna stood up hastily. "That'll be the inspector. I'd better leave you to it. Don't forget your coffee, now." She gave a rapid curtsey and hurriedly exited to the hall.

5

Hallmets led Lesser and Larsson into the study. It was about the same size as the sitting-room. By the window to the front of the house was a large table, an upright wooden chair pulled up to it. In the inner corner opposite was a stove coated in dark blue ceramic tiles. By the stove, a tall standard lamp overlooking it, was an armchair, upholstered in a dark red cloth, partnered by a low table, and opposite it another armchair of the same old-fashioned style. Against the other walls stood bookshelves of dark wood, with cupboards below them.

And, standing with his back to the warm stove, a big man with a fleshy face and close-cropped black hair. He wore a dark suit that barely succeeded in containing his body, the buttons of his waistcoat clearly straining to hold it closed. His face was wide and red, and his eyes seemed to be only tiny points of light within it. A black pencil moustache formed a bushy tuft under his bulbous nose. From his large ears, black hair could also be seen sprouting. The man was looking at him, but there was no sign of welcome on his face.

"You must be Hallmets," said the man, "I know this one, it's Sergeant Lesser."

"I'm Chief Inspector Hallmets. This is *Inspector* Lesser, and Sergeant Larsson. I'm guessing that you're Inspector Einmann. I'm pleased to meet you." Hallmets held out his hand, but the man ignored it.

"A simple case of suicide," he grunted, "And you people from Tallinn can't keep your noses out of it. Do you think we're all stupid down here?"

"No-one is suggesting you are stupid, inspector, nor that

people of Viljandimaa are inferior in any way from those in any other part of Estonia. I believe Colonel Reinart from the Ministry of the Interior has already been in touch, to explain why he has asked us to attend this case."

"Some toff who's never done a day's work in his life, but knows the right people, I'll bet. These bloody secret policemen are …"

"I'm not interested in your opinion of the colonel," interrupted Hallmets. "Kindly keep it to yourself. And a word of advice. Giving vent to such opinions could get you into deep trouble. We're not political police. As you should be aware, the Special Crimes Unit is made up of experienced detectives from all parts of the country, including Inspector Lesser and Sergeant Larsson."

"Women! In the police. How the hell's she going to break up a bunch of drunks on a rampage?"

"You'd be surprised. However, that's not her job. It's solving crimes. That's the point of the SCU."

"So what are you doing here? This isn't a crime. OK, it's an 'unexpected death'" – he wagged his fingers to indicate the quotation marks – "But there's nothing mysterious about it, and I've solved it, so you're wasting your time. I've just finished writing up my report, and it'll be with the examining magistrate first thing in the morning. End of story. I'm sorry you wasted your journey coming down here. Actually no, I'm not, you shouldn't have bothered setting out in the first place. Now, is there anything else you want? I've got to get back to town now. I've other work to be doing."

"That's fine," said Hallmets quietly, "Go right ahead, and don't mind us. We'll just hang on here a while though, and take a look around, maybe have a chat with the staff, and so on. You know the kind of stuff detectives do. Just so we can form our own opinion, and report back to the Ministry. And I'd appreciate a copy of your report, too. I'm sure your typist has enough carbon paper. No need to go out of your way to get it to me. One of my people will be at Viljandi Police Station by now, so it can just be passed to him. I expect you've already had a message from Captain Kruus, asking you to assist us. Colonel Reinart's first call, as protocol demands, will have been to the local Chief of Police."

Einmann's jaw dropped, or at least sank into his double chin. He paused, and they could almost hear the cog wheels turning in his head as he sought to process this information. The thuggish expression melted away to be replaced by one of shiftiness. His weasel eyes slunk from one of them to the other, lingering longest on Larsson. "All right," he said, "You and your Tallinn pals have got it planned, to make sure us bumpkins jump when you say so. Well, I'll tell you what my report says, then I'll get back to town to get it typed and submitted. And of course I'll give a copy to your goon at the station. You can stay here as long as you like and do whatever 'detecting'" – again he emphasised the quote with his fingers – "you want." He pulled his notebook from his inside pocket, and flicked through the pages, peering closely, until he found the one he wanted. "I'm only going to read this once. Here we go:

"I was informed at 08.10 this morning, Friday 29th November 1935, that an unexpected death had been reported to the duty sergeant at Viljandi Police Station. The deceased was Arnold Madrus, retired general, residing at Rauakivi Castle, Viljandimaa County. I immediately proceeded by car to the aforementioned residence, accompanied by Officers Juurup and Anvelt.

WINTER BlOOD

We arrived there at 09.05. We were met by Raud Kirik, servant of the deceased, who showed us the body, which had been left *in situ* for us to examine. I ascertained that the presumed deceased was in fact dead before proceeding further. *Härra* Kirik informed me that he had already summoned by telephone the deceased's usual doctor, to certify the death. The body had been discovered at approx. 7.40 by Jaak and Eda Pirn, employees of the deceased. The body was covered by snow, which points to death occurring sometime during the night, and therefore probably several hours, before it was discovered. It was clear that death was caused by a wound from a cavalry sabre which had pierced the body right through, entering at the lower chest area and exiting through the back. Given that none of the resident staff, that is *Härra* and *Proua* Pirn, *Härra* Kirik, and Anna Mäesalu, heard anything during the night, and the mode of death and position of the body, it seems likely that *Härra* Madrus entered the forecourt sometime earlier in the night and fell upon his sword, in the manner of defeated generals throughout history. No note from the deceased was found, and in view of the general's standing and reputation, I believe we should not seek the causes of his suicide, but accept it as the final decision of his distinguished career. I therefore recommend that no further investigation take place, and that his death be announced to the public with some discretion, and the exact circumstances withheld. Dated 29 November 1935, 15.00 hours."

Einmann snapped the notebook shut and thrust it back into his inside pocket, nodded coldly to Hallmets, and marched to the door, opened it and slammed it shut behind him.

6

"Well, he hasn't changed!" said Lesser. "He arrived when I was still a sergeant. He was in Valga before that. Rumour had it they'd had enough of him there and got him transferred."

"What's he like, as a policeman?" asked Hallmets.

"He likes a quick solution to a case, tends to jump to conclusions. Doesn't waste time considering all the possibilities, and generally thinks he knows better. Oh, and he's also got a chip on his shoulder. Even back then, he couldn't understand why he hadn't been promoted to DCI. And I think you'll have gathered his attitude to women."

"Sadly, he's not alone," muttered Larsson. "So what do we do now, chief?"

Hallmets looked at his watch. "Three fifteen. It'll be dark not long after four, so we should really have a look at the spot where the body was found, while there's still some light." He pulled the bell-cord half way along the wall.

A few moments later Anna reappeared. "Can I get you something?"

"Not at the moment, Anna," said Hallmets, "But we'd like to see exactly where the general's body was found, while it's still light. I guess that Eda's in the kitchen at the moment?"

"Yes," said the girl, "And Jaak's there too."

"That's even better. Can you introduce us to them?"

Anna nodded. "It's this way then. Just follow me." She led them back through the sitting room and into the hall. There was no sign of either Einmann or Juurup; Hallmets guessed that all three of the officers from Viljandi had returned there. From the hall she opened the left hand door at the rear, and led them into a large kitchen. It would, as usual, be the warmest room in the house, with the iron range at the far end lit first thing in the morning, and kept alight until last thing at night. A stocky middle-aged woman with a red face was busy pummelling dough with a chunky fist on the big wooden table in the middle of the room. By a window, Lembit was sitting on a wooden chair, one leg crossed over the other, drinking from an earthenware mug. In another chair next to him sat a small weather-beaten man in later middle age, smoking a pipe. Eda looked up at them, but didn't stop kneading the dough. Lembit put down the mug and stood up, giving Hallmets a salute. The other man merely moved his eyes to observe the visitors, then nodded and sucked his pipe again.

"Eda, Jaak," said Anna, "These are the police from Tallinn. They're wanting to know …"

"Thank you, Anna," cut in Hallmets, "We'll take it from here." He introduced his colleagues to Eda and Jaak, and motioned Lembit to sit down again. "*Härra* and *Proua* Pirn, we're from the Special Crimes Unit in Tallinn. We've been asked to report to the Interior Ministry on the general's death, since it was somewhat unusual. That means we may ask you some of the same questions Inspector Einmann asked. I apologise for that. Firstly, we'd like you to show us exactly where you discovered the general's body, and tell us how it happened."

It didn't take long to tell, and soon Eda, Jaak, Anna and the three police officers were standing in the forecourt in the gently falling snow. Five minutes later they were back in the warm kitchen, sitting round the wide, well-used table. Lembit had not moved.

"Thank you for your help," said Hallmets, "Please don't disturb that area. We'll clear the snow tomorrow and see if there's anything underneath. The general was a well-known figure, so naturally his death, being so dramatic, could raise some questions. That means we have to be sure we get the answers right. Our inquiries could take a few days to complete, so I'm going to leave Sergeant Larsson here overnight, to make sure nothing is disturbed."

"I'll make up a bed for her right away," said Anna, getting up.

"No, thank you, Anna. I'm afraid she'll have to stay awake. Just in case anything unusual takes place. Now, at this point I need a little background information. *Härra* and *Proua* Pirn, you came to work for the general not long after he'd taken up residence here."

"Yes," said Eda, "That were back in '22. Baron von Winkelstein was a big supporter of the German mercenaries. His son was killed fighting for them, down in Latvia somewhere. The baron was with the Germans too, and fled to Germany after Võnnu. His wife and the two daughters had already locked up the house and moved into Tallinn, to stay with relatives. After the war the family were offered the same deal as the other barons: they could have the house and one farm, provided they lived there and worked it. Like most of 'em, they chose to scuttle off to their Fatherland. The government divided up the estate and carved several farms out of it, for our own people. What was left was the house and the gardens, and they offered those to the general, same as they did to some of the other people who'd been high up during the War. As a sort of reward, I suppose. Though I'm not sure what he did during the War, he weren't well-known like Laidoner or Põdder."

"So you didn't work for the von Winkelsteins?"

"No. The servants went off with the family. The families who were left, those who wanted, got farms that had been part of the estate."

"Old Mati Hamann, over at Rauaküla," said Jaak, "He were the stableman. Then there was …"

"They don't want to know about them, Jaak," said Eda, "That were afore the general's time. See, they, I mean the general, I suppose, put a notice in the paper, asking for a cook and a handyman. Must be a married couple, so's they can live in the cottage. And that were us."

"Who was it who interviewed and hired you, then?" asked Hallmets, "Was it the general himself?"

"No, no, it were Raud Kirik who did that," Eda went on. "He were there in advance, to get everything ready, like. It were a month or two before the general himself showed up. He were very pleased with the place. At that time Raud did the finances, ordered food, and so on, and whilst his adding up was spot on, he couldn't handle the farmers and the merchants, and they swindled him right, left and centre. We had to tell the general, and after that he put me in charge of the household finances, which is just what a housekeeper should be doing. But Raud, he didn't take it so well. He felt he'd been demoted like, in the general's opinion. But I think the general knew him well enough. See, Raud had been his batman or something like that during the war. He said once that the general had saved his life during the conflict. He could have got himself a job as a teacher, he said, but instead he stayed here."

"Just as well for him," growled Jaak, "He'd have got himself into trouble sooner or later."

"Why would that be?" asked Hallmets.

"He has airs and graces. Always knows best. The way he treats Eda and Anna. I've had to have words with him more than once. See, anywhere but here, he'd soon fall out with everybody. In the castle here, the general kept him under control. As I said, he knew what Raud were like."

"Where is *Härra* Kirik, by the way?"

"He were here this morning," said Eda, "We called him after we found the body, and he phoned for the police and the doctor. Then he was interviewed by that inspector. He must have gone over to his room."

"We'll have a word with him in a minute. By the way, where is the general's body at the moment?"

"The doctor certified him dead, and called for a van to take him into town."

"Good. There'll need to be a post-mortem."

"The inspector said that wouldn't be necessary, it were obvious he'd killed himself. Like Julius Caesar, he said."

"But Julius Caesar didn't kill himself," said Anna, "He was murdered! I saw it at the theatre, just last year."

"You think the general were murdered?" asked Jaak.

"I think we mustn't jump to any conclusions," said Hallmets, "At the moment it's not clear exactly what happened. Inspector Einmann's gone to submit his report, and will no doubt include his own interpretation of what happened. But it'll take a while longer to be sure, and to understand why it happened."

"So that the history books get it right?" asked Anna.

"Exactly. I think we'd like a chat with *Härra* Kirik now. Anna, I wonder if you could take Inspector Lesser over to the stables, and he'll invite him to come over here. After we've had a word, the inspector and I will go on to

Viljandi."

"You'd best not be leaving that too late," said Jaak. "That road can be deceptive sometimes. I've warned Lembit here about the spots he needs to watch out." Lembit nodded sagely.

Anna led Lesser towards the far end of the kitchen and through a door into a passage.

"Would you be wanting something to eat before you go," asked Eda, "I've got a nice meat loaf that I just made yesterday. I can boil some potatoes too."

"No thanks," replied Hallmets, "It's kind of you to offer, but we'll get something back in town later. There is something you can do for me, though, Eda. Can you show Sergeant Larsson the general's bedroom."

Eda led Larsson out of the kitchen towards the hallway.

A minute later Anna and Lesser returned. "Kirik's not there, chief," said Lesser, "Should we search the house for him?"

But before Hallmets could reply, a flustered Eda rushed into the room. "You'll need to go up to the general's room, chief inspector. Raud was in there. The sergeant's with him now."

"Henno, come on," ordered Hallmets, "Everyone else, just wait here please. Oh, Eda, you'll have to show us the way."

7

Eda led them out into the hall and up the staircase, turning right at the top into a corridor, and opening the first door on the left. Hallmets asked her to return to the kitchen, and went in, followed by Lesser.

The bedroom was simply furnished. Against the side wall stood a wooden single bed, with a dark red quilt on it, and two pillows in dark red cases. At the other side wall was a dressing table and a wardrobe. In the middle of the rear wall was the window, which, Hallmets guessed, looked over the bluff at the rear of the house onto the lake. Now all that was visible were slowly falling snowflakes. Flanking the window were two wooden armchairs. On the left one sat Sergeant Larsson. On the other was a tall slim dark-haired clean-shaven man, staring at the floor. He looked up as the two officers came in.

"This is Raud Kirik," said Larsson, "This is where he was sitting when Eda and I came in." She turned to the man. "This is Chief Inspector Hallmets and Inspector Lesser." She stood up, "I'll keep an eye on things downstairs." She left the room.

Hallmets took the seat she'd vacated. Meanwhile Lesser went over to the bed, turned back the covers, and began to examine it.

"*Härra* Kirik," Hallmets began, "Perhaps you'd begin by explaining what you're doing here. You will be aware that the circumstances of General Madrus' death have still to be fully investigated, and this room is therefore part of the area we need to examine."

The man looked up, and Hallmets could see his eyes

were red. He'd been crying. "I just wanted to be near where he'd been, that's all. When Jaak called me out to see the body, I couldn't believe it. When I called the police and the doctor, it was as if I were in a trance. I held myself together when the doctor came and then the police. Once the inspector said he was finished with me, I let the horror of it hit me. I'd kept it at bay till then, you see. So I came up here, to grieve in peace, without those peasants seeing me. He took me under his wing in the army, made me his batman, kept me with him ever since. He saved my life, you know."

"Tell me about it," asked Hallmets quietly. Meanwhile Lesser moved across the room and began discreetly to examine the dressing table.

"It was during the war. I was caught up in things, not thinking straight, I lost my temper, did something I shouldn't have. The army regulations were very strict. Anyway, the general intervened, and sorted everything out. That's when I became his batman."

"And you've been with the general ever since?"

"Yes, that's right." He stared at the floor.

"Did you see or hear anything last night, *Härra* Kirik?"

"No. It was just a normal day. The general and I played a couple of games of chess after dinner, and then, it must have been about eight thirty, I went back to my apartment. I had a drink of brandy and read a book. *The Four Just Men*, by Edgar Wallace."

"In English or Estonian?"

"Oh, in English. I like to keep practising. English is the language of the future, you know."

"So you read, then what time did you go to bed?"

"About ten. I read for a little, then lay down. I must have fallen asleep right away. I'd just got up this morning, about quarter past seven, when the buzzer went. There's a buzzer, you see, so that the general can summon me whenever he wants something. Anyway, it was Jaak. He'd found … well, you know. And then I went out and saw him and called the doctor and the police."

"Thank you. I'd like a bit of background now. What exactly is your job here?"

"I was his manservant, butler, driver, librarian, secretary …"

"What about the secretary who came in twice a week? What was his name?"

"Villem Jonsson. Yes. I did the general's letters and formal correspondence. But he got Villem in when he decided to write his book."

"He was writing a book? What was it about?"

"It was his memoirs. I offered to help him, but I can only type very slowly and I don't know shorthand. So he got Jonsson in. That way he could dictate to him and then get it typed up quickly."

"Did you know *Härra* Jonsson, before this?"

"No, not at all, I'd never met him. The general put an advert in the paper. He was the only one who applied. I suppose that was because it was only two days a week. But in the end he agreed to pay Villem for four, so that he could do another two days at home, typing up the material."

"Is he local, or did he come to Viljandi to take the job?"

"I don't know. He's well educated – at the university in Tartu – so he's probably lost some of his local accent."

"Where does he live?"

"He lodges in town somewhere. He comes here on a bike."

"Do you know the address?"

"No, sorry. He said once that it was near the station. That's all I know."

"How old is he?"

"Oh, in his twenties I'd say. Not long out of university I suspect."

"About General Madrus's memoirs. How long ago did he start on it?"

"About six months or so. He started writing it out himself, but after a couple of weeks he asked me if I could type it. As I said, I was too slow, so he decided to hire someone with shorthand and typing skills. I put the advert in the paper."

"Just in Viljandi?"

"No, it was in the Tartu edition too."

"Have you read any of the general's book?"

"Only the very first chapter, about his ancestors and his birth. Once Villem was hired, he said he'd show me the whole thing when he'd got it finished. He wanted me to be his First Reader, he said, so that I could read it as a whole without any peeks before that, and give him an honest comment on it. As far as I know, he'd not finished it yet."

"Do you know where he kept the work on the book?"

"In his study, I'd guess. That's where they closeted themselves two days a week."

"Have you looked for it?"

"No, of course not!" said Kirik, and Hallmets knew he was lying.

"Please go downstairs now. The general's private rooms will have to be locked, so I'm afraid you won't be able to enter them. One of my officers will be in the house at all times, day or night. Please stay here at the estate until our investigation is completed. I'm saying this to all the staff, not just you. Shall we go?"

8

When they got back to the kitchen, Hallmets asked Kirik to sit at the table.

"Thank you, *Härra* Kirik, Now I'm going to ask you all to wait here whilst your living quarters are searched."

"Hey, what's that for?" demanded Jaak, "We had nothing to do with the old boy's death."

"I'm not suggesting you did. But I'd like to put you firmly in the clear, and this is the easiest way to do it."

"I don't mind," said Anna, "But I'd rather it were Eva who did it. She'll know how to treat a girl's private possessions."

Larsson had been establishing rapport while he'd been upstairs, thought Hallmets. Excellent. He noticed that Jaak was looking worried now. "We're not interested in minor breaches of the legal code that may be revealed," he explained, "All we're looking for is anything that might be related to the general's death." Jaak nodded slowly.

"Look here, this is intolerable," said Kirik, "I won't stand for it."

"Do you have something to hide, *Härra* Kirik?"

"No, of course not, but …"

"But what?"

"Look, can I speak to you somewhere else? In private."

Hallmets led him into the hallway and closed the kitchen door. "Please be brief, sir, we want to get this over as quickly as possible, and before we return to Viljandi."

"Yes, of course. Look, there are materials which might be construed as, er, compromising, and I promise you they are entirely for my own use, and I even keep them locked up."

"Thank you. I'll bear that in mind. Where are they kept?"

"In a locked cupboard, by the bed."

"May I have the key?"

"But I've told you what's in it. Surely you can take my word for it. There's nothing else there, I promise you."

"I'm sorry, sir, we'll have to check. If you object to the search, I will get a warrant tomorrow. But until then you'll be confined to a room here in the castle, to avoid the suspicion that you've tampered with potential evidence. And with the search results being officially itemised, your personal materials may be addressed less flexibly than they would be today."

Kirik said nothing, but dug his right hand into his trouser pocket and produced a small brass key, which he dropped into Hallmets' awaiting palm.

"Thank you. This will be returned to you as soon as we're satisfied that the contents of the cupboard are not relevant to our enquiries."

"Please, don't let those peasants see them," pleaded Kirik, "They wouldn't understand. They resent my intelligence and favour with the general as it is."

"Your privacy will be respected as much as possible, *Härra* Kirik."

Back in the kitchen, Hallmets asked Lesser to search Kirik's apartment, and Larsson Anna's room.

While they were gone he asked, "Think back over the last couple of weeks. What visitors did the general have. Apart from the secretary and the doctor."

"That'll all be in his diary," said Eda. "It's in his study, it's usually laid out on his writing desk, so I can check it to see if we need to get anything ready."

"I 'ad to build a kennel once, when a pal of the general's brought his dog," added Jaak, "Big ugly brute it was, but gentle as a lamb when you got to know it."

"Chief Inspector" said Kirik, "At the moment the diary's in my apartment."

Jaak and Eda stared at him suspiciously. "It don't ought to be there," growled Jaak. "You're up to no good, Kirik. That's what I think."

"We don't need any speculation right now," said Hallmets firmly, "Exactly where is it, *Härra* Kirik?"

"In the cupboard I mentioned to you before."

"Where he keeps his dirty books," sneered Jaak.

"How do you know what's in *Härra* Kirik's bedside cupboard, *Härra* Pirn?"

"I were cleaning the place," said Eda, "He'd left it unlocked. Disgusting stuff. Naked women. In all sorts of poses. Perverts like him should be locked up."

"Or castrated," added Jaak.

"Let me ask another question," said Hallmets. "Were there any casual visitors to the house? I mean people who didn't want to see the general, but yourselves."

There was silence for few moments.

"There was a chap came round selling brushes," said Eda, "That was the week before last. I didn't take anything."

"Were the brushes the usual sort?" asked Hallmets.

"Oh yes, we just didn't need anything right now. He's been before, usually comes around every six months or so."

"OK. Anyone else?"

"The vet came to check the horses," said Jaak. "There's only a couple, they're getting on now, like the general. But he liked to ride round the garden every now and then, made him feel like he was a baron, I reckon."

"You know the vet?"

"Oh, yes, everyone knows Dr Heinemann."

There was silence again.

"Thank you. I think that's enough questions for today," said Hallmets. He'd clearly need to interview Kirik again, without the others present. "We'll talk to you all again tomorrow."

By this time Larsson had returned. "Nothing suspicious in Anna's room," she said, and Anna looked suitably relieved.

Five minutes later Lesser opened the door he'd left by, and motioned Hallmets into the corridor. He was carrying a leather-bound book, a large cloth-bound album, and a leather wallet. "I found the general's diary. An interesting photo album, which could probably put Kirik inside for a year or two. And a nice little nest-egg under the mattress. Four thousand kroons in cash, in this wallet. Nothing else suspicious."

"Okay. We'll give him the money back and hang on to the album and the diary." He took the items from Lesser. "Can you help Eva go through the Pirns' place now. I think we should be getting away soon."

Lesser waited in the corridor whilst Hallmets returned to the kitchen. "Sergeant Larsson," he said, "Could you help the inspector take a look round the Pirns' cottage." Then to Kirik, "Thank you, sir. We have the general's diary now. We'll take it to Viljandi with us for a closer examination. And we'll hang on to this album for the moment too."

"Now look here, …" began Kirik, then controlled himself and shut his mouth. "Yes, all right." he whispered.

Eda stared at him as if he was dirt.

"Sergeant Larsson will be staying here until the morning," said Hallmets. "You will follow her instructions to the letter. If not, you will be in serious trouble. *Härra* Kirik, you will go to your apartment now, and remain there until we ask you to come out."

"But I haven't had dinner yet."

"I'm sure you have some emergency supplies in your apartment. Please leave now."

Kirik looked pained, but got up and left via the back door.

"Now, *Härra* and *Proua* Pirn, as soon as we've gone you may make a meal here, for yourselves, Anna and the sergeant. Then you should go to your cottage and wait there until we return tomorrow. Anna, Sergeant Larsson will decide when you should go up to your room. Is that clear?" They nodded. "Lembit, can you get the car ready, so that we can be off as soon as we can."

Lembit saluted. "No problem, sir. Right away." He picked up his leather coat, his cap and his gloves, and went out.

Larsson and Lesser were back ten minutes later. Lesser nodded to Hallmets. "There's nothing of interest to us in the cottage." Jaak looked suitably relieved.

"Alright, we'll get off now," said Hallmets, "Sergeant Larsson will see us out."

In the hallway, he briefed Larsson: "Base yourself in the study – that gives a good view of the forecourt. I'm sure Anna will get you some blankets. Before you eat, get Anna to take you round the whole house, so that you see all the rooms. We'll have a look at the outbuildings in the morning. Anna can stay with you in the study until she goes to bed. Then take a walk round the house every half hour, just to check there's nothing odd going on. Any questions?"

"No, chief, that sounds fine. I take it the phone's not been fixed yet."

There was a receiver on a small table in the hall. Hallmets picked it up, tapped the hook several times, and listened. Nothing. "No, so if anything happens, just deal with it. I'll see what we can do to get some people out to mend the line tomorrow. See you then."

9

The car was waiting outside the main door, and as soon as they were in, they set off. It was still snowing lightly, but it was already darkening, so Lembit had the headlights on.

As they were about to emerge onto the road, a car came round the sharp bend just before the gate, slithered across the road, and just avoided drifting into theditch alongside. After that it slowed down and proceeded at a crawl, with Hallmets' car having to creep along behind.

"I'd like to go a little bit faster," said Lembit, "But I daren't try to overtake. So just relax, we'll get there sooner or later."

Twenty minutes and no incidents later they crawled into the outskirts of the town, and passed the railway station. By now the snow had stopped, though it still lay on the roads. The car in front soon turned off, and they went on along the now empty street, passing a cemetery, and then a bridge over a river.

"OK," said Lesser, "We're on Vaksali Street. From here it's the second on the right." They turned into an unassuming road, with few houses. "This is Tasuja Street," said Lesser, "Keep going. It's the villa right at the end."

They stopped in front of a two-story whitewashed villa "Here we are," announced Lesser, "Police Headquarters. I should add that our hotel is only ten minutes' walk from here."

Hallmets asked Lembit to leave the car there, and they entered the building. He hoped it would be warmer inside than it had been in the car.

A large man with a generous white moustache, whose uniform showed him to be a sergeant, sat at a desk in the small entrance hall. Behind him, he was flanked by two doors, the one on his left of white-painted plywood, the other of dark polished oak. "Good evening, gentlemen," he said as Lembit shut the door behind them. "Now you folks don't look like criminals or drunks, or good citizens about to complain about something. And one of you is mighty familiar. Henno Lesser, I think!" He stood up and shook Lesser warmly by the hand. "And this will be DCI Hallmets." He saluted to Hallmets. "Sergeant Lauk at your service, sir!"

"Pleased to meet you, sergeant," said Hallmets, holding out his hand, which Lauk shook with a smile. "Has my colleague arrived?"

"He has indeed. It was good to meet Ilmar Hekk again after so long. The Invisible Man, we used to call him. He wasn't based here, but they used to bring him in for surveillance operations. I've assigned the special incident room to your team. Inspector Lesser'll know where it is."

"And Inspector Einmann?"

"Well now, you've missed him, sir. He's always out of the door at five on the dot. And now" – he looked at his large steel pocket watch – "it's eighteen minutes past. But he did give me a note to pass on to you." He handed Hallmets a thin brown envelope.

"Thanks." He slipped the envelope into the inside pocket of his jacket. "I may see you later, sergeant."

"No problem, sir, I'm here till late tonight."

Lesser led him past the desk, through the heavy oak door into a corridor with whitewashed walls, on both sides of which large boards were covered in notices, of wanted men (and women), lost dogs, missing youths, and general announcements of every type. About ten paces down the corridor Lesser opened a door on the left and beckoned Hallmets in.

They found themselves in a warm room with a stove in the corner and a window in the opposite wall, with a curtain of coarse cloth drawn across it. Sat at a bare wooden table was Hekk. He stood up to greet them.

"It's not exactly busy here, boss," said Hekk, "Though this is the non-public side of the building. By the way, Ants phoned earlier. Seems he's dug up some stuff about General Madrus. Said he'll hang on till you call him."

"Okay. I'll do that now. Is there a phone anywhere?"

"Yes. End of the corridor, on the right. Use phone number one, it's an outside line, connects directly to the exchange here. Number two is internal to the station, and you'd have to put your call through via the reception desk."

"Thanks, Ilmar. Henno," – he addressed Lesser – "While I'm phoning, can you bring Ilmar up to date on where we are with the general?"

"Will do, chief," said Lesser.

"I'll see if I can rustle up some coffee," said Lembit.

"The mess room's the last door on the left," said Hekk. He already had a mug on the table in front of him.

Hallmets hung his coat and hat on a hook in the corner of the room, and stood in front of the stove warming his hands for a few moments, then went down the corridor. The last door on the right had a piece of card pinned to it with 'Telephone' written on it in black wax crayon. It was a small room with no window. There was a small table with two black bakelite telephones on it and an upright wooden chair on either side. The telephones were numbered 1 and 2.

Hallmets picked up the handset of phone number 1 and tapped the cradle down a few times to be connected to the exchange. He gave the number of Police Headquarters in Tallinn, and, once connected, asked to be put through to the Special Crimes Unit. Marta had gone home, but Kadakas picked up. He explained that he'd put together a timeline of the general's life, and could send it the next morning via the teletype machine. Marta had typed it out for him, and would take it to the teletype operator, who would be in around eight.

Having thanked Kadakas and rung off, Hallmets went back to the reception desk, and asked Lauk if they could find the address of a Villem Jonsson.

"Hmm. Our secretary Juta will be in tomorrow morning. She can find it in the files. The name doesn't ring a bell so he's not one of our regulars. If he's anywhere in the files, Juta will find him. Otherwise you'd have to look in the county voters' register. But unfortunately it's not arranged alphabetically, but by street. So unless you know what district he lives in, the only thing you can do is just go through the whole thing. I suppose you've a fifty percent chance of finding him before you get to the middle."

"I think he lives in the town somewhere."

"It's not so bad then. The register is arranged by parishes, so you can start with the ones that cover the town. Oh, but how long's he been here?"

"I don't know. He worked for the general for the last five months or so. But I don't know if he was in Viljandi before that."

"Is it urgent?"

"We'd like to locate him tonight if possible."

"OK. I'll let you into the archive room and point you to

the relevant material, but do put everything back exactly where you found it, or Juta won't be very pleased. Come on."

Lauk led Hallmets back into the corridor, into a room opposite the incident room, and switched on the light. The room was square, with whitewashed walls and ceiling and no windows. The left wall was fully shelved, with books, bound files and cardboard folders on it, the far wall had a row of grey filing cabinets against it, and the right wall had a table and two chairs. A single bulb on a wire in the centre of the ceiling lit the room, but there was an additional electric lamp on the table.

Five minutes later they were all at work, looking at different sources. The recorded crimes' register was a bound volume, so Hekk took that through to the incident room, along with the voters' roll. Lesser worked his way through the material in the filing cabinets, whilst Hallmets went through the telephone directory, the trades register, and any other list of people he could find.

Two hours later, they were no further on. No Villem Jonsson was to be found. He was not on the voters' roll, or in the file of recent additions. He had committed no crimes, and had no contacts with the police for any reason. He was not in any of the other files or volumes.

"So," concluded Hallmets, once they'd put everything back and sat round the incident room table, "Is he trying to keep a low profile, or is he simply not a permanent resident in the town?"

"We can check the lodging houses," suggested Lesser. "The fact that it was near the station would be a help."

"Good idea. We'll do that tomorrow. We certainly need to have a chat with him. I'd like to know what the general put into his memoirs."

"You think it may have some link to his death?" asked Hekk.

"He must have died for some reason, whether it was murder or suicide."

"You think it may have been murder?" asked Lesser.

"I'm finding it hard to imagine why he would kill himself in such a public manner. Was he making some sort of statement, and if so, for whom. The same thing applies if it was murder. Whoever did it was making a point which they hoped others would recognise."

Hallmets remembered he'd not read the letter from Einmann. He took it out and extracted a single sheet of thin grey paper from the envelope. The others watched expectantly.

"A message from Inspector Einmann." He glanced through it. "OK. I'll read it out. 'My report going to Examining Magistrate tomorrow. Post Mortem 11.00.' That's it. Well, the post-mortem may help us. I'll go myself. Henno, can you take Ilmar to the castle first thing in the morning and take charge of things there. Search the whole place, starting with the general's study. We're looking for any letters of his, any document referring to Villem Jonsson, or any of the staff for that matter, or anything about his book. Later this evening I'll go through the general's diary. But it's high time we got to our hotel and had something to eat. I'm sorry, I didn't intend to keep you all here this late."

"I'll say goodnight at this point," said Lesser, "There's a meal waiting for me at my cousin's. I gave her a ring from here earlier to say I'd be late, but I don't want to keep them waiting too long. They won't eat till I arrive."

By half past eight Hallmets, Hekk and Lembit had gone

to the hotel and checked in, then headed for the dining room, where they were soon presented with plates of sauerkraut with pork and barley, and mashed potatoes. And beer from a local brewery. They didn't talk about the case. Even though there was no-one else in the room, it was normal practice not to mention their work in any public place.

After the meal Hallmets phoned Kirsti, to let her know he was settled into the hotel. He didn't mention the case. There were at least two telephone operators between himself and their house, who might be tempted, either from boredom or curiosity, to listen in. After that he sat himself in the warm hotel lounge with a glass of brandy, and read the general's diary.

It wasn't as helpful as he had hoped. Knowing the general was writing his memoirs, Hallmets had assumed he would have kept a detailed diary. If so, this wasn't it. Each week had one two-page spread, with Monday, Tuesday and Wednesday on the left sheet and Thursday, Friday, Saturday and Sunday on the right. Appointments and events were noted extremely briefly, sometimes simply a time and a name. Occasionally there was a place. This would take some time and effort to decipher.

Hekk and Lembit were still chatting in the dining room when he passed the doorway on his way to the staircase. He arranged to meet them for breakfast at 7.15 and wished them all good night.

10

Saturday, 30th November

It was still dark outside when Hallmets came down for breakfast at quarter past seven. He wondered if they were the only guests staying there. Lembit was already at a table, and Hallmets joined him.

"*Tere hommikust!*" he greeted the driver.

"Good morning to you too, boss. I've been out for a quick walk around the block. Chilly, and a bit icy, but no more snow in the night. The ice'll be the main danger on the road today."

"Hope you didn't have too late a night."

"No, we weren't long after you, boss. And I'm clear as a bell up here," – he tapped his temple – "I don't drink, see. Me and the missus, we took the pledge six years ago, when our first was born. Never regretted it since, although it's been very tempting at times. You know, have just one glass. The important thing's to have something else to drink that actually tastes good, so I always have a bottle of the wife's blueberry elixir with me. Looks good, tastes good, and does you good. And not a drop of alcohol in it."

"I wish I'd been drinking that," said Hekk, who'd just arrived, "I'll need lots of coffee just to wake myself up."

Hallmets and Hekk walked to the police station at eight fifteen, while Lembit took the car round. Sergeant Lauk had been replaced at the reception desk by a young uniformed officer, who leapt to his feet to salute when they arrived. He introduced himself as Officer Talvik, and told them that Inspector Lesser was waiting in the incident room. While they were introducing themselves to Talvik, the outside door opened again and Einmann swept in. He pushed past Lembit, who was at the edge of the group, gave a vague response to Talvik's salute, and went into the corridor without a word to anyone.

"Well, there goes Mr Friendly!" commented Hekk, "Is he like that all the time?"

Talvik smiled. "Yes," he whispered, as if afraid Einmann might hear him, "I'm afraid so."

Hallmets asked the others to go on through to the incident room, then asked Talvik where he could collect a teleprinter message that he was expecting.

"No problem, sir," said Talvik, "Juta is already here. She'll paste the tape onto paper and bring it down as soon as it arrives. By the way, our mess room is at the end of the corridor on the left. If you want coffee, you can make it there. But if you're going to be here for a few days, it might be a good idea to put something into the kitty."

"We found it," said Hallmets, "But I'll see something goes into the kitty. Oh, there is one other thing. The telephone line to Rauakivi Castle. Do you know if anything's being done to get it repaired?"

"Yes, sir. Sergeant Lauk spoke to the phone people yesterday afternoon, and they're going to fix it this morning."

"Good. That's very helpful, officer. I'll get back to you if there's anything else we need."

In the incident room. Hallmets outlined the events of the previous day, then went on to the tasks for the day. "We're going to have to cover a lot of ground today. I'll stay here. The post-mortem is at eleven. Then I'll see if I can find *Härra* Jonsson. We may need help from the people here."

"Einmann's an asshole," said Lesser, "But he's not typical. Standards are still very high for entry into the police force, and most of us are proud that that's what we are. Lauk is a good man, and he has a lot of influence with the cops here. A lot more than Einmann."

"That's good to know," said Hallmets, "Henno, can you and Ilmar go to the castle with Lembit. Start by clearing the area where the body was found and see if there's anything there. Then search the place from top to bottom. Interview the staff again, find out their movements the day before the body was found. Kirik is hiding something, so pay special attention to him. If he wants his album back he's going to have to be more co-operative. The phone line should be restored sometime this morning, so give me a ring if anything dramatic happens. I'll get over there once I'm clear here."

"No problem, chief," said Lesser.

"Lembit, once you've delivered the others, can you bring Sergeant Larsson back here, so she can get some sleep. By the way, did you pick up anything useful yesterday?"

"Yes, boss. I had a good nose around the stables, once I'd parked the car under cover. Can't say there's anything there that looked suspicious. The old boy's car was there, it's a Mercedes 170 sedan. Very nice motor. Not as big as a limo, that suggests to me that he wanted a comfortable drive from A to B rather than something that would impress the natives. Only a few years old, too, that model's only been around since '31. Nothing there that shouldn't be, but that's just me having a quick nose around. The others certainly don't like Kirik at all, but I reckon they're afraid of him too. He's a hard one to read all right. I'd bet a hundred kroons he's hiding something."

"Thanks, Lembit, that's useful. Oh, Henno, one more thing. Can you can get a description of Jonsson from the staff. Just in case I can't find him at this end."

"Okay chief," said Lesser, "I'll get that done first, and send it back with Eva."

"That would be good. I'll see you all later."

After the others had filed out Hallmets sat for a few moments considering what to do next. There was a knock on the door and a woman came in. She was perhaps in her mid-thirties, slim and rather short with bobbed brown hair, and a serious expression. "DCI Hallmets?" she asked.

"Yes. You must be Juta. I'm pleased to meet you." He held out his hand and she shook it.

"I've a message that's just come from Tallinn, on the teleprinter. Quite a long one, so I've cut the tape and pasted it up in here." She put a brown cardboard folder on the table. "Any other help you need, just let me know. My room is the first on the right at the top of the stairs."

"Thanks, Juta. There is something else. I've a list here of the resident staff at Rauakivi Castle. I wonder if you could check whether any of them have previous form. There are only four. Sergeant Lauk gave us permission to look for another one in the files last night, but we didn't find him."

"I noticed," she said drily. "*Härra* Jonsson. What do you know about him?"

"Only that he lives in lodgings near the railway station. Do you keep a list of lodging houses?"

"Yes. Quite a lot of our, ah, customers seem to have temporary addresses. It's in my office. Come up and I'll have a look."

Hallmets followed her along the corridor and up the wooden staircase at the end. A little way along the upstairs corridor was a door marked 'J. Kala.' She led the way into a warm room, well lit by windows on two sides. This must be one of the best rooms in the building, thought Hallmets. Juta went straight to a filing cabinet in one corner, opened the top drawer, and pulled out a large notebook. "We keep a list of them in here. They're supposed to register with the county, but there are always some who don't, either because they're only having lodgers temporarily, to get over a hard patch, or to avoid the inspections. So we add the ones we hear about to the book as well. You say near the station. Let me have a look."

She turned the pages of the book, occasionally jotting down a name and address. "What sort of person is this Jonsson? Respectable? Ex-con? Old? Young?"

"He's quite young, maybe mid to late twenties, and educated. Works part-time for the late general Madrus as a secretary."

"That's useful. He has an income and is, shall we say, respectable. In that case we can exclude what we might regard as doss-houses, and look, for the moment at least, at the more respectable establishments." She crossed out four of the names on her list. "We also note what kind of lodgers each one prefers. Age, sex, occupation, and so on." She continued turning the pages, shaking her head every so often. Hallmets sat himself on a chair in the corner of the room and waited.

The entries only occupied half the book, so Juta was soon finished. She held out a sheet of paper. "I've boiled it down to these three as the most likely. They are widows who take in only young men with professional jobs, the accommodation is of good quality, and the houses located in streets where more respectable citizens live, but also not far from the station. If you don't strike lucky with them, come back and we can widen the search a bit more."

Hallmets took the paper and thanked her.

"That's what I'm here for," she said.

"One other thing," he added, "General Madrus' post-mortem. Where would that be taking place?"

"The mortuary's at the new hospital, out at Jämejala, just off the Tallinn road a couple of kilometres out. It's signposted from the main road."

"Thanks. By the way, can I make a donation to the kitty, for coffee and so on?"

"That would be very helpful." She opened a drawer and took out a tin. 'Kawe Chocolates' was printed on the lid in swirling letters. He handed her two ten-kroon notes. "That's very generous," she commented, "Depending how long you're all here, I might give some of it back."

"If there's any left over, put it in the Christmas Fund."

Back in the incident room downstairs, with a cup of coffee laced with cream, Hallmets looked at the list. *Proua* Krauss, Naituse Street 22; *Proua* Vilms, Itaalia Street 17; and *Proua* Mölder, Belgia Street 46. He'd try all three later in the day.

He opened the folder Juta had brought down earlier. The paper tape was pasted onto blank sheets of paper in perfectly straight lines. It provided an outline of the life of General Madrus:

Born 1875 Arnold Jaan Madrus at Pajuküla Farm, Viljandi County. Father Jakob Madrus, farmer. Mother

Inge Madrus, nee Villak. Attended local primary school, then gymnasium in Viljandi. Left at 16. Worked on farm. 1895 joined Zubitsky Regiment as junior officer. Served mainly in Caucasus and Poland. Regular promotions up to Captain (1904). Moved to Military Supplies 1905. Promoted to Lieutenant-Colonel (1914). 1914-16 Galician campaign and Brusilov offensive (in Supplies). Feb.1918 Resigned from Russian Army & returned Estonia. Jan. 1919 Joined Estonian National Army as Colonel in Supplies Division. Remained in Army after War, in Supplies Directorate. Promoted Lieutenant-General 1928. Retired 1931. Married 1904 Elena Labjankova, four children. Wife and 2 children died 1918 flu. Survivors Vitus b. 1906, present whereabouts unknown, and Sirje, b. 1907, now married to Urmas Kangemees, address in Valga. No political affiliations recorded for Madrus. Will keep looking. AK

Now they had an outline of the man's life. It was a start. He went down to the telephone room and got connected to Tallinn again. He thanked Kadakas for what he'd supplied, and asked him to check the newspaper archive references to General Madrus.

11

Shortly after ten, Eva Larsson arrived. Hallmets asked her how things had gone overnight.

"Nothing untoward to report. I had a good chat with Anna during the evening. She was very relieved I was in the house overnight, otherwise it would have been just her in her attic room. I asked her again whether she'd heard anything in the house the previous night. She eventually admitted she'd taken something to help her sleep, and wouldn't have heard a couple of elks fighting in the next room. She's desperate to get away from the place. She thinks it's cursed."

"Where did she get that from?"

"Apparently there's a story that the man who built it, the first Baron von Winkelstein, murdered his wife and walled up her body somewhere. Apparently she did disappear. But it's also possible that she'd had enough, and simply cleared off. But that doesn't make such a good story."

"Quite. What was Anna taking to make her sleep through everything?"

"Morphine. She has a cousin who works at the hospital, and slips her the occasional bottle. She swears she's very careful with it, only takes it to help her sleep, and isn't addicted. I'm inclined to believe her. But the sooner she's out of there, the better. She wanted to come back with me this morning, but I told her they all had to stay till we'd sorted out what happened."

"What does she think happened?"

"She's convinced the general was murdered. He seemed to her to be too unimaginative a type to think of killing himself in such a dramatic way. Or even of killing himself."

"Interesting. Did she say anything else about Jonsson?"

"She says she didn't have a lot to do with him. But he was well-educated, she could tell that from the way he spoke, the words he used. And he was always very polite."

"What are the others doing?"

"They're searching the whole place. Then they'll question the staff again."

"Good. I think you should go back to the hotel now and get some sleep."

"Not right now, chief. I dozed a bit in the night, and had a cold shower this morning in the general's bathroom. After it had been searched, of course. I'd rather get on with something, if you don't mind."

"Alright. But if you feel you need a rest, just go back to the hotel."

"Do you want me to spend the night in the castle again tonight?"

"No. I'll ask Ilmar to take tonight's shift. You need a good night's sleep at some point, if you're to stay sharp. Here's what I'd like you to do now." He handed over the diary. "Check through all the appointments recorded here and see if you can identify who he was meeting and where. Note any you think we should follow up. I'll need to get off in a few minutes to get to the PM out at the hospital. I'll see you when I get back."

Ten minutes later he was in the car on the way to the hospital at Jämejala küla. It was only a few kilometres out of town, so it didn't take long to get there. The main hospital building, constructed in the years after independence, was attractive on the outside, airy and bright on the inside. But the mortuary wasn't there; it was in a low stone windowless building that looked like a survivor from the farm which perhaps once stood here. Only the whitewash on the exterior looked recent.

As he entered the building, he steeled himself for an encounter with Inspector Einmann. But the voice that greeted him was altogether other than that of the sullen inspector.

"*Tere, Ülemkomissar!* How are things up in the big city?"

"*Tere Professor!* I didn't expect to see you here." Hallmets had encountered Professor von Stallenborg at many an autopsy. Thinning white hair, glasses with thick lenses, and an irrepressible sense of the absurd.

"*Härra* Hallmets, please, how many qualified pathologists do you think there are in a country the size of ours? I'll tell you the answer. Two! Ah, here's my assistant!"

He gestured towards a young man who didn't look more than eighteen. He was thin, clean shaven, with curly black hair and a very pale complexion, and a serious expression.

"Meet Dr Kaljo Visnapuu, junior pathologist. Top of his class in the medical faculty. Why he wants to minister to the dead rather than the living, I've no idea."

Hallmets shook the young man's hand. "Tell me, *Härra Doktor,* why *do* you want to minister to the dead rather than the living?"

"I'm really not very good with people," he said hesitantly, "At least here I don't have to engage in conversation with the patients. And they don't mind you looking inside them. I think I'm more of a researcher than a practitioner."

"That's not a bad thing," said Hallmets, "Somebody's got to do the research, otherwise our knowledge is not advanced. At least here you're linking it to real people, even if they're dead. By the way, *Härra Professor,* where's Inspector Einmann? I thought he'd be here."

"Einmann! You must be joking! He can't be bothered with detail, he just wants conclusions. More than that, he wants the conclusions he's already thought of. And if he doesn't get them, he throws his dummy out the pram. So, let's get down to business." He led them over to a steel-topped table on which a body lay, covered by a sheet, and whipped the sheet off in one dramatic and well-practised movement. "Here's the old boy, anyway. Fine figure of a man, eh?"

The general, even in death, looked like a general. That is to say, he was tall, not running to fat, and not bald. He had a fine head of grey hair, as well as a thick moustache, trained outwards on each side, which nevertheless must have interfered with his eating, and a beard rather longer than it needed to be. At least, that was Hallmets' impression.

"First thing," said the professor, "Is that there are no scars on his body. That's not what you'd expect of a military man. Either he was very lucky, or he kept well away from the action."

"He was in Supplies."

"Ah. No need to get his hands dirty then."

"Hmm. Well, what have you got for me?"

"Nothing very tricky here," said the professor, "Okay, Doctor V., you tell him."

The young man cleared his throat. "Well. As you can observe, we've already made a preliminary examination and extracted some of the internal organs. Starting with the stomach contents, …"

"No, no, he doesn't want all that stuff. Not unless the old boy was poisoned. Which he wasn't. He's a policeman. What does he want to know? Number one?"

"Er, how did he die?" answered Visnapuu, as if remembering something he'd memorised for an exam.

"And number two?"

"When did he die?"

"Exactly. So, oblige our chief inspector here, who is, by the way, probably the sharpest investigator in our country, and tell him what he wants to know."

"Um, yes, he was killed by a gunshot in the chest, sometime between 8 p.m. and 2 a.m. Approximately."

"He was shot?" asked Hallmets.

"Ah!" quipped the professor, "I note your ears are in full working order, and yet you question them. Have faith! As to our client here, as my colleague here has stated so concisely, he was shot."

"And the sabre?"

"Yes, that was carefully inserted into the wound afterwards. Although there is some minor cutting of flesh contingent upon its passage through the body. Not really a major concern of ours, but I think you'd be wanting to explain why that was done. No doubt to create an effect. But to what end? There's the mystery, eh?"

"Quite so. Did you find the bullet that killed him?"

"Sadly not. It passed through the body, and may still be at the scene of the shooting. Wherever that was. But that's your job. Our job is simply to tell you he wasn't doing a Brutus or Cassius."

"Thanks. Anything else I should know?"

"Not right now, but we haven't finished yet. Want a look inside?"

"No, it's okay. Just send me the final report. And maybe a copy to Einmann as well. It might persuade him the general didn't fall on his sword."

"Oh dear. Poor Inspector Einmann. He likes a simple solution. Now he'll probably go off in a huff. Or try to poison you. Come on, Kaljo, let's get slicing. I'll be in touch, Chief Inspector."

12

Meanwhile, on a steamer crossing the Gulf of Finland, Jaan Kallas sipped his coffee. He sat in the ship's buffet, at a table right by a window, so that he could watch the water. It was grey and thick, sluggish, as if unwilling to be disturbed by the ship's passing. It was cold out there. Kallas knew that the icebreakers had cleared a passage out of Tallinn harbour to the gulf, and the same thing would be happening by Helsinki. Outside of the shallower coastal waters, the gulf was clear of ice. Further east however, the approaches to Leningrad would already be choked. Tallinn and Helsinki were bustling ports because they could be kept ice-free right through the winter.

He took a sip from the squat glass of brandy by his coffee cup. Most of the other customers in the buffet were also taking the opportunity to have a last drink at Estonian prices; once they arrived in Finland, booze was significantly more expensive, a legacy of the Finns' long and sad relationship with alcohol. From 1919 it had been banned altogether, but that hadn't solved the problem, and prohibition ended in 1932. The current high prices were another attempt to deal with it. Most of the travellers on the boat would have several bottles in their luggage.

For Kallas, the trip made a break from the drudge of journalism under a dictatorship. "Investigative" wasn't a word favoured by the National Propaganda Service, which administered the censorship of Estonia's newspapers. The country's leading newspaper, *Postimees*, had been taken over by the state shortly after the institution of the state of emergency, and that bold and ruthless act served as warning to the others: keep in line, if you want to stay in existence. That applied to *Pealinna Uudised* as much as any of the others. Eirik Hunt, the editor, made it clear to his staff that they weren't going to rock the boat. "We want to be here when all this comes to an end," he'd said to them, "And one day it will." His words were to be prophetic, though not in the way he thought.

Kallas had been affected more than many others. Sport, fashion, motoring, and the doings of the rich and famous were largely unaffected by the censorship. It was mainly politics and crime reporting that were affected. This had hit Kallas, a veteran reporter who liked to investigate and to speculate, badly.

It had also affected his book sales. After the case which had brought Hallmets to national attention two years previously, Kallas, who had been beaten up by rogue cops during his investigation, had written a best-selling account of the whole case. As soon as the censorship was inaugurated, his book was one of the first to be affected. It wasn't banned, as much of it showed the police in a very positive light. However, his publishers were forced to make significant cuts, to minimise the activities of the rogue police officers involved, and in particular to remove any reference to their leader, Inspector Indrek Lepp. The unacceptable behaviour was to be restricted to two low-level individuals, and Lepp left out of the story altogether.

However, there was no such overt censorship in Finland, though publishers still had to be careful, given the right-wing political climate. Kallas' Finnish publisher produced a Finnish translation of the original book, with a strapline, "Complete and Unexpurgated!" This wasn't a hundred percent true, but there was a lot less left out. The purpose of his trip today was to visit a Helsinki bookshop, make a short speech and sign copies of the book. He'd submitted his copy to the paper for today before leaving, and Hunt had no objection. Indeed, the trip would be useful for him too, for Kallas would be able to see what was happening in Finland, and buy some of the foreign papers that were unavailable in Tallinn. Even if they couldn't print it, it was useful to see what was going on in the rest of the world.

Threading its way between the islands which screened the Finnish coast, the steamer made the busy harbour and reached the Estonia Pier. At the kiosk in the terminal he bought a copy of *Helsingin Sanomat*, the country's biggest newspaper, plus a couple of Swedish papers. He couldn't read much Swedish himself, but someone back at the paper would be able to. There were German papers there too, but since the Nazis had come to power, the German media were less trustworthy.

The tram stop was right outside the terminal, and in a few minutes he had reached the large square facing the main railway station. Every time he came, he had to stop for a moment to take in the dramatic modern building. Built of warm pinkish granite, the main entrance, under a great semicircular arch, was flanked by monumental figures from Finnish mythology, four in all, each clasping a large globe, which lit up at night. It was for him the most impressive building in the capital, and if he had time to kill, he always resorted to one of the cafes on the square.

His session at the bookshop, not far from the station, started at twelve. Finnish and Estonian are closely related, but not so close that speakers of one can automatically understand the other. However Kallas had mastered enough Finnish for the modest audience to understand him, and to respond to questions, without needing a translator. He enjoyed the event, as some of those there were keen to chat about what was going on in Estonia. He still had to be careful, as it was always possible that the Estonian political police had sent someone over to listen in. He signed a few copies for purchasers, and a few more for the shop, and was out not long after one.

He decided to have lunch in one of the cafes on the square. From his seat by the window, he was able to watch what was going on there. As he finished his plate of meatballs with turnip and potato, he noticed that a crowd was beginning to form, and, as his coffee and brandy (three times what it had cost on the ship) arrived, he could see placards being raised: 'Support the veterans,' 'Jobs for all,' 'Down with the Reds.' He guessed these were supporters of IKL, successor to the right-wing, and now-banned, Lapua Movement.

He wiped his moustache with his napkin, paid his bill and moved out into the square. It was bitterly cold, and he wished he'd brought his fur-lined winter hat with its ear-flaps, rather than the more stylish but less practical fedora he was wearing. He pulled his woollen scarf – knitted by an aunt now in her 80s – tighter around his neck, took his fur-lined leather gloves from his overcoat pockets and put them on. That was better. He reckoned there were perhaps a hundred and fifty people in the crowd. He moved round the square to get a better look.

Then a placard near the edge of the crowd caught his attention: 'Solidarity with the Estonian Patriots.' There could be no doubt about what that referred to: the Vaps Movement, banned the previous year, as soon as

Konstantin Päts had seized power. But what did it mean? Why declare their solidarity now?

He walked further round the edge of the square. The organisers of the demonstration would be lurking at the back somewhere, ready to vanish if the police appeared. Sure enough, behind the crowd, a small gaggle of men were apparently just having a chat. There was no indication that they had anything to do with the demonstrators. Kallas moved a little closer to get a better look at them. Yes, there was a youngish man, clean-shaven, fresh-faced and well-dressed: Artur Sirk, the former leader of Vaps, and instigator of its drift towards fascism. He had been arrested when Vaps had been banned, but then mysteriously escaped from Tallinn's supposedly escape-proof Patarei Prison. So, he thought, Sirk is working with the Finnish fascists now, and only two hours by boat from Tallinn. Is he up to something? Before the censorship, Jaan Kallas would have had a field day with this, writing a graphic description, and adding plenty of speculation as to what was going on. But now, as far as the Estonian authorities were concerned, this event would simply not have happened.

Then, at the rear of the little group, he noticed another figure, who'd been looking the other way, turning round, and Kallas' heart skipped a beat. A tall thin man in a brown overcoat, and even though a fur hat with ear flaps and a thick scarf meant that only his face was visible, that was enough. A skeletal face, the skin unnaturally pale, clean-shaven, so that his ginger hair was not visible: Indrek Lepp! The man who had ordered him to be seized by his henchmen on a Tallinn Street in broad daylight, taken to Police Headquarters, and beaten up. And perhaps worse, if he hadn't been rescued by DCI Hallmets and a couple of his people. So, Lepp was involved with the fascists too. His reporter's intuition told him something was brewing here, something that might have implications for Estonia.

Suddenly he froze. Lepp was staring straight at him, his green eyes burrowing into his own with a burning intensity. He'd been recognised. Lepp turned to Sirk, said something to him, then began to make his way through the passers-by, heading in Kallas' direction. Kallas turned and made off. He didn't want to run, and tried to look casual, but he hadn't got more than a few metres when a sinewy hand gripped his arm like a vice.

"Kallas! You piece of scum," hissed Lepp, "Who told you to come here?"

Kallas thought quickly. He tried to force a smile. "A little bird told me. So what are you planning, *Härra* Lepp, with your pal Artur? Have you a few words for the press?"

Lepp clamped his arm even tighter. "Only this. You won't get back to Tallinn alive. You have my word on that." With that he suddenly punched Kallas in the stomach with his other hand.

Kallas gasped and doubled over, then fell down onto the cobbled surface of the square. It took him a while to get his breath back. Meanwhile several well-meaning Finns had surrounded him, and were asking how he was. One woman speculated that he'd had a heart attack, and they should call an ambulance. "I'm okay," he eventually managed to wheeze, "Anybody see that man?"

But no-one had. By holding Kallas close to him, Lepp had delivered the blow unobserved, then vanished as Kallas fell. Gradually his breath came back, although his stomach was still sore. He assured his helpers that he'd be fine, he just needed to sit down for a while. An elderly man helped him to his feet again, and after expressing his thanks, he headed for the café.

13

Half way there, Lepp's words came back to him: You won't get back to Tallinn alive! He abandoned the café plan, and headed for the tram stop instead. The sooner he could get to the ferry terminal the better. He wasn't a coward, but he wasn't a fool either, and Lepp wasn't someone who issued idle threats. And now he was really convinced that something big was going on. Lepp had not wanted to be seen by him, that was clear.

He reached the tram stop, and didn't have long to wait before a tram arrived that would take him to the harbour. Kallas was first on board. There were a few people behind him, and just as the last one had boarded two men ran up and jumped on. They sat by the door. A solidly built man with a hard face and a scar on his cheek, and a small thin man with the look of a weasel. Kallas looked at the men. The big man stared back expressionlessly; the small man smiled, showing his bad teeth, and winked at him. He knew immediately that Lepp had sent these men.

At least they couldn't assault him on the tram, thought Kallas. He'd be safe till they got to the terminal. But what then? He daren't even go to the toilet, they'd get him there for sure. He couldn't go out onto the pier to look at the ships in the harbour, they'd probably knife him and throw him into the water. The big man was the muscle, the little one probably carried the knife.

The tram drew up outside the terminal building. There were still about ten people on board. He thought of getting out first and dodging round the other side of the tram. But these men weren't both dopes; at least one of them would be watching him all the way to the terminal doorway, and that was only about four metres away. So he stuck with the rest and went through the glass-panelled doors into the building, followed the corridor into the buffet, and sat himself at a table opposite the counter. Here he was quite visible to everyone, and hopefully safe. The thugs wouldn't attack him here.

They didn't. Instead, they sat themselves down at his table. First the little one, who leered at him, and said, "You don't mind if we sit here, do you? We like to have company, don't we, Matti?" Then the big man sat down too, directing his expressionless gaze at Kallas.

"I'm Antti," the little man went on, "And this is Matti. You don't know us and we don't know you. That's the way we like it, but I don't mind telling you who we are because you're not going to live to remember. We've been told you're a reporter for a socialist rag in Tallinn. We can't have you makin' up all sorts of lies, getting our pals into trouble. So we're just going to make sure you never get back to Tallinn. See, we complement each other. Matti's big and he's got a lot of strength. I'm small but I've got a lot more up here." He tapped his temple with his right hand. "And between us, we're going to do a lot of damage to you."

This didn't sound so good. The only positive he could draw from it was that the names and the accent told him they were Finns rather than Estonians. At least on the boat he'd be back in Estonia, even if it was just a small bit of it floating on the water.

Kallas shunted his chair back so that his legs weren't under the table, where they might be in range of Antti's putative knife. It was always possible that one of the thugs carried a gun, but they weren't likely to use it in the buffet. "Well, gentlemen," he said, "I'm going to get a cup of coffee and something to eat." He didn't feel very hungry, but felt he should keep the initiative somehow. He got up and made for the counter.

In a moment Antti was behind him. "You know what? I fancy a cuppa meself. I'm right behind you, squire!"

Kallas ordered a cup of coffee and a *kiluvõileib*, an open sandwich of sprats on rye bread with slices of boiled egg on top. He took them back to the table and started eating. In a moment Antti was back with coffee and a pasty of some sort. Matti looked at him. "What about me, Antti? I'm hungry too."

"All right," sneered Antti, "Here's some money. Go and get something. Not too much, mind. I think the boat'll be in soon." As the big man shuffled off towards the counter, Antti smiled at Kallas. "Even one of us can take you out. But with two it's more enjoyable. Matti likes to break things, you know, fingers and so on, while I prefer to cut them. Very slowly."

Kallas chose not to respond, but forced himself to eat, and look nonchalant. Five minutes later Matti was back with a glass of beer and a plate of salmon soup with a big chunk of rye bread balanced on the rim. As he started slurping it noisily, Kallas noticed the boat coming in, and people at other tables getting ready to move.

"Time to go!" he announced, getting to his feet at the same time as four young men at the next table. He skipped in front of them and joined the flow up the stairs to queue at the gate for the boat. Antti jumped to his feet too, knocking his coffee onto Matti's lap. Matti grabbed his arm with a shout of anger. "Hey, what the hell was that for?"

Kallas didn't hear the rest. He joined the queue, with the four men behind him. They looked like working men, each carrying a canvas overnight bag and a toolbox. He greeted them, asked if they've been to Tallinn before. As a reporter, he knew how to get on with people. The main thing, he'd learned, was to listen to them, and empathise. Soon they'd introduced themselves and explained they were going over to do some renovation work in a church in Tartu. They expected to spend about a week there. They'd not been to Tartu before, although two of them had been for short trips to Tallinn.

Kallas couldn't see Antti and Matti. Perhaps they'd given up, now he was on the boat, or forgotten to get tickets, or Matti had insisted on finishing his meal. However, a few minutes later, there was a commotion further back in the queue and the two of them pushed their way up towards him. However, the workmen weren't having queue jumpers. "Where do you think you're going?" said the one who seemed to be the leader. Koivo was his name.

"We're just joining our friend here!" said Antti, pointing to Kallas.

"I've never seen these men in my life!" said Kallas

"We were having lunch with you," said Antti slyly.

"You may have been sitting at the same table, but I don't know you."

"Course you do! We're old pals, you and me!" Antti winked at the workers, as if to share a secret.

"Then what's my name?" said Kallas.

Antti had to stop and think.

"You don't even know your supposed pal's name," said Koivo, "Bugger off to the back of the queue, both of you. We don't like queue-jumpers." General murmurs of agreement came from people further back in the line. "Get to the back, you two!" shouted a distinguished looking man. "Filthy communists!" shouted a middle-aged woman. "Look out!" came another voice, "They're probably pickpockets." Antti scowled at Kallas, and drew a finger across his throat. "We'll see you later," he sneered, and turned to lead Matti back to the end of the line.

"Thanks Koivo," said Kallas, "Those two have been bothering me since I arrived at the terminal. I don't know what they're up to."

The gate was opened, and as their passports were checked, the passengers moved towards the gangway onto the deck of the boat, most heading straight for the interior. Kallas accepted Koivo's invitation to join them for a drink in the buffet, and soon they were ensconced at a table in one corner. So far so good. As long as he stayed with Koivo and his companions, he was safe. The question was, how far would the two thugs go. If their orders were to eliminate him, they might simply keep tracking him until they got him alone. In which case he needed to lose them once they reached Tallinn. But at least then he'd be on his home ground. He knew the city like the back of his hand.

He noticed the two men come in and take a table at the other end of the room. People were staring at the wet patch at the front of Matti's trousers, and he didn't look too happy. Kallas had an idea. He'd been on the boat many times, and knew the two men behind the bar. He offered to buy his new friends a drink, and went up to the bar. One of the barmen, whose name he remembered was Siegfried, greeted him. He explained that the big man over there with the wet patch was a notorious drunk from Helsinki who frequently got into fights, and that his friend was a pickpocket. As a crime reporter he'd seen them both in court more than once. Siegfried thanked him, and left the buffet, returning in a few minutes with two hefty crew members. The two thugs were ordered to leave the buffet and sit out on the benches on the open deck.

Siegfried thanked Kallas for pointing them out. "We try to run a clean ship here, *Härra* Kallas, and these types need to get the message they're not welcome. The big man had obviously already wet himself, and if he'd had more to drink, goodness knows what might have happened."

Kallas was able to relax a little more. The question now was whether the thugs would continue to follow him, in which case he'd have to try to lose them in the maze of alleys in the old town.

The ship arrived in Tallinn and they filed down the gangplank onto Estonian soil, and queued to show their passports and pass through customs. As Koivo and his group had their passports checked carefully, Kallas noticed Antti and Matti, now looking very chilled, working their way up towards him again. Antti came up behind him and whispered, "Now we've gotcha, eh?" Kallas passed through the check with the two close behind him and exited the terminal onto the quayside. The two thugs appeared on either side of him and grabbed his arms tightly. Antti hissed into his ear, "Now you're coming with us."

"Excuse me, Jaan," called a voice, "Aren't you going to show us the way to the station? We were waiting for you." Koivo and his three companions stood by the quayside a few metres ahead of him.

"He's coming with us," said Antti.

"Yeah, you want an argument?" growled Matti.

"Give me a hand here, lads," called Kallas, "These two are trying to rob me." He tried to get away, but the two men held him tight. At least, they did until Koivo punched Antti on the nose and then kicked his legs from under him. As he fell, one of the others gave him a shove, and he disappeared over the edge of the quay and hit the dark and icy water with a dull splash.

Matti let go of Kallas. "You threw him in the water," he said, "It serves him right for spilling his coffee on me. And I had to leave most of my lunch behind."

Two policemen appeared around the corner of a warehouse and headed in their direction. The harbour was well-patrolled.

"You better get back to Helsinki in a hurry, unless you want to stay here for a long time," said Kallas. The big man took the hint, and began to lope back towards the terminal.

"Everything alright here?" asked one of the patrolmen.

"Yes, thank you, officer," said Kallas. "These two men were giving me some trouble. They'd followed me all the way from Helsinki. One of them fell into the harbour. He was trying to pick my pocket, but these gentlemen came to my rescue."

"Okay," said the officer. "You leave it with us now, sir. We'll fish him out and put him on the next boat back to Finland. We don't want that sort here." He saluted, and the two officers strolled towards the rusty iron rungs where a sodden Antti was trying to drag himself out of the water.

Kallas was happy to accompany his new friends to the railway station and see them off to Tartu.

As he walked back to the newspaper office, he

considered what had happened. He'd have to keep his ear to the ground, something was going on. But what?

14

After leaving the hospital, Hallmets decided to have a look at the three possible addresses Juta had given him for Villem Jonsson. All three were in an area between the railway station and the town centre, an area of wide streets with generously-sized houses of wood sprinkled along their length.

He started at Naituse Street 22. A middle-aged man in his shirt sleeves answered the door, wiping his hands on a rag. He noticed the car and looked suspiciously at Hallmets. "Yes, do you want something?"

"*Härra* Krauss?"

"What if I am?"

Hallmets introduced himself, and showed his ID. "We're trying to locate a young man named Villem Jonsson. I was wondering if he had lodgings here."

"Hmm. The name don't ring a bell with me. But the wife'll know for sure. Wait there, I'll get her." He disappeared indoors, and a few moments later a large, smiling, woman appeared.

"Don't mind Krauss," she said, "He's suspicious of everybody. He said you were looking for someone."

"Yes, that's right. A young man, mid-twenties, name of Villem Jonsson. Would he be lodging here?"

She thought for a moment, wiping her hands absent-mindedly on her apron. "No. We don't have anyone of that name. Nor have had in the past either. But you could try *Proua* Vilms, she's in Itaalia Street, or maybe *Proua* Mölder on Belgia Street. I can't remember the numbers, but most folks there will direct you."

Hallmets thanked and went on to Itaalia Street 17. Here

a young man answered the door, explained that he was one of the lodgers, and no, he'd not heard of a Villem Jonsson. He fetched *Proua* Vilms, a tired-looking woman with grey hair under a black headscarf, who said the same thing. She didn't offer any further recommendations.

The wooden building at Belgia Street 46 had been painted dark green, and the paint had faded over time into a comfortable shade which discreetly showed the texture of the wooden planks, without shouting about it. A window on the ground floor was open, and a cat sat on the sill watching Hallmets as he exited the car.

He knocked on the door, and after perhaps half a minute, he heard a woman's voice from within: "All right, keep your hat on, I'm coming. But I'm not buying anything."

Footsteps approached and the door opened to reveal a woman of rather solid proportions, a pink face and grey hair tied back in a bun, a coarse grey apron over her black dress, and a frown. She looked at him, and then the car caught her eye. So, not just a tall distinguished-looking man, but a tall distinguished-looking man with a distinguished-looking car, and a chauffeur busily polishing the headlamps.

Her expression changed to a polite smile. "What can I do for you, sir? If it's about the house, I'm afraid it's not for sale. But there are still plenty of vacant plots where you could build a new one." She gestured vaguely along the road.

"I'm sorry to bother you. My name is Hallmets, Detective Chief Inspector Hallmets." He showed her his ID. "It's *Proua* Mölder, is that right?"

"Yes, I'm Epp Mölder." Now she was puzzled. "Not one of my lads in trouble, I hope. Please, do come in. What am I thinking of, just standing at the door."

She led him through a corridor to a small room at the back of the house which seemed to be her snug. There was a window to the back of the building looking onto a garden, in which the snow still covered what looked like dug-over patches of earth on either side of a path leading to a clump of fruit trees. She noticed him looking out the window. "It's a nice garden, isn't it? I grow plenty of veg in the spring and summer, and there's apples and plums from the trees. I'm sorry the room's a bit chilly, I only put the fire on in the evening, when I can have a sit-down." Two padded armchairs flanked the fireplace, one of which had a low table by it. On the table were a couple of magazines, *Today's Estonian Woman* and *Knitting for All Ages*.

"Please, take a seat." She indicated the seat without the lamp and the table, and Hallmets eased himself gently into it. He was wary of armchairs that looked soft and inviting; sometimes you sank in further than you wanted. But this one was quite firm, and he was able to relax in the knowledge that he'd be able to get out of it again whenever he wanted.

"Thank you, *Proua* Mölder. This is simply a routine enquiry, in connection with a case we're looking at just now. I'll come straight to the point. Do you have a lodger named Villem Jonsson?"

"Villem? Oh yes, he's one of mine all right. I hope he's not in any trouble."

"He may have some information that could help us, that's all. Tell me, how long have you been taking in lodgers?"

"Oh, ten years now. Ever since my Albert retired. He had the garage out on the Tartu Road. He saw from the start that cars were going to be big. Got in there when he was still young. Any car you like, he could fix it. Anyway, when he retired, he said to me, Epp, he said, even if I go, you'll still have the house. That'll help you make a living. He'd foreseen it, you see, I mean, that he'd go first, so as soon as he retired, he got the place converted so that we could run it as a lodging house. We did that for four years, then he took ill, and soon he was gone. It were a blessing really, he was in a lot of pain towards the end. But we'd got the routine established, so I could keep on running the place, and it's done me fine so far. I have to get a man in for the maintenance now, of course. Albert could fix anything, you know."

"So how many lodgers do you have at the moment?"

"I have seven right now. That's as many as I can deal with, and it pays me enough to live on."

"Are they all men?"

"Good heavens, yes! A mixed lodging house is asking for trouble, I can tell you. Young men and women under the same roof, well, you just think of it! I don't need to say any more, do I?"

"Of course not. Villem Jonsson. What's your impression of him?"

"A very nice lad. No trouble at all. Pays his rent on time. And keeps himself neat and tidy, and clean. I like my lads to be clean and able to present themselves well."

"How long's Villem been with you?" asked Hallmets.

"Oh, not so long I suppose. About six months. He came here to get a job. I don't think he was long out of the university. He seems very well educated. He works for that general out at Rauakivi Castle. As a secretary."

"Is it a full-time job?"

"No, he only has to be at the castle Tuesdays and

Thursdays. I know that 'cause he has to be up early those days. But he does another two days, typing up and correcting stuff. The general's memoirs, he said. He gets paid for the four days, so that gives him enough to pay the rent. All day Wednesday and Friday I hear him upstairs tap-tap-tapping away on his typewriter."

"Does he tell you how the book is coming on?"

"He says it's hard work, but they're making progress. He's very involved in it. I think he must know more about the general by now than anyone else. Barring the general himself, of course."

"Is he here at the moment?"

"No, I'm afraid not. He goes home every weekend, off on Saturday morning, back on Monday afternoon. Such a good lad. Some of them, you know, they get away from home, and they never think of visiting their families."

"It's a pity I've missed him. If you don't mind, *Proua* Mölder, I'd like to have a look at his room."

"Oh dear, he's done something, hasn't he?"

"No, no, he's done nothing wrong at all. But, as I said, he may have some information relating to a case we're working on. The thing is, he himself may not regard it as important, so he may have just left it in his room."

"Oh, well, if that's it, I suppose it's all right. Come along, then. It's upstairs."

She led him up a bare wooden staircase to a corridor on the upper floor. "Six of the boys are up here, three at the front and three at the back," explained *Proua* Mölder, "The other one is downstairs, at the front, next to the lounge. They do appreciate the lounge. They need a space to relax and chat. Otherwise they'd be getting up to no good. There's two bathrooms up here, at that end, next door to each other. All the boys use them. That was one of the changes Albert made. 'You can't have them queueing for the toilet,' he used to say. I've got a little bathroom all to myself at the back downstairs. You do need a bit of privacy when you've got a lot of lodgers."

It was the third room along, facing the rear of the house. A small, rather bare room, containing a narrow bed against the left wall, a wardrobe and dressing table against the right wall, and, by the window, a table with an upright chair by it. On the table sat a large typewriter, its body painted blue, the name 'Olympia' embossed in white on the plate above the roller, and by it a neat pile of blank sheets of paper.

"It's a very good typewriter," said Hallmets, "German, I think. Does he leave it here all the time?"

"Oh yes. He says it's too heavy to carry about, and in any case, he doesn't work when he's home. But the typewriter's his prize possession. Says it took him months to save up for it."

"Do you mind if I have a little look round on my own now, *Proua* Mölder. What we're looking for is confidential. If you'll wait downstairs, I'll only be a few minutes."

Proua Mölder was clearly reluctant to leave, but Hallmets had spoken with a quiet authority that could not be argued with. "Yes, of course," she mumbled, "Er, do let me know when you're done. So's I can tidy the room, and lock it." Hallmets smiled assent, and she retreated.

He waited until he heard her steps going down the stairs, before starting to examine the room.

The result was disappointing. He could find nothing of the work on the general's book. Jonsson must have taken everything with him. But why do that if he were only away for the weekend, and said he didn't take work away with him. Unless it was very near completion and he'd taken a draft of the whole thing to read through. He may also have been under instruction from the general not to leave anything lying around.

He went back downstairs, and found *Proua* Mölder in her little den at the back of the house. He thanked her for letting him into the room. "One other thing," he added, "Do you happen to have Villem's parents' address? We still need to talk with him, in case he can help us."

"Oh yes, I keep good records. Albert insisted on that. 'If any of them skips it,' he said, 'we need to be able to find someone to pay what they owe.' That's usually the parents, of course." She took a set of keys from her apron pocket, and opened the single door of a cupboard in the corner of the room. From the top shelf she extracted a thick notebook with plain cardboard covers. "I keep all my records in here," she said, flicking through the pages, "Here it is. Jonsson. Soo Street 34, Võru."

15

Back at the police station, he found Larsson still there, and asked if she'd had any luck with the diary.

"Not a lot, chief. There's very little detail on his activities. If he goes to Tallinn, he just writes 'Tallinn,' which doesn't help. His meetings locally are just what you might expect: Independence Day vigil, speech at the war memorial, address to the Women's Voluntary Defence Organisation, prize-giving at the gymnasium, annual Chamber of Commerce lunch, and so on. In terms of folks visiting him, either he didn't get many visitors, or he just didn't put them all in his diary. How did the PM go?"

"Someone shot him in the chest, then pushed the sabre through the wound."

"Interesting. So it was murder, as Anna thought."

"Yes. How are you feeling, Eva? Do you need some sleep?"

"I'm OK for the moment. I'll get to bed early this evening."

"Right. I need to check out an address. It's Jonsson's parents. Thanks to Juta, I managed to track down his lodgings, but he's gone home for the weekend. The address is in Võru, so I'll leave a message with the police there to track them down and ask him to stay there. Then let's get some lunch, and after that we'll go back to the castle."

Hallmets put a call through to the Võru police station, and asked the desk sergeant there if a couple of officers could visit Soo Street 34 and see if Villem Jonsson was there. If he was there, they should ask him to remain at that address until an officer from Hallmets' unit could get over to Võru to interview him, hopefully on the following day. If not, they should ask the parents where he was.

Then he and Larsson walked up Jaama Street, past the bus station, to the market square, and a homely cafe, where Hallmets enjoyed a bacon and mushroom pie and Larsson a carrot and onion pie with their coffees. It wasn't snowing, but it was very cold, and the iron grey sky hanging oppressively over the town was keeping its own counsel about what it was going to do next.

As soon as they arrived at the castle, Hallmets called the team together to see where they were. They met in the general's sitting-room. Anna appeared with coffee and pastries. Lesser assured Hallmets they'd been given a good lunch by Eda Pirn.

Hallmets reported on the post-mortem, his search for Villem Jonsson, and the general's diary, finishing with Kadakas' information on the general. He asked Lesser to summarise what had been happening at the castle.

"We spent most of the morning searching the place, including all the outbuildings. That included going through the Pirns' cottage and Kirik's apartment again, though that was probably a waste of time, since they've had time and opportunity to get rid of anything they don't want us to find. We haven't got round to interviewing anybody yet."

"Did the search reveal anything useful?" asked Hallmets.

"Most of what was in the house – furniture, books, fishing gear, even paintings – was left behind by the von Winkelsteins. The general hasn't added very much that's his own. Maybe he liked living in the baronial ambience."

"Or," added Hallmets, "As a military man, he didn't

actually have much that was his own."

"Having lost most of his family," put in Larsson, "Maybe there wasn't much left to build an identity on."

Lesser cleared his throat and carried on. "I think the general's study and his bedroom had already been searched, before we arrived. That seemed to me the case when I went through his bedroom yesterday. Too untidy for a lifelong military man. And no personal papers at all. Considering he was writing his memoirs, you would expect old diaries, or notes, or even correspondence with his publisher. But there's nothing. And the cupboard in the study is suspiciously empty; I'm guessing that's where his papers were. But the door hasn't been forced. Somebody opened it with a key, took the stuff out, and locked it again. Kirik claimed he didn't have a key, so we had to force it open. However, we did have one piece of luck. This was tucked down the side of the armchair in the study. It may have just slipped down there, or someone may have put it there."

He passed a business card to Hallmets, who looked at both sides, before commenting. "Rist and Pistoda, publishers, Lai Street, Tallinn. Hopefully, they were publishing the general's memoirs. I'll go up to Tallinn tomorrow to see what else we can find out about the general's past. Then I can pay Rist and Pistoda a visit on Monday morning. The card shows they must have some connection with the general. Even if they turned down his memoirs, they may know who else he was talking to. Thanks, Henno. We've only two real trails to follow so far. Either it was, as Colonel Reinart suspects, political, or it was something in his memoirs that someone didn't like. The other avenue we need to look at is his family. We should contact the surviving son and daughter, in case they're involved. I'll ask Ants to track them down. Unless *Härra* Kirik has that information."

"Actually," said Lesser, "I think Dr Kirss, that's my cousin's husband, may be able to help there. He mentioned to me last night that he'd done some legal work for the general. I didn't want to quiz him there and then, as it would probably be better coming from you, on an official basis."

"Thanks. Perhaps if I come over some time this evening?"

"That'll be fine. He's usually home by half past six."

"Right. We need to interview Kirik and the Pirns in more depth now. Not forgetting Anna too. We should go through their movements on the night before last, then if there was anything odd they noticed the last week or two, and finally who visited the general here recently. Henno, if you can take the Pirns, Eva takes Anna, and Ilmar and I will take Kirik. It's now 3.15. That way, we'll hopefully get away before it gets too late."

16

Lesser interviewed the Pirns in the kitchen, Larsson talked to Eva in her room in the attic, and Hallmets and Hekk interviewed Kirik in the general's sitting-room. Hallmets and Hekk took one of the sofas flanking the fireplace, and Hekk invited Kirik to sit on the other. Kirik treated him to a patronising smile as he made himself comfortable.

"Thank you for coming to see us, *Härra* Kirik," said Hallmets, "Officer Hekk will be asking you a few more questions. We just want to clarify some of the things you've already told us. I'll take notes, if you don't mind."

Kirik smiled again. "Of course, chief inspector. Anything to help." He smiled indulgently at Hekk, as if permitting him to begin. Hallmets took out his leather-bound notebook, and fountain pen.

Hekk nodded. "Thank you, sir." He gave the impression of being a small-town clerk somewhat out of his depth at finding himself a policeman. "Um, I wonder if you could begin by taking us through exactly what you did the night before last. Er, that would be the night of the 28th to 29th November, 1935."

"Of course. Well, as I already told the Chief Inspector, it was just another ordinary day. I had various administrative tasks to do during the day, then ..."

"Sorry, sir," said Hekk, "Can you tell us what these administrative tasks were?"

"The usual thing. Make sure the maid had tidied up the house properly. She's a bit of an idler, that one," he said as an aside to Hallmets. "Then I ordered Jaak to clear the snow from the courtyard. Then I met the general, to go through what he was going to do for the day."

"And what was that, sir?"

"Not a lot, really. He was going to do his usual walk around the estate, to make sure everything was in order. Then write a letter to the municipality, about keeping the road to town clear of snow. The general was always very careful about things. That's why he was so good during the war, at keeping the troops supplied. He always noticed the details. Had a good memory too."

"Still?" asked Hekk.

Kirik seemed affronted by Hekk's temerity in asking such a question. "Naturally. He was still as sharp as a tack."

"Did you always accompany him on his inspection?"

"Oh, yes, of course. To note down what needed doing."

"And was the estate in good order?"

"Yes, everything seemed fine, if rather wet underfoot. But no mysterious footprints in the snow, or anything like that." He smirked. "Then he wrote his letter, or rather dictated it me. I typed it out, and he signed it. By then it was lunch-time."

"Did the general take his lunch on his own?"

"Of course." Kirik looked at Hallmets as if to sympathise with the chief inspector for having such a clod as an underling. "The rest of us had lunch in the kitchen."

"And after lunch?" continued Hekk

"I took the general's letter into town and delivered it to the town hall. That way they couldn't pretend they never got it. I got a couple of things at the shops, and had a coffee at one of the cafés on Market Square. When I got back, the general was still asleep in his chair in the study. He usually read and then had a snooze after lunch."

"And then?"

100

"I think once the general woke up, he had a cup of coffee, and read for a while. The maid will confirm that, I'm sure. I polished the car and checked the fuel and water levels, and cleaned the spark plugs and the distributor. The car had been misfiring a bit on the road to town. Then after dinner, the general asked me to play a couple of games of chess with him. At about eight thirty, I returned to my apartment. I had a glass of brandy and read a book. *The Four Just Men*, by Edgar Wallace. I went to bed at about ten. And slept, until Jaak buzzed me in the morning. Then, when I saw what he'd found, I called the police."

"What did the general do after you left him? Did he have a routine?"

"Yes. He would have read a bit more, with a cup of cocoa, and gone to bed about nine-thirty."

"Did you hear or see anything unusual during the night?"

"I told you, I was asleep."

"Thank you, sir. Did you notice anything unusual over the last couple of weeks?"

"Such as what?"

"Any change in the general's demeanour or routine, unexpected visitors, any occurrence that struck you as odd."

"No. Nothing at all. Anyway, what's all the fuss about? The general killed himself. Inspector Einmann said so. Cut-and-dried, he said."

"We have to make sure everything's clear," said Hallmets. "Officer Hekk, please continue."

"Yes, sir. *Härra* Kirik, do you remember any of the visitors who came here in the last couple of weeks?"

"Sorry, I'm afraid I don't."

"How many were there? Just give me a rough idea. Five, ten, twenty, a hundred."

"I don't know, maybe half a dozen. The general didn't get a lot of visitors."

"And you can't remember who any of them were?"

Kirik opened his mouth to say something, then shut it again. "Well, I think the minister from the parish church was out one day."

"Can you give us his name?"

"Eh? Oh, Viinapuu, no, Veinberg, that's it, Dr. Veinberg. And then there was Dr Kirss, the lawyer."

"Do you know why the general wanted to see him?"

"I've no idea. That's all I can remember."

"Thank you, sir. Do you happen to have *Härra* Jonsson's parents' address?"

"No, I don't. I think it was in Võru somewhere. I've answered enough questions. I'd like to go now."

"Not quite yet, sir," said Hallmets, "Let's talk about you now, shall we, *Härra* Kirik. What did you do before the war?"

"What's that got to do with anything?"

"Just answer the question, sir."

Kirik looked uneasy. "Oh, this and that. I did all sorts of things. I even worked on a fishing boat for six months."

"Don't worry, sir, we can easily find out. One other question. Do any of the staff possess any firearms?"

Kirik looked relieved at the change of subject. "The usual for an estate. The general had a hunting rifle and a shotgun, for shooting birds. Probably still had his service revolver, too. I handed mine in when we left the army. Pirn has a shotgun too, for killing vermin."

"Thank you for your co-operation, *Härra* Kirik. Please remain here on the estate until we advise you otherwise."

WINTER BlOOD

17

It was after four when the team assembled again in the sitting room. Hallmets asked Hekk to report on their interview with Raud Kirik, then added his own comments. "Kirik is certainly a suspect. I'm pretty sure he's not telling us everything. We need to look into his background. So, Henno, what did you learn from the Pirns?"

"Not much more than you, chief. On the night of the killing, they went over to their cottage once they'd done the dishes and tidied up after the general's dinner. That was about seven forty-five."

"What about the general's cocoa?" asked Hekk.

"That was Anna's job," put in Larsson.

"Then," continued Lesser, "They listened to the radio for an hour. It was the weekly programme for smallholders. This week's was about keeping chickens, they said. We can check that. It finished at nine, and then Jaak walked round the outside of the buildings, to check that all was okay. The light was on in the general's sitting-room, but the curtains were closed, and Jaak says he'd never have peered in, even if they had been open. There was also a light on in the kitchen – I'm guessing that was Anna – and also in Kirik's apartment. There was no-one creeping about suspiciously, and it hadn't started snowing yet, so no footprints to see. Then they went to bed. Jaak says he read the newspaper for a while, and Eda was reading a novel. *The Three Keys*, by Eirik Laidsaar."

"It's a good one," said Hekk, "Came out just this year. From Loodus. Most of what they publish is foreign authors, so it's good to see a thriller writer of our own. Sorry, Henno, do carry on."

"Thank you, Ilmar. Anyway, they turned the lamp off at about ten, and slept well. Noticed nothing until Jaak went out in the morning and found the general. About the visitors, they say the same as Kirik, there weren't many. Eda's in the kitchen a lot, and she remembers all the visitors she had to make coffee for. I made a list. I'll read it out:

Monday 18th November, afternoon: Dr Kirss.

Wednesday 20th November, afternoon: Colonel Janno, from the Army Pension Scheme.

Thursday 21st November, *Härra* and *Proua* Sinakas, for dinner. They're the general's neighbours, their house is further up the road. He owns a furniture workshop in town.

Friday 22nd November, afternoon: Rev. Dr. Veinberg. Eda thinks it was to discuss the arrangements for the Christmas services.

Saturday 23rd November, morning: Dr. Kirss again. Eda thinks it was to do with the general's will. That may be pure speculation on her part, but I suspect she also listens at doors.

Monday 25th November, afternoon, Professor Strelkov, from Tartu University. She thinks he's writing a history book, and was asking the general about the war.

And finally Wednesday 27th November, afternoon: *Härra* Sepp. She doesn't know who he is, or what it was about."

"Mr. Smith," said Larsson, "A common name. Or a fake one?"

"Unfortunately she didn't see him. It's Anna who takes the coffee through. However Eda says there may be visitors she doesn't know about. Kirik usually answers the front door when someone is expected, and if they don't get coffee, she may miss them completely if she's in the kitchen or the wash-house."

"What's your impression of the Pirns, Henno?" asked Hallmets.

"I'd say they're pretty much on the level. Probably making a few extra kroons selling produce from the estate on the side, but no big secrets to hide."

"Thanks, Henno. Okay, Eva, what have got from Anna?"

"She's quite sharp, I'd say, chief. She waited in the kitchen, until she heard the general go up to his bedroom. Then she went to the sitting-room, damped down the fire, and tidied up. After that she checked all the downstairs rooms to make sure the windows were shut, and there was nothing that needed putting away. She got up to her room not long after ten, and went to bed soon afterwards. With a spoonful of morphine syrup. She's got a similar list of guests to Eda, except, unlike Eda, she saw them all when she brought through their coffee, or, with the Sinikas couple, dinner. She can also describe what they look like. She recognised *Härra* and *Proua* Sinikas, and Drs Kirss and Veinberg, as they've been here before. She thinks Professor Strelkov had been before too, but it must have months ago. She'd never seen *Härra* Sepp before, and doesn't know who he is. But she has given me a description of him, which may be useful."

"Let's hear it, Eva, in case it rings any bells," said Hallmets.

"Average height, middle-aged, she thinks, black hair, right hand parting, carefully-trimmed moustache, a scar on the back of his left hand, that might be useful. She says he was dressed 'like a bank manager,' in a rather old fashioned suit with a high winged collar and bow tie. He was also wearing *pince nez* when she saw him, with a thin gold chain attached. And spats on his shoes. He was sitting on one of the sofas, and there was a briefcase lying on the empty seat by him, and a couple of papers on top of it. Both he and the general were silent when she set out the coffee and pastries. The general thanked her when she was finished. Sepp remained silent throughout, but watched her surreptitiously."

"Anyone recognise him?" asked Hallmets. Heads shook all round. "We'll have to ask Kirik and the Pirns about him. I'm meeting with Dr Kirss this evening. Henno, can you check out *Härra* and *Proua* Sinikas and the pastor."

"No problem with the pastor, chief. He was already in the job before I worked here. He must be about seventy now. I can't see him bumping off the general. I'll certainly talk to him, though, the general may have said something to him. I've never met *Härra* and *Proua* Sinikas, so we can pay them a call too. What shall we do with the staff here?"

"We've no reason to keep them incommunicado. Tell them they must continue to live in the castle or in Viljandi. We can keep them here overnight, and tell them that in the morning. Ilmar, can you do a night shift here? I doubt if anything will happen, but you never know."

"Anna will be relieved to hear that," said Larsson. "But I've another question. Who owns the castle? Was it given to the general, in which case his son and daughter should inherit it, or was it simply lent to him by the state for his lifetime, in which case it reverts to them. I'm just thinking about who benefits from his death."

"That's a good question. I'll ask Dr Kirss this evening. Clearly it'll affect the staff, as well as the general's offspring. There's just one other thing. I think the general was shot inside the house. A noise outside would have wakened the Pirns or Kirik. Inside, there was only Anna, and she was sedated. But the question is, where? Here's a possible scenario. A secret visitor comes during the night, and knocks at the front door."

"Why not the kitchen?" asked Hekk, "Wouldn't that be more private?"

"That's true, but I don't think the kitchen was a part of the house which the general considered his own. If he was expecting the visitor, I think he'd want to see him, or her, on his own territory, as it were, his own rooms in the house. That means the hallway, the sitting-room, the study and his bedroom. I don't see the bedroom being the site, given the way he was fully dressed."

"Why did he have a coat on, if he invited the visitor in?" asked Lesser.

"The coat was open when he was found. I think the killer put it on him, then dragged him out into the courtyard."

"At least we can rule out a burglar. No burglar I know would go to the trouble of staging a suicide. And most burglars I know don't carry guns."

"I think you're right, Henno," replied Hallmets, "It looks like someone came to see him, and then killed him. And then set up the suicide pose. What we don't know is whether they came with the intention of killing him, or whether they were not satisfied with the result of their meeting, and then decided to kill him. So the hallway, sitting-room and study will need searching again. This time we're looking for a bullet, probably stuck in the wall somewhere, and any indications of violence. Scratches on the wall, that sort of thing."

"What if we don't find it?" said Larsson.

"Let's not worry about that unless it happens. I think it's time we were getting back to town. Tomorrow morning I'll head back to Tallinn, on the train, so Lembit and the car can stay here. On Monday I'll check out Rist and Pistoda, the publishers. Hopefully they'll have some of the text of the general's memoirs. And I'll also see if I can track down Colonel Janno."

18

They were back at the police station by 5.30 after another crawl along the dark and icy road. There was a note awaiting Hallmets from Dr Kirss, inviting him to his home for dinner that evening at 7.00. Lesser headed off to his cousin's, with instructions to pass on Hallmets' acceptance of the dinner invitation, while Hallmets and Larsson returned to the hotel, where Lembit had already gone with the car.

After a wash and a change of clothes, Hallmets met Lembit, and they set off. It only took Lembit ten minutes to find the right house, a wooden building of two stories on Uueveski Street. Hallmets realised that Lesser could walk from there to the police station in fifteen or twenty minutes. He asked Lembit to collect him at nine thirty; he didn't want to overstay his welcome. And, given that even when they arrived, with no street lights, it was pitch dark, he didn't trust himself to find the way back to the hotel on foot, despite having the printed street map the hotel had given him, which made the layout of Viljandi look deceptively simple.

He was welcomed by the lawyer and his wife. Dr Kirss, tall and stooping slightly, reminded Hallmets of Jaan Tõnisson, the leader of the Liberal Party, now prohibited from any political activity. Dr Kirss was probably in his fifties and his hair and beard still a rich black. With his thick glasses magnifying his eyes, he gave the impression of a slightly mad professor. His wife Greete, perhaps ten years younger, was shorter, and slim, with a face of perfect classical proportions that could have been created by a Greek sculptor, except that she didn't look like she was made of stone, and had a disarming smile and a way of emphasising whatever she said with balletic gestures of her hands. Only when she paused, and looked thoughtful, did he see a resemblance to Henno Lesser.

The meal, served by the Kirss's 20-year old daughter Liina, was excellent: a soup of smoked mushrooms, pork chops with potatoes and stewed apple, and a cheesecake with mixed berries. The berries and mushrooms had been picked in the autumn, the apples grown in the garden. Town-dwelling Estonians kept up the traditions of self-sufficiency of their parents and grandparents.

During the meal the conversation did not touch upon General Madrus. There were plenty of other things to talk about. After his legal studies at Tartu University, Dr Kirss had spent two years at the University of Frankfurt, studying criminology, and he had several friends in Germany. The messages he was receiving about the Nazi regime and its approach to law were very depressing. One of his friends, who was Jewish, had already left the country, and his letters now came from Los Angeles. Another, who'd become a member of the Hessian *Landtag* for the Social Democratic Party, was now incarcerated in a concentration camp. Others were finding it increasingly hard to cope with the use of the law as a political weapon. 'Law is subject to the Will of the *Führer*, whose voice is that of the German People,' was the Nazi line, 'All enemies of the *Führer* are therefore criminals.' Hallmets had visited Germany in the 1920s, and knew that this approach would also place many policemen in a difficult position.

After the meal, they moved to the sitting room, and Greete offered them a glass of locally-distilled plum brandy. Then she excused herself, saying she should help

Liina with the washing-up, leaving the two policemen and the lawyer. Now Hallmets felt able to raise the topic he wanted to discuss.

"Thank you, Dr Kirss, for the opportunity to raise this matter. You will realise that what we say now is confidential."

"Of course," nodded Kirss, "I heard on the grapevine only today that General Madrus has died. Inspector Einmann apparently believes he killed himself."

"I'm afraid that's very unlikely. He was shot in the chest, that's what killed him. The sabre was added later. However, I think Inspector Einmann had not, when he allowed his views to become known, been aware of the post-mortem result."

"Ah. Einmann does tend to jump to conclusions. How can I help you?"

"I think you already know. You visited General Madrus on the afternoon of Monday the 18th November and the morning of Saturday the 23rd. Your conversation may be relevant to our investigation. I'd be grateful if you could tell me what you talked about."

"There is the matter of client confidentiality, chief inspector. On the other hand, you're about to tell me my client is dead, and his doings are the subject of a murder investigation, so I'll agree, under protest of course ..." He smiled.

"Naturally. That is noted."

"Thank you. It was about his will. It was five years since he last changed it. At that time his son, Vitus, was made the executor. But, since then he had lost touch with Vitus. And since he had no way of contacting him, he wanted to make Sirje the executor."

"Sorry to interrupt. What happened with Vitus? Was

there a falling out?"

"He wouldn't say. Only that he'd lost touch with him."

"Did he say when?"

"'A few years ago' was all he would say. Said he'd expected him to reappear, but he never did."

"Did he seem sad about that?"

"He tried to hide it, but, yes, I think he regretted whatever had passed between them. But he was too proud to do anything about it. I suggested putting a call for Vitus in the newspapers, and he hesitated before turning it down. 'Not just yet,' he said 'Maybe in a month or two.'"

"I presume he left his money to Vitus and Sirje."

"Yes. Apart from a cash sum to Raud Kirik. 10,000 kroons."

"Worth killing for, no doubt about that. How much did he leave?"

"He had about a hundred thousand in bonds and other investments. But there was also a question mark over the castle. He thought it would be part of the inheritance and wondered whether he should allocate it specifically to Vitus, as his eldest, or let the two of them decide what to do with it. I had to ask him what proof he had that he actually owned the place. He'd simply signed the document they pushed under his nose when they granted it to him, without reading it, and he assumed it was a gift. I told him I'd have to check that out, especially as he said he didn't have a copy of the document. That's the main reason I went over again on the Saturday. I'd gone to Tartu, to the National Archives, and they were able to show me the document. In fact it turned out they'd only awarded him the use of the place, and not its ownership. So it now reverts to the state. I'll have to write to somebody in Tallinn to let them know. The sooner we can hand over the responsibility for it, and the staff, to someone else, the better. Otherwise it'll be a drain on the general's estate. We daren't just shut the place down and abandon it, as the deed says it has to be returned to the state in the condition in which it was received."

"I'm guessing the general wasn't too pleased about that, I mean the fact that he didn't own the castle."

"You're right, it was a major disappointment. He'd rather seen himself as a successor to the German barons, and his bubble was somewhat punctured, knowing that his baronial estate was only borrowed."

"So what was the upshot of the second meeting?"

"I was to redraw the will, clarifying the appendix relating to the general's assets. I had also told him we had to take steps to locate Vitus, since if the general were to die and Vitus be unavailable, it could cause problems with the settlement. He said we'd discuss that when I came back. Luckily he signed the updated will I brought him on the Saturday, so Sirje is now the executor. Sorry, but I'm afraid that's all I can tell you."

"That's been very helpful. Is there anything else you might have heard about the general or the castle, that might be relevant?"

"Let me think. You know the place is haunted, but I don't think that's relevant. The only question mark I'd raise is about his man Kirik. I've met him a couple of times at the castle, and I must admit there's something about him I just don't find quite right. Anyway, what about another brandy? Or a coffee? Perhaps both would be the best solution."

Lembit arrived punctually at 9.30, and took him back to the hotel, driving very slowly on the icy roads. "You've got the right idea, getting the train tomorrow, boss. The road's going to be bad after a night of this."

Back at the hotel, he phoned Kirsti. She was pleased to hear he'd be home the next day. They arranged to meet at the *Alt-Revaler* café at one o'clock for lunch. He went to bed, and had no sooner begun to consider the various hypotheses surrounding the general's death that he fell into a deep sleep.

19

Sunday 1st December

The following morning it was freezing cold. Ice was everywhere; long icicles hung from the gutters, and ice particles glittered everywhere in the early sun. The slush on the roads had frozen solid, and Lembit had to drive at a snail's pace to get Hallmets to the railway station. He made the 9.30 am to Tallinn. Being Sunday, it was not an express. It was very cold in the compartment, and the supposed heating seemed to have little effect. But at least there was no-one else there, and he had time to think.

He recognised that this was the phase in the case when the questions multiplied. That was actually a good sign, because it meant there were lots of leads emerging. And somewhere amongst those questions was one that led to the truth, the one answer that made sense of everything. But the next stage was the difficult one: snipping off all the dead ends until one question remained. That usually took a lot of time and legwork, and that was where they were right now. He had three lines to follow: the political one, although there was little evidence of that so far; the memoirs, and that meant talking to the publishers and the missing secretary; and the family, which meant searching for a son who'd been missing for some years. All that represented a great deal of legwork. But also plenty of thinking, creating and discussing hypotheses that fitted the facts or might explain them. Without that creative aspect, he knew that many policemen would end up like Einmann, simply grabbing at the first explanation that came to mind.

The train rattled on through the frosted countryside,

passing marshes, woods, fields, villages, stopping at tiny stations for people whose only lifeline to the capital was this railway. Hallmets had bought a newspaper at the station in Viljandi, more out of habit than interest in what it might say. As usual, President Päts was on the front page, taking the salute at a march-past of nurses, firemen, and other public servants. What kind of state needed a march-past of nurses and firemen? How did that save lives or put out fires? He quickly leafed through the pages, and satisfied himself that there was no mention of General Madrus' death.

At last, after two and a half hours, the train crawled into the Baltic Station in Tallinn. Hallmets' first move was to the station cafe, to get a coffee and a hot pie, and try to warm up. Coming out of the building twenty minutes later, he saw in front of him the outline of Toompea Hill, where all the government buildings were, in the midst of them the tower of the cathedral which gave the hill its name. He remembered the time he'd emerged from that same station entrance two years ago, to investigate the case of a senior police officer who'd been found impaled on the roof of a kiosk. But this time Lembit and Ants weren't waiting at the foot of the steps to whisk him down to the Interior Ministry and Police headquarters on Pikk Street. Today a brisk walk might keep him warm.

Fifteen minutes later he was in his office. At least the heating was working here. Marta wasn't in, it being Sunday, and there was no sign of Kadakas. He decided he might as well go straight to the *Alt-Revaler.*

He settled down at a table near the window facing onto Town Hall Square, where he could watch the passers-by. A glass of brandy would help him relax.

He was suddenly torn from his thoughts by a tapping on the cafe window right in front of him. He looked up. Kirsti was waving at him from the street and smiling. She came in.

"Sorry I'm late, my love," she said, as she reached the table, and stooped to give him a kiss on the cheek.

"No problem, Kirsti. I've had plenty to think about whilst I was waiting."

"And a little drink, too, I see."

"Just a little nip to keep me going. It was bitterly cold on the train up from Viljandi. Anyway, what would you like to eat?"

Hallmets had blood sausage with sautéed cabbage, Kirsti *rosolje*, a salad of herring, beetroot and potato. Over coffee they made small-talk. Hallmets knew better than to talk about a case in a public place, and Kirsti knew better than to ask about it.

He asked her how the last few days had been. There'd been no problems at home. "But," Kirsti went on, "Something a bit worrying at work."

"Oh yes, what was that?"

"We were sent a list of books to be put in a special section, where readers are only allowed if they have a pass signed by the Principal. These are books considered 'unsuitable for young people' or 'hostile to the Fatherland.' The Special Section has to be in the basement, so we had to identify a space and clear all the shelves. This afternoon we'll have to go through the list and assemble the books. What a waste of time. They all look fairly innocuous, as far as I can see."

"But it's a bad sign, when we're told what books we can and can't read. At least we've not started to burn them here. By the way, talking of books, have you come across

Rist and Pistoda, the publishers."

"Rist and Pistoda? We probably don't have any of their books in the library; they mostly do fiction or popular history. And westerns, I think. But I've seen plenty of their books in the bookshops. You have too, you've just never wondered who the publishers were. They don't have any of the top authors, maybe they're not big enough."

"That explains why they didn't publish yours."

"Very amusing, darling. Now I remember why I married you."

"I'm so glad to hear it. So, how's the great work coming on? You'll have had some time to get on with it while I've been away."

Kirsti had had her first novel, *The Bishop's Gold*, a historical thriller set in the time of the Teutonic Knights, published the previous year, and was now working on another, this time set in the period of Swedish rule in the seventeenth century. A mysterious Scots mercenary limps off a ship in the harbour of Tallinn. He has the key to a secret, and people are hunting him. Matilda, the daughter of Baron von Greindorff, helps the man to hide in the basement of her father's manor house. But the pursuers are closing in. And the Baron is suspicious, and worried, for he has a secret too.

"The problem is," confided Kirsti, "I can't think what the baron's secret could be."

"Maybe he walled up his wife in the basement."

"No, no. It's not that kind of story. The baron's not a bad person, I think he must have done something wrong a long time ago, and is still feeling guilty."

"Maybe he killed the Scotsman's father, in a duel, then married his mother, so that the final revelation is the Scot and the baron's daughter are brother and sister."

"You're not taking this seriously, Jüri. That wouldn't do at all. They're supposed to get married at the end, and then the Scot discovers that he is really the Earl of Keltie. And they live happily ever after. It's no good asking you about these things, you always bring crime into it."

Hallmets knew better than to respond to this. He changed the subject. "When you worked at the University in Tartu, did you come across a Professor Strelkov?"

Kirsti thought about it. "Yes, I did. Russian History was his subject. Quiet, but knowledgeable. And rather sad, too. You know, he lost a son and daughter during the war. They were students at St. Petersburg University. They were killed by the Bolsheviks during the revolution. He was already here, in Tartu, he'd been appointed before the world war broke out. They were trying to get out of Russia, back to Tartu, when they were killed. I don't know the details, he never talked about it. That was all I heard from colleagues. Perhaps he's retired now. Is he relevant to your case?"

"He might be. I may have to go down and see him."

"Do give him my regards if you do."

20

Just before half past two Hallmets got back to his office. Two people were waiting, sitting at the big table in the unit workroom. One was Ants Kadakas, the other Jaan Kallas. They both got up as he came in.

"K and K," said Hallmets, as he hung up his coat, "I can't take you in alphabetical order."

"I think you should hear what *Härra* Kallas has to say, chief," said Kadakas. "I was over at *Pealinna Uudised* this morning, to see if I could find anything more about General Madrus, and ..."

"I ran into Ants in the archive," said Kallas, sitting down again, "And thought you were the person I should share this with. If times were different, I'd just have written about it, and we'd have had an exclusive this morning. As it is, we have to pretend that everything's lovely. I could take it to Colonel Reinart, I suppose, but I don't trust him. I know you'll do the right thing. But there's always a price. Mine is a cup of coffee."

Ants had anticipated Hallmets' response. "I'm onto it," he called, as he disappeared into the little kitchen off the workroom.

And over coffee, and pastries, Kallas told Hallmets of his trip to Finland the previous day.

"Lepp," concluded Hallmets grimly, "So the bad penny has turned up again. Lapua, or whatever they call themselves now, would be just his cup of tea. But this demonstration, expressing solidarity with people over here, and with Sirk in evidence, is worrying. What do you think, Jaan?"

"I think they're planning something. The fact they tried

to kill me may just represent Lepp's psychotic mind, but I think it's more than that. Lepp drew Sirk's attention to me before he came after me, and he made it plain I would die before I got back here. They both wanted me dead, because they knew I'd recognised both of them. They didn't want news of the rally getting back here."

"So why have it at all. Why not just make their secret plans, er, in secret?"

"This event was for the Finns. They're rallying support so that when it happens, people in Finland will not be surprised, and will show support for their cause."

"What cause would that be?"

"I think you know that already, Jüri. Replacing our benevolent dictatorship with something more akin to Herr Hitler's regime. And if that happened, it wouldn't be good for us, and for a lot of other good people. I can already imagine Lepp, in a black uniform, sitting in Colonel Reinart's office, signing off the lists of executions. Now and then, maybe he'll do one himself, just to keep his hand in. The question now is, though, what do we do with this information?"

"I think the only thing we can do is take it to the colonel. Let me talk with him. He may be aware of it already from his own sources, but maybe not what you've seen."

"Does General Madrus' death have anything to do with this?"

"How do you know about that?"

"I can assure you Ants never mentioned it. He almost collapsed when I asked him about it. You'll need to train him to keep a straight face." They both glanced at Kadakas, who blushed, and looked at the table. "No," went on Kallas, "As you know, I have ears all over the country, and I still use them, and reward them. It's worth being well-informed, even if I can't use the information I collect. Not yet, anyway. Somebody called me from Viljandi this morning, told me the general had topped himself, fallen on his sword, like someone out of a Roman tragedy. It didn't take me long to find out that Ants had been looking him up, but, as I said, the boy did well, wouldn't say a word more. So, come on Jüri, what's the story. Have you been down to check it out?"

Hallmets only hesitated long enough to take a sip of his coffee. "Alright, Jaan, I'll tell you, but not a word to anyone else, do you understand?"

"I'm a wise old monkey, my lips are sealed."

"Madrus was murdered. Shot in the chest. Then the sword was artistically applied by his killer. But right now we don't know who that was. We're following a number of leads. But you could be helpful here, Jaan. Did you ever meet the general?"

"Sorry, I only saw him at a distance. Luckily I didn't have to report on the tedious official events he usually attended. And as far as I'm aware, he wasn't involved in any crime. He seemed to me like a pretty boring type. An army bureaucrat. Never said anything controversial, always just what was expected of him, never stepped out of line. I've no idea what went on in his head."

"You didn't come across him during the war?" Kallas had been a war correspondent, sending back reports from the front line that more than once had the military censors complaining about him. But no-one stopped him, because when the Estonians achieved a success, he was always there, with a report that conveyed the effort and the sacrifice that lay behind the triumphs.

"Not that I can remember. I'll have to check my files."

Kallas kept detailed records of all the investigations he had done, all the notes he had taken, the whispers he had heard, and the reports he had filed, from the very beginning of his career. It was an archive that had stood him in good stead on many occasions, when he had more dots to join together, and did a faster job of it than his rivals in the other papers. "I'll get back to you tomorrow if I can. I better get off now, and see what nonsense they want me to produce for tomorrow's edition."

As soon as Kallas had gone, Hallmets thanked Kadakas for the potted biography of the general he'd sent down to Viljandi, and asked what he'd got that morning.

"Not a great deal more, chief. As *Härra* Kallas says, General Madrus is only reported attending official events, being present at rallies and march-pasts, or making speeches at war memorials on the days of commemoration. No scandal at all, that I could find. Most of the stuff that's available is about after the war. The first newspaper article I could find him mentioned in is in 1920. Before that there's nothing. The details I got for the biography came from the Defence Ministry and the Government Information Office."

"So here's a man who seems to be completely boring, and yet someone stages an elaborate tableau of his death. There must surely have been more to him."

"I'll keep looking, I'm just not sure where to look."

"Good point. Tell you what, leave it for the moment, see if you can get me the address for the general's daughter, Sirje Kangamees."

"I'm pretty sure I wrote it down. I'll check through my notes."

Given that it was a Sunday, Hallmets didn't expect Colonel Reinart to be at his desk. But he was mistaken. His phone call resulted in an immediate invitation next door to the Interior Ministry. He began by reporting the port-mortem result.

Reinart nodded. "Well, well. Who do you suspect?"

"It's too early to say right now, colonel. There's no smoking gun or obvious solution, so we have to do it the hard way, and that takes time. I can't even tell you yet whether there's a political aspect, or if it's something else altogether. We're still trying to build up a picture of the general himself. What sort of man he was. Which is how one of my officers ran into Jaan Kallas down at the *Pealinna Uudised* offices. And *Härra* Kallas had an interesting experience yesterday, which he passed on to me." And he told the colonel what Kallas had seen and experienced.

The colonel made notes as Hallmets spoke. Finally he put his pencil down. "Thanks for passing this on, chief inspector. We've been getting reports that the Vaps folk are planning something. Apparently it's going to happen quite soon. But I hadn't realised that Lapua were involved. This is very useful intelligence. We knew Artur Sirk was in Finland. It doesn't surprise me he was mixing with that lot. But Lepp, hmm, that's very unfortunate. I thought he'd had the sense to make himself scarce after that business two years ago. Do keep me up to date on your investigation. Madrus' death is a complication we can do without at the moment."

"One other thing, colonel. I'm finding it hard to get details of what the general actually did during the war. Do you have anything on that?"

Reinart opened the top drawer of his immaculately

polished desk, and pulled out a slim file. "Let me have a look," he muttered, running his finger down the pages, until finally it stopped. "Hmm. As you say, not a great deal. Tells us only that he was in the Russian Imperial Supply Corps. Mind you, Hallmets, the failure of supply chains was one of the reasons the Russian armies did so badly against the Germans. Anyway, it says here that he resigned from the Russian Army in February 1918, and later in that year applied to join our army. After various placements, he was assigned to the Supply Directorate in January 1919."

"Eleven months months later," observed Hallmets. "I wonder what he was doing for those months. And what were these 'various placements?' That's rather vague."

"I doubt it's that important," said Reinart, "Things were pretty chaotic at that time. I'd guess that 'various placements' just means they don't have any record of what he was doing then. I think his political views could be the key to his death. If we can find out what they were."

21

By the time he was back in Police Headquarters it was almost four o'clock. Kadakas had found the address for Sirje and Urmas Kangamees, in Estonia's southern border town of Valga. Hallmets asked him to phone Lesser at Rauakivi Castle and pass on the address. A few minutes later, the call to Lesser had been transferred to Hallmets' phone.

"Afternoon, chief. Ants just gave me the Kangamees family's address in Valga. Thanks for that. In fact, we already had it this morning. Einmann had told Sergeant Lauk to contact them and let Sirje know her father was dead. He explained to her that we're now handling the case, and she called me here. She's already contacted Dr Kirss to find out how much the general left, and is going to see him tomorrow morning. If the roads are passable, that is. It may snow again during the night. I've arranged to talk to her at the police station tomorrow afternoon at two. She was wanting to stay at the castle, but I told her it was out of bounds till we've finished there. She wasn't very pleased. 'I'm paying for those servants now,' she said, 'They'll just be sitting around doing nothing, no doubt raiding my father's wine cellar every mealtime.' She doesn't sound that bothered about her father's death. 'Had to happen one day,' she said. But she's a bit peeved it happened the way it did. She'd have preferred the 'respected former soldier dies peacefully in bed' scenario. So now she wants us to keep the whole thing hushed up. She doesn't want the words 'suicide' or 'murder' to get into circulation. I told her the papers would have to sit on the story until there was an outcome to the investigation."

"That's useful. How are you getting on with things at the castle?"

"Found the bullet, or should I say the probable bullet. In the study. Embedded in one of the books on his bookshelf. Julius Caesar's *De Bello Gallico,* annotated edition edited by Professor Kaalmann. It's about a metre and a half above the floor. Looks like the killer is sitting in one of the armchairs, and the general in the other. Then at some point the general stands up, and at that point the killer shoots, so that the bullet has a slightly upward trajectory that takes it to the bookshelf. If that's right, it suggests the general invited the killer into his study and offered him a seat. We searched the study, the sitting room, and the hallway, and no sign of another bullet."

"Good. At least we know where it happened. Did you get the bullet off to Einer Sepp to examine?"

"Yes. I sent Lembit with it the police station, and Lauk sent a man with it on a motor bike up to Tallinn. Should have reached there by now, if the roads aren't blocked. I left a message for Einar to get onto it as a priority."

"What about the general's neighbours?"

"I went over to see them this morning. They don't have very much to do with the general. They think he's a bit of a snob, taking on airs and graces as master of the Rauakivi estate. He invites them over once a year, for dinner. They think he believes it's the duty of a mansion-owner to keep in touch with lesser beings in the neighbourhood. The evening was rather boring, only enlivened when the general, after a few glasses of French wine, got talking about politics. According to them, he was very disappointed with the current regime. 'Our present leader has no imagination at all,' said the general, 'Boredom will become compulsory, nothing will change.

Compare that to what Hitler's doing in Germany. Now there's a man with imagination. And a vision for his country. Päts is still a peasant at heart, a man of yesterday. Vaps would have taken us forward into a future we could be proud of.' Needless to say, *Härra* and *Proua* Sinikas were rather worried by this, and left not long afterwards."

"Okay," said Hallmets. He didn't know who might be listening on the line, and wanted to cut off this line of discussion. "I'm glad the general didn't express these views in public. What about the pastor?"

"Oh, yes. I'm due to see him in the morning. He tends to be rather busy on Sundays. By the way, I'm not sure there's more we can do here at the castle. I told Anna she could go back to town and stay there if she wants, and the others they could stay in their own quarters, on the estate, but can go out and about. But no-one should enter the castle. We've sealed all the doors. And Lembit disabled the general's car. In case it's needed for evidence, I told Kirik."

"That's excellent. I had an interesting chat with Jaan Kallas, the reporter, this morning, and I've kept Colonel Reinart up to date. Tomorrow morning, I'll go to the publishers in the morning, then see what we can learn from Colonel Janno at the Defence Ministry. So I don't think I'm going to be back in Viljandi till at least Tuesday. I'll give you a ring tomorrow sometime. By the way, I hope you don't mind meeting *Proua* Kangamees without me."

"No problem, chief. I'll let you know how it goes."

It was now half past four, and already dark outside. At least it wasn't snowing. But Hallmets could feel the cold seeping into the building. He sent Kadakas home, and set off himself for the station. He could feel the ice on the pavement and had to walk carefully. He got the electric train to Nõmme at five, and was at home by ten to six, warming his hands by the fire and listening to Kirsti prepare their dinner. Juhan went off after the meal to get some work done for school that was due in the next morning. Why did he always do things at the last minute, thought his father. But he said nothing, and looked forward to a pleasant evening with his wife.

22

Monday 2nd December

On his walk with Kirsti from home to the railway station at Nõmme, Hallmets bought a couple of newspapers, *Postimees* and *Pealinna Uudised*. He'd reached his office by half past eight, and scanned the two papers. Both reported the death of General Madrus. However, the event was not highlighted; the reports were buried in the lower half of a page towards the middle, and no details were given of how he died. The report in *Postimees* gave the announcement and a brief overview of the general's career. The report in *Pealinna Uudised* was, Hallmets noted, written by Jaan Kallas. Given that Kallas was a well-known crime reporter, the editor, Eirik Hunt, was sailing close to the wind by putting Kallas's name to the piece. The article repeated the official announcement, sent to all the papers by the National Propaganda Service. Ignoring the general's career history, the article went on: *General Madrus was a well-known figure in Viljandi, appearing on the platform on many official occasions. His speeches, memorable for their wit and erudition, will be sadly missed by the denizens of that fair city. The general was familiar locally as the proprietor of Rauakivi Castle, whose park is a favourite place of leisure and exercise for those in Viljandi County. We hope to bring you more information about this sad occurrence as it reaches us.* So, thought Hallmets, Kallas was setting his claim on the Madrus story. That reminded him he would have to talk with the reporter again, and see if his digging had revealed anything more about the general.

Just after nine fifteen he walked down Pikk Street, turned left to walk alongside St. Olav's Church, and left again to head up Lai Street. He reckoned Rist and Pistoda shouldn't be too far up. An odd name, Rist and Pistoda: cross and dagger. Was there a Mr Cross and a Mr Dagger? Or did they specialise in religious books with a twist at the end?

The offices of Rist and Pistoda were on the first floor, above a shoe shop. Hallmets greeted the young woman at the reception desk and introduced himself. "I'm looking for whoever's in charge," he said, "It's about a case we're pursuing."

"Ah, that would be *Härra* Rist. Yes, of course he's here. Just a moment." She went down a short corridor to a door, tapped on it and leaned in for a few seconds, then came back. "No problem, he'll see you right away. The room at the end, just go on in."

Toomas Rist was a small man in his fifties with a rotund figure suggestive of a love of good food. He had a small black moustache, an almost bald head, glasses in round tortoiseshell frames, and smiling eyes. He sat at a desk which looked ancient enough to be a family heirloom. Behind him an array of bookshelves displayed, Hallmets guessed, the products of Rist and Pistoda. Rist beamed at Hallmets as he came in, and stood up to shake hands. "Chief Inspector, I'm so pleased to meet you. I still remember how you solved the Vaher case the year before last. I followed Jaan Kallas's articles in the paper. I read his book too. Absolutely thrilling. It's a pity he didn't come to us with it. Please, do take a seat." He motioned towards two leather armchairs flanking a coffee table under the window, and, when Hallmets had sat, he took the other.

"I've asked Riina to bring us some coffee. But I don't know how I can be of help."

Hallmets took from his inside pocket the card found in Madrus' study, and handed it to Rist. "This card was found in Rauakivi Castle, the home of General Madrus. We believe the general is writing his memoirs. And that you were going to publish them."

Rist turned as white as the ice on the window ledge outside. "Er, I can't imagine where he might have got it. We're certainly not publishing anything by him. I don't even know who he is. What did you say his name was?"

Hallmets was about to tell Rist that a copy of the morning's paper was lying on his desk. Then the penny dropped. Rist had assumed he was working with the political police, and Madrus must have done something to annoy the regime. "I'm sorry, *Härra* Rist," he explained, as amiably as he could, "I think I should clarify things a bit. This is not, I stress, a political issue. It's a purely criminal matter. As you no doubt read in today's paper, General Madrus has died. There are some questions about his death that have raised issues of possible criminal behaviour, and we are investigating the general's activities and contacts in the last few months. We already know that he was writing his memoirs, and believe you to be the publishers."

"So you know about the book?"

"Obviously. And I'd like you tell me all about it. Just in case it's relevant to our investigation."

"Are you absolutely sure the book is relevant?"

"I don't know, *Härra* Rist. That's why I'm asking you about it. Please don't misunderstand me. I'm not suggesting that there is anything illegal in your relationship to General Madrus as his publisher. But there may be information in the book which might be of help to us."

Rist paused for a few moments, as if working out what to say next. "All right. I apologise if I seemed rather reluctant to admit to our contact with General Madrus. You must understand that publishing is a competitive business. We have to be quite secretive about what we're doing, or the others will try to get in on the act, or even pre-empt us. I had a bad experience just last year, with *Gunfight at Cactus Ridge*. Do you know it?"

Hallmets shook his head. "I would guess it's a western. Not my cup of tea, sorry."

"Not at all," smiled Rist, "You see, I got a deal with a German publisher to publish an Estonian translation. The author, by the way, is German, Heinz Kletterer, he's very popular in Germany. Westerns are big there, and I felt sure they'd be big here too. Well, even though I kept things scrupulously quiet here, word nevertheless must have got out, probably at the German end, and the next thing we knew Vahva Editions in Tartu had announced they were launching *Gunslingers of Dodge City*, by Ray O'Flahertig."

"Odd name. Is he Irish, or American?"

"Neither. His real name is Leopold Schlechtmeier, he lives in Vienna. Never been to America in his life. Unlike Heinz Kletterer, I might add, who's been there several times. Well, at least twice. Anyway, *Gunslingers* was published a month before *Gunfight*. Really messed up our launch, I can tell you. We'd planned a big do in a farmhouse done up like a western saloon, with a couple of Swedes who juggle with six-shooters before shooting apples off each other's heads. And what do you think Vahva Editions did? Exactly that. Except for the jugglers, of course. They had some girls who dressed as Red Indians, rather more scantily I think, and performed acrobatics on a canoe moored in the river. Pathetic."

"Did it affect your sales?"

"Of course. I mean we did well enough from *Gunfight*, Kletterer is the better writer, and since the translator was already working on *Sheriff of Tumbleweed County*, we were able to get that one out quickly. We've not done badly out of westerns."

"And crime?"

"Oh yes, we do that too. We're too small to get the big names, you know, Agatha Christie, Edgar Wallace, Conan Doyle, Chesterton. We almost got that Belgian, Simenon, he's quite popular. Ah, here's Riina with the coffee. And some cakes, too. She's a wonder." He beamed at Riina, as she set down the tray on the coffee table."

After the first sip, Hallmets tried to steer Rist back to the point of his visit. "What about true crime, does that go down well?"

"Oh, yes. There's not much real crime here, I mean in Estonia, but we did well with a couple of books about the atrocities committed by the Reds during the Civil War in Russia, and I'm working on the rights to a book about gangsters in New York, *Machine-Guns at Breakfast*. Of course, everybody saw *Scarface* at the cinema, and …"

"What about General Madrus's book? Tell me about that."

Rist frowned at the interruption to his exposition, but quickly regained his composure and refocused his enthusiasm. "You'll keep this quiet, won't you? I mean, if we can get something out fairly soon, while he's in the news, it could do very well."

"*Härra* Rist, I'm going to share something with you that

is confidential, and which you must not repeat to anyone. We have reason to believe that the general was killed by person or persons at present unknown."

Rist's eyes opened wide. "You mean he was murdered?"

"Exactly. And what you said a few moments ago gives you a perfect motive for eliminating him, doesn't it?" smiled Hallmets.

"What? Look, I can assure you, I had nothing to do with it. Not at all. I don't believe in violence of any sort. Please, I'm sure I was here or at home whenever it happened. Riina will confirm my appointments here last week. My wife will tell you about the weekend. And our daughter. You can't really think that …"

"Calm down, *Härra* Rist, I'm sure your alibi is secure. But you see how Madrus's book could be linked to this attack on him. For instance, what if he revealed something there that someone didn't want to come out? That's why I want to know what was in there. But start by telling me what contact you had with him. From the beginning."

"Yes, of course. He approached me several months ago, March I think it was, said he was writing his memoirs, and would we be interested in publishing them. He said someone had recommended us to him. Naturally I asked for some details, and a look at what he'd done so far. I'd heard his name of course, but I couldn't have told you what he did in the war, or afterwards. I presumed it would be mainly about his exploits during the war. I thought right away of a title, *The Heat of Battle*. Not bad, eh. But the samples he sent weren't very good. His writing style varied between turgid and incoherent. And the synopsis he produced wasn't very gripping. It seemed to have very little about the war, and plenty about his upbringing and early life, and his rather tedious life since. Er, and his political opinions."

"His political opinions?"

"Yes, he seemed to be dissatisfied with just about everything that's happened since the war. But that isn't what readers want, you see. They want actions, not opinions. And negative opinions are the worst – they just put people off. So I invited him to come up here, went through it all with him, and explained exactly what we wanted. I told him that voicing his political opinions would be unwise in the present circumstances. If he were to present his analysis of the current situation, or his vision for the future, that might be okay, as long as it was positive, forward-looking, even inspiring. And of course, not in any way critical of the current regime. I also suggested he might be wise to hire a secretary to organise the book, and perhaps even write it for him. All he'd have to do then was simply tell his story to the secretary. He said he'd think about it, and I got a letter a fortnight later saying he'd done just what I advised."

"Did he then send any more material."

"Just a couple of chapters. The early stuff again, but this time much more readable. He'd clearly got the right sort of person for the job. There was also a chapter on his experiences during the war. Nicely written but too bland and much too short. I told him he needed to get a lot more about the war, that was what readers were going to be interested in. In fact I told him at least fifty percent of the text should be about the war. No-one would be that interested in his early life, and only a few in what he'd done afterwards. Well, that was three months ago, and I've had nothing since. I actually wrote to him just last week asking for a full draft as soon as he could get it to me. I didn't get a reply."

"May I see the material he did send?"

"Just a moment." Rist got up and went over towards his desk, next to which, tucked into the corner of the room, was a large safe. He opened it and leaned in, eventually pulling out a thick brown envelope. "This is all the stuff we've had from him." He hesitated, then handed it to Hallmets. "You must understand, chief inspector, that I'm giving you this on the strict understanding that you keep it completely confidential. And that you return it as soon as possible. As I said, if Madrus is in the news, it will do well. But only if we can get the whole book. We'll have to try to contact his secretary. And his executors, of course. Any deal would have to be with them now."

"Many thanks for this, *Härra* Rist. I promise I'll get it back to you as soon as I can. I won't take up any more of your time." Hallmets rose to go.

Rist rose too. "My pleasure, chief inspector. By the way, you sound like a literate man, and I'm sure you didn't get where you are without a few adventures. Have you thought of writing your own memoirs? I'm sure they'd do very well."

"I'm rather busy at the moment, but get back to me once I've retired. By the way, is there a *Härra* Pistoda?"

"What? Oh, I see. No, no, there's just me. But I thought, Rist Publishing doesn't sound very gripping, does it. But *Rist ja Pistoda*, Cross and Dagger, well now, that has a bit of ring to it, doesn't it. And suggests we publish stuff that's, well, exciting, eh?"

23

Hallmets was soon back at Police HQ. Marta told him Kadakas had gone to the State Library to see if there was anything relating to General Madrus. Hallmets sat down in his office with a cup of coffee, and opened the envelope containing the material Rist had given him. He extracted a bundle of typed sheets.

He began with the general's life before the war: his childhood and youth, and his joining the Imperial Russian Army (Estonia at that time being part of the Russian Empire) as a junior officer in the supplies division. None of it was gripping. The chapter on the war he put aside to read more carefully, and turned to the only other chapter, entitled 'My Life in the New Estonia'.

It wasn't an easy read, mainly because the general's ability to express himself was limited, and his sometimes incoherent rants were everywhere. However, Hallmets now had a clearer idea of what was going on in his head. And didn't like it much. It seemed that Madrus thoroughly disliked communists, socialists, liberals, Jews, gypsies, intellectuals, artists, Russians and Lithuanians. And the unemployed. And women – but only those who 'got above themselves.' Who he liked was less easy to discern, as he much preferred denunciation to appreciation.

One thing, or rather, place, he did approve of was Estonia. This could be inferred from the references to various groups as 'a danger to our country' or 'a bacillus intent on infecting our beautiful Fatherland' or 'parasites sucking the sap from the great tree that is Estonia.' However, the kind of Estonia he wanted didn't sound like a lot of fun. Lots of people would be excluded, and the rest would no doubt be told exactly what to do.

Hallmets could now see why Toomas Rist was so irritated with Madrus. But he could also see why Reinart might suspect him of sympathy for the Vaps Movement, whose journal *Võitleja*, Fighter, seemed to espouse similar views, though rather more coherently put. As a serving officer, of course, Madrus could not express any political views. He had instead bottled them up, and poured them all onto these pages. The question for Hallmets was, had the general, since his retirement, done anything other than spew his prejudices onto paper. Clearly he had done nothing in public, or Reinart would have known it. But had there been more going on in private? He would have to have another conversation with Raud Kirik.

Finally he looked at the chapter about Madrus's part in the War of Independence. He described how, having reached the rank of major, he had resigned from the Russian Imperial Army after the October Revolution, as did many Estonian officers. By then it had become clear that the options facing Estonia were to be part of Communist Russia, to be part of a German Baltic Grand Duchy, or to be an independent state. The war had been fought by the Estonians on two fronts, against the Red Army invading from Russia, and the German mercenaries led by General von der Goltz coming from the south. Being familiar with supply work, he was immediately assigned to the Supplies Division, and worked there throughout the war, 'making sure our boys at the front got exactly what they needed at exactly the right time.' But it was all very vague. Very few details were given of any of the strategies the general used. The anecdotes given were all well known to Hallmets, and did not personally involve Madrus. And in particular, he had glossed over the period between his resignation from the Imperial Army and his appointment to the Supplies Division of the Estonian Army. They needed to find out more about Madrus' part in the war.

It now seemed clear to Hallmets that the general would have had some sympathy for the amateur fascism of the Vaps movement. But had he been a secret member of the group, as well as a private sympathiser? Vaps had hoped that General Laidoner, the hero of the Independence War, would lead them into the 1934 presidential election. But Laidoner had refused, and eventually agreed to stand for another party. General Larka, a less charismatic figure, and one-time minister of War, had then been nominated as Vaps's presidential candidate. At no time was General Madrus mentioned as a possibility for the role.

Why then might his political views now have got him killed? Unless there was some sort of power struggle going on within the movement's supporters, and, as Colonel Reinart suspected, they were plotting something new. It was also just possible that Madrus had been killed by an agent of the current regime. In that case, however, the colonel would have been aware of it, and would not have called Hallmets in to investigate. He would simply have gone along with Einmann's verdict of suicide, and suppressed the post-mortem result.

He picked up the phone again and asked Marta to get Jaan Kallas for him. However, Kallas was out, so he left a message asking him to focus on the first year of the general's war service.

Just after half past twelve, Colonel Reinart phoned. "This is a secure line," he announced, "It runs direct from my building to yours, no exchanges in between. And we've got a special warning system, that can tell if the switchboard operators at either building are listening in. So here's the number to use if you need to talk to me. Keep the number to yourself, and phone directly from your office, rather than through your secretary. I'm sure she's perfectly trustworthy, but the fewer people who know, the better. Anyway, any luck with these publishers?"

Hallmets reported on his meeting with Rist and his reading of the fragments of the memoirs Rist had given him.

"So he had strong opinions," commented the colonel, "I thought as much. The ones who keep their views quiet are always the most dangerous. I'm surprised we didn't pick up on any of it. By the way, I checked up on Toomas Rist. After what you've told me, it doesn't surprise me he was publishing the memoirs. Rist was a member of Vaps. He was actually on the Tallinn District Committee. We're still keeping an eye on him."

"Having strong views and acting on them are two different things, colonel. But someone may have thought General Madrus was going to act on his views."

"You're not suggesting we killed him, are you?"

"Hardly, colonel. Your people would have done it more subtly, I suspect. But perhaps Madrus had got wind of this current plot. What if Madrus wanted a role, and he wasn't welcome?"

"Interesting. Let me know what develops. I'll get back to you if I hear anything that might help you."

It was time for lunch, so he went down to the canteen on the ground floor, and had a mushroom pie with fried potatoes and peas. He finished off with a coffee and a chocolate biscuit, then returned to his office. As he entered the workroom, he saw that Kadakas had returned.

"Any luck this morning, Ants?" he asked.

"Nothing new, sir. And that's a whole morning gone."

"That's what a lot of police work is like, Ants. But it's never time wasted. It's told us there's been very little in the papers about Madrus that interests us. Have you had lunch?"

"No, er, not yet, chief. But if you want me to do something else ..."

"No, you go and get something to eat now. Once you're back, we're going to pay a call on Colonel Janno, at the Defence Ministry."

"Yes, sir, of course. I've been there a few times. When I was in the military. OK. I'll grab some lunch. I won't be long."

"There's no rush, Ants. No point us arriving during his lunch hour."

24

Hallmets soon confirmed that Colonel Janno was Head of the Pensions Department in the Defence Ministry. He thought of phoning to make an appointment. Then he decided to walk to the Defence Ministry – after all, they only had to walk one block up Pikk Street, then turn to the right into Pagari Street. It was often useful to approach people when they weren't expecting you. And if the colonel wasn't in, the fresh air would do them good. Kadakas was back by half past one, and they were outside the looming bulk of the Defence Ministry by ten to two.

At reception they only had to wait five minutes before a young woman arrived to take them up to the colonel's office. It didn't take her long to notice Kadakas. "Ants!" she cooed, "Long time no see. So you're a policeman now."

Kadakas blushed. "*Tere*, Katriin. Er, how are you?"

"The better for seeing you again, Ants." Her eyes devoured him.

"Shouldn't you introduce us, Ants?" said Hallmets, with a smile.

"Oh, er, yes, er, Katriin, this is Chief Inspector Hallmets, Head of the Special Crimes Unit. Chief Inspector, this is Katriin Kellermann, she works in the Pensions Department, as, er ..."

Katriin gave Hallmets a firm handshake. "Personal Assistant to Colonel Janno. If you'll come this way. It's no good just telling people to come up. The Pensions Department is the least important part of the ministry, so it's miles away, and in the attic."

Ten minutes later they were in the department foyer.

Hallmets asked Kadakas if he'd mind waiting there for a short while. He thought he'd get more out of Colonel Janno by himself, as two war veterans having a chat. Kadakas didn't mind at all, and Katriin's eyes lit up. But she collected herself, and ushered Hallmets into the colonel's office.

The office was very much like his own, except that being on the top floor and on a corner, with windows on both sides, it was full of light, with fine views along Lai Street and Pagari Street. The colonel, a stout man with well-oiled brown hair and a fine moustache, rose to shake hands. "Hallmets. Yes, thought I recognised the name. You sorted out that Vaher business a couple of years ago. It was in all the papers. Also mentioned you'd played a part at Võnnu. I think a good few chaps wanted you to stay on in the army after the war."

"There were other things that needed doing too. I'm guessing you stayed on."

"Too right. Trouble is, armies aren't the same in peacetime. They get to be just like any other big organisation. And need people to look after the pensions. Still, it enables me to keep in touch with lots of old comrades. That's interesting. I mean, to see what happens to men when they leave the army. Some just get on with something else, others can't cope. Mainly, I think, because they've got so used to having their behaviour prescribed from morning till night, that they don't know how to organise themselves any more. Ah, here's Katriin with some coffee."

After a first sip of his coffee, Hallmets raised the matter he'd come about. "Tell me, colonel, how did General Madrus take to retirement?"

"Aha! So that's what it's about? I missed the

announcement of his death in the paper this morning, so I was rather surprised when I had a phone call about the general this morning."

"Oh yes? Who from?"

"A Dr Kirss. Lawyer for the general's daughter. They want the old boy's financial situation sorted out as soon as possible. I must admit, it's better for us to find out right away, I mean, if a chap's died. Sometimes the family don't tell us till months later, having pocketed the dead man's pension in the meantime. Then we have a devil of a job clawing it back, I can tell you. Usually costs more to recover the money than if we'd just let them keep it. Anyway, all I know is that General Madrus passed away three days ago. Must have been a sudden illness; he was hale and hearty when I saw him, and that was just a couple of weeks ago."

"On the afternoon of Wednesday the 20th of November, I think."

"How on earth did you know that?"

"I must ask you to keep this confidential, colonel, but General Madrus did not die a natural death. In fact, it's become clear that he was murdered."

"Good Lord! Who killed him?"

"At this point in time, that's not clear. Given his rank, and national significance, I've been asked to investigate. Naturally we've interviewed his staff, and are looking into his recent visitors, to see if anyone can throw any light on the matter. So I'd be grateful if you could tell me about your visit of the 20th. Please rest assured, I'm not suggesting there was anything suspicious about it at all. But you may have noticed something that will help us. I often find ex-military people have very sharp eyes."

This flattery worked well. The colonel beamed. "Yes, of

course. Got to keep your eyes open if you want to stay alive, eh?"

"Exactly. So I've just a couple of questions."

"Fire away, old chap."

"First, can you tell me why you were there?"

"That's not a difficult one. As I said, I like to keep in touch with our pensioners. However, Madrus was a bit of a special case. Not only did he get a rather generous pension, but he also had a large house on loan from the state. So part of my job was to make sure he was looking after the estate properly, you know, not letting it run to seed. He gets an allowance, sorry, he got an allowance for that, staff and upkeep and so on. So I was just doing a routine check. There's a list of things I go through. Though most of the questions were answered by that man of his, ..."

"Raud Kirik."

"Yes, that's him. Odd sort. Not quite sure what to make of him."

"How often did you visit General Madrus?"

"Every six months. May and November."

"Any problems this time?"

"I always have to repeat the same reminder, that the estate is on loan from the state, but the poor man kept insisting that he owned the place. Apart from that, everything was as it should be. I had a look round and it all looked well cared for."

"He didn't seem excited or worried about anything this time?"

"Hmm. Well, now you mention it, I think he was actually more upbeat than usual. Didn't argue too much about the status of the place. In fact, he said, 'Well, it'll all be sorted out quite soon.' When I asked what he meant by that, he told me not to worry. The other thing he was keen to talk about was his politics. He's usually fairly circumspect, but this time it was just the opposite. Rather unwise, I'd say. Not the sort of views you want to blow a trumpet about these days, if you get my drift."

"Yes, quite. I'm aware that some of his private opinions were quite extreme."

"I had to tell him to ease off, you know, in case any of the staff were listening. He stopped, but then he said, 'Thank goodness I won't have to be quiet for much longer.' Yes, I would say he was looking forward to something, I'm just not sure what."

"He had no requests that were out of the ordinary?"

"No, as I said, he actually had fewer queries than usual. Even offered me a glass of brandy with my coffee. He certainly didn't seem afraid that anything untoward might happen to him."

"That's very helpful, thanks. There's one other thing you might be able to help me with. I'm trying to trace the general's career, in case there's anything there that might help us. I know he was in Supplies in the Russian Imperial Army, and later on in our own, but it's not clear what he was doing between February 1918 and January 1919. He doesn't seem to have been assigned to Supplies Division until then. Have you any idea?"

"Hmm. Let me think. Well, I don't know the details, but I suspect if he volunteered for our army any time in 1918, he'd have been given a combat command. You see, right at the beginning, in the second half of 1918, the only chaps with previous military experience were the ones who left the Russian Army after the revolution and joined us to fight the Reds. So they were all sent to combat units. That was where the need was. Then, after a few months, it would become apparent which ones weren't suited to combat command, and the army leadership would shuffle them into more suitable posts. And by then it was also becoming clearer which of the volunteers – chaps like yourself – were potential command material."

"So how would I find out which units he served with during late 1918?"

"His file will tell you that. It'll be down in the basement, in Archives."

"But I saw his file at the Interior Ministry, and it wasn't specific at all. It simply referred to 'various placements.'"

"Ah. well, you see, there are two versions of every file, the shallow version and the deep one. The deep one never strays from our archives. If anyone asks for someone's file, we give them a copy of the shallow one, it's usually quite slim, just the basic information, and a career outline. The Interior Ministry are the worst, I have to say, they never return anything we send them. So what you've seen is the shallow file for General Madrus. But if you go down to the basement, with a note from me, they'll let you look at, but not take away, his deep file. That should give you the information you seek."

Hallmets left the colonel's office to find Kadakas and Katriin on either side of Katriin's desk, both leaning over towards each other, deep in quiet conversation. They both jumped.

"Thanks for waiting, Ants," said Hallmets briskly, "Now we need to get down to the archives in the basement."

Kadakas jumped to his feet. So did Katriin. "I'll show you the way down," she said, "Otherwise you'll never find it. Do you have a permit from the colonel?"

Hallmets held up the piece of paper Colonel Janno had

given him.

25

Four floors down, and many winding corridors and turnings later, Katriin led them triumphantly into a small office with no name plate, which smelt of the mustiness of old paper. Behind a desk sat a man with a grey beard and moustache, and an old Russian Imperial cap.

"Ah, Katriin. The flower of the forest, come to brighten our day. And bringing guests from the outside world."

"*Tere*, Frants! I'm glad to see you well. These are two policemen, who want to consult a file." She turned to Hallmets. "Frants is the gatekeeper. You must show him your credentials if you want to go further. Goodbye, chief inspector." She gave Kadakas a kiss on the cheek. "See you soon, Antsie!" And with a wave to all was gone.

Frants winked at Kadakas, "Who's a lucky boy, then? Another fly for the spider. Well, now, gentlemen, as the lovely Katriin said, you don't get past here without identification."

They both showed their police badges.

"That was the easy bit," smiled Frants, "Now you have to fill in the form."

Twenty minutes later, having scrutinised the completed form carefully, he handed it back and pointed to a narrow door next to his desk. "Through there, gentlemen. It's been a pleasure to meet you. Perhaps I'll never see you again."

The door led them to a dim corridor with another door at the end. When he opened it, Hallmets was astonished. The room they found themselves in was, despite the fact that the light outside had faded, large and well-lit. During the day, it would be even brighter, illuminated by large windows on both sides. A smart middle-aged woman sat at a reception desk.

"Come in, gentlemen. Can I have your forms, please?"

"We didn't expect this," said Hallmets, handing over the form. "Not after ..."

She smiled. "Frants makes sure our time isn't wasted. And he's very good when it comes to throwing out trouble-makers. Not that we get many, of course. Now, what have we got here. General Madrus, eh? You'll need a chit from a senior official to see that one."

Hallmets handed over the form Colonel Janno had given him.

"That'll do nicely," she said. "Take a seat over there, and I'll give you a call when the file's been brought up." She pointed to a row of chairs against the wall by the door.

Ten minutes later, the receptionist called them over again. "If you go to table six, the file is waiting for you. Removal of any material from the file is strictly prohibited. You may make notes, but only in pencil on an official pad." She handed each of them a pencil and a note pad. "Nothing else is to be placed on the table. Please indicate as soon as you're finished, so that the file and your notebooks can be checked. Note that the archive will close to visitors at four thirty pm, so you must be finished by twenty past." She pointed them to an empty table with a thick file sitting on it, and two chairs.

"We're never going to get through all this, sir," whispered Kadakas. "There's piles of it. And it's already nearly half past three."

"Don't panic, Ants. First, we know it's here, and we, I mean you, can always come back and consult it again.

Second, all we need to do now is take a brief skim through it, and then focus on what he did between February 1918 and January 1919. You take the pad and I'll dictate anything that needs written down. But we'll have to keep our voices down. We don't want to be thrown out for making too much noise."

The skim-through showed that most of the file would not add much that would be useful to them. It covered what they knew already, but in much greater detail. Even after Madrus had retired, every official speech he had made was listed, and often the full text provided. Cuttings from newspapers were also included.

Then they homed in on the period of interest. It told an interesting story. Madrus, along with many other fellow-Estonians in Russian service, had resigned in February 1918 and returned to their homes in Estonia. It now seemed that Russia's collapse could lead to Estonia's independence, and Estonian political activists, including Jaan Tõnisson and Konstantin Päts, began to prepare for that. However, it soon became clear that the Bolsheviks did not intend to give up control of their Baltic dominions, and therefore, later in 1918, an Estonian Army was formed, and volunteers sought. Naturally those who had seen service in the Imperial Army were welcomed, and given lead roles, so that when fighting started, the Estonians would be led by experienced men. Although his role in the Imperial Forces had been in supply, Major Madrus, as he was then, joined the new Estonian National Army in January 1919, and was made second-in-command of the 19th regiment, with the rank of lieutenant-colonel. The regiment successfully resisted the Red Army's initial advance in the south-east of the country, and then began to move forward. In March 1919, however, Madrus was transferred to the Supplies Division, and moved to its headquarters near Tallinn. No reason was given in the letter of notification, signed by the Commander-in-Chief, General Laidoner, a copy of which was included in the file.

"This is useful, as far as it goes," concluded Hallmets, "But we need more. We should look at Raud Kirik's file too. We don't have time today, so can you come back tomorrow morning and do that? No need to come to the office first, go straight to the Ministry. I think Colonel Janno's chit should cover Kirik too. He was the general's batman after all. If there's a problem, ask them to phone me, and I'll talk to Janno. Come on, let's go."

Kadakas seemed more than willing to return to Pagari Street the next day; Hallmets wondered whether the smiling Katriin had anything to do with this. Outside the Defence Ministry, he told Kadakas he could go home. It was nearly half past four.

He walked back to Pikk Street and his office. He needed to call Lesser and see how things were moving down in Viljandi. He reached him at the police station there, and brought him up to date on his activities in Tallinn.

"Thanks, chief. Some interesting developments to report from down here. I phoned the castle this morning, but, of course no-one answered. I should have realised the only phones would be in the castle itself. So I sent Eva and Ilmar out there with the car to see how things were. Half an hour later I got a call from Eva. Looks like *Härra* Kirik has done a bunk overnight. Ilmar and Eva talked with the Pirns. They think they saw movement and a light at Kirik's apartment last night, and wondered if he had a visitor. This morning they'd seen no sign of him, which is

154

unusual, as he's usually out and about quite early. Ilmar and Eva went over to the stables to check him out. No answer at his door, but Ilmar got it open. No sign of our man. No evidence of disturbance, so if he went, it was of his own volition. They checked out the grounds, in case he was somewhere on the estate, either alive or dead, but not a sign of him. Then they searched the house again, in case he knew some way in that we hadn't sealed. But no dice there either. The car's still there. But he could have got a taxi to collect him at the end of the drive, or simply walked into Viljandi."

"Hmm. That's not good. OK, what about the general's daughter?"

"I was hoping to talk with her this afternoon. But she phoned up and put it off. She was too bogged down in the legal stuff. However, I'm meeting her tomorrow at two, and that's definite, I've made that clear to her. So it's been a rather frustrating day. Anything else I need to know from your end?"

"Yes. Can you raise the general's war experience with his daughter, and also ask what she knows about Kirik. I'm hoping to have another chat with *Härra* Rist tomorrow morning, and Ants is going back to the MoD archive to see what else he can dig up on the general's war record, especially the period from from January to March 1919. There may be nothing important there, but we need to check. I'll call you again tomorrow, Henno."

He asked Marta to call *Härra* Rist and request a meeting at ten o'clock the following morning. This was granted with enthusiasm. Maybe *Härra* Rist thinks I'm going to write a book for him after all, thought Hallmets.

26

Tuesday 3rd December

He wasn't wrong. Toomas Rist was as welcoming as he had been the last time Hallmets had called. "Do come in, Chief Inspector. I hope your swift return here means that you've decided to pen some memoirs for us."

"Sadly not, *Härra* Rist. I just want to clarify a few things that came up during our previous conversation."

"Ah. Well, do come into my office. It's time for coffee, too."

Over coffee and pastries, Rist opened the conversation: "There was nothing more in the paper this morning about General Madrus. Are you any closer to knowing what happened to him?"

"I'm afraid I still can't give you any further details of the general's death until the case has been resolved. I'm sure you understand."

"Of course. So how can I help you?"

"You mentioned the general's political views yesterday. I want to know how closely Madrus was involved with the Vaps Movement?"

Rist paused to think hard before he replied. "We were discussing General Madrus's book, not his political activities. I was very surprised to see the stuff he had written in those draft chapters. And in any case, how would I know if he had any links to Vaps?"

"I was informed yesterday, *Härra* Rist, by a very reliable source, that you were on the Tallinn district committee of the movement. Don't you think someone in your position would have been aware of such a high-profile sympathiser."

Rist paled. "I'm not sure what this has to do with your investigation, chief inspector."

"I need to be aware of any possible aspect of General Madrus's life that could have had a connection with his death."

"You're suggesting he may have been attacked on account of his political opinions?"

"It's a possibility we can't ignore. That's why I'm asking you about it. Let me reassure you, by the way, that I'm going to treat this conversation as 'off the record.' I don't want to get you into trouble with anyone."

Rist looked relieved. "Thank you, chief inspector. I appreciate that, I really do. All right. Yes, I admit I was on the local committee, it wasn't secret, at the time. Naturally, I was interrogated by the political police last year; it wasn't a pleasant experience, I can assure you. But I think in the end they concluded I was harmless, so I wasn't charged. Though they did warn me they were going to keep an eye on me." Rist sipped his coffee and considered his words. "All right. General Madrus, as a public servant, was not a member of the Movement. But I can tell you that he fully supported our ideals and aims. That's why I was so disappointed at the crude and incoherent manner in which he expressed himself in his book. I had hoped he would make a more cogent case for our approach."

"I've been told he was more closely involved." Hallmets didn't know whether Madrus was more closely involved. But it stood to reason that a retired general who sympathised would not simply be ignored by the Vaps hierarchy.

Rist frowned. "Hmm. The political police are well-informed. We didn't know who their spies were. Well, if they know about it, there's hardly any point in denying it. He was one of our advisers on security issues. He had a very clear idea of what people want from the forces of law and order. I remember him saying, at a meeting, that only two types of crime matter to ordinary people: violence and theft. And of those two, violence matters more than theft. Above all, people want to walk the streets in safety, to have confidence that nothing bad will befall them or their loved ones. That's why crimes of violence must be seen to be dealt with, effectively and without mercy. When there's a violent incident, a public one, there must be an arrest and a sentence, and the sentence must be tough. Most people believe that will keep violence under control. It doesn't even matter, he said, if the wrong person is convicted, as long as they look plausible. Of course, that doesn't necessarily mean sending innocent people to jail. You'll know yourself as a policeman that there are plenty of crooks out there who've got away with murder and more, and they're the ones you go for, because they will look plausible."

"So it's all a matter of public belief in the system?"

"Yes, that's it. The public want stability and order. Who doesn't? They're fed up of self-serving politicians who aren't thinking of the nation as a whole, all struggling to get their own snouts into the trough. To us, the Movement, that is, the answer is simple. Remember your Roman history. Livy's tale of Cinncinnatus, who's called from his plough when the city is threatened, takes up the dictatorship, deals with the threat – Etruscans, Celts or whoever it was – then lays down his powers and goes back to the farm. Someone who can lead the nation during a time of trouble."

"Like Hitler?"

"No, no, not at all. Hitler will give people the certainty they want, that's true. But I think he'll go too far. He's a little man who's caught up in his own mythology. He'll never want to give up the power. He'll enjoy being an autocrat. No, he's the wrong type altogether."

"Did you have an Estonian Cinncinnatus in mind?"

"Yes. There was someone who fitted the bill."

"Ah. General Laidoner?"

"Exactly. He led us in the War of Independence, and then laid down the supreme command and retired to civilian life. And when the Reds attempted their coup in 1924 he took up again the supreme command, and then once more laid it down, when the emergency was dealt with. He still has more personal prestige than any other person in Estonia. We approached him, but he wasn't willing. He preferred to stand for the Smallholders' Association."

"You didn't think any of the politicians could take the role?"

"Come, come, chief inspector, that doesn't take much thinking about. There were only two who commanded enough popular support, Jaan Tõnisson and Konstantin Päts. Tõnisson is a great idealist, but he's an old-fashioned liberal who hasn't really got to grips with the twentieth century. Look how long it took him to get off the gold standard. And Päts, well, he's got a lot of support among the farmers, that's true, but we felt there was something not quite trustworthy about him. I'm not saying any more, except that it turned out we were right."

"But didn't he do what you were wanting to do, set up an authoritarian state?"

"No. He has simply arrested the flow of history for a

few years. He has no vision of what Estonia might become. Of what we might have made it. And we would have done it with the people's consent. The story that we were planning a coup was nonsense."

"So there was no plan to approach General Madrus, when Laidoner turned you down?"

"I believe it was raised at the executive committee. Once Laidoner said no, the choice was difficult. There was no-one with the right level of standing with the people, and who also shared our ideals. Madrus' name was mentioned, but it was felt he lacked charisma. And I also heard it said that his war record was not wholly good."

"Do you know why?"

"No. I suppose they thought being away from the front organising supplies wasn't the same as being involved in combat. Like yourself, for instance. Your actions at Võnnu turned the battle around. Don't you, privately, share our ideals of order and stability, shaped by a vision of a future Estonia?" Rist smiled benignly.

"I think those are admirable goals. But I don't think the way you get them is by having a dictatorship. Once you start telling people just what to do, you take away from them any responsibility for their own behaviour. And to me, accepting responsibility for your own actions is the basis of all morality, because you have to think about what's right and what's wrong. It doesn't mean you do good things all the time, but it does mean that when you do something that's wrong, you accept responsibility for it. You personally. Once you've broken that link to personal responsibility, morality is gone. Right behaviour then becomes just doing whatever you're told."

"How do you apply that to dealing with criminals?"

"Every crime is an act of personal decision-making. People choose to commit crimes. And there are always reasons. Sometimes we can sympathise with them: a poor man who steals a loaf of bread to feed his family, a wife who kills the husband who's been beating her regularly for years. More often we don't. But the fact remains, there are always reasons why a crime is committed. Therefore, if a crime is committed, we need to find who did it and what his – and it's mainly his – reasons are. And that may point to lessons we can learn to try and stop that crime happening again. If the poor man steals bread to feed his family, increasing the sentence, even making it a capital offence, won't stop poor men stealing bread. But if we remove the poverty that was the main trigger for his stealing, it won't happen any more. So, if there's a murder, finding a random criminal and executing him may make people feel good, but it doesn't tell us what's behind it, and how we can stop it happening again."

"You make your case very convincingly, chief inspector. I don't agree with all your views, but what you've said tells me that you're thoughtful and articulate. In short, a publisher's dream. And with your background, we could have a real best-seller! Please do think about it."

Hallmets laughed. "I will. Just one more question. What did you think of General Madrus personally?"

"I think we were wise not to go for him. He'd have been a useless dictator! Anyway, chief inspector, no more politics, please. Now you will join me in a drink." Rist opened a glass-fonted cabinet and took out a bottle of brandy and a couple of shot glasses.

27

Returning to HQ, he found Kadakas waiting for him, eager to report his findings on Raud Kirik from the Ministry of Defence archive. Kirik was born and grew up on his parents' farm near the town of Paide, in central Estonia. In late 1918 he'd volunteered for the new Estonian Army, and been allocated to the 19th Regiment, soon being promoted to Corporal and then Sergeant. In March 1919, along with the then Lieutenant-Colonel Madrus, he was however transferred into the Supplies Division. A letter attached to the transfer notice made it clear that this was at Lieutenant-Colonel Madrus' specific request. After that, his career paralleled that of Madrus. He never advanced beyond sergeant and left the army at the same time as the general.

Sadly, as with the general, detail was lacking about the period up to March 1919. The only information there was a pencilled list of places and dates. Kadakas guessed that these were where Kirik, and whichever elements of the 19th Regiment he was with, were located on the dates recorded. But one of the entries had been marked, by an almost invisible dash in the margin of the page. "Almost as if someone had marked it to come back to, and then forgotten to rub out his mark," suggested Kadakas. He pointed to the name and date on his copy: Hapsaküla, 17th January 1919. "They had a big history of the war, in several volumes, so I looked it up there, but there's no mention of the place."

"Well-spotted, Ants," said Hallmets, "That could be important. I don't recognise the name myself, but it looks from the other place names on the list that the 19th were at that time in a different sector than I was. I'd say at that time they were fighting the Reds at the bottom end of Lake Peipus, near Petseri."

"Could someone you know have been there?" asked Kadakas.

"Good question. Let me think about it. But Jaan Kallas was a correspondent throughout the war. He may have come across it. I think we should ask him first. I know he keeps good records of everything he wrote."

Hallmets phoned Kallas, but he was still unavailable. He left a message giving the name – Hapsaküla – and the date – 17th January 1919.

He tried to cast his mind back to the war years. It wasn't hard. The occasion when a Red sabre had sliced off the two outside fingers of his left hand was burned in his memory. Contacting the men who'd been under his command wouldn't help – he knew where they'd been, but it wasn't where Kirik and Madrus were. He tried to remember officers he'd encountered who'd been in the south-east sector. A name came into his mind – Kaljusaar. He'd met him at a briefing meeting somewhere near the Russian border in the summer of 1919. Later on he was, like Hallmets involved in the decisive battle at Võnnu. He might know something. But how to find him.

"We need to find a Major Kaljusaar," he said to Kadakas.

"Wouldn't Colonel Janno have his details? If he'd stayed on in the army, that is."

"Of course. Good thinking."

"Er, why don't I give Katriin a ring, sir?" suggested Kadakas.

Hallmets smiled. "She may not even need to consult the colonel."

Kadakas seemed to spend a lot of time on the phone talking in a low voice to Katriin. Eventually he rang off, and said to Hallmets, "She'll have a look herself, sir, and get back to me as soon as she's got something."

Twenty minutes later, the call came for Kadakas. "We're in luck, sir," he reported, "Katriin found him. He stayed on in the army, promoted to colonel in 1923, left on medical grounds in 1928, due to a wound that was giving him trouble. He's receiving a pension from the Defence Ministry, so they have his address. He lives here in Tallinn, out at Kitseküla, on the south side of the city, beyond the Luther furniture factory."

"Good work, Ants. Let's pay him a call right now. We'll collect a car from the pool. How's your driving?"

Evald Kaljusaar's house was a comfortable wooden house of one storey. In response to Hallmets' authoritative knocking on the iron door-knocker shaped like an eagle's head, a voice from inside, "Okay. Hang on there. I'm coming." The door creaked open to reveal a tall grey-haired man leaning on a walking-stick. He stared at Hallmets, frowning. "I know you, but I can't put a name to you. From the war, I think, eh?"

"Hallmets. Jüri Hallmets. Detective Chief Inspector. I joined the police after the war."

"Glad to meet you," said the older man. "Wait a minute. Weren't you at Võnnu?"

Hallmets smiled, "Yes, colonel, I think we were both wounded there. Your unit had a hard time, I think."

"It was tricky. Those Germans could be so persistent. Yes, I got a nasty shot in the knee. Bit of a mess, but they cleaned it up. Just can't bend the leg any more. Still, at least it's still there. What about yourself?"

"Only lost a couple of fingers," said Hallmets, "Ruined my career as a concert pianist."

"What?" asked Kadakas, "Were you really …"

"Course he wasn't," laughed Kaljusaar, "But you've got to joke about these things. And there are men worse off than us two. At least our minds are still intact. Well, don't just stand there! Come on in. You'll have some coffee of course? I assume this isn't a social call. Especially as your batman – or whatever you call them in the police – is with you."

"This is Officer Kadakas, colonel. You're right, I'm here on business. And we'd love some coffee. Thank you."

Having been introduced to Kaljusaar's wife Naima, and now ensconced in the colonel's study at the rear of the house, and supplied with coffee and sweet biscuits, Hallmets could begin. "I'm in charge of the Special Crimes Unit, and we've been asked to look into General Madrus's death. Keep this to yourself, but it wasn't a simple matter, and we need to find out what circumstances could have brought it about. In particular, we're looking at the first few months of 1919. When he was serving in the south-east sector, in a combat role. Before he was transferred to Supplies. Can you remember anything about him?"

"Hmm. Madrus. Let me think." Kaljusaar went over to the bookcase which stood against the wall, awkwardly swinging one straight leg as he walked, and fetched a tall volume from the middle shelf. He brought it over and opened it up on the low coffee table. "This should help. It's an atlas of the war. If I recognise the place names, it might bring back a few memories."

"You've never been tempted to write your memoirs?" asked Hallmets, as the colonel leafed through the volume.

"Me? No. Plenty of others have done that already. And now, well, in the current climate I wouldn't be able to say half the things I'd like to. Nowadays you've got to give the officially approved account. It's all about nostalgia, and heroism, and memorials to the glorious dead. You can't mention the mistakes, the stupidities, the needless deaths, the atrocities. You can't criticise any of the decisions made. Mostly they were good ones, of course, or the best under the circumstances. But now and then, well, you know how it was. People in the middle of things don't always see the big picture, and people back at HQ don't always appreciate what's going on at the front. Ah! Here we are. The south-eastern sector. That was a difficult one. The landscape didn't help: forests, bogs, swollen streams, waterlogged fields, isolated villages. And then when the temperature dropped, it could get very chilly, and the ice made everything treacherous. Madrus? Yes, yes, I remember now. He was a lieutenant-colonel then. They'd put him into a combat role straight away. He'd been in the Russian Imperial Army, so they assumed he'd know what he was doing. In his case, that was a mistake. Pretty soon they shunted him into Supplies. I believe he was quite successful there – we always managed to get the stuff we needed."

"What can you remember about his combat actions?"

Kaljusaar stared at the map. "I was with the 26th. I think he was with the 19th."

"That's right," confirmed Hallmets. Kadakas watched the colonel intently.

Kaljusaar finally tapped the map with his finger, and then pointed to an area. "Yes, I think the 19th saw some action here. A tricky spot all right. The Reds were well dug in, but they managed to get them out, eventually. It

166

was all very messy. The Reds didn't just fall back in an organised body, like a proper army. They tended to sort of disintegrate, then gather somewhere else. So you could never be quite sure you'd got rid of them all. Anyway that's where Madrus was."

Hallmets peered at the map. "Hapsaküla?" said Hallmets innocently, pointing at the name, "Does that bring anything to mind?"

"Funny you should mention Hapsaküla. It does ring a bell. Something happened there all right. Was there a fight? I don't think so. But you're right, Madrus was there. I met a veteran years later who told me something. Now what was it?"

"Some sort of incident?"

"Atrocities. Yes, that was it. As you'll know, the Reds were a pretty savage bunch. They deliberately used terror as a weapon, to cow the local populace. Killing, raping, maiming, torture, the more vicious the better. And in the cold light of day, not the heat of battle. This man told me some of things the Reds had done there. In that village. Raping the women then crucifying them. Can you imagine that? Killing children. My God, awful stuff. I saw some of it myself, where I was. So if you caught the bastards, you just had to shoot them or hang them. I think it was all too much for Madrus. He lost his nerve, lost his ability to command. You'll know yourself that if you can't take these things, and stay calm and in command, you lose the respect of your men. And their trust. Yes, I'm sure that's why they moved him into Supplies. Lost his nerve. But they covered it up, you see. Every move had to be presented as part of the big plan, a step in the right direction. For morale. So his move to Supplies was presented as promotion."

"Anything else you can remember about what he did around that time?"

Kaljusaar stared at the map for along time. "Sorry, that's it, really. I was quite focused on my own bit of the action. You'd have to find some vets from the 19th to give you the story. But be warned, if there's anything dodgy went on, they'll clam up as soon as you look at them."

"What do you mean by dodgy?"

"Same as what you no doubt encountered. Mostly pinching stuff. I don't mean just picking fruit off a farmer's trees, I mean stripping all the valuables from his house. And then claiming the Reds did it. Which was plausible, of course. Difficult to disprove unless you caught them red-handed. And sometimes the stuff they took was useful to us. Especially food. Care for some lunch, by the way?"

"No thanks, colonel. That's been very helpful. I hope it didn't bring back memories that are too unpleasant."

"We all live with these memories, chief inspector. They never go away. You just have to keep them at the back of your mind as much as you can. And stay busy, that's the way to play it."

Kadakas drove them back to Headquarters. Leaving the car there, they walked to the *Alt-Revaler* for some late lunch.

28

Jaan Kallas was back in his flat on Kreutzwald Street, just off the main Narva Road by eleven. He'd already compiled his copy for the evening edition, merely rehashing some press releases from the Propaganda Office. He would have to be back at the office that evening to file his copy for the following morning. Until then, he was free. He had made the second bedroom of his two-bedroom flat into his study. Here he kept copies of all the material he'd ever filed, even the garbage he was now obliged to write. The collection was indexed, so that he could home in on a piece he was looking for without wasting too much time.

It was not so easy this morning, though. A search for General Madrus in the index had pointed him to several articles mentioning the general in passing from later stages of his career. Having skimmed these, he concluded there was nothing relevant to his death. Next he looked at his material from the first half of 1919. He was soon transported back to those difficult days when the outcome of the war was still far from clear, and it was with difficulty that he forced himself to move from one piece to the next. The writing was sharper in those days too, he noted. Spare and expressive, whether it was capturing the voices and feelings of the men at the front, or analysing the strategic and tactical choices made by the commanders of the army. He'd definitely got more prolix, as well as putting on more weight, once the war was won.

At 11.45 his phone rang. Kristiina from reception at *Pealinna Uudised*. A message from DCI Hallmets: 'Hapsaküla, 17th January 1919.' That was all.

But it was enough. He moved into the middle of January. He'd been covering a wide area then, moving around behind the lines, then darting forward to capture what was going on. A fearless reporter, crawling along trenches under fire, ducking behind walls and lurking in burnt out buildings as he interviewed those at the heart of the fighting. He'd even on a couple of occasions managed to interview Red or German prisoners, before they were taken away for further interrogation, or summary execution after a military trial.

There was not much about Madrus and his unit, but Kallas did go to Hapsaküla on the 19th of January, after hearing of a particularly unpleasant atrocity committed by the Reds. He dug out the article.

Horrific Red Atrocity
from special correspondent Jaan Kallas
Hearing from returning soldiers of our army of a terrible atrocity, I got here yesterday, in time to see the naked corpses of women from the village of Hapsaküla. All that happened was observed by an old man who hid in a ruined building. The Reds, he told me, arrived one week ago. All men who remained there, from the age of twelve up, were shot dead on the edge of communal grave pits. After the men it was the turn of the children. All children under the age of twelve were thrown into the grave pit alive, and clubbed to death with rifle butts if they attempted to crawl out. The women were forced to fill in the pit. Then they were subjected to multiple rapes, before being crucified naked, nailed onto the wooden walls of buildings. Six more young people, four men and two women were later found in a cottage in the village. Two had been beheaded. The others had been tied to chairs and tortured, before being finally stabbed to death with

170

bayonets.

The Reds then withdrew from the village to take their foul terror elsewhere. Many of our soldiers were physically sick when they moved into the village the following day. They left the horrific spectacle until correspondents could arrive to record the scene. "We have the descriptions of the killers, and they will face justice when we catch them," commented Colonel Renner, commander of the 19th Regiment. His second-in-command, Lieutenant-colonel Madrus, whose advance units discovered the ghastly scene, was not available for interview.

When I asked an ordinary soldier, who refused to give his name, what his reaction was, he explained, "I puked up. We all did." When I asked him if any of the Reds had been apprehended, he was pulled away by a sergeant, who said his men were too shocked to make any further comment.

Kallas read the account two or three times, to try to bring the scene back to him. He succeeded only too well, but still needed a stiff brandy to stop himself shaking. There were no other pieces referring to the incident, or to the village. A pencilled note recorded that a week later he had tried to return there, but found it had been declared out of bounds.

Why had he wanted to return, he asked himself. The first time he'd been there he had seen the mass grave, the crucifixions, and the bodies in the cottage. Was there something else he'd missed, or did he want to look again at something he'd seen the first time?

He put the typed copy of his text into an envelope and left the flat. He needed some fresh air. He also wanted to get his information to DCI Hallmets as soon as he could. He didn't know how this information related to General Madrus, but Hallmets might have found other parts of the jigsaw. He knew the *Alt-Revaler* was Hallmets' favoured spot for lunch and headed there on the off-chance he would find him there.

But as he made his way along Narva Road towards the Old Town, he glanced across the street, and felt a chill run down his spine. On the other side of the road, heading in the same direction, was the tall, slim, almost cadaverous figure of Indrek Lepp. He was striding out at a rapid pace, followed by Antti and Matti, who were struggling to keep up with him.

Kallas was faced with a choice: should he continue to the *Alt-Revaler*, in the hope that Hallmets would be there, or follow Lepp and his creatures, to see where they went. So far he didn't have to choose, as the three were heading in the same direction as Kallas, along Narva Road towards the old Viru Gate, which would take them into the Old Town.

They passed the National Theatre, and then reached the Viru Gate. But once through the gate, the threesome turned sharp left, to follow the alley which ran inside the mediaeval city wall. Kallas now had to make a decision. The safest option would be to find Hallmets and report the matter to him. But Kallas hadn't got where he was by always taking the safest option. His journalist's nose led him after the trio, and into the narrow lane. He kept well behind them. He knew the biggest danger was Lepp, whom he guessed was always vigilant, and might glance around at any moment. He therefore held himself well back, delaying over lighting a cigarette until two men in long homespun coats, perhaps farmers come into town for

172

the market, had passed him, before following.

The alley was dim. On the left the old city wall rose steeply above him, on the right decrepit two-storeyed houses of dark and crumbling stone formed a continuous line. The lowering sky seemed to absorb the light from the space between them. The wet cobbles of the roadway felt slimy beneath his feet.

He did not have to tail them for long. He saw them, from a distance, stop at a door, then disappear inside. Carefully he moved forward, keeping behind the two farmers, strolling at what seemed a snail's pace, as they discussed the merits and demerits of a new breed of cow they'd recently encountered. At last they passed the doorway that interested Kallas and he stood in front of it. The building seemed as decrepit as the others in the alley. The small panes of the two downstairs windows were obscured by grime and dust, although he thought he could see blinds drawn down behind them. The door between them was as old as the house, with brown paint, cracked and blistered, peeling off in some places. A rusty iron knocker hung in its centre. Fixed on the wall beside the door was a wooden plaque about 20 cm square. Carved in small capitals in the plaque, in letters that at one time had been inlaid with black paint, of which tiny traces remained, were the words: H. WEBER and below: CONSULTANT.

Kallas was wondering what sort of consultant Herr Weber might be, when he sensed rather than saw a movement of the blind on the window to his right. He instantly turned and began to move away in the direction he had come. But a squeaking told him the door was opening. Glancing back, he saw a big man emerge from the door. Matti! No doubt Antti would be right behind him.

"Hey, Kallas, hang on there, old buddy, we'd like a chat," shouted Matti.

Kallas took to his heels. He wasn't a coward, but he knew when the odds weren't good. There was no-one in the alley, apart from an old man hobbling along with a stick. He picked up speed. But the cobbles were slippery, with ice or slime, and after about a dozen steps he slipped, lost his balance, and fell sideways, his head narrowly missing the base of the old city wall.

As he struggled to get back to his feet he heard footsteps approach.

"Want a hand up, old pal," said Matti.

"*Härra* Lepp wants a little word with you," said Antti, "But first we'll have a little fun, eh, Matti?"

"Sounds good to me," said Matti, giving Kallas a vicious kick in the back. He rolled onto the cobblestones again, groaning.

"Maybe a kick in the head will help his thinking," suggested Antti.

"Yeah," agreed Matti.

Kallas covered the sides of his head with his hands.

"*Härra* Kallas!" called a new voice, "Are you all right?"

It was the old man with the stick.

"Clear off, Grandad," sneered Antti. "He's a pal of ours, and we're giving him all the help he needs."

The old man's response was as swift as it was unexpected. He suddenly thrust his heavy walking-stick into Antti's stomach, causing him to double up and fall onto the road. Then he spun the stick in the air, so he was holding the end, and swung it club-like to connect the handle with Matti's temple. He staggered to his left two paces and collapsed into a heap. Meanwhile Antti was back on his feet, gasping for breath, but already wielding a knife. The stick's handle swung again to hit his knee with a sharp crack. Antti dropped the knife and fell onto the cobbles, screaming and clutching his knee.

"Time to go," said the old man, seizing Kallas' arm and almost dragging him along the alley. In minutes they'd reached the Viru Gate again, and the man pulled Kallas behind a flower-seller's booth.

"Are you OK?" he asked.

"Yes, more or less," answered Kallas, "Thank you. I think you saved my life. That's a hell of a stick you've got."

"Yes, the handle's weighted with lead, Gives it a bit more oomph."

"Who are you, anyway? I don't know you, but you seem to know me. And you're not as old as you looked." Close up, he could see the powder that greyed the man's hair, and he'd felt the man's strength as he'd pulled him along.

"Lieutenant Tamm at your service. Political police. I've been following these three all day. Probably blown my cover now, but we can't have them beating up innocent citizens. Especially one of our best journalists."

"So you knew they were here?"

"We do like to keep well-informed. I'll need to report now, but you'll be OK from here, there are too many people about for them to try anything. Cheerio!"

Lieutenant Tamm slipped away and seemed to vanish immediately into the crowd.

Kallas took his advice, and moved on up Viru Street, past shoppers peering into the shop windows. At the top of Viru Street he turned right into Raekoja Plats, dominated by the elegant mediaeval town hall with its graceful minaret-like tower.

Across the square he reached the *Alt-Revaler*, and even before he entered he spotted, at his usual table by the window, *Ülemkomissar* Hallmets. Inside the cafe door, as he hung up his coat, he noticed another officer with Hallmets. That was the ex-soldier Kadakas.

Hallmets had already seen him, and gave him a discreet wave. "Jaan, do come and join us," he said, "The meat balls are good. Swedish, apparently. I'm not sure what makes them Swedish. We'll talk once we've eaten."

Kallas sat on the vacant chair at their table, facing the window, Hallmets on his right, Kadakas on his left. He leaned towards Hallmets and whispered, "I've just seen Lepp ..."

Hallmets put a finger to his lips. "So, he's here," he muttered, "Anyway, Jaan, have some lunch. Then we'll go somewhere where we can talk."

Back in the workroom at Police HQ, they sat round the big oak table, with cups of coffee and glasses of brandy. Kallas first told them what had happened to him earlier.

"So," commented Hallmets, "Something's going on all right. But it sounds like Reinart and his people are already onto it. Will they just let it run, in order to sweep up as many of the plotters as they can at the last minute?"

"Could Reinart have engineered the whole thing?" asked Kallas, "To strengthen the regime."

"Nothing's impossible. But I think involving the Finns would be too much of a complication for him. It's more likely Sirk and his Finnish pals cooked it up. Reinart probably has spies amongst the former Vaps people, and got wind of it quite soon. But he doesn't know all the details, hence his worry about whether Madrus had been

176

involved. But Lepp's a problem for Reinart, because he was earlier very publicly made out to be a great policeman. If he's caught, I suspect Reinart would prefer to have him quietly eliminated."

"You say *if* he's caught?"

"Lepp's no fool. If he has any suspicion the police are onto him, he may vanish immediately."

"Could what happened today tell him that?"

"Perhaps. Though, as far as we know, Lepp didn't witness it. He was presumably waiting for our two pals to bring you back to the house. I hate to think what your 'little chat' would have been like. I suspect torture and maybe execution could have come into it. So what he will get is a garbled version of Tamm's intervention from the two thugs. He will undoubtedly become more wary, but if there's a big prize to be won, I doubt it'll put him off yet."

"Will they come after me, then?"

"I don't think so. The thugs may want revenge, and Lepp doesn't like you at all. But he'll assume you've reported your Finnish experience to somebody, and probably also what happened today, so there's no point in shutting you up any more. He's also not easily distracted from his main goal. Mind you, he'll certainly have both of us on his death list if he takes over from Reinart. But you should be careful, just in case Antti and Matti decide to do something on their own. Another brandy?"

"Yes please. There's something else I've got for you, an article I wrote in 1919."

Kallas showed Hallmets and Kadakas the article. They read it carefully.

"There's something odd here," said Hallmets, "Why were six people taken to a cottage and tortured. It doesn't make sense. Especially as two of them were women. Why were these people segregated from the rest?"

"Could they have been Estonian soldiers?" suggested Kadakas, "Though I don't think any women were at the front line."

"Russian whites?" suggested Kallas, "Hiding in the village. Maybe the Reds only found them later. But you're right, it's curious. Maybe that's why I wanted to go back – to take another look at the cottage."

"It may be," said Hallmets, "that this Hapsaküla incident was what triggered Madrus's transfer away from a combat role."

"Do you think it has anything to do with his killing? Reds getting their revenge for their atrocity being discovered and publicised, perhaps. But then, they weren't usually that bothered when the results of their terror were uncovered. And they were elsewhere by then, so it was very infrequently that anyone was punished for the atrocities."

"Could Lepp's reappearance have anything to do with Madrus's death?" asked Kadakas, "It does seem rather a coincidence."

"Yes, that's possible," observed Hallmets, "If there was something going on and Madrus heard about it. They may even have tried to involve him. We need to find this *Härra* Sepp, who visited him just two days before he was found dead."

"Who's he?" asked Kallas.

"We don't know. Maybe you've come across him, Jaan. Average height, thin, middle-aged, short black hair, parted on the right, clean shaven, he has a scar on the back of his left hand. Our witness says he was dressed 'like a bank manager,' in a rather old fashioned suit with a high winged collar and bow tie. He was also wearing *pince nez* when she saw him, with a thin gold chain attached. And spats on his shoes. Ring any bells?"

Kallas jotted the details down in his notebook. "No-one immediately jumps out at me. I'll have a think, maybe ask around too. One of my colleagues may know him. Could he have been an envoy for the plotters?"

"Right now we have absolutely no idea. So any help you can give us would be appreciated. I can't offer you an exclusive interview on it, as you know exclusive interviews aren't allowed any more."

"I'm not bothered about that. But I need to keep my brain sharpened, and copying the stuff spewed out by the propaganda office doesn't exercise anybody's brain."

29

The afternoon crawled past. The leaden sky foreshadowed snow, and then it came, filling the air with drifting flecks of white, and seeming to silence all the sounds of the city beyond his window. In the muffling hug of snow, all human activity seemed to slow down. Sluggish cars dragged themselves along unwillingly, people in the streets seemed frozen every time he looked down. He tried to make progress on his report, to sum up where they were, yet, as if dampened by the snow, the words refused to come, and when they did, did not seem right.

He was relieved when, not long after four, Marta phoned to tell him Inspector Lesser was on the line.

"Henno. Good to hear from you. How are things down there?"

"One or two things to report, chief. First, Eva and I had an interesting chat with Sirje Kangamees, the general's daughter. She lives in Valga. Her husband Urmas is a Head of the Roads Department in the Valgamaa county administration. She was quite unhappy that you weren't there – she felt she should have been interviewed by the man in charge – but we managed to get past that. And once she got going, it was hard to get a word in.

"Before we could get on to anything else, she had to unload her anger about the status of the estate. Like her father, she thought the castle and the land had been gifted to the family by the state, and she was shocked to find out from Aarne, I mean Dr Kirss, that that wasn't so. She was ready to take legal action against the local authorities here, but Aarne told her it would have to be the Estonian government, and specifically the Ministry of Defence, who signed the lease agreement with the general. The estate was, it seems, taken over after its abandonment by the von Winkelsteins, by the Land Commission, then passed over to the Ministry, along with several other estates. Some of them were used for army facilities and training, a few were presented to individuals who had outstanding service in the War."

"Like General Laidoner?"

"Yes. Except that he was given his estate as a gift. This is where the confusion arose, as Madrus thought his was a gift too. Aarne says he tried to tell him several times that it wasn't, but Madrus just didn't want to listen. Now *Proua* Kangamees seems to have the same problem. But we eventually exhausted that topic."

"I'm relieved to hear it. That was Colonel Janno's impression too. So, what could she tell us about the general?"

"She wasn't very complimentary. Growing up with him can't have been easy. A lot of the time he was absent, and when he did come home, he was often bad-tempered. He didn't seem very interested in his children at all. She thinks he paid no attention to her because she was a girl. She says he was worse with his son, that's Vitus Madrus. He wanted him to go into the army when he grew up, and was always trying to toughen him up, to make a man of him. But Vitus just wasn't the type. He was more interested in art and literature than fighting, and that made his father even more angry. According to her, Madrus beat the boy frequently. When he was nearing the end of his time at the gymnasium, Madrus booked the boy a place in the Military College. Not long after his eighteenth birthday, in the spring of 1924, a month before he would finish at the gymnasium, Vitus disappeared. He left the house as usual to get the bus into Viljandi, and never came back. He didn't turn up at the school. Naturally the general reported him missing and demanded that the police track him down, but they couldn't find him. It seems he went straight from the bus terminus to the railway station and got the next train to Tallinn. But where he got off the train, no-one knew."

"And if he went all the way to Tallinn, he could have gone to Finland, Sweden, even Russia."

"Exactly. And he's never been seen nor heard of since. My guess is that, as you suggest, he got out of Estonia as soon as he could."

"So he could conceivably have come back and killed his father," observed Hallmets. "Do we have a picture of him?"

"Sirje said she didn't have any pictures of him, but I don't believe her. Once she'd gone, I called the gymnasium. They keep all the end-of-year class photographs, so the secretary there is going to search through them, and will hopefully get back to me tomorrow. Sirje was very vague about what he looked like then, deliberately so, I think. She certainly doesn't want us to go looking for him."

"I take it she has an alibi for the night of the murder."

"Yes. She and her husband went to the theatre. The local Dramatic Society were putting on a play by Shakespeare. *Macbeth*. It was the opening night."

"Very appropriate. A play about a murder," commented Hallmets.

"Then they went to a drinks reception with the Dramatic Society. Her husband is on the committee. After that, at about 11 pm, they went home. It's possible they could then have driven up here and killed the general. But I don't think she hated him enough to kill him. He'd largely ignored her, and she reciprocated. She hadn't seen him face-to-face for years."

"She could, I suppose, have known all the time where Vitus was, and kept in touch with him. And even put him up if he came to Estonia. It's conceivable that he came back, stayed with his sister, then came up to Viljandi to kill his father."

"But why come back and do it after all these years?" asked Lesser.

"Maybe they were getting fed up waiting for him to die, and decided to hasten his departure. But I agree, it's not very convincing. OK. Keep an eye on her, and once we get the picture of Vitus, we can circulate it. Any sign of Kirik, by the way?"

"Nothing, chief. Ilmar went back to the estate, just in case he was hiding out somewhere. But no luck at all."

"Maybe we should get a call out for him later tomorrow. I'll go down to Tartu then to speak to Professor Strelkov. Then I hope to come over to Viljandi. There's a possible event in the general's past that may be linked to his death. There also seem to be events going on which I'd rather not talk about on the phone. But I'll fill you in tomorrow."

The decision to go to Tartu had been made as he was talking. He could take the train down and get Lembit to come over from Viljandi with the car for him.

He went through to the workroom. Kadakas immediately stood up. "Permission to report, sir!"

"Remember this isn't the army, Ants. Sit down and tell me what you've got." Hallmets sat down at the big table. Before trying to tackle his report, he'd asked Kadakas to phone the police in Võru, as they'd not responded to his request that they check out the address *Proua* Mölder had given him for Villem Jonsson's parents in Võru.

"The address exists all right, er, chief. Soo Street 34. The cops checked it out today. The people who live there are called Jonsson. But they don't have a son called Villem. Two daughters, and no sons."

"Very clever. He must have looked up people called Jonsson in the phone book and given *Proua* Mölder their address. The only risk would be that she phoned them up to check his *bona fides*. She probably just checked the phone book to satisfy herself that they lived at that address."

"So his real name may not be Jonsson at all?"

"That's right. Another complication. OK, see if you find an address for a Professor Strelkov. He lives in or near Tartu, so start there. He may well be in the phone book."

Meanwhile he asked Marta to book him a single ticket to Tartu for the 08.30 train the following morning. That was the express which only made a couple of stops and would get him into Tartu by 10.30. He'd pick up the ticket on his way home.

Ten minutes later Kadakas had found three Strelkovs who lived in Tartu. However, only one had himself listed as 'Prof. Dr. Dr. A. Strelkov.' Hallmets recognised the street name. It was near the Botanic Garden, close to the river.

Hallmets phoned him up. After three rings the phone was picked up. "Yes?"

"*Proua* Strelkov?"

"*Doktor* Strelkova. I am a doctor of medicine. Do you wish to speak to myself or my husband?"

"It was your husband, that is, Professor Strelkov, I'd like to talk to."

"Who may I say is calling?"

"*Ülemkomissar* Hallmets, from the Special Crimes Unit in Tallinn. I'd like to ask the professor about some events during the War." It had occurred to Hallmets that a professor of history might be able to shed more light on the Hapsaküla incident. If the professor was talking to Madrus, he suspected it was probably to do with some historical research. That suggested that the professor's period of expertise was the not-so-distant past, perhaps even the War.

"My husband is busy and cannot come to the phone. Perhaps you could phone tomorrow morning."

"In fact, I shall be in Tartu tomorrow morning and would like to talk to him in person, if that's possible. I'll be arriving at about 10.30, on the train from Tallinn.

There was a pause. "All right. What about eleven o'clock? We are near the river, so it will take you perhaps twenty minutes to walk from the station."

"I'll probably get a taxi, so I should be there on time. Thank you."

The professor's wife is very protective of her husband, thought Hallmets. He asked Marta to phone Viljandi and ask Lembit to meet him at Tartu's main police station at 1.00 pm, to drive him him back there, and also to let the hotel know he'd be back.

Kirsti was pleased to see him home again for another night. And now that he was home, he could talk freely to her about the case.

"You seem to have quite a lot of missing people. Kirik, Jonsson, and now the general's son. Maybe they're all in it together. You know, like *Murder on the Orient Express*. It only came out last year, maybe they all read it and ..."

"I must admit, that's a possibility we hadn't got round to thinking about. I mean, that they were all involved in some sort of plot, not that they got the idea from Agatha Christie. Talking of plots, are you any further with Baron von Greindorff?"

30

Wednesday 4th December

It had snowed in the night, and the next morning everything lay beneath a white blanket, dully gleaming under the grey bulk of solid-looking cloud. It seemed to Hallmets, as he and Kirsti walked to the station at Nõmme, that all sound was muffled by the snow: footsteps, voices, sounds of traffic, and the clunks and scrapes as the shops pushed up their shutters and got ready to open.

He wasn't sure whether the train into Tallinn would run. The snow looked thick on the tracks; but nevertheless, albeit a little late, the train arrived, and they and the other commuters waiting on the platform, got on board, and wiped gloved hands on the misted windows, to catch a glimpse of the snow-bound landscape as they headed into the city.

At the Baltic Station in Tallinn there was no question of the 8.30 train to Valga, via Tartu, being cancelled or even delayed. Snow was, after all, a normal part of the winter experience. He was relieved to see that the papers carried no further reference to General Madrus, instead focusing on the President's speech welcoming a delegation of furniture designers from Poland, who had arrived to attend a conference in Tallinn. "Furniture design," said the great man, "is the way into the future, and the liberation of mankind from discomfort. Thus will new energy and creativity be released. Furniture, not fighting; wardrobes, not war." Hallmets could not disagree with this sentiment.

As the train sped through snow-clad fields and snow-laden forests, past snow-veiled villages and towns, he thought over the case yet again. The vanishing of witnesses was worrying, and though he did not consider Kirsti's suggestion that they were all in it together very likely, it gnawed at the edge of his consciousness, threatening to push its way into his thinking when he least expected.

It was with relief that he stepped off the train in Tartu, admiring again the magnificent wooden station building, with its wide awning for the shelter of passengers, dating from Tsarist times. And, walking down the steps from its main entrance, passing what was in spring and summer an attractive garden, he was tempted to turn left, and pass the house of Jaan Tõnisson. Fifteen minutes walk beyond Tõnisson's house, and a right turn and then a left would bring him to the house he and his family had lived in for many years. It was a familiar walk, and he turned to the left instinctively, before correcting himself, and instead headed for the taxi rank. On a good day he'd have enjoyed the walk down to the town centre and the bridge over the *Emajõgi* – the 'mother river' – and reached Professor Strelkov's on time. But not today.

He reached the professor's place – one of the older houses on the south side of the river – shortly before eleven. As he exited the taxi, and paid the driver, he noticed that *Proua* Strelkova was already waiting at the open door. A tall, thin woman, with the pasty complexion that he always associated with Russians, and an expression worthy of a prison wardress.

"*Härra* Hallmets, I presume," she said as he arrived at the door. It was a statement, not a question. "Come this way." That was an order, not a request.

The living-room was warm, and a log fire crackled in

the fireplace. An older man rose from an armchair to greet him. Grey hair and beard, not quite as tall as his wife, he smiled, although Hallmets sensed an underlying layer of sadness.

"Chief Inspector, I'm very pleased to see you. I have, of course, heard about your exploits." He held out his hand, and shook hands. Noticing Hallmets' other hand, with the third and fourth fingers missing, he paused. "Yes, of course, you too were in the war. Did you lose anyone?"

"I was lucky," replied Hallmets, "Only two fingers and several friends."

Silence fell, and Hallmets noticed that Strelkov's wife had left the room.

The professor coughed politely. "And I do believe I met your wife a few times at the university. In the library, wasn't she? A very pleasant girl, from Scotland. How is she now?"

"She's fine, and remembers you, professor. She sends her warmest greetings."

"Thank you. Now, how can I help you? Something about the war, Ludmilla said."

At that point the professor's wife returned with coffee and home-made biscuits for her husband and his guest. She poured the coffee, and then left, after a meaningful frown at her husband. "Don't exert yourself too much, dear," she muttered, then to Hallmets, "No more than thirty minutes, please. He mustn't overdo it. He has to watch his heart."

"Don't fuss, dear," said the professor, as he waved her out of the room.

Once they'd sipped their coffee and the professor nibbled on a biscuit – "I can't take coffee on an empty stomach," he explained – Hallmets decided to raise the topic he was interested in.

"Professor, am I right in thinking the War is one of your specialisms?"

"Yes, that's right. When I taught at St. Petersburg, recent history was frowned upon, unless it glorified the Tsarist State. That's why I moved to Tartu in 1914. My colleagues thought it was a downward move, they didn't rate Tartu. But the atmosphere was healthier. But then came the War. My eldest son and daughter were just starting their studies at St. Petersburg. I told them to come to Tartu, but they liked the life in the capital, the theatre and so on, so they stayed. Too long, as it turned out. They were killed by the Reds in early 1919. Only our younger son was left alive. He was only seven, so naturally he had come with us to Tartu.

"Living through the War, and our loss, taught me that these events must never be forgotten. So I made it my business to study them, what made them happen, how they happened. And how they can be avoided in future. Historians tend to shy away from recent history, because often it's politically sensitive, so I ploughed a lone furrow. But my classes here were popular; young Estonians wanted to know what had happened, to think about how their state came into being. Anyway, I retired a couple of years ago – my heart's a bit dodgy – but I continue my researches, and am hoping to complete another book."

He took another sip of coffee. "So if you're wanting to know something about the war, you've come to the right man."

"I'm glad to hear that, professor. I'm particularly interested in one event. On the 17th of January 1919, at a village called Hapsaküla. There was some sort of atrocity,

I believe."

The professor took a bite of his biscuit and chewed slowly, nodding. Then he put the biscuit down on its plate. "Early 1919 was a bad time. It was still touch and go, particularly at the Eastern end of the front, where the Reds were strongest. Some villages changed hands more than once. Whilst for the Estonians this was a War of Liberation, to drive out the foreign rulers, for the Red Army it was simply a civil war, and all their opponents, whether the Germans, the White Russians, or the Estonians and Latvians, they clumped together as 'Whites,' that is, enemies of the revolution. They did not recognise the desire of the Baltic peoples for independence, and wanted to restore the Tsarist Empire as a communist one. But, instead of trying to woo people to their new state, the policy adopted, quite deliberately, and with encouragement from Lenin and Trotsky, was Terror. In that, they behaved just like the Tsars before them. And Terror meant just that, to carry out any acts which would frighten the population into obeying them. So in areas where they captured territory, atrocities were common. I'm sorry, what was the place you mentioned?"

"Hapsaküla. It's near the Russian border."

"It doesn't ring a bell. But as I said, atrocities in that area were common. I'd have to take a look in my files, and see what I've got on it. By the way, can I ask why you're so interested in this particular event. Do you know the place? Were you there during the War?"

"No. I was further West, with the Latvians, fighting the Germans."

"Hallmets! Of course, I should have made the connection. You were at Võnnu, weren't you?"

"Yes, that's right."

The professor laughed. "If you don't mind, chief inspector, I'd very much like to interview you. It's important that my book about the War shows how the soldiers in the field saw it, not just the politicians and the generals."

"I'd be happy to. But, about Hapsaküla?"

"You didn't tell me why you were interested in that particular village."

Hallmets paused. "It's come up in an investigation. I'm afraid I can't tell you more than that. But I would be grateful to know what you can tell me about it."

The professor nodded. "Of course. I'll just be a moment." He got up, with some difficulty, and left the room. Soon Hallmets could hear the professor and his wife talking quietly, in Russian.

After another five minutes, the professor's wife came in. "I'm sorry, *Härra* Hallmets, but I've ordered my husband to rest now. He is always tempted to overdo it, when he finds something interesting, and then tires himself out. It's not good for his heart. But there is no need to worry about your request. He will see to it when I think he is able, and send you the information you asked for. May I order a taxi for you?"

"I'm sorry, *Proua* Strelkova, but I have one more question I must ask your husband. This cannot wait, as it is directly related to a murder investigation."

"I'm afraid that's absolutely impossible." Hallmets recognised the authoritative voice of the doctor protecting a patient.

"This is important for us, so I'd be obliged to refer the matter to the examining magistrate. I'm sure he'll decide on the proper course of action."

"This is outrageous!" shrilled *Proua* Strelkova, "I will

not ..."

"Ludmilla, please be quiet." The professor stood in the doorway. "Your histrionics are more likely to give me a heart attack than the chief inspector's questions." He sat down again, and turned to Hallmets. "I'm sorry, chief inspector, I'll send the information you asked for within the next two or three days. My files are rather extensive and it will take me a while to go through them, and I won't be able to start until after my afternoon rest. But if this is about something else, I don't mind answering a quick question now."

His wife scowled at Hallmets and stalked out of the room.

"Thank you, professor. There's just one question, and it's very simple. You visited General Madrus on the afternoon of Monday 25th November at Rauakivi Castle. Can you tell me the purpose of your visit?"

"Ah. I should have realised that was the investigation you were referring to. I noticed the general's recent death in the paper, but didn't realise there was anything about it which required investigation. But of course, what we read in the papers is never the whole truth. I must say, he seemed in perfectly good health when I saw him. Anyway, the reason for my visit. There has been much written about the military events of the War, some of it by me, I must admit. But my next book will focus on what made the military success possible."

"The quality and dedication of our fighting men?"

"I expressed myself badly. I've written previously about the experiences of our fighting men. So I'm looking now at the logistics that enabled them to have the weapons, the ammunition, the food, the clothing and other equipment they needed. And the transportation systems that enabled them to be where they were needed at the time they were needed. General Madrus was a senior officer in the Supplies Division, and I wanted to get an overview of the supply issues from him. He kindly agreed to talk to me, and I must say his information was most useful in helping me grasp the big picture, so to speak, of the whole supply question. Most useful indeed. Would you like a copy of the notes I made of our conversation? Once they're typed up I can send you a carbon copy."

"Thank you, that would be useful. It will, of course be returned to you. Can I ask if your conversation touched upon the general's military activity before he was attached to the Supplies Division? This was in the early part of 1919."

The professor paused to think. "No. He gave me the impression that he was attached to Supplies Division as soon as he volunteered. After all, that's what he had been doing in the Imperial Army. Not so successfully, I think, but then he was subordinate to others. Russian aristocrats with little experience or even interest in supply issues, who thought weapons and food could just be magicked up from nowhere."

"Thank you. Did the general touch on any other matters? His personal life, or his political opinions, for instance?"

"I make it clear to everyone whom I interview for my research that I am interested only in the historical events they can illuminate, and I do not wish to discuss the current political situation. I find this deters people from saying things they might afterwards regret. And we didn't talk about his personal life. Of course I commiserated him on the loss of his wife and hoped he was not too lonely in the castle. He assured me he had plenty to do keeping the estate in order, and with his official duties."

"Did he mention that he was writing his memoirs?"

"No, he did not. How very interesting. I'm sure they'd be worth reading. Though memoirs can be deceptive, you understand. They do tend towards the rewriting of history, in which the writer's part is naturally exaggerated. They must therefore be carefully checked against other sources to extract the nuggets they may contain. I wonder how far he'd got with them."

"A final question. Did he seem worried about anything?"

"I'm not sure how we'd define 'worried,' and how worry is manifested. I guess different people show worry in different ways. All I can say is that the general was serious and thoughtful. There were no obvious signs of agitation or inability to concentrate on what I was asking him. That's really all I can say."

"That's most helpful, professor. I'll leave it there, and let you get your rest. Please do apologise to your wife for my insisting to ask about your talk with the general."

Professor Strelkov showed Hallmets out of the house. There was no sign of his wife.

31

It was not snowing, so Hallmets chose to walk from the Strelkovs' house to the police station. He soon reached the zone where broom-wielders had cleared the pavements of snow, and crossed the bridge over the river back into the city centre.

Reaching the police station, he was greeted by several former colleagues. He was also handed a note by the duty sergeant, asking him to phone Viljandi police station. Sergeant Lauk took the call.

"Good morning, Sir. About your request for transport from Valga, I'm afraid there was a lot of snow overnight, and the road to Tartu is blocked not far from here. Lembit was all for having a go, but I told him it was not on. I hope you don't mind that, Sir, but there's no point risking lives, as well as vehicles."

"That's fine, sergeant, I agree with you. Is there any way of getting over there?"

"Hmm. You could always take the train back to Tallinn, then down here. The trains are still running. However, the road from here to Valga is still clear. If you were to get the next train down to Valga, Lembit may be able pick you up there."

"That sounds like sound advice. Many thanks, sergeant. If Lembit can get himself to the police station in Valga, I can meet him there. Please let him know. Also can you ask him to bring *Proua* Kangamees' address. I'd like a word with her if she happens to be in."

He was planning to have lunch in Tartu, but found himself instead in a police car being driven to the station to catch the one o'clock train to Valga. Fortunately there had been time to buy a ham and cheese pie and a bar of chocolate from the cafe next door to the police station, and a thermos flask of coffee was meanwhile conjured up for him in the kitchen at the police station. Thus equipped, and having purchased a couple of newspapers at the stall in the station building, he awaited the train, on its way down from Tallinn.

Not long after the train had pulled out of the station, the snow arrived. Nothing was visible from the carriage window. Indeed, the wind was hurling the snow against the side of the train facing eastwards, so that the window was soon covered by an icy skin of freezing snow. Looking westwards, all he could see were the swirling flakes. Towns, villages, forests, fields, the homes of the rich and the hovels of the poor, all became equal in being expunged from sight. The town of Elva was passed unseen, and Hallmets tackled his lunch. The pie was tasty, the coffee hot, and the chocolate comforting. He kept most of the chocolate and half the coffee, just in case.

The train was forced to slow down, and a one-hour journey stretched towards two. But after ninety minutes the snow eased off, and the outside world reappeared. And ten minutes later they were in Valga. One train a day went on to Riga, but not this one.

As he emerged from the station, he saw the familiar black Volvo, and was greeted by Lembit. "Good to see you, chief. Glad you got through."

"Thanks Lembit. How was your journey down here?"

"A bit hairy in places, especially on the road out of Viljandi down to Karksi. Once I hit the Pärnu road it wasn't so bad. Nevertheless, the quicker we get out the better. I can take you straight to the Kangamees place now. It's not far."

The villa where Urmas and Sirje Kangamees lived was, thankfully, not far from the town centre. A maid ushered Hallmets into an expensively furnished living-room, whilst Lembit was directed through to the kitchen. The living-room fireplace was bare, but Hallmets noticed the radiator under the window. Central heating was still a luxury few could afford. *Härra* Kangamees could not be doing badly.

"I'm afraid *Härra* Kangamees is out," said the maid, "But *Proua* Kangamees will see you, in a few moments. Can I bring you some coffee?"

Hallmets sat on a sofa, and waited. The coffee was most welcome, coming as it did with a sweet pastry with chocolate paste in the centre. Hallmets had time to eat all of it before Sirje Kangamees finally appeared. She had, it seemed, been spending some time on her appearance. A woman of average height and slim build, her dark hair was long and straight, with a fringe, which reminded him of Claudette Colbert in Cecil B. de Mille's epic movie *Cleopatra*, which he'd seen with Kirsti earlier that year. She was wearing a violet cashmere jumper, a grey woollen skirt and silk stockings. A small and rather grotesque dog, with a flat scowling face, long off-white hair, and very short legs, scuttled in after her. A whiff of expensive perfume reached Hallmets as he stood to introduce himself.

She shook his hand, clasping it a little longer than was perhaps necessary. Her hand was soft and cool, and Hallmets noted as he removed his hand traces of some cream recently applied to hers.

"Chief Inspector Hallmets." She emphasised the 'chief.' "I do appreciate you coming to see me. I was very disappointed that I was only able to speak to your subordinate the other day. No doubt he relayed to you all that was said at our meeting. But do sit down, please." She sat herself down on a soft armchair, and lifted the dog onto her lap.

"Thank you. Inspector Lesser has reported to me, yes. So this is more of a courtesy call, to assure you that we intend to get to the bottom of your father's death."

"Thank you. Though I'm not sure you ever will get to the bottom of it, as you say, I think too many people disliked him."

"Did they include your brother Vitus?"

She smiled. "I disliked him too, chief inspector. If you're going to include Vitus in your list of suspects, I should be there too."

"Naturally. But the difference is that we know where you are. Do you have any idea where Vitus is? If he can be eliminated as a suspect, it would enable us to focus our investigation."

She hesitated, and Hallmets was now certain she knew more than she was saying. "Please, *Proua* Kangamees, it would really help us. And Vitus too."

She hesitated again, bit her lip, then, put the dog on the floor, came over and sat next to Hallmets on the sofa. The dog growled suspiciously at him, then scrambled back onto the armchair. Now she seemed to notice his left hand for the first time. She stared at the scar tissue on the edge of the hand, where the third and fourth fingers should have been rooted. "Was that in the War?"

"Yes. A Russian sabre. I was lucky. I've got three fingers left."

"What about the man who did it?"

"He wasn't so lucky."

"You killed him with your own sabre?"

"I had a revolver."

Hallmets sensed she was putting off what might be a difficult conversation. "Tell me about Vitus. You're in touch with him, aren't you?"

"Yes," she admitted in a tiny voice.

"For how long?"

"Ever since he left home. We've always kept in touch. We were close as children. You don't lose that. He wasn't good at dealing with Father's constant criticisms. I supported him as much as I could, tried to protect his psyche. Father never understood him, never even made the effort. He'd thought of running away, ever since he was fifteen. I persuaded him to hang on, I thought he was too young, he wouldn't have been able to cope. By the time he was eighteen, he was ready. And he couldn't wait any longer. I helped him get away, gave him what little money I'd saved up. I even told Father I thought I'd seen him at school that day, just to delay his realisation that Vitus had gone. Father's reaction to his going was typical. Rather than asking what might have led Vitus to go, he raged at him, called him an ungrateful cur, and then set up a manhunt as if Vitus were an escaped prisoner." She smiled. "But by then he was too late. I was always the better organiser of the two of us, and I put together the plan for his escape. I bought his train ticket, so that when the police went with his description to the railway station, no-one recognised it."

"How did you get him out of the country?"

She laughed. "Father helped us there, unwittingly. He was occasionally sent on missions abroad, to our allies, or the League of Nations, and he had a fantasy that he'd be seconded to New York as a delegate for a few months. So he got passports for us all. He kept them in the safe in his study, but I knew where they were; I'd spied on him opening the safe, and knew the combination. Even if I'd not seen him, I could have guessed it. 1875. The year of his birth. Imagination was not one of my father's attributes. He never was sent to New York, of course. He always thought he was more important than he really was. God knows why they gave him that estate. But now it looks as if they only lent it to him. Bastards!"

"You were telling me how Vitus got out."

"Oh yes. I got his passport from the safe the afternoon before, while Father was out somewhere. I'd got the timetables of the boats to Sweden, and made sure he had enough money for the ticket. I thought if they suspected he might leave the country, the first idea would be that he'd gone to Finland. He made it to Stockholm with very little money left. Then his own skills kicked in. I was a good organiser, but Vitus was good at languages – he'd studied Russian, German and English at school – and also very personable. He could get on with people. All except his own father that is! He got a job as a steward on a Swedish cruise ship. He soon picked up Swedish, I guess. Free trips to the Mediterranean, the Norwegian fjords, even the Scottish islands. He knew how to be servile to the rich, and had a good time. He did that for three or four years, and that was when he discovered himself, what his talents and dreams were."

"What were they?"

"Acting. His dream was to be a film star, but he hasn't made that yet. He got minor parts in regional theatres in Sweden, then a permanent position in the Royal Theatre in Uppsala."

"I'm guessing he'd changed his name by then."

ALLAN MARTIN

"He needed a passport to get the cruise liner jobs. But he claimed to be a refugee from Russia, and got himself registered with the League of Nations Refugee Commission, who supplied him with a temporary ID card. Victor Yeltsky, he called himself. Four years later, that would be 1928, he got a Swedish passport, and changed his name again. The Swedes had no objection to immigrants Swedifying their names; they thought it helped them fit in. Now he was ..." She stopped, She had realised she was telling Hallmets the whole story. "I don't think I should say any more."

"It's too late, *Proua* Kangamees. With what you've given me, we can find him." Hallmets didn't believe that himself, but was able to say it with such authority that Sirje Kangamees did. Her head fell into her hands. "But I'd rather hear the whole story from you. *Proua* Kangamees, ..."

"Please, call me Sirje."

"Let me ask you this before you go on, Sirje. Do you think Vitus killed his Father?"

She raised her head. Tears were streaming down her face. Hallmets produced his handkerchief and offered it to her. She wiped her face. "I don't know," she said, "I just don't know."

"Would the boy you knew at home have killed his father?"

"No. He was never a violent boy. He hated violence."

"Then it's more than likely that he's innocent. Go with your instinct. That's why it's imperative that we find him. It would be even better if he came to us voluntarily. By not coming into the open, he attracts suspicion to himself. I take it you've been in touch regularly?"

"Yes. We write to each other at least once a month,

sometimes more."

"So he knows that his father is dead?"

"Yes."

"And how he died?"

"Yes, I told him all about it."

"Told him?"

"Yes. No. I mean, I wrote to him."

"Where?"

She hesitated. Hallmets could hear the clock on the mantelpiece ticking.

"Riga. He's in Riga at the moment."

"So he came up to meet you, didn't he? Or did you go to Riga?"

"No. I mean, all right, yes, we met over the border, in Valka, in a cafe."

Hallmets knew that after independence there had been a dispute about the border between Estonia and Latvia. Both had claimed the town known to the Estonians as Valga and to the Latvians as Valka, which had a mixed population. The Estonians and Latvians living there had got on well together before independence. But the two states could not agree on how to deal with such a mixed area. They finally appealed to the new League of Nations to solve the dispute, and a delegation, led by a British general, had come to investigate. The upshot was predictable: the arbitrators simply drew a line dividing the town in two. The border fence now divided Estonian Valga from Latvian Valka. All Sirje had to do to meet her brother on foreign soil was to show her passport at the frontier gate and walk into Valka.

"When was this?"

"Sunday morning. I contacted him on Saturday morning, as soon as Sergeant Lauk had phoned me from

Viljandi to tell me about Father's death, and he came up the next morning to Valka to meet me."

"Does Vitus live in Riga now?"

"No, no, he's now with the Citizens' Theatre in Stockholm. But they're currently doing a short season in Latvia. I phoned his hotel to arrange to meet him."

"Describe your meeting with him. How did he seem?"

"He didn't confess to murder, if that's what you mean. And didn't fidget or keep glancing over his shoulder. At that time, of course, we weren't sure what had happened. Sergeant Lauk had been rather vague, only saying there were some puzzling circumstances. But I have to admit that neither of us were particularly affected by Father's death. It was more that a source of sad memories had gone. Neither of us had had anything to do with him. I'm afraid we talked more about how much money he might have left. That sounds rather mercenary, doesn't it? I also wanted to see more of Vitus. He'd not visited Estonia since he'd left. He was keen to come back for a visit, and also to settle the legal affairs, but wanted to wait until the dust had settled a little."

"Listen, Sirje, I need to talk with him. But I don't mind meeting him in Valka, or even in Riga, if he feels safer not being in Estonia. And there will be no underhand attempt to kidnap him, I can assure you. Could you contact him, and arrange something?"

She stared at the floor. "You haven't asked me for his present name," she murmured.

"I'd rather he told me himself."

"All right. I'll see what I can do. I'm guessing you'd want to meet him sooner rather than later. Where can I contact you? I don't want to call the police station. People say their calls there are recorded."

"I'm staying for the next few nights at the Elk Tavern in Viljandi. You could get me there. Or leave a message with Dr Kirss. I'm sure he's trustworthy. But don't think I'll keep this secret from my colleagues. It's part of our investigation. And I trust them too. However, it will stay within our team, I can assure you of that."

Her "Okay" was barely audible.

"Just one other question, Sirje. Did your father ever talk about his experiences during the War?"

"Not since I left to go to the Nursing School. Before that, while I was still at home, hardly at all, and Vitus and I were just not interested. I did hear him boasting to visitors of how many mortar shells they'd moved in one week, and stuff like that."

"Nothing about the first part of 1919, after he joined the Estonian Army but before he was moved to the Supplies Division. For a few months he was involved in actual combat."

"I didn't know that."

"Or a place called Hapsaküla?"

"Hapsaküla. Now that does bring back a memory. When I was about sixteen, I once heard him talking to Raud Kirik, that servant of his. They were having a heated discussion in his study. At one point I heard Kirik say to him, 'We still remember Hapsaküla, General. It'll never go away.' At that point, unfortunately, I leant my ear a bit closer to the keyhole and the door swung open. I pretended there was someone at the door. After that, whenever he and Kirik were in the study, the door was locked. Why is that important? Did something happen there?"

"We're not sure yet; it may not be relevant at all. However I think I'd better be going now. My driver

Lembit will be itching to get on the road. We need to get over to Viljandi, and the snow is making the roads very difficult. It's now quarter to four, and it'll soon be dark."

"You're welcome to stay the night here if you can't get through."

"Thank you, Sirje, I'll remember that."

32

Hallmets sat in the front of the car with Lembit, so they could talk as they travelled. The light was already fading as they drove through Valga. For a while the road out of the town ran alongside the high, steel-mesh fence marking the frontier with Latvia.

"Well," Hallmets asked, "Did you pick up anything useful, Lembit?"

"One or two things, boss. I had a nice chat with Ana, the maid. She reckons they're spending more than they have. Everything's got to be the best. You wouldn't believe what they paid for that monstrosity of a dog. I'd have had a look at the car, but he's taken it to work. Ana reckons it's posher than this one. German, she thinks."

"What about their movements in the last few days?"

"Ana says they went to the theatre on the evening of the 28th. Then they were at some reception to do with the theatre. They got back home about one in the morning, and she reckons both of them were fairly well-oiled. If that's the case, I don't see them driving through the night to top the old boy, then coming back again in the snow. Plus Ana would certainly have noticed. She says they went straight to bed, and nothing wakened her during the night. The house is not so big that she wouldn't have noticed."

"And no-one else was staying with them that night?"

"I reckon Ana would have said so if there was."

"Anything else?"

"Ana says that on Saturday morning *Proua* Kangamees got a phone call from the police telling her about the general's death. It fair put her into a worry, and she locked herself in her husband's study to make a phone call. The next morning she went out without telling Ana where she was going. That was very unusual, especially on a Sunday, when they usually slept in. Ana says she seemed quite excited when she went out. And when *Proua* Kangamees got back, she'd obviously got something on her mind. She even forgot to tell Ana to walk the dog, and it did a pee on the living-room carpet. Poor old Ana had to clear that up, of course, and take the dog out. Then, this morning, she locked herself in the study again to phone. Ana tried to listen at the door, but couldn't hear very much. But she reckons the way she was talking, the tone and so forth, whoever it was, she knew them pretty well. Ana wonders if there's another man on the scene. Mind you, boss, housemaids do tend to have over-active imaginations."

By now it was getting dark. They were heading westwards along the Pärnu road, and the going was not too bad; it looked like a snow-plough had been out earlier that day. The worst section of the journey would be when they reached the turn-off north to Viljandi.

Their worst fears were confirmed when they reached the junction at Karksi, 60 kilometres from Valga. A handwritten sign on a wooden board stated that the road was closed at Sultsi, twenty kilometres up. That meant another 50 kilometres to the junction where the main road from Pärnu branched off to Viljandi. From here it would be another fifty to Viljandi. In the darkness their speed was reduced further.

"Will the battery last?" asked Hallmets. "If it runs down the headlights'll go out."

"Don't worry, boss, this is a Swedish car, they're

designed to cope with this sort of weather. But we better not use the heater unless we have to. If it starts snowing and we need the wipers on too, that's when it might get sticky."

They finally reached the junction, without encountering any other traffic. Lembit turned tentatively into the dark mouth of the road. "Looks like this one's been ploughed too," he said, after a few minutes, "Let's hope for the best."

And things were satisfactory for the next 25 kilometres. Then the snow started, swirling around the car, then throwing itself at the windscreen, then spiralling away again before returning to batter one side or other of the vehicle. They were now crawling along, both of them peering into the faint beam cast by the headlights, which seemed to be absorbed by the pillars of moving snow that drifted from one side of the road to the other.

Near Pinska, only three kilometres from Viljandi, their luck ran out. Coming around a corner, Lembit slithered the car to a halt. Ahead of them a lorry lay on its side against the right-hand verge, its cargo of empty milk churns filling the rest of the carriageway.

Lembit got out to have a look, then returned to report. "Sorry, boss, we can't get past. The driver's not there, that means he's walked on in the hope of getting someone with a tractor in Pinska to get him upright and give him a tow. They'll have to collect the churns, too, or one of them could cause a nasty accident. I reckon our best bet is to leave the car here and walk into Viljandi. We should be able to do it in about an hour."

Lembit produced a thick sheepskin coat, with fur hat and gloves to match, and a pair of thick felt boots from the storage space at the back of the car. "I've got more of these in the back, that I keep for emergencies. Do you need anything, boss?"

Hallmets himself had a good quality woollen overcoat over his suit, plus a cashmere scarf Kirsti had bought him as a birthday present, a fur hat and fur-lined leather gloves. "A pair of boots would be good. These brogues are very comfortable, but not designed for snow."

Lembit went back to the rear again, and soon came back with another pair of felt boots. "Here we are, boss, these should do the job."

Thus suitably attired, they set off, working their way in the still swirling snow between the scattered churns, some of which, driven by the wind, were still rolling about.

In fifteen minutes they had groped their way to the first houses of Pinska, close enough to Viljandi to be considered a suburb. The newly installed street lighting lifted their spirits, and gave them an incentive to keep going, and soon they arrived at a pavement which had earlier that day been swept clear, and on which the snow was not too thick. Their pace increased, and more powerful street-lights signalled the main streets of the town. Now they were striding out in the anticipation of arrival at the hotel.

And they reached it at quarter past ten. The door was already locked and bolted, but Lembit by a few strong raps on the iron knocker soon roused the landlord, who, once he'd recognised that these two exhausted and snow-covered figures were actually guests at his hotel, welcomed them into the warm interior, slamming the heavy door on the winter outside. Fires were lit in their bedrooms, and mine host's wife repaired to the kitchen to make something hot.

Relieved of their coats and boots, they came to the

lounge, where Ilmar Hekk was still sitting in front of the fire enjoying a warming brandy before going to bed. Two more armchairs were pulled up, and more brandies ordered, to aid the recovery from their ordeal.

"Good to see you, chief," said Hekk, "Eva's already gone to bed. We thought you might have decided to spend the night in Valga."

"It's thanks to Lembit that we made it here," answered Hallmets, "Without his spare boots I'd have frostbite by now. It's good to see some friendly faces, and a warm room." He raised his glass. "*Terviseks!*" They raised their glasses.

He excused himself and went to the telephone booth by the reception desk to call home and let Kirsti know he was safe and sound. "Thank Goodness," she said, "I was beginning to wonder where you were. Especially in this weather. It's snowing up here too." Hallmets gave her a brief account of his day, and asked how things were at home.

"We're okay. The snow didn't start till Juhan and I were both home, and Juhan brought in some more wood to make sure we had a good fire going. There was a concert on the wireless too, the National Orchestra playing Haydn and Mozart. Juhan got on with some homework and I tried to do a bit of writing."

"More luck with the baron?"

"Yes. I think I've worked out his secret now. Twenty-five years previously he had himself hidden a fugitive in the house, in this case a young Estonian woman fleeing from the church authorities who accused her of witchcraft. In fact she was a midwife who also practised many of the old folk remedies. That led me into a whole back story about how the young man – he hasn't become the baron yet – falls in love with her, and invents for her a new identity as a distant cousin from Germany. In the end he marries her. So, at the end of the main plot, his daughter discovers not only that her father made the same sort of decisions that she did, and also that she herself is half-Estonian. How does that sound?"

"I'd say that's perfect. Well done. I'm always impressed by your creativity."

"It's my Celtic heritage, I think. Well, you should get something to eat now, and get properly warmed up. Let me know when you're coming back to Tallinn. See you soon, I hope. Love you."

"Love you too, Kirsti. I'll be in touch."

When he got back to the lounge Lembit was already tucking into a hot meat pie with fried cabbage and leek. His own plate waited on the table, with a metal lid on to keep it warm. A fresh glass of brandy awaited him too.

"Want a report on what's been happening here?" asked Hekk.

"No, thanks, Ilmar," replied Hallmets, "I'm too tired to take it in. We'll have a meeting first thing tomorrow at the police station, and we can share everything then."

Half an hour later he lay in bed, and began to think about the meeting next morning. But he'd only got to item 1 when he fell asleep.

33

Thursday 5th December

He awoke from a deep sleep and drowsily stared at the alarm clock. Ten past eight! He should have been up at seven, but had forgotten to set the alarm last night. A cold wash helped to wake him up, and he was downstairs by quarter to nine. Here he found Hekk and Larsson waiting in the lounge. They'd had breakfast, and were ready to go to the police station.

"Morning, chief," said Larsson, "I was glad to hear you made it last night. We decided not to wake you up, let you get a good sleep. I took the liberty of telling Henno you'd set the meeting time for ten. I hope that was OK."

"That's fine. Thanks, Eva. Why don't you two get over to the police station. I'll come on as soon as I've had some breakfast. We can start the meeting as soon as I arrive. By the way, where's Lembit. Did he sleep in too?"

"'Fraid not, boss," said Hekk, "He's already gone off with a patrol car to see if he can get the Volvo back here."

The morning was dry and crisp and cold. The snow on the roads would frozen by now. But at least the cloud was thinner and not suggesting more snow. The walk along the icy pavement helped to wake him up and clear his mind.

Sergeant Lauk greeted Hallmets like a long-lost brother when he reached the police station at 9.25. "Good to see you, sir. We heard about your journey last night. Must have been awful. Mind you, I remember times during the War when we were snowed up for days in ruined hovels. But at least we were better off than the Reds. There's more than once we found a Red patrol lying in the snow, and all of them frozen to death for want of good coats and boots. And sense too."

After the distribution of hot coffee, the team meeting got under way. There was plenty to report. Hallmets brought them up to date with his activities in Tallinn, Tartu and Valga. Then he asked Lesser to report on progress in Viljandi.

"It's been more plodding here, but I think we're a little further on. First, it does look as if Kirik's done a bunk. We've been to the bus and train stations again with his description, and tried the hotels and boarding houses, in case he came into town, but no positive identifications. I'm guessing that a car fetched him off"

"Do we have a photo of him?"

"Ilmar and I searched his quarters," said Larsson, "And the general's study, but no sign of anything. The only photos Kirik had were the ones in his albums. However, the local newspaper have pictures of public events at which the general spoke. I went over and had a look. There are some with Kirik standing in the background, and Toomas, the paper's photographer, copied the bit with him in it and blew it up. We've a couple of upper body and head shots, but they're not that clear."

"If only he had a couple of duelling scars, or a broken nose," observed Hekk.

"Anna, the maid, helped us in the end," continued Larsson, "She offered to sketch him from memory. Painting's her hobby. She's got some real artistic talent there, and she's very observant too. She produced a very good likeness of him in ink. Toomas photographed it, and we've now got copies that can be circulated more widely."

"I sent a request to the Border Police," added Lesser, "To alert the ports, the airport, and all the border crossings, and hold him if he tries to leave the country. Trouble is, he may already be gone."

"Could he be involved in this possible plot that Colonel Reinart is worried about?" suggested Hekk, "It sounds as if Madrus wasn't seriously considered for the figurehead. But what if he'd got very bitter about that and threatened to turn them all in? Then Kirik, who was still loyal to the plotters, was ordered to kill him."

"I don't see him doing that," said Larsson. "The impression I got was that he was really cut up when the general died. He may be a good actor, but I felt he was genuinely shocked. And even fearful. As if they would come after him next. Maybe that's why he fled, because he thinks they're after him too."

"Okay. Maybe he knows about the plot too," added Hekk, "He's not going to give it away, but *they* don't know that. They fear that in revenge for the general, he might give them away. So better to be on the safe side and get rid of him too. So he goes into hiding."

"But if Madrus was killed because they feared he'd give it away, and it wasn't Kirik, then who was it?" asked Lesser.

"What about this mysterious *Härra* Sepp?" suggested Larsson. "I also got Anna to draw a sketch of him. Two in fact, one of him sitting in the chair, and the other just of his face. None of the local officers recognised him. Sergeant Lauk got a couple of them to go through the files here, but they didn't turn anyone up."

"An emissary from the plotters in Tallinn?" put in Hekk, "Sent to get a sense of the general's loyalty, maybe even offer him a minor role in the new regime. But the general turns him down, so a couple of days later Sepp comes back and finishes him off."

"That's possible," said Hallmets. "Our problem is that we've now got four missing people: Kirik, Jonsson, Sepp and Vitus Madrus. We need to start finding them if we're to get this investigation moving again. Henno, what else have you got?"

"Regarding Jonsson," Lesser continued his report, "or whatever his real name is. I talked to the other lodgers at *Proua* Mölder's place, to see what else they could tell us. That was quite useful. They said they often chatted in the lounge in the evenings, and that included Jonsson. He told them he'd been at Tartu Uni, and finished four years ago. He said he'd studied History and Literature. Unfortunately we don't have a picture of him either, but Eva's going to get Anna to sketch him from memory today. It may be that Professor Strelkov could recognise him from the sketch. Or one of the other staff in either of those two subjects."

"Good idea," commented Hallmets, "If he stayed at the Uni for the full course, someone will have supervised his dissertation, and seen him quite often. The only problem might be if he was just making it up, and never went to the Uni at all. Did *Proua* Mölder ask him for any references?"

"Yes. She dug them out for us. One is on University notepaper from a Dr Naarits, in the Literature Department, and praises Villem Jonsson as a talented and diligent student. I phoned the Uni yesterday and talked with Dr Naarits. He keeps carbon copies of all the references he issues, and there is none for a Villem Jonsson. The reference must be forged."

"However," said Hallmets, "Dr Naarits may recognise

the sketch and give us a name. What about the other reference?"

"That was from a Dr Andreas Jonsson, a lawyer in Pärnu, on his office notepaper. This Dr Jonsson claimed to be Villem Jonsson's uncle, and said he'd worked in his office for three years after finishing at the university. I called Dr Jonsson yesterday. He has no nephew called Villem Jonsson, and does not think it a good idea to employ your own relatives. One of us will have to go over to Pärnu and see him, with Anna's sketch. It may be that Jonsson was in fact employed there, under a different name. That would give him the opportunity to purloin some of the firm's notepaper, and to copy the boss's signature."

"So Jonsson has some skills as a forger," said Hallmets, "It's certainly worth seeing Dr Jonsson. What about Dr Veinberg, the pastor? Why was he seeing the general?"

"He wasn't very helpful, I'm afraid. He was most apologetic, but explained that the reason for his visit to General Madrus and their conversation were confidential, and concerned a private spiritual matter. I asked if the general wanted to make a confession. Veinberg only smiled. He's one of the old school, and once he's given you his decision, that's it. No hints or clues. Sorry."

"A private spiritual matter," said Hallmets. "It does suggest some sort of personal crisis. There are things you see a lawyer for, and things you see a clergyman for."

"He might have been putting his house in order, as it were, in advance of dying," put in Larsson. "Could he have had a terminal illness?"

"There was no evidence of that from the post-mortem. Eva, can you get the sketch of Jonsson from Anna. I can ring Professor Strelkov, and see if he remembers Jonsson.

I'm hoping that Sirje Kangamees will get in touch this morning, and that Vitus is willing to meet me in Valka. We can try the university today, too. About Kirik, we have his military record; it shows he was born in a farm near Paide. I think it's worth someone going up there and tracking down the parents, or any other family. He may be hiding out there."

"Why don't I go?" suggested Lesser, "As an inspector, I'll be able to get more help from the local police."

"I know that area pretty well," added Hekk, "Maybe I should go too?"

"Good idea," said Hallmets, "Are the trains still running?"

Hekk nipped out of the room. They sipped their coffees, now lukewarm. He was back in a couple of minutes. "According to Sergeant Lauk, they were delayed yesterday, but are back on today."

"Right," said Hallmets, "Here's what we'll do. Henno and Ilmar, get yourselves to Paide today. Stay there tonight and call me sometime tomorrow. Eva and myself will stay here for the moment, though I feel the investigation is moving away from Viljandi, along with all the suspects."

34

The meeting ended at eleven. Lembit had by then returned with the car, and was checking it over for ill-effects of its overnight in the open. A message was also awaiting Hallmets from Sergeant Lauk, that Dr Kirss had phoned, and he should call him back, at his home, once his meeting was over.

He called the lawyer immediately.

"Thank you for calling, chief inspector. I asked the sergeant to leave a message as he said you were in a meeting, and I know how inconvenient it can be to be dragged out of things just at the wrong moment. I've been contacted by *Proua* Kangamees, who wants me to pass on this message to you. Here it is: 'Kafejnīca Latvija. Friday 11 am. Macbeth.' I assume it means something to you. Please do not explain it to me. Have a good day."

Hallmets guessed Sirje Kangamees would not need a response. He decided to take Larsson with him to the meeting with Vitus. He needed a witness to the conversation, and two heads would remember more of it than one. And a woman would be less of a threat than a male officer.

He asked Larsson to visit Anna as planned, and get the sketch of Jonsson, and she set off. There was no point in contacting the lawyer in Pärnu until she got back. They'd have to show him the fake reference and the sketch of Villem Jonsson. He might recognise the face or even the style of the signature. Hallmets would have to call on him in person; he might be the sort of lawyer who only talked to the man in charge.

Lesser and Hekk didn't need to leave yet, as their train

was at twelve. That would give Lesser time to phone the police in Paide and ask them to send a car to pick him and Hekk up at the station in Türi, the nearest stop on the railway, only eighteen kilometres from Paide.

On the table in front of him were the sketches of Kirik and Sepp, the originals and five photographs of each. He studied Kirik's face: thin, with hooded eyes, and a thin straight mouth, that together seemed to give out an aura of distance, or perhaps arrogance, looking past you to someone more important. Or fear, looking behind you to see who might be there, lurking in the background, waiting to strike.

He turned to Sepp. And noticed that the two pictures of the same man somehow showed two different men. He looked closely from one to the other and back, before the penny dropped. The sketch of Sepp sitting in the chair invited you to take in the whole man, especially how he sat and how he was dressed. And this suggested a middle-aged man, of a rather prim old-fashioned disposition: the upright position, hands on knees, the careful parting, neat moustache, furrowed brow, and thoughtful expression. And one with a fashion sense to match: the suit with a high winged collar and bow tie, the *pince nez*, the spats. But looking at the sketch of the face, he saw, as Anna had, another man, a younger man beneath the mask. The eyes bright, almost sparkling, despite the furrowed brows, skin smooth and fresh, lips slightly parted, as if holding back a tendency to smile. Anna truly was a talented artist.

He went to the reception desk and asked Sergeant Lauk if he could get a couple of men to take Sepp's picture to the railway and bus stations, taxi drivers and cafes in the town centre, and see if anyone recognised him.

"No problem, sir," said Lauk, "Juurup and Talvik are

available. I'll send them off right away."

"By the way," remarked Hallmets, "I haven't seen Inspector Einmann recently."

"No, sir. Curiously, the day after the general's post-mortem, he decided to take some leave owing to him. He won't be back until next week."

Hallmets went along the corridor to the telephone room. First he called Professor Strelkov. His wife answered the phone. She made it clear her husband was resting and could not answer the phone. Hallmets asked when he would be available. "Perhaps you could phone in a few days," she said, "He was really tired out yesterday. And says that it will take a while to find the information you wanted." Then she rang off. He asked the operator to connect the number again. This time the phone was not answered. He considered asking the Tartu police to send a car round to bring the professor into the police station to answer the phone. But it was too early to alienate him, and in fact the problem could well be his wife. Had the professor answered the phone, he might have been perfectly willing to talk.

Next he tried the university in Tartu. The switchboard put him through to the records office, and a woman answered. He explained who he was, and that he was trying to find a former student of the University named Villem Jonsson, who'd been there between 1927 and 1931 or thereabouts.

"I'm sorry," she replied, "We don't give out confidential information over the telephone. I'm sure you can understand why. Please put your request in writing, including why you seek the information requested, and it will be dealt with as soon as we have time. Thank you for your call." And the line was cut.

He pondered what to do about that. He could see the university's point of view; anyone could phone up and pretend to be an official. He thought of sending a telegram, but the same caveat would apply. A letter on official notepaper with a clear, and therefore checkable, identification of the sender, was what they needed. He was about to go up to Juta's office to dictate a letter, but stopped himself, and went back to the incident room. In his briefcase he always kept a folder containing some official notepaper from the Special Crimes Unit. That, he thought, might have more sway than a letter from Viljandi police station, and it also gave the correct return address.

Juta accepted the alien notepaper without demur and typed out the request on the spot. "*Härra* Jonsson is proving elusive," she commented, as Hallmets signed the letter, "I wonder what his real name is."

The letter would go to the post office with the other mail that afternoon, and, unless the trains were cancelled, would be delivered tomorrow. Whether his request would be dealt with then, or left until Monday, was anybody's guess. So he needed to try a few more shots.

He phoned the university again and asked to be put through to the History Department. He asked to speak to a member of the academic staff, and was told they were in a meeting, but should be finished by half past twelve, at which point, as was usual after a staff meeting, they all went out for lunch. He was advised to try his luck later that afternoon.

He was put back to the switchboard operator and for the Literature department. The secretary who answered asked what he wanted. He explained, and added that perhaps Dr. Naarits would be able to help. She thought about it for a few moments, then said, "Sorry, Dr. Naarits isn't in today.

In fact, he won't be back in till Monday. But I can put you through to Dr. Roosna instead." He thanked her and heard the phone ring again.

"Yes, what do you want?"

"My name is Hallmets. Chief Inspector Hallmets, from the Special Crimes Unit in Tallinn. Can I ask who I'm talking to?"

"This is Dr. Roosna, docent in German Literature. I'm very busy at the moment, so please tell me what you want, preferably in less than thirty words."

"I'm trying to find out if there was, between the years 1927 and 1931, or thereabouts, a student in the Literature Department named Villem Jonsson. He also studied History."

"Thank you. That was twenty-nine words. I'm impressed. You should be an academic."

"I was a teacher once, in a different world to this one."

"Ah. I can check the departmental log books for those years, but they're not in alphabetical order, so it'll take a few minutes while I run my finger through them. Can I call you back?"

Hallmets gave him the number for the outside line phone, and rang off. Then went back to the incident room. He wedged the doors open, so that he'd hear the phone ringing. Ten minutes later it rang.

"*Guten Tag, Herr Hallmets!*" said Dr Roosna breezily.

Hallmets thought he'd better answer in German. Academics could be eccentric. "*Ja, hier ist Hallmets. Guten tag Herr Doktor. Haben Sie etwas gefunden?*"

"*Ach, bitte*, please, Chief Inspector, forgive me, I'm so used to speaking in German with my students. But your German is good."

"I've been there a few times. It's a most interesting

country."

"Indeed. So sad what's happening there now. Burning books, banning authors. Great writers like Thomas Mann having to flee abroad. I dare not send my students there now, you know. I'm trying to get them placements in Switzerland, but the Swiss are so suspicious, though the universities do all they can to help. It's a sad world we live in. And a dangerous one."

"You're right, *Herr Doktor*. Tell me, did you find Villem Jonsson?"

"Maybe. Four Jonssons altogether in that period, but only one Villem. He was studying Literature, but his other subject was Economics. He was an older man too, forty-one when he started attending. Could he be the one you want?"

"No, I'm afraid not. The person we're looking for is the usual student age. But thanks for your help. We may come over next week and ask you to look at some pictures of a young man, to see if you recognise him as a former student. Thank you so much for your help."

"No problem. It gave me a break from my research. Good luck with your researches too."

Hallmets was not surprised at Dr Roosna's lack of success. He now suspected that 'Villem Jonsson' may have borrowed the name of his fellow student for later use.

He decided to bring up to date his outline report on the investigation. The disappearance of four individuals connected with the case didn't look good. But at least they were now getting sketches of three of them, and if all went to plan he would meet the fourth tomorrow.

Not long after twelve, Larsson came back with the

224

sketch of Villem Jonsson. He seemed an ordinary young man with no distinguishing features. Not the sort who would stand out in a crowd of students. Nevertheless, someone at the university might recognise him. One of the team was going to have to get over to Tartu. But that wasn't going to happen until next week.

He and Larsson bought hot pies and pastries from a local baker for lunch and ate in the incident room with coffee. Hallmets asked Larsson how she thought things were going.

"Getting these pictures has made a big difference," she said, "Now we can visualise the people involved, and these are the ones who matter, I think. One of these four – Kirik, Jonsson, Sepp and Vitus Madrus – holds the key to all this. If we can get these pictures widely disseminated, I think we'll home in on them."

"What if they've left the country?"

"I don't see Kirik or Jonsson leaving the country. Kirik has no roots anywhere else. Jonsson I don't think needs to. He can vanish easily inside Estonia. Vitus, well, he's not that far away. Sepp I haven't a clue about. He's the enigma. He could have entered the country, done the killing, left right away, and be anywhere in Europe by now. For all we know, he could be a professional assassin, or even an agent of a foreign power. And yet, the manner of the general's death doesn't suggest a professional hit. The business with the sabre is surely telling us something. So I'm inclined, on balance, to think Sepp is still around too."

"I hope you're right, Eva. But we have to careful with the pictures. We don't want to alert our suspects that we've got accurate images of them. Putting them in the papers might give us some genuine sightings, as well as ten times as many mistaken ones, but will also drive our quarry further into hiding. Tell you what, could you persuade the newspaper photographer to give us half a dozen of Villem Jonsson? We may have to go to a printer if we need lots. Or we could use that photostatic machine they've got at Pikk Street, although the copies it produces aren't always that sharp."

"I'll go there now. I'm sure Toomas will be happy to do it, provided he's not too busy."

"One other thing, Eva. I'd like you to come with me tomorrow to my meeting with Vitus in Valka. I need someone else there who'll be able to remember what's said."

"I'm up for that, chief. Sounds like a nice trip, if the weather's not too bad, that is."

With everyone out, he phoned Kirsti to say hello. Then got back to his report.

35

Jaan Kallas was fed up. He'd spent the morning chasing up a veteran of the 19th Regiment whom he found in another article he'd written in May 1919. He found the man in a musty-smelling room in a decrepit building near the harbour in Tallinn. The man welcomed him in, offered him vodka, and rambled on about his War memories. But when Kallas mentioned Hapsaküla, the man's memory suddenly failed him, and he took a long swig of vodka and said he'd run out of steam and could Kallas go now. He didn't want to talk about the War any more. And what about the twenty kroons Kallas had promised him for the interview. Kallas gave him ten and offered another twenty if the man would tell him what happened at Hapsaküla. "I don't want to talk about it. Now clear off," said the man. Kallas gave him another ten kroons and left. By the time he turned the corner of the street, Kallas reckoned the man was out of his door on the way to the booze shop.

Now he was ensconced in a bar near the harbour, wondering what to do next. Given it was lunch time, it wasn't a difficult decision. He went for blood sausage and turnip, and a dark beer alleged to have been invented by nuns.

He'd almost finished the food, and had just taken a long swig of his beer when someone came in. Kallas was in a dark corner – his favourite position in any eating or drinking establishment – so the newcomer didn't see him. A slim man with straw-coloured hair and a toothbrush moustache, rather poorly trimmed, wearing an overcoat that had seen better days. Kallas recognised a man down on his luck. But he also recognised the man himself. Artur

Simm, a former colleague of Kallas's who'd been involved in some very murky stuff a couple of years ago, and been sacked by the *Pealinna Uudised* as a result. He remembered the paper's editor Eirik Hunt saying to the assembled staff afterwards, "The point of reporters is to report the news, to question the news, to interpret the news, but not to *be* the news." He hadn't seen Simm since his departure. Until now.

He watched Simm buy a drink, scrabbling in the pockets of his coat for enough change, then looking round for an empty table. His eyes drifted round the room until they met Kallas's. Then he stopped, as if hypnotised.

Kallas signalled for Simm to come over. "Sit down Artur. Long time no see."

Simm sat down resignedly, put his glass of brandy on the table. "Hello, Jaan," he muttered, without enthusiasm. He drank half the contents of the glass.

"You look awful," said Kallas, "What's happened to you? And your finger?" He'd noticed that the fourth finger on Simm's left hand was missing. He knew it had been shattered by a thug back in 1933, but the last time he'd seen it, it was just under a bandage.

"It went septic. They thought gangrene might set in, so they cut it off. That was just the beginning. Everything went wrong after that. Marju threw me out. She said I was drinking too much, had no self-discipline. I couldn't get a job in Tallinn. Worked on a farm for a couple of months picking fruit. Drifted around. Got arrested for being a vagrant in Pärnu, spent a couple of weeks in jail. I guess that was the low point. Eventually I went to Finland, got a job for an organisation, writing press releases. That saved me. It doesn't pay a lot, but it's a job. I suppose you're just the same, writing for the paper."

"Yeah. Except that we can only write what the Propaganda Commission says is okay. Or just copy what they tell us to write. It's no fun."

They were both silent for a while, then Simm drained the rest of his brandy, and started to get up.

"Have another, on me," said Kallas.

Simm hesitated, then sat down again. Kallas signalled the barman for another brandy and a beer for himself. Simm accepted a meat pie, and then three more brandies. At last he began to relax, and talk about his new life in Helsinki. He had a room in a lodging house, and got enough money to make ends meet, and buy the occasional bottle of brandy, at the inflated Finnish prices.

"Well," said Kallas, "At least you can buy a few bottles here to take back."

"I wish," said Simm, "But things are going to get better soon. I might even come back to Estonia."

"That sounds positive. Are you getting another job?"

Simm touched the side of his nose. "Something really big's coming up. Everything will change. I might even get your job." He sniggered and emptied his glass, then put it down, but it missed the table, and smashed on the floor. The barman looked over sharply. His ears must be attuned to the sound of breaking glass, thought Kallas, as he signalled that he'd pay for the glass.

"I'm impressed," he said to Simm, "You must be in at the top then. But what do the Finns want over here?"

"Shnot the Finns," slurred Artur, "It'sh Vaps, but the Finns are helping. When Sirk's in charge here, I'll be in line for a good job. Maybe I'll be the Propar..., Propoggan ..., Poppa goblin Committee, eh?" He slid off his seat onto the floor.

The barman helped get Simm to the door and out into

the fresh air, and Kallas propped him up and managed to get him moving. He didn't want to be seen hanging around outside a pub with a drunk. He was able to get Simm walking after a fashion, and could hold him up – he noticed the other man was pitifully thin.

It took twenty minutes to get to Kreutzwald Street. It took some effort to get Simm up to the third floor and Kallas's door. Once inside, he deposited Simm on the sofa, where he promptly fell asleep.

He woke up two hours later, and Kallas encouraged him to have a shower. He looked more presentable after that, and thanked Kallas profusely for the food and drinks and hospitality. "I won't forget this, Jaan," he said, "I need to get off now, I'm late for a meeting. But when we're in charge I'll put in a word for you. Make sure they don't put you in jail. All the best."

"Sure thing, Artur. Come up any time."

Once Simm had gone, Kallas made himself some coffee, and pondered. It was clear something was planned by some ex-Vaps people and that the right wing in Finland were offering assistance. And Artur Sirk, the former Vaps leader, was involved. That explained why Lepp had been so angry when Kallas saw Sirk at the demonstration in Helsinki. It seemed he now had some very important information. But what to do with it?

He decided to call Hallmets and talk with him again. But when he phoned Pikk Street and spoke to Marta, she told him the chief inspector had been in Tartu the previous day and was now in Viljandi. He'd told her he'd probably be back in a couple of days. If Kallas phoned again, say tomorrow afternoon, she might know more. Or she could give him the number of the police station in Viljandi.

Kallas took the number, thanked her, and said he'd think

about it.

36

At half past two Larsson was back from the newspaper office with six copies of Anna's sketch of Villem Jonsson. Hallmets asked her to go to Jonsson's lodgings and check with *Proua* Mölder and the lodgers that it did look like him. "Let's be sure that the man who lived there and the man who did the secretarial work for General Madrus are definitely the same person."

At three fifteen Juurup and Talvik came to report. Hallmets recognised them from his first visit to Rauakivi Castle. They'd had no luck with the picture of Sepp. Hallmets thanked them, and was still staring at Sepp's image when Larsson returned at half past.

"Did the guys have any luck with Sepp?" she asked.

"Not a sausage!"

"It's very odd. Those clothes would have been distinctive."

"Perhaps they were supposed to be. I think *Härra* Sepp deliberately dressed like that for his meeting with the general because he knew he would be seen there by the general's servants. He may have passed through Viljandi wearing much more ordinary clothes, then changed into these rather old-fashioned ones when he arrived at the castle, perhaps by the wall round the courtyard, before going to knock on the door. He might have had a bag which he put his normal clothes in, which he left hidden, then collected on the way back."

"Or maybe he just wore a rather ordinary overcoat, and took it off when he arrived. No need to do any changing then."

"That makes even more sense, Eva. We'll try again,

using the face only. But not today. Anyway, how did you get on?"

Larsson confirmed that the part-time secretary and the lodger were the same person.

At five to four Lesser phoned from Paide. "*Tere*, Chief. We got here about two, and we're fixed up at an inn. The local cops identified Kirik's parents' farm, and drove us out to it. It's now run by Kirik's elder brother Kaarel Kirik. His father died six years ago, his mother is still alive and lives at the farm too. We spoke to the brother. A man of few words, typical suspicious farmer. Said he hadn't seen Raud since their father's funeral. He wouldn't let us talk to his mother, said she wasn't quite with it any more."

"Do you believe him?"

"I don't think so. He was too cagey, even for a farmer. I'm sure Kirik's there, or he was there. It's possible he only stayed at the farm a couple of nights, then moved on somewhere else. If that's the case, his brother could have driven him to Türi – he's got a van – and dropped him at the station. He could even have gone the other way, over to Tapa, to pick up the train from Tartu up to Tallinn or down to Tartu or Valga."

"Or he could still be hiding out at the farm."

"That's possible too. A search would cause a lot of disturbance, and I suspect Kirik would sneak away before we got near him. I didn't get the impression the brother liked Raud very much. But families are funny. They could hide him for months, even years. Or kick him out right away. Tomorrow we'll try the bus station and the taxis with his picture, then go over to Türi again and try at the railway station."

"Thanks, Henno. That's a good idea. Ask the local

police to keep a rather obvious eye on the farm. It might panic him if he's still there. Let me know how you get on."

Next Hallmets phoned Kadakas in Tallinn. He'd tried without success to find more out about Hapsaküla. He'd managed to find one of the general's former colleagues in the Supplies Division; however this man had not encountered Madrus before his move to Supplies, and said that Madrus never talked about his combat experience, only ever saying that it was useful for a supply officer to be aware of what it was like at the front.

"But," Kadakas concluded, "I did find something else, or rather, er, Katriin found it. Apparently, General Madrus has an apartment in Tallinn, not far from the Paks Margareeta Tower. It wasn't provided by the Army, so he must have bought it himself. But kept it very quiet. Katriin found it in the Army Personnel Lodgings Record. Officers have to log all the places they stay when on active service, and on three occasions Madrus gave the address of the flat. I checked it with the local authority and found he is registered as the owner. It may be worth searching the place; he may have kept his confidential stuff there."

"Good work, Ants. Or rather, thank Katriin for me. And you're right, the place needs to be searched. Can you discreetly check it out tomorrow. It's possible either Kirik or Jonsson could be there. Or even Sepp."

He went back to the workroom. Larsson was drinking coffee, Lembit was reading the newspaper. Hallmets passed on what Lesser and Kadakas had told him. "This flat owned by Madrus in Tallinn could be very important," he concluded, "I've asked Ants to keep an eye on it, but once we're done here we should get up to Tallinn, and have a good look at the place."

"So what's the plan for tomorrow, chief?" asked Larsson.

"The meeting with Vitus is at eleven, so I'd say we should get off by half past eight. Earlier if we can. We'll just have to hope it doesn't snow overnight."

The atmosphere at the hotel was rather subdued that evening. Hallmets, Larsson and Lembit were now the only guests, and the proprietor asked how long they'd be staying. Hallmets told him he'd let him know later that evening. Over dinner, he asked Lembit whether it was feasible to drive back up to Tallinn after the meeting with Vitus. He sensed that the general's flat was a crucial discovery, and the sooner they could get into it the better.

"Well, boss," replied the driver, "It all depends. If the snow keeps off and the roads aren't too icy, it would be doable. I'd suggest going back from Valga via Pärnu rather than via Tartu. The distance is about the same, but the Pärnu road's a good one, and being further west and nearer the sea, it's less likely to get blocked by snow. It would certainly be better if we had our bags with us, rather than having to come back here on the way."

"We'll check out in the morning then."

"And, of course," added Lembit, "It also depends on how long you want to spend in Valka."

"That I can't predict. But if we're meeting Vitus at eleven, we should hopefully be away by one. That would get us most of the way while it's still light."

"What about the lawyer in Pärnu, chief?" asked Larsson, "We were going to run Jonsson's picture past him."

"Good point. I'll have to give him a ring, see if there's

any chance we can drop in tomorrow afternoon."

After dinner Hallmets called the police station, and the ever-obliging Sergeant Lauk found Dr Andreas Jonsson's home phone number. Then he called Dr Jonsson. The lawyer was very irritated to have to be interrupted in the middle of a game of bridge. But he was even more irritated to learn the cause of his interruption.

"Yes, yes, I'm aware of this fake reference. Another policeman alerted me to it the other day. Have you arrested the man yet? Forgery is a criminal offence."

"We haven't yet tracked this individual down, sir. However we now have an artist's drawing of him, and we'd like to run that past you. It would seem a reasonable conjecture that the man may have worked in your office at one time. That would have given him the opportunity to purloin some of your notepaper and also to become familiar with your signature."

"Yes, I see what you mean, chief inspector. Yes, that's even worse. The blackguard accepts your wages, then betrays the trust you've put in him. Well, of course, I'd very much like to look at the picture. And if I recognise him, there'll be hell to pay, I can assure you."

"I have a meeting in Valga tomorrow morning. But if you're available mid-afternoon, I could drop by on my way back to Tallinn and show you the pictures. But don't worry if that's not possible. In that case I would leave the picture with the Pärnu police, and someone would come to see you at your office or your home whenever it would be convenient."

"No, no. Tomorrow afternoon will be fine. The sooner the better, eh? I'm usually at home on a Friday afternoon anyway."

Next Hallmets phoned Kirsti, and told her he'd back the following evening. She was pleased to hear it. Then he told the proprietor they'd be checking out the following morning. The man was relieved; tomorrow he'd be able to close the hotel for the rest of December, and relax.

After that he went for a walk round the town. He needed to unwind. The night was clear and cold, and a full moon cast its unworldly light on the buildings. He had to be careful, as the streets were icy, but thankfully the pavements had been salted that afternoon. When he came to the square with the old water tower in one corner, and the white walls of the town hall gleaming in the moonlight, he saw the Christmas Tree in front of it, festooned with tiny glowing lanterns. He guessed it had been erected that day, rather early for the festive season.

Then, as if they'd been waiting for him to arrive, the singing began. A choir had arranged themselves on the town hall steps, presumably to celebrate the arrival of the tree, and familiar Christmas hymns resounded round the square. Other people, individuals like himself, couples and whole families drifted over to watch and listen. It took him back to his own childhood, the voices drawing back the curtain of the years, to another town square thirty-one years ago, at the end of 1904. He remembered holding his youngest sister's hand, and closing his eyes to let the words of the songs fill his whole being.

That had been a good year. He was doing well at the local school, and his teacher had told his parents he would benefit from a full secondary education. They should think about sending him to the gymnasium in Tartu. That would be a fateful decision, for it meant he'd have to lodge during the week in the city. The pastor had agreed with the teacher. He had been teaching Jüri Latin that year, and some knowledge of the language would be very helpful to his application to the gymnasium. The harvest had been good, and the outlook for the farm was positive. Jüri knew his father would have preferred him to stay at home, and help with the never-ending tasks that a farm presented. But he also knew his father wanted what was best for Jüri, not himself. Besides, his younger brother Siim would still be there, and he was more of a farmer's son than Jüri, more at home in the field than the classroom. And his two sisters would be there too, they could already milk the cows, and look after the chickens.

No-one realised that the year after that would be a bad one. Comprehensive defeat of the Russian Imperial forces by the Japanese army in the Far East laid bare the dysfunctional organisation of the Empire, and sparked revolt in both the cities and the countryside. Even in Estonia, the wealthiest and most westernised of the Empire's provinces, the arthritic shudders of the ageing Empire's disintegration were felt. In the countryside the tension was palpable. Hallmets remembered his father reading to the whole family the newspaper account of the events of 16th October, when Russian soldiers were ordered to shoot at a crowd of peaceful demonstrators in Tallinn, killing 94 people.

Now that time was a world away. But the Christmas songs were the same. Hallmets wondered what the next years would bring. He did not see the peace and happiness celebrated in the songs. Hitler's Germany and Stalin's Russia would see to that. But the singing encouraged him. No matter the regime, the Estonian people had continued to sing their own songs in their own language. That reminded them who they were, and they would not forget.

37

Friday 6th December

It was quarter past eight when the car set off, with Hallmets and Larsson well wrapped up in blankets behind Lembit. The sun had come out, but it was freezing cold, and the roads were still treacherous. Lembit had to drive with extreme care. He told Hallmets that the snow ploughs had been out the previous day, and they should be able to negotiate the shorter route from Viljandi to Valga, via Karksi. That should give them, as long as there were no blockages, a good chance of reaching Valga in time for the meeting with Vitus. The weather forecast suggested it would be sunny but cold all day, and that was encouraging too.

The journey ran as planned, through a glistening landscape of frozen snow, from which trees and buildings tentatively peeped out, as if wondering when the day was going to warm up.

They arrived in Valga at half past ten. The meeting was not until eleven, but nevertheless there was no time to waste; they still had to get into another country. Lembit, who seemed to be familiar with every town in Estonia – perhaps even the villages too – dropped Hallmets and Larsson on Sepa Street, at the corner of the road which led perhaps forty metres to the frontier. He explained that he would park the car at the main police station on Vabaduse Street, less than a hundred metres away in the town centre. He himself would wait at the Balti Kohvik, a café on Uus Street, just round the corner from where he was leaving them.

Hallmets had already decided that he and Larsson would cross the border as private citizens, not as police personnel. If they went officially, they should have given notice both to the Estonian Border Police, who manned the frontier post on the Valga side, and to the Latvian Interior Ministry in Riga, who would liaise with the Latvian Police and Border Control Agency. This process would take several days, and once they entered Latvia, they would first have to explain exactly what they were doing to a CID officer, who would then accompany them to the meeting. Vitus had agreed to meet one man; a woman accompanying the man might just be acceptable, but two men and a woman, that started to look like a posse. And Vitus would vanish.

For private citizens, provided their papers were in order, things were more relaxed. Plenty of people in both Valga and Valka had relatives on the other side. Arriving at the Estonian frontier post, they showed their passports, which gave no indication of their occupation. Asked why they were going to Latvia, Hallmets decided to stay as near the truth as possible. They were going to meet up with an old friend who was an actor with the Stockholm Citizens Theatre. As the group were in Riga only until the weekend, their friend had arranged to meet up with them today in Valka for a catch-up chat and lunch together.

"What is your actor friend's name?" asked the border guard.

"Björn Smærgaard," answered Larsson, with a smile. "He's very well-known. I think he's been in films too. You must have heard of him."

The official shook his head and waved them on towards the open gateway a few metres further down the road.

"Who's Björn Smærgaard?" asked Hallmets quietly, as

they walked on.

"You know I always do my homework, chief," said Larsson. "He's one of the actors at the Stockholm Citizens Theatre. I called them yesterday, and asked who their star actors were. But whether he's Vitus, I've no idea."

A few metres beyond the gate they reached the Latvian border post. The Latvian guards would only speak Latvian, however both Hallmets and Larsson had picked up enough through previous contacts with Latvians to be able to follow what they were saying.

"*Pases, lūdzu,*" said the guard.

They handed over their passports.

The man looked briefly at them. "How long are you staying in Latvia?"

"Only a couple of hours," answered Larsson, "We're meeting a friend in Valka for lunch."

The guard nodded, "Okay," and handed the passports back. He no doubt assumed his opposite number on the Estonian side had asked more questions and was satisfied. Why should he go to the trouble of asking them again?

Now they had ten minutes to reach the café. The road led slightly downhill from the frontier and over a bridge across a stream, and then into Valka. They could see no obvious centre of the town ahead of them, but after five minutes came to a row of shops on the right hand side, among which they spotted the Kafejnīca Latvija.

Hallmets led the way in. There were seven small tables in the room, five of them occupied. A buzz of conversation in both Latvian and Estonian filled the air. This was clearly a frequently used rendezvous for families and friends split by the frontier in 1920. Hallmets glanced around. Only one table had one occupant. It was by the window on the left side as Hallmets saw it, and slightly separated from the other tables to allow easy passage to the kitchen. Sitting at it was a man, reading a book, a cup of coffee on the table by him. The volume was Shakespeare's *Macbeth*. The man was about thirty, clean-shaven, with fair hair and glasses, and paid no attention to him. Yet Hallmets recognised him.

"Good day, *Härra* Sepp," he said.

Now the man did look up, his mouth open in surprise. He quickly collected himself, as a good actor does. "I'm afraid you must be mistaken. My name is not Sepp."

Hallmets held out his hand and smiled. "Of course. I'm Jüri Hallmets. I'm pleased to meet you, Vitus. Thank you for coming."

Vitus stood and shook Hallmets' hand. "My name is now Axel Hellerby. Please, sit down."

Hallmets sat down and motioned Larsson over. "This is my colleague, Eva Larsson. She is not here to kidnap you, only to listen to our conversation, and remember what was said."

Vitus looked, first suspiciously, them more appreciatively, at Larsson. "Maybe you *should* kidnap me," he said to her, "I'm sure you'd enjoy it. Do sit down. Can I offer you a coffee?"

A waitress had materialised by the table, and Vitus ordered two coffees. "Something to eat?" asked the waitress. "Not just yet," answered Hallmets.

While they waited for the coffee, no-one spoke. But Larsson took the drawings of Sepp from her bag and put them on the table. Vitus looked at them carefully.

The coffees arrived. Hallmets thanked Vitus. Then gestured at the pictures. "Of course, Vitus, we know your name is not Sepp. That was only a name you used when

242

you visited your father. On the afternoon of Wednesday 27th November. You were the last visitor he had before he died, did you know that?"

"It's a good likeness, isn't it. Even got my scar, too." He turned his left hand over to show them the thin white line running across it. "My father did that, you know. With a whip. When I was eleven." His glance strayed across the table to Hallmets' left hand. "But I shouldn't complain, should I? It's only a scratch compared to yours. In the War, I take it?"

"A Red sabre. I shouldn't complain either. I've still got the other three fingers. The drawings, by the way, are by Anna, the general's maid."

"She's got talent. And a nice bottom too. I'm sorry, *Proua* Larsson, I forgot myself. I do apologise."

"Accepted," smiled Larsson.

"To answer your earlier question," said Hallmets, "Yes, of course it makes you a suspect. But that doesn't mean we want to arrest you and pin the crime on you. Following a crime, the task for the police is to establish who all the suspects are. Then to eliminate them all. Except one. Your willingness to meet us today gives me hope that we will be able to cross you off our list at some point. There are still other names on it."

"Like that creep Kirik?"

Hallmets smiled. "No comment. So let's not beat about the bush. I suspect you had a story ready for us that didn't include *Härra* Sepp's visit to the general. Now you'll have to include it. But first, I'd like to go back a bit further. *Proua* Kangamees has given me a good idea of your history. Did you meet your father at all between the time you left home and a week ago Saturday?"

"No. That was the first time. I had no desire to meet

him. As a figure in my life, he faded away quite quickly, especially after I left Victor Yeltsky behind in '28. Those years on the liners, they were chaotic, fantastic and awful at the same time. Building a storehouse of experiences, and asking myself who the hell I was every day of it. And at the end I knew the answer, and it wasn't Victor Yeltsky. Axel Hellerby is the person I wanted to be, the person I have become. I'd be obliged if you'd call me that, by the way. I'm not Vitus Madrus any more."

"Thank you, *Härra* Hellerby. So what made you decide to visit your father?"

"As I guess you know, Sirje had helped me get away, and we remained in touch from then on. It was Sirje who persuaded me to see him. He'd had a couple of illnesses, and she reckoned another bout of something might take him off altogether. And that maybe there could be some sort of reconciliation before that happened. Not so that we could be one big happy family again, but so that we could draw a line under the anger and the pain, accept that we were now only acquaintances with some shared blood, and do what we could, as relatives, to support each other. Sirje also was conscious that there would be legal issues when our father died, and didn't want me to be left out. So I agreed for her to set up a meeting. That's what happened on the 27th."

"So what was the Sepp business all about? Why the disguise?"

"Sirje had talked in very general terms with Father about a possible meeting, and his response wasn't very encouraging. He wanted me to fall on my knees and beg forgiveness for all the trouble I'd caused him. I couldn't do that. But Sirje thought his anger was about a me that he'd made up in his head, and once we were face to face,

244

he would have to see me as I was, as Axel Hellerby, not Vitus Madrus. So she organised *Härra* Sepp's visit. He was supposed to be a film producer who wanted to use the castle as the location for a film about Mary Queen of Scots; and was going to offer lots of money for the privilege. Father bought into that right away and the meeting was set up. I dressed for the part from the theatre's costume store. I agree it was a bit over the top. I came up to Valka the previous day – the show didn't start till the Friday – and stayed overnight with Sirje and Urmas. Then I borrowed Urmas's car and drove up to Viljandi. I parked the car near the station and got a taxi to the castle. I wore an overcoat over my costume.

"Father was very pleased to meet '*Härra* Sepp' and welcomed me in. I waited until the maid – Anna you said her name was – had served the coffee before revealing who I really was. Of course, we'd overdone the build-up, and he was disappointed that I wasn't a rich film mogul. Just his only son! At least he didn't fly off the handle. I think his rage at me had died away without him realising it. There was no big hug and tears of thankfulness either. It was like meeting an old man who vaguely remembered you from a long time ago. So in the end we struggled for things to say. I think I did most of the talking, and he just nodded, as if it was all rather puzzling. I was waiting for him to say, 'And who are you again?' But he did know me, and in the end we were able to talk in a friendly manner, albeit about rather superficial things. No great soul-searching reconciliation like you get in novels, or plays. But I gave him my address, and when I rose to go he thanked me for coming, and said we should keep in touch. He even asked me what I wanted him to call me. I told him he could stick with Vitus, I don't think he'd have been able to call me anything else."

"Thank you, *Härra* Hellerby. That's cleared a few things up for us."

"You said I was the last person to see him alive? That would make me a strong suspect, wouldn't it?"

"Not necessarily. I said you were the last person to visit him before he died. In fact, his staff saw him alive and well after your visit. And he was not killed until sometime on the Thursday night, the 28th November. His body was found early on Friday morning by one of the staff. So you'll understand that I do have to ask you where you were on that Thursday night."

"Yes, of course. That's not a problem. We were rehearsing that evening; the dress rehearsal before we opened the next day. *Macbeth*, do you know it?"

"I've seen it a number of times. Both here and in Scotland." Vitus raised his eyebrows. "And may I ask what you did after that?"

"Er, I spent the night with another member of our group. I can give you her name if it's really necessary."

"I'm afraid it is. Because of your close relationship to the general, it's essential that we have clear testimony to support your account of your movements. Well, I think that's all we need to ask you, *Härra* Hellerby. May we pay for our coffees?"

"Of course not. You probably don't even have any Latvian money."

38

They crossed the border again at half past twelve, and found the Balti Kohvik in Valga without too much difficulty. Lembit was just having his lunch, so they joined him. By ten past one they were on the road again.

The sun had risen as high as it was going to get on a December day, but it had taken a little of the iciness off the road surface, and Lembit was able to make good progress.

"What did you think of Vitus?" Hallmets asked Larsson.

"Well, chief, I have to confess that he's rather attractive. And knows it. But I'm guessing that wasn't the angle you were looking for. I think he's on the level. The story had a ring of truth about it. We can corroborate it with Sirje and her husband. And with his theatrical associates. We could easily find out if he ducked out of rehearsals for a whole night, the day before the play opened. Why is everybody going to see *Macbeth* these days? They should go to see something more jolly; after all, it's nearly Christmas."

"Yes, I tend to agree. About Vitus's story: can you do the checking with *Proua* and *Härra* Kangamees. And the theatrical people. The fact you speak Swedish will help there."

"No problem, chief. I can get on to it tomorrow."

They reached the outskirts of Pärnu not long after three. To Hallmets, it was the sort of place he'd like to retire to, when that day finally came. The pace of life in the old resort town by the coast was slower than in the capital, and the cafés seemed to be places where you could linger over a coffee and a chat, instead of bolting down the coffee when it was still too hot and rushing off to the next meeting or crime scene.

Dr Jonsson lived in a modern villa on Aisa Street, a leafy avenue close to the town centre. The lawyer himself came to the door and took in at once the upmarket car and uniformed driver at the gate behind the two detectives. The 'Chief' of 'Chief Inspector' also had an impact; this wasn't just any old plain clothes cop, this was a top man, with a car and a driver and an attractive aide to prove it. Dr Jonsson welcomed Hallmets and Larsson in. "It's a bit too cold for your driver to sit in the car. He can come through to the kitchen and have a hot drink." He led them through the hallway and then left into his study, one wall lined with the usual leather-bound law books. In a corner three comfortable chairs were arranged round a coffee table; this was clearly a place he met his clients.

"Sometimes my clients prefer not to be seen coming to my office in town. There are lots of people just sitting around in cafés taking note of who goes past. Not out of nosiness, you understand, but for want of something better to do." Dr Jonsson was of average build and height, but his steely grey moustache and piercing gaze gave him an air of authority.

Hallmets tried to avoid wondering who these clients were, and focus on why they were here. But before he opened his mouth, a woman brought in coffee and pastries.

"It's good to see women in the police force," said *Proua* Jonsson, on being introduced to Larsson, "We need more women in all the professions. I hope you pull your weight, too. We're not just accessories for men."

"I think Sergeant Larsson used to work here in Pärnu," said her husband.

"Yes, that's right," Larsson confirmed. "A very nice place to work. Very different from Tallinn."

"I'll let you get on with it," said *Proua* Jonsson, "You won't want to delay too long if you've still to get to Tallinn this afternoon, while there's still a bit of daylight."

Once she'd left the room, Larsson took the picture of Villem Jonsson from her bag, and handed them to the lawyer. "Would you like to have a look at this sketch, *Härra Doktor.* It's an artist's impression of the person who forged the reference from you. The artist has seen this individual many times, so she is familiar with his appearance and his expressions."

Dr. Jonsson took the pictures and studied them. Then he went to the door and called his wife. "Inge! Come through and have a look at this."

Proua Jonsson was soon back, and took the sheet from her husband.

"Do you think it's him?" he asked her.

"Oh yes, no doubt about it. It's Oskar all right."

The lawyer gave the drawing back to Larsson. "Yes. It's a good sketch of him. I recognised him right away, but wanted Inge to see it, to corroborate the identification. His name is, well, at least it was when we knew him, Oskar Kitsnik. He worked in the office for three months, during the summer, four years ago. He had written to me, saying he was at the university in Tartu, he was hoping to enter the legal profession once he'd completed his studies, and he was looking to gain a flavour of the work in a legal office. He did not want to be paid, and would not mind doing menial tasks. He enclosed a letter from his tutor, a Dr. Naarits. Are you going to tell me that was forged?"

"Probably. This person, using a different name, forged another reference from Dr Naarits. Do you still have the letter?"

"Yes, I suppose so. It'll be in the filing cabinet at the office. Would you like me to send it to you?"

"That would be very helpful, thank you," said Larsson, "Could you tell us what sort of duties did Oskar have?"

"Oh, just very low-level stuff. Copying legal papers, making coffee, delivering documents to clients, that sort of thing. But it would certainly have been easy for him to snaffle a few sheets of our notepaper. And he'd see my signature often enough."

"What was your impression of him?"

"A very polite and well-presented young man. Actually, I thought he would make a good lawyer. He did whatever he was asked without demur, and did his best to do it well. He was always pleasant, and got on well with everyone in the office. I even invited him here for dinner a couple of times. Inge felt he might not be getting enough to eat."

"We formed a very positive impression of him," added his wife, shaking her head, "I suppose we're lucky he didn't forge any cheques."

"That would have been harder," said her husband, "The cheques are kept in the safe, and have to be signed by myself, and also by my chief clerk."

"Did he ask for a reference when he left?" asked Larsson.

"Yes, he did. I gave him a very positive one."

"So he'd have a good example of your signature, as well as your style, to copy," said his wife.

"It does look like that," said Larsson.

"So why didn't he use my reference?" asked Dr Jonsson, "After all, it was genuine."

Hallmets came in at this point. "This young man, whatever his name is, is a suspect in a murder case." The lawyer just stared, his wife gasped. Hallmets went on: "It now seems that he has used a number of names for different purposes. It may be that he did not want to use the name Kitsnik again. I doubt it was his real name. We will of course check the name Oskar Kitsnik with the university, but I suspect there will not be a student with that name. Or if there is, it will not be him. However, we have a good likeness of him here, and we're sure that, if he was a student at the university, we should be able to identify him. It would be harder for him to get into the university and get all the way through using a fake name. Though not totally impossible. And it's also even possible that he only worked in one of the university offices, and was not registered as a student. However, we will be able to find these things out. And eventually, we'll track him down."

"Please let me know when you do," said Dr Jonsson.

"One more thing," asked Larsson, "Did he ever say where his home was?"

"If I remember, he gave an address in Tartu which I assumed was his student lodgings. When he came over for an interview – I wouldn't have taken him solely on the basis of his letter – I naturally asked him that. He said his family lived in Tallinn, that his father was a senior clerk in the office of the Luther Furniture Factory."

Larsson took that down in her notebook. "That's very useful. We can check that. And what about his accent? Did he sound like he came from Tallinn?"

Proua Jonsson answered: "People from Tallinn sound like they come from anywhere, or even nowhere. But he didn't have an obvious northern accent, nor an obviously southern one either. I think he made an effort to speak without an accent. And he never used dialect words, always spoke official Estonian, if you see what I mean."

"And people did comment on how well-spoken he was," added her husband. "But why should someone with so many advantages want to be a criminal?"

"That's the question we have to answer," said Hallmets.

It was four o'clock by the time they got going, and getting dark. The sky was clear, and the cold bitter. Already a full moon was beginning to rise, and, as the day faded into darkness, it cast a gleam onto the road that enabled Lembit to see further ahead than he would with only the car's headlights to rely on.

The road turned inland again to run almost directly north to the capital. The traffic they had encountered in Pärnu soon died away, leaving the road virtually deserted. It was still necessary to be on the alert, as round the next bend they might meet a farm cart heading homeward, or the bus from Tallinn to Pärnu, or a solitary car heading south.

In the event there was a bus, just one, which they met thirty kilometres on their way. And no other traffic until, nearly two hours later, they reached the outskirts of Tallinn. Hallmets had Lembit drop him at his home in Nõmme, on the way into the city, and arranged to meet the team the following morning.

It was good to be with his family again. Liisa, their daughter, had come home from Tartu for the weekend, so all four of them were now at home. Over dinner, Hallmets asked Liisa if she'd encountered Professor Strelkov.

"We had a few lectures from him in the first year History course, on the Independence War. He seemed to know all about it. But he was over our heads some of the time, expecting us to know all sorts of background stuff and related events in the rest of Europe. He also had a tendency to quote German and Russian sources in the original, rather than translating them for us. I guess he's more used to his research students than us."

"What about Dr Naarits?"

"Oh, he's really nice. I did his Estonian Literature course last year. He really knows how to explain things at the right level, and didn't demand that we read every single Estonian book there ever was. Some of the books we had to read were even interesting. He started off with *Prince Gabriel and the Last Days of the Pirita Convent*, that was a real hoot. And some of Eduard Vilde's short stories were good. But this year he wants us to read *Truth and Justice* by A. H. Tammsaare, all five volumes. I know everyone says it's a great work, but it's at least thirty centimetres thick. I read Volume 1 last term, and I have to admit I wasn't gripped by it. Even Mum's book's better."

"Well," said Kirsti, "Rated higher than Tammsaare. That's the best compliment an author can have. Maybe I'll be nominated for the Nobel Prize next."

"They should make a film of your book, Mum," added Liisa, "Who would you want to play the minstrel. What about Clark Gable?"

39

Saturday 7th December

Hallmets reached police headquarters at ten past eight. He was surprised to find Kadakas already there.

"You haven't been here all night, Ants?" he asked.

"Oh no, sir, I just thought I'd get in early today in case there was a lot to do. I'm beginning to think we're closing in, I'm just not sure on whom."

"Well, the good news is that we've reduced the number of suspects to two. Vitus turned out to be *Härra* Sepp, and I'm reasonably sure he didn't do it. That just leaves Kirik and Jonsson. So you're right, we are closing in."

Larsson was in a few minutes later, so Hallmets called a meeting right away.

He first summarised the current position. Essentially they now had two suspects, Kirik and Jonsson. "We'll keep calling Jonsson that until we know his real name. Both he and Kirik are in hiding, but we don't know why. One of them is hiding from us, I'm pretty sure of that, but which one, we don't know yet. The other one could also be hiding from us, but for different reasons, or could even be hiding from the other one. Or they both be in it together, and both be hiding from us for the same reason, and even in the same place."

"Where do you think they are?" asked Larsson.

"My guess is that Kirik is at the family farm near Paide. We'll see what Henno and Ilmar have to tell us this afternoon."

"Could he have come into Tallinn, and be at the general's apartment?" asked Larsson, "We know he was close to the general, so he may well have known about it."

"That's also possible. Any sign of him there yesterday, Ants?"

"No. I wandered down there every half hour and hung around for a bit. But no sign of movement during the day, and no lights on after dark."

"That doesn't mean there's no-one there," said Hallmets, "Kirik would, I suspect, be very careful."

"Why don't we raid the place right away?" suggested Larsson.

"That's very tempting. I can't see any advantage in delaying, especially as we don't know whether Kirik is there or not. If not, and we wait to try and catch him there, we could be waiting a long time."

"What about Jonsson?" asked Larsson.

"We can't get any further on him till the university opens up again on Monday. And the furniture factory. So there's not a lot we can do about him today. I'm hoping Henno will phone before he and Ilmar set off from Paide. Then I can decide about raiding the flat. If we go with that, we'll do it this afternoon, once they're back. For the moment, Ants, can you keep a watch on the apartment. I'll send someone over to keep you up-to-date on what's happening."

Hallmets asked Larsson to contact the furniture factory, in case there was someone in who might know *Härra* Kitsnik.

At 8.50 Lesser phoned from the railway station at Türi. "Yesterday we checked out the bus station in Paide and the bus and train station here in Türi, but no luck. Kirik could well still be on the farm. But we'd need a big operation to raid the place. There are hidey-holes all over the farm buildings, and he could easily slip through our fingers."

Hallmets told Lesser about the general's apartment, and that he intended to raid it that afternoon. He asked Lesser when he and Hekk would be back.

"The local cops gave us a lift here, and the train goes at nine, so we should be back here by half past ten. We wouldn't want to miss out on the raid."

Not long after half past nine Larsson reported that she had managed to speak to a secretary at the furniture factory, who'd been there many years and knew all the office staff. She swore there'd never been a senior clerk, or even a junior clerk, called Kitsnik.

Hallmets dictated to Marta a letter to the Legal Office of the Interior Ministry requesting a warrant to search the flat, and gave it to Larsson to deliver. It wouldn't take long to get there, but it all depended on whether the duty magistrate was willing to act on it. Some he knew simply agreed to everything, others could be very difficult. However Larsson could provide further details about the investigation if necessary.

He debated whether to inform Colonel Reinart, and in the end decided it was worth the risk. The risk being that the colonel would insist on his own people carrying out the raid, and would only tell Hallmets what he thought he should know. He phoned the colonel, on his secure line. First of all he updated him on the case so far, stressing that fact that they now had only two suspects. Finally he mentioned the apartment, and that he proposed to search it that afternoon.

There was silence at the other end of the line. "OK," said the colonel cautiously, "But I'd like a couple of my own men to go in with you, to identify and requisition any material that might fall within our sphere of competence.

I'm sure you realise that I could take over the search myself, and keep your people out. But I want to work *with* you. We're both on the same side here, even though we're pursuing different lines of inquiry. You want to understand the general's murder. I want to to see if he's connected to this plot that's currently being cooked up. Who knows, we might even be able to kill two birds with one stone. I'll nip downstairs and make sure there's no trouble with the warrant. What time were you thinking of?"

Reinart, like a good secret policeman, wanted to go in after dark. Hallmets felt that people creeping round the flat with torches in the middle of the night would arouse more suspicion in the neighbourhood than a discreetly managed raid in broad daylight. On top of which, people were likely to be out and about, so a few people wandering into an apartment block wouldn't arouse much suspicion. They agreed on 1 pm. Reinart's officers would come round to Police HQ at half past twelve so they could all go in together.

Hallmets had another thought. He didn't know whether Sirje Kangamees knew about the apartment. It seemed like the general had wanted to keep it very quiet. He also hadn't said anything to her yet about the meeting with Vitus. He guessed Vitus would already have reported the gist of the meeting to her, but it would be polite to keep her in the loop from his end. He phoned her up.

"*Proua* Kangamees, Chief Inspector Hallmets here. First, can I thank you for arranging the meeting with Vitus. He may well have already been in touch with you about it, but may I say it was very helpful to our investigation, and, once we get the corroboration Vitus has offered us for his movements, I think we'll be able to eliminate him from our investigation."

Sirje Kangamees confirmed that Vitus had phoned her late on Friday afternoon to give her an account of the meeting. She said he had seemed satisfied with the intentions of the two officers and was keen to co-operate with them to establish his innocence. She was grateful for the chief inspector's discretion, and would help in any way she could. As long as the truth, whatever it was, was kept under a bushel, and did not attract a scandal which would ruin the general's posthumous reputation.

Hallmets then got round to the apartment. "I don't know if you are aware of it, *Proua* Kangamees, but your father owned an apartment here in Tallinn, near the Paks Margareeta Tower."

"What? A flat in Tallinn. No, I certainly knew nothing about that. Did he keep a mistress there?"

"Not that we are aware of. But he did keep its existence very secret, and we want to know why. I therefore plan to search the place this afternoon."

"Oh. Do I have a say in this? I really would like to see it myself first."

"I'm very sorry, *Proua* Kangamees, but that just isn't possible. My team is investigating a very serious murder, and it is imperative that we see what's in there as soon as possible. Any visit by you before we go in could place you under suspicion. We will obviously have to search very carefully, in case there are documents hidden there, but I will make sure the apartment is restored fully to the state we found it."

"I see. Well, when can I see it then?"

"I'll let you when that's possible. However, I can give you the address now. It's worth letting Dr Kirss know, so that he can get on to the legal matters, and officially take ownership on behalf of the general's estate."

Lesser and Hekk arrived at ten to eleven, directly from the railway station. Five minutes later Larsson was back with the search warrant. Colonel Reinart's endorsement made it impossible for the magistrate to refuse it. Magistrates who had opposed the regime had been retired or moved to other posts, and those who remained knew that the political police were not to be disobeyed.

Now came that period of tense anticipation, when no-one could concentrate on anything because they were all focused on the flat. What revelations they might find there. Or plans for the coup attempt, as Colonel Reinart no doubt hoped. Perhaps even a gang of conspirators huddled round the dining-room table, trying to remember how to wire up the bomb correctly. Maybe a cache of letters and photographs which would reveal scandals involving members of the government, just the thing Jaan Kallas would have been interested in. Or, as Sirje Kangamees had supposed, a scantily-clad courtesan lounging on a lushly-draped bed, unaware of the general's demise. On the other hand, they had to remember that all they might find could be a mound of dirty dishes in the sink and a basket full of unwashed clothes. Imaginations could run riot as the tension grew.

Hallmets sent Hekk out to tell Kadakas what was happening. He was soon back to say Kadakas was waiting. Hekk had had a quiet word with the concierge and obtained his co-operation, and silence. There was no sign of Kirik.

At half past eleven Hallmets told them all to go and get an early lunch, and be back by twelve fifteen. He himself went down to the canteen and brought back an open sandwich of herring and boiled egg on dark rye bread. He needed to be near the phone in case anything happened in the minutes leading up to the raid.

The others were back by ten past twelve, and at quarter past Colonel Reinart arrived, accompanied by a younger man. The contrast between the two could not have been greater. As usual the colonel was in uniform, everything he wore looking as if it just been delivered from the laundry that morning. His riding boots had been polished to a high sheen, matching the gleam of the oil on his carefully groomed hair, and Clark Gable himself would have envied the colonel's moustache. The other man looked like someone the colonel had bumped into in the street on his way over, and brought along merely to contrast with himself. He wore baggy trousers and an old tweed jacket of a faded shade of brown, a grey shirt with a soft collar and no tie. And a flat cap of the sort workers in many countries wore.

"I thought I might come along myself," announced the colonel with a smile, "Just in case something interesting turns up. Oh, and this is Lieutenant Tamm, who's coming with us too."

The younger man nodded and gave a casual hint of a salute. "Good to meet you, chief inspector. I've heard a lot about you."

Read my file too, thought Hallmets, but "Pleased to meet you, lieutenant," was all he said, as they shook hands.

He introduced the two men to the rest of his team. Then another thought struck him, and he turned to the colonel. "Colonel, I'm shamed, as we all are, by your impeccable turnout. However, this is supposed to be an undercover operation, and your uniform could attract some attention. Perhaps you have an overcoat."

"Ah, yes, good point, Hallmets. Perhaps, lieutenant, you could nip back to my office and ask Roosa to give you my overcoat."

"If your overcoat is as smart as the rest of your dress," put in Hallmets, "It won't help. But there's no need for the lieutenant to go back. We keep some old clothes here for the very purpose of making us look ordinary. Ilmar, you're the master of merging with the crowd, do you think we've got something in the wardrobe that'll suit the colonel?"

Hekk looked the colonel up and down. "I'm sure I can find something, chief. Give me five minutes." He left the room.

"I'm sure Ilmar will find something suitable," said Hallmets. "By the way, lieutenant, I believe you saved my friend Jaan Kallas from a couple of thugs a few days ago. He's very grateful."

Tamm smiled. "Thank you. If I hadn't been tagging along, tailing those two, it could have got very nasty. You should tell him not to be too adventurous. We've got this in hand."

As Hallmets was wondering what to say next, the door opened, and Hekk came in, carrying an old and very scruffy overcoat, and battered felt hat. "I think this coat will do," he said, "But it needs a hat to go with it. Would you like to try them on, sir?"

The colonel looked at the coat in disgust. "I can smell it from here," he said, "Do you really expect me to wear that?"

"Only until we get into the apartment," said Hallmets, "Then you can give it back to us. It looks as if it'll fit, anyway. You don't need to put it on until we set off."

The colonel was clearly uncomfortable in the

workroom, amongst the other ranks, as it were, so Hallmets invited him into his office.

"Where are you with the coup, colonel?" he asked again.

"Between ourselves, we know pretty much who everyone is, and we've got them under surveillance. What we don't yet know is exactly what their plans are. And, especially, what the timescale is. The president will be at Kadriorg Palace as usual this weekend, but we've doubled his guard. And the army units just outside the city have been put on alert, just in case."

40

At 12.45 Colonel Reinart was persuaded to don the old coat and hat. The coat was a long one, so that his gleaming boots were mostly covered. "I'll certainly have to send my uniform to the laundry after wearing this over it," complained the colonel. "God knows what's crawling about in it." Hallmets asked Larsson to wait, in case they found something at the flat that required immediate action elsewhere. The he and the others set off. Hekk had an old rucksack slung over his shoulder.

Out of the building, they headed on down Pikk Street towards the Paks Margareeta Tower, which guarded one of the gateways though the old city wall. The street was narrow, and old buildings, opening directly onto it, were squeezed together on both sides. There were plenty of people about, and cars on the roadway, so they had to walk in single file along the narrow pavement. Before they reached the gateway, Hallmets signed for them to stop, and indicated a building on the left, a former merchant's house, five storeys tall, with its gable facing the street, and the pulley beam still projecting from the loft, where goods would be stored. The merchant himself, and his family, would have lived in the bottom two floors, with other goods, such as wine, in the basement.

Kadakas, who'd been leaning on the wall outside, straightened up. He turned to the closed wooden door to the building gave three knocks, and after a short pause, opened the door and went in to hold it open. He closed it once they'd all come in.

They were now in a hallway. At a desk on the right of the door sat the concierge, a thin man with a pock-marked face. Running his eyes along the group of strangers, the man suddenly perked up. "Inspector Lesser! Fancy seeing you here. And this time you ain't after me."

"Tannberg! Good to see you," said Lesser, shaking hands with the man. "Must be a while since you were inside."

"Five years since they let me out, sir. I was only in for four. Good behaviour, see. And I've been as good as gold since, you take my word for it. And being a former, er, unauthorised visitor to people's homes, I know how to keep this place safe, all right. Not a single burglary since I started here. Mind you, I think that's partly 'cause the word's got around that I work here, and nobody wants to cause trouble for me. Officer Hekk here tells me there's a top secret operation on. Well, don't you worry, inspector, Mum's the word. Old Tannberg knows how to keep his trap shut."

"Good," said Lesser. "It's the apartment owned by General Madrus that we want to look at."

"Oh yes, him what died just recent. Killed himself, that's what folks was saying. Mind you, the papers was very quiet about it. I'd bet there was a woman involved."

"Did he ever bring a woman here?" asked Lesser.

"Well, no. Mind you he weren't here that often. Hardly any visitors either. I don't reckon he were a very sociable type. Hardly ever said a word to me. Still, that meant he were satisfied with the service."

"When was he last here?"

"Hmm. Must have been quite a while ago, maybe three weeks. He were only here for a couple of days."

"Any visitors?"

"Only one, a young lad. Very well spoken. Educated. Told me he were the general's secretary. See, I make it my business to know who all the visitors are. That's how the folks who live here like it. They don't want people drifting in and out just whenever they feel like it. So any stranger who comes in doesn't get past me till I've asked them a few questions. If they're legit, I call up to the apartment, and they tell me whether to send them up or not. Otherwise I make sure they push off. Especially salesmen, but I can spot them as soon as they open the door."

Hallmets produced the sketch of Jonsson. "Was this the young man?"

Tannberg looked at the picture. "Aye, that were him. Has he been up to no good then, seeing as you've got his picture?"

"We're just keeping an eye open for him," said Lesser, "So if you do happen to see him in the next week or two, do give me a ring. I'll make it worth your while."

"Will do, sir. You can count on Old Tannberg. I'm guessing you're wanting a look around the general's apartment, then. So you'll be needing the key." He opened a small drawer on the right side of his desk, rummaged about, and pulled out a key. There was no tag on it.

"How do you know that's the right one?" asked Lesser.

"Well, sir, I used to be very familiar with keys, I can memorise the shape of the bit, that's the part at the end that turns to work the lock. Much more secure than if I labelled them all. I've also got a few keys in here that don't even belong to this building. Clever, eh? Anyway, this is the one you want. Flat 6, two floors up and on the right. There's no name on the door. I'll give you a ring on the phone if anyone arrives and wants to go there. Come to think of it, the general being dead – bless his soul – it would be suspicious if anyone was to come looking for him, wouldn't it? Well, have fun, gentlemen!" He placed the key on the desk, and Lesser picked it up, gave Tannberg a nod, and led the way up the stairs.

The block was well-looked after, and smelt vaguely of furniture polish. The stairs from the ground floor to the first were even carpeted. However, the stairs from the first floor up to the second were narrower, and Hallmets remembered that in the merchant's original house, these stairs would have led from the family living quarters up to the servants quarters and the storerooms. He guessed the flats from here on up would be less opulent than the ones on the ground and first floors. Still they would not be cheap to buy, especially as the block was very convenient both for the city centre and the harbour area, which was only a couple of minutes' walk from the gateway by the Paks Margareeta Tower.

There were only two doors on the landing. On the left, a brass plate on the solid wooden door read, 'Flat 5' and beneath that, 'J. Haussmann.' By contrast, the door on the right only had a brass number 6 fixed in the centre at eye height. Lesser turned the key in the lock, and opened the door.

It was clear even in the hallway that the flat was sparsely furnished. A single hook on the wall was available for hanging a coat. A small mat below it was for leaving shoes. On it still sat a pair of worn and muddy shoes. On the other wall a mirror at head height, with a brush and comb on a small shelf below it. The carpet was threadbare and the lampshade looked as if it had been there since the days of the Tsars. If the rest of the place was this bare, thought Hallmets, it wouldn't take long to search. Especially with six people. The cold from outside had seeped into the flat, too.

Despite the cold, Colonel Reinart immediately removed the coat and hat and hung them on the coat-hook. He peered in the mirror to check his hair, and reached for the brush, but immediately checked himself, left it where it was, and smoothed his hair with one hand.

Four doors led to other rooms. All were closed. Remembering their orientation vis-a-vis the street, Hallmets opened the first on the right, which he guessed would be the living-room.

He stopped in the doorway. The room was as minimally furnished as the hallway, with a single armchair under a standard lamp in front of the ceramic stove, and a low table beside it. At the other side of the room, near the window, stood a dining table with a single upright chair. The only other items of furniture were a low, grey metal two-drawer filing cabinet, set in the corner of the room, and some bookshelves against the wall next to it, above a shallow cupboard.

In the upright chair by the table sat Raud Kirik, dressed only in his underwear. Long combinations and a vest. His arms and legs were tied to the chair, and the handle of a knife protruded from his chest.

Hallmets stepped into the room, and let the others come in. He asked Hekk to check for signs of life.

Hekk checked the eyes, looked for pulse in the neck, and took out a mirror which he held in front of the nose and mouth. "Dead as a doornail, I'd say," he said, confirming officially what the others could already see, "Cause of death appears to be a dagger in the heart. Looks like a bayonet. No other obvious signs of violence."

"OK," said Hallmets, "Nobody touches the body. This is now a crime scene, so we need to be very careful what we do touch. There might be fingerprints. Ants, can you go down to the concierge and use his phone to call HQ and summon the duty doctor, and Einar Sepp and any other forensic people he can get hold of. Then get back there yourself and let Eva know what's happened."

"What's wrong with the phone up here?" asked the colonel, "It's rather more private."

"There may be prints on it. And we'll have to tell *Härra* Tannberg anyway. I'm sure he can be warned to keep quiet about it for the moment. At least till we've examined the place and got the body away." He nodded to Kadakas, who slipped out of the room, followed by Lesser.

"Who is he?" asked the colonel.

"Raud Kirik, the general's assistant, and former military colleague. We've been looking for him."

Lesser came back in. "No more corpses in the other rooms, chief."

"Can we get on with the search now?" asked Reinart irritably, glancing over at the filing cabinet.

"It's not so simple now," said Hallmets. "As I said, this is now a crime scene, so we must disturb as little as possible, in case traces of the perpetrator can be found. However, I understand your priorities, colonel. I think, under the circumstances, it should be all right to search the filing cabinet. I suggest Ilmar and Henno check out the other rooms for anything we might have to look more closely at. But before we do anything, let's remember that we respect the general's property and put things back where we found them. The general's family will be taking possession of the place once we give them the word, and I've assured them that we'll leave the place neat and tidy. And the less we touch the better, till the forensic people are done."

Lesser and Hekk went off to the other rooms, while Hallmets and Colonel Reinart remained in the living-room. Tamm made a beeline for the filing cabinet. "It's locked," he announced, as if surprised.

"Well, for heaven's sake, Tamm, get it open somehow," urged the colonel, "Didn't you bring a screwdriver?"

"I don't think we need to wreck it," said Hallmets, "I'm sure we can get it open for you." He called Hekk in from the kitchen, and indicated the cabinet.

"That won't give us much trouble," muttered Hekk, as he took a bunch of tools on a ring from his overcoat pocket. "It's just a standard filing cabinet. No special features." In less than a minute, they heard the lock click open. "Unless it's booby-trapped," said Hekk, as he pulled the bottom drawer out. Colonel Reinart and Tamm jumped back two metres, whilst Hallmets remained where he was, aware of Hekk's sense of humour. "There you go, gentlemen," said Hekk, pocketing the tools, and heading back towards the kitchen.

As Reinart and Tamm knelt down to go through the filing cabinet, Hallmets decided to have a look round the rest of the living-room. It didn't take long, and he soon found himself looking at the bookshelves. The general wasn't evidently a big reader. There were a couple of accounts of the Independence War, well-thumbed, and a history of Estonia, which looked unread. A copy of a Russian translation of *Macbeth*. Hallmets picked it off the shelf and flicked through it. A folded sheet of paper fell out and fluttered down to the floor. He bent down, picked it up, and opened it out. The message was typed in red, and was unsigned:

We know what you did.

We will come for you.
Blood for blood.

He took an envelope from his pocket and slipped the note into it. He would have to get it checked for fingerprints, but doubted that it would reveal anything. Most people who sent anonymous messages had the sense to avoid handling them. He checked the first pages of the book; there was no inscription or Ex Libris plate. How had the general come by it? Had the book, including its message, been given to him? Or had he received the message and hidden it in the first book that came to hand. He took the book as well; he'd have to go through it later to make sure there was nothing written on any of the pages.

There were also a few well-read thrillers. He noticed an Estonian translation of John Buchan's *The 39 Steps*. Hallmets remembered having seen the film starring Robert Donat at the cinema that autumn; he'd taken the whole family and they all enjoyed it. It was a particular thrill for Kirsti, seeing something set in her native Scotland. She even recognised some of the places. He flicked all the books, but nothing else fell out.

The cupboard below was unlocked. On the top shelf were a bottle of ink, a fountain pen, and some paper and envelopes, as well as a stick of sealing wax. On the middle shelf lay an army-issue leather holster. He picked it up and extracted the revolver from it, opened it up and sniffed. It hadn't been used recently. He put it back, next to the box of cartridges. At the bottom of the cupboard lay a bundle of papers. Hallmets pulled them out. It was a typed copy of a book. The title on the first page:

Organising War and Peace: a Life in Military Supplies

WINTER BlOOD

by Arnold Madrus

He looked at the date printed below: 8 November 1935. So, this was a more up-to-date version than the one Rist the publisher had given him. Possibly the result of Jonsson's secretarial efforts. Was that why Jonsson had visited the general – to present him with the latest version of his memoir? Hallmets picked the bundle out; he'd have to go through that later.

He went over to the table. Reinart was sitting at it going through a pile of papers taken from a folder. Tamm was still lifting folders out of the filing cabinet and flicking through them. He had a notepad on the floor beside him, and was noting down the title and contents of each one. A pile of folders already beside him showed there was plenty there.

"Any luck?" asked Hallmets.

"Lots of documents about his army career," said Reinart. "Nothing that interests us yet. But of course, we'll have to take it all away and go through it page by page, just in case. It's awfully tedious. I'm glad it won't have to be me."

"Anything about the first half of 1919, when he was on active combat duty," Hallmets asked Tamm.

"Hang on, I'll check through my list." He ran his finger down the list on his notepad, and looked up again. "No, nothing so far. There's nothing before the middle of 1919."

"What about yourself?" asked Reinart, not looking up from the page he was reading.

"Just a threatening letter and a copy of his memoirs," answered Hallmets.

"A death threat?" asked Tamm, "Can I see it?"

Hallmets took the letter out of the envelope and, holding it in the top right corner, showed it to him. Tamm held out his hand to take it, but Hallmets pulled it away. "Sorry, please don't touch it. I'll need to get it checked for fingerprints." He showed it to the colonel too.

"'We know what you did,'" said Reinart, "That suggests some sort of revenge killing. That's a relief. I feared his death was going to be about politics. Did you say his memoirs too? Anything political in them?"

"I think I told you the version I'd got from Rist had a lot of political ranting in it, but nothing very specific, and no reference to any political activity of his own. This is a later version written up, I suspect, by Villem Jonsson. My guess is that the rants will have disappeared, but there still won't be any revelations about what he's up to now. Don't worry, colonel, if there are, I'll contact you right away."

Reinart was about to reply, when he was interrupted by a shout from Tamm. "Whoa! This looks interesting. It was right at the back. The file's called 'Vaps 1930-1934.' Do you want a look, colonel?"

"Yes, please, pass it over here. I've seen enough of this one." He thrust the papers he was looking at back into their folder, seized the one Tamm was passing him, and opened it to see what was inside. "Ah, this is more like it. Correspondence with Sirk and other folks in Vaps. 'Dear Artur ...' Now we're getting somewhere."

But now Lesser and Hekk were coming back in. Hallmets asked them what they'd found.

"The bedroom's as sparse as here," reported Lesser, "Just a bed, bedside table, wardrobe, dressing table and chair. Nothing hidden in or under the bed. Full dress uniform in the wardrobe, plus a pair of trousers and an overcoat, some underwear and shirts in the dressing table drawers. Nothing hidden in either. Nothing on the bedside table; one drawer, containing a pencil and a note pad. Nothing written on the pad – he must have taken the sheets away with him when he tore them off. Maybe reminders to do things. But I'm pretty sure the bed's been slept in recently."

"What about the bathroom?"

"Shaving gear, hair cream, Eau de Cologne, bottle of aspirin, and a bottle of sleeping pills. It just says 'Sleeping Pills. Take one as required.' on the label. Should we get them analysed?"

"Yes, that's probably worth doing, bring them along. Anything hidden anywhere?"

"No. I checked above the cistern, under the sink, and so on."

"OK. What about the kitchen?"

"I suspect the general ate out all the time he was here. There was tea and coffee, and several bottles of Scotch whisky, but that was it. Oh, and a tin of corned beef and a tin of biscuits. Some crockery and cutlery, two of each. Cupboards mostly empty, apart from a couple of brushes and a bottle of bleach. I guess he had someone come in at intervals and clean the place. No evidence that he did it himself."

Hallmets thanked them and showed them the anonymous note and the memoirs. He put the note back into its envelope and into his jacket pocket, and handed the memoirs to Hekk, who had produced from his rucksack a canvas bag with a fold over top with a padlock dangling from it. He put the memoirs into it and clicked the padlock shut.

"Should we look under the carpets?" asked Hekk.

"I suppose so," said Hallmets, "Though I can't imagine

General Madrus hiding anything there. It would be too obvious, if anyone else were looking."

As he expected, nothing was found under the carpets. Hallmets decided they'd done enough. If there was anything else, the forensic searchers might find it."

As if on cue, there was a rap at the door. Hekk went to answer it, and led a tall thin man with a drooping moustache into the room. Behind him, another figure lurked in the hallway.

"I believe you have a possible corpse," said the tall man.

"Ah, Dr. Klaas, do come in," said Hallmets, "He's over there. Einar, you're there too. Come on in." Einar Sepp, the forensics technician, slouched in, a small man in shabby clothing, in contrast to Dr Klaas. "Is there anyone to help you?"

"Sorry. Saturday's not a good day. But Ago should be here soon."

As Sepp began to look for likely sites of fingerprints, Dr Klaas had finished his examination. "No question about it. He's dead all right. Probably for a day, maybe even two, given the low temperature in here. Looks like a stabbing, but you'll have to wait for the PM to see if there's anything else." And he was off.

Not long afterwards Ago, the police photographer, arrived, and began the laborious process of recording the scene. Hallmets decided it was time his team left. He asked the colonel if he and Tamm wanted to stay on.

"No, no," said the colonel, "We can go through this stuff more comfortably back at the Ministry. Did you bring a bag, Tamm? There's lots of this material."

"Er, no, Sir. You didn't ask me to ..."

"Yes, all right," hissed the colonel, "Look, chief inspector, you don't happen to have any spare bags, do you?"

Hallmets signalled to Hekk, who produced two more of the canvas bags and handed them to Tamm. "Ilmar," he added, "Can you hang on here till the technicians have finished, then put a seal on the door. I'll leave you the key to lock up. Don't forget to bring that old hat and coat back too."

Ten minutes later Hallmets, Lesser, Reinart and Tamm left the flat. Down at the entrance, they found Tannberg drinking coffee. Hallmets waited until Reinart and Tamm left, then closed the outside door.

"You'll be aware, *Härra* Tannberg, that we found a dead body in the flat. I trust you will not mention this to anyone, until you see it reported in the newspapers."

"That'll be the day," laughed Tannberg, "But don't you worry, sir. I know how to keep my mouth shut."

"Thank you. But we do need to ask a few more questions. You see, both the dead man, and his killer, seem to have got into the apartment without you noticing. How do you think that happened?"

"Well, sir, I can't be at the door all day and night. See, if there's a job needs doing in one of the flats, I have to go and do it. Then there's nobody at the door, and I suppose anyone could creep up the stairs. Then I goes off duty at ten, until seven the next morning. The outside door's locked, of course, but anyone with a key could get in. Then there's my day off, that's Sunday, and ..."

"Not quite as secure as you made out earlier, then? Did anyone go up to the general's flat in the last few days?"

"No, no-one. Though, now you come to mention it, yesterday morning there was something odd. I got a phone call from some sort of agency in Tartu, said they were phoning on behalf of Professor Linnamees, he's on the third floor, right above the general. But he's away at the moment, some sort of research trip. To Turkey, I think. An old temple. See, he's a big expert on these ..."

"Just tell us what happened," interrupted Lesser.

"No worries, chief. Well, they said the prof had been in touch to say he thought there was a funny smell in the toilet, and would I check it out, and get right back to them. Offered me twenty kroons to do it, said that was their normal rate. So I went up right away and checked. There was no odd smell at all, the prof must have imagined it. Or maybe he'd farted and not noticed it, then smelt it later. I dunno. Anyway, when I got back downstairs again, I could have sworn the front door had been open. It was colder, and there was a few leaves had blown in from the street. So I phoned the number they gave, and guess what, ..."

"It was a public phone box," said Lesser.

Tannberg's face dropped. "How did you know that, chief? And I never even got my twenty kroons. All that effort for nothing."

"What time was this?" asked Hallmets.

"Hmm. Quite early it was, about quarter past seven, I think."

"Before Ants had started observing the place," said Hallmets.

"A perfect way of getting you away from the door," Lesser said to Tannberg. "But that's very helpful. We may have to talk with you again. Meanwhile, if anyone asks about the general or his flat, call me immediately. Meanwhile, once our technicians have finished, the flat will be sealed. After that, no-one is to go there, until we remove the seal." He handed over a couple of sheets of paper. "This is a notification for you. Can you sign both sheets and give me one back. It just says you are aware the flat has been sealed and that no-one is to enter."

Tannberg glanced through the form, produced a pencil from his top drawer, and signed the two copies, then handed one back to Lesser. "Good to do business with you, *Härra* Lesser. And don't you worry, sir, anyone comes in here asking about Flat 6, I'll be in touch. It's nice to have some excitement now and then."

41

Jaan Kallas woke up. What the hell was that noise? Someone was banging on his door. He glanced at the clock. 2 pm. He must have dozed off. He got out of his armchair, and made for the front door. Though he had no intention of opening it just because someone was trying to bash it in.

"Stop that bloody racket right now," he shouted, "Who the hell are you and what do you want? If you're up to no good, I'll call the police right now!"

"It's me, Artur. Artur Simm. Please, Jaan, let me in."

Kallas did not fear Simm, so he drew back the three strong bolts on the door, opened it, and let the other man slip past him and into his living-room, where he slumped into the other armchair, panting heavily. Kallas rebolted the door, then came into the room.

"Thanks, Jaan. Just give me a moment," Simm gasped, "I think they're after me."

"You look like you need a drink, Artur. How about some snaps, and maybe a beer to wash it down? Then, once you've calmed down, you can tell me all about it."

Artur downed a double shot of the brandy in one go, then grabbed the beer and drank half of it. He shook his head, and seemed to calm down. "Thanks, Jaan, you're a real pal. I needed that."

"That's OK. You're lucky you caught me in. I have to go out soon to file my copy for tomorrow morning." He caught the signs of panic in Simm's eyes. "But don't worry, you can stay here if you want. As long as you like. But you really need to tell me what's going on. What are you afraid of? Who's after you?"

"They knew I talked with you. They must have seen me the other day. Now they think I've told you all about the coup."

"Relax, Artur, you didn't tell me anything about a coup."

"But they think I did. Lepp interrogated me."

Kallas couldn't stop himself. "Well, well. What's his role in all this?"

"Oh God. He's one of the leaders. He's going to run the secret police once we're in power."

"It doesn't sound as if you're part of 'we' any more, Artur. Have they thrown you out?"

"I don't know. Lepp was asking why I was talking to you, what I'd said. Trouble was, I couldn't remember what we talked about. Then he said you'd been following him, so I must have told you about him."

"I did follow him, but that was nothing to do with you. I just caught sight of him one day, near the Viru Gate and wondered what he was up to. His two Finnish thugs came after me, but luckily a guy who was passing by rescued me."

"He thinks I put you onto him. He also said you were spying on him in Helsinki. He says you'll be among the first to die when we're in power."

"I don't think you'll last that long, Artur, once he's in power. It sounds to me as if you need to be making yourself scarce right now. If he even suspects you've given the game away, your life's not worth a lot. His Finnish pals followed me onto the boat from Helsinki to Tallinn, and would have done for me if they could. I managed to put one over on them, but frankly, Artur, you wouldn't stand a chance. Don't you have any relatives who live in the middle of nowhere?"

"Not really. I never kept in touch with them. If I'd still been with Marju, her family are out in the country. But they never thought a great deal of me. Marju's father thought she was wasting herself on me. Maybe he was right."

"Stop feeling sorry for yourself, Artur, that won't get you anywhere. You need to take a good look at where you are now and identify a reasonable way forward. Things are never going to go back to what they were before, so you need to focus on the future. If you don't, you probably won't have one. Look at the positives. You're still a reasonably young man. You've got some skills. Maybe you need to start a new life somewhere else."

"But where?"

"Don't be pathetic, Artur, use your bloody brain. You're the only person who can get you out of the mess you're in. But you've got to face it like a grown-up. I'm happy to help you, but only if you can accept your responsibilities and make your own decisions. And base them on reality and not wishful thinking. Now, you can stay here for the next few days if you want to lie low. But if I think you're just wallowing in it and not working out what to do next, you're out. And that's a promise. Now, it's time we had some coffee. When was the last time you ate anything?"

After some coffee along with bread and cheese, and then a sweet pastry, Artur began to recover an appearance of normality. "Jaan," he said, "You're my only friend. I'm so grateful to you. I want to tell you what's going on, I need to share it with someone."

"Tell me whatever you want," said Kallas, "I'm listening. Sometimes it's better to get these things off your chest."

"Remember I told I'd got a job in Helsinki, writing press releases?"

"Yes."

"It was Lepp who offered me the job. He knew I'd been sacked by *Pealinna Uudised,* and even that Marju didn't want me any more. I was in a doss-house near the harbour, and one day I was just hanging around the harbour wondering what to do next, ..."

"Feeling sorry for yourself?"

"... when Lepp just appeared out of nowhere. 'You need a job,' he said, 'I've got one. Do you want it?' I just said yes. 'Right,' he said, 'Follow me.' and he marched me straight on to the Helsinki boat. He took me to a house there and allocated me a room. There was a comfortable bed, and regular meals. The job was simple; he wanted me to write press releases for this political organisation, ..."

"The Patriotic People's Movement?"

"Yes, that was it. But in fact it was Lepp who wrote the press releases. All I had to do was circulate them to the various newspapers and radio stations, and pretend that I'd written them. Once he had to be somewhere else, so I wrote the press release, and he was furious, told me my job wasn't to think, it was to obey. I was frightened. After that I just did whatever he told me. Any job was better than no job, Jaan."

"That isn't always the case, Artur. Anyway, go on."

"Eventually he told me there was something big planned, and I soon heard from others that ex-Vaps people were planning a coup here. Once it was launched, the Finns would come over in force and help. Lepp told me I would be the liaison with the press when it happened. He'd feed me the press releases to issue as the coup took place. 'Do this well,' he said, 'And you'll get a job with the Propaganda Commission, our Propaganda Commission, that is, and you'll be able to tell arseholes like Jaan Kallas what you think of them. Not that he'll be alive very long to hear you.'"

"So when's this coup supposed to happen?"

"I don't know. Quite soon, I think. No-one knows exactly when, apart from the Central Committee. Maybe they haven't even decided yet. They're having a meeting tomorrow, that's probably when they'll fix the date."

"Where do they meet?"

"I think they have each meeting at a different address. Just ordinary houses, I suppose. They don't want to attract attention. I'm not supposed to know, I'm not a member. But I did overhear someone mention Volta Street, that's next to the electrical goods factory."

"All right, Artur. I'm going out now, I need to do my copy for tomorrow. I'll be back about ten. Once I've gone, lock the door, that lock should keep most people out. But just to be on the safe side, bolt the door on the inside, all three bolts. And don't open up to anyone, no matter who they claim to be. I'll phone when I'm leaving the paper, and when I get back, I'll knock on the door and tell you it's me. There are plenty of books to read, or you could listen to the radio. Or, even better, think about what you're going to do for the rest of your life."

42

The team assembled at three in the workroom. The radiators kept the room warm, and hot pies and coffee had helped them all warm up again after the raid.

"All right, everybody," Hallmets began, "Things have moved forward. We now have only one suspect. Problem is, we don't know who he is yet. I think we have to assume that Jonsson killed Kirik. There are signs the bed had been slept in. So either Kirik was already staying there, and Jonsson arrived, perhaps early yesterday morning, or Jonsson was staying there, and Kirik arrived yesterday morning. At any rate, the upshot of their meeting was fatal for Kirik. However, we've got good likenesses of both of them, so we can check out the bus and railway station, taxi ranks, and so on, to see if we can pick up a trace of any of them. Henno, I think you need to go back to Paide, and talk to Kirik's brother. I guess once he knows Kirik's dead he'll be more co-operative. That should tell us which of them was waiting at the flat."

"But we still don't know what's driving all this," said Kadakas.

"We're getting closer. The note in the book may have been for either the general or for Kirik, maybe even both of them. It does look like an act of vengeance. And that points back to the War again. I'll have a good look at the latest version of the general's memoirs and see if that gets us any closer. Henno, anything from the technicians?"

"Einar did find some fingerprints. But they're all Kirik's."

"That suggests he was the one who slept there," concluded Hallmets. "And Jonsson just came in for the kill. Talking of which, what about the dagger?"

"Estonian Army bayonet, as used in the War."

"As with the sabre. Weapons from the War."

"Looks like it's all pointing that way, chief," agreed Lesser.

"So, here's the plan," said Hallmets, "Tomorrow's Sunday. We'll concentrate on trying to trace Kirik and Jonsson here, while Henno goes to Paide to talk with Kirik's brother. The other thing we need to do is get Jonsson's picture round the university. If he was ever there, somebody will recognise him. The place will be shut tomorrow, so some of us should get down there on Monday Once we know who he really is, our chances of catching him will improve. We should also get his picture to all the police stations, and the Border Police, with a request to detain him. But we don't want anything in the papers yet – that could easily send him into hiding."

"He may have skipped the country already," observed Hekk sadly.

"Let's just hope he hasn't. For what it's worth, I don't think we're dealing with a professional killer here, the sort who can disappear, then reappear in another country with a new identity."

"He's not done badly with fake identities so far," commented Larsson.

"That's true. But I suspect that's been opportunistic rather than professional. I'm saying that partly to encourage us. If this man were a professional, we've probably already lost him."

Hallmets spent the next two hours reading the new version of the general's memoirs. He had to admit, the quality of the writing was dramatically improved. There was no doubt Jonsson had talent as a writer. But the content had changed too. The political rants had gone, and the rambling accounts of early life which would have bored the reader to death within the first three chapters, as well as the tedious and repetitious accounts of the movements of bags of grain or pairs of boots from A to B. But it was also clear that Jonsson had questioned the general closely, to get his account of events in proper order. Events which had been vague were sharpened up. The general's role was made clearer. His feelings about events were also now included. As he read, Hallmets could not but admire the job Jonsson had done in turning an incoherent, irritating, and mostly desperately dull account into a real book. If Jonsson didn't end up hanged or in jail for life, there was a career out there for him.

Best of all, there was now a whole chapter devoted to what happened to Colonel Madrus during his few months of actual combat. The cup of coffee beside him grew cold as Hallmets turned the pages to get closer to Hapsaküla. And then, there it was.

We entered the village. The Reds had fled, and the whole place was eerily silent. The crucifixions were the first thing we saw. Women had been stripped and nailed by the hands onto the sides of barns. We could also imagine what must have happened to them before their terrible deaths. How could any human beings have committed such acts? And yet there they were before us. I felt we should bury them immediately, and most of the men agreed. But Colonel Renner ordered that they should remain until the atrocity was made known to the world. The cold would preserve them for a few days, long enough for the press to be summoned to view the awful spectacle.

'Otherwise,' he said to us, 'No-one will believe us. No-one would believe such evil were possible.'

That was not all. An old man, who had hidden in his woodshed, led us to the mass grave, where the bodies of men, women and children lay uncovered except by the snow. And in a house not far off, there were more bodies. By now, some of the men were physically sick. All were angry. All knew this could happen in their own village if the Reds got there. This was the reality of the Red Terror. But it did not make our men cower in fear, and run away. It made them furious, and mad for vengeance. Only the discipline enforced by our officers and NCOs prevented some of them from riding after the retreating Reds to take their revenge on any stragglers.

In the next few days the world learned about Hapsaküla, as photographers recorded the vile tableaux and reporters described it with all the vividness of the most gothic novels, or of the Book of Revelation. For truly this was the work of Satan himself. Who were the Reds but his cohorts, no longer men but demons, who must be hunted down and destroyed. And so, as horror passed into anger, we moved on, steeled to destroy the Red horde.

And then he was past it. Three paragraphs, but it was clear from Jonsson's telling of it, that it was a turning point for the general. Reading the next paragraphs, it seemed almost as if Madrus had lost interest in the War. Far from the enthusiastic pursuit of the Red Army that he'd expected after reading about Hapsaküla, it seemed that the fire had gone, even from the general's words. The psychological impact had left him unable to command, though this was never admitted. Instead he expressed his relief at being moved not long afterwards out of a combat

286

role and into the Supplies Division, where he knew his real skills lay.

Had the sight of the atrocities simply been too much for a sensitive man? Yet there was no evidence that Madrus had been a particularly sensitive individual. Had the events perhaps exposed his incompetence as an officer? An inability to distance himself from the emotions that the atrocity would arouse? That was possible, although Madrus had not seemed a particularly emotional type, and his children's testimony seemed to back that up.

This account added nothing to the facts Hallmets already possessed regarding the incident. But from the general's account, or at least its interpretation by Jonsson, he now knew that Hapsaküla had left an indelible mark upon the man.

43

It was almost five, and he was thinking about reading the rest of the book at home, when the phone rang.

"*Tere*, Jüri. Jaan Kallas here. Look, is there any chance we can meet as soon as possible. I've got some news for you. Can you make the *Alt-Revaler* in ten minutes?"

He accepted the invitation, then phoned Kirsti to say he'd be home a bit later, told those team members still there that he'd see them in the morning, and set off through the icy streets.

Kallas was waiting in one of the high-backed armchairs in the innermost, and warmest, part of the café. Hallmets pulled the one opposite a bit closer. He'd ordered and collected a coffee on the way past the counter.

"*Tere*, Jaan. Everything OK?"

Kallas glanced around to make sure there was no-one within listening distance, and spoke in a low voice. "Artur Simm turned up at my flat this afternoon. In a hell of a state. He said the plotters think he'd spilled everything about the plot to me. Then he gave me quite a bit of it. Lepp has told him we're for the chop once he's head of the political police, and lots of others will follow. Lepp also promised Artur he'd be a member of the Propaganda Commission. But the main thing is that their so-called Central Committee is meeting tomorrow evening, at a house in Volta Street."

"Right. Before we do anything else, just tell me everything Simm said to you."

Kallas added whatever else he could remember of his conversation with Artur Simm.

"Are you sure Simm hadn't been followed to your

place?"

Kallas looked blank for a moment. "*Kurat!* I hadn't thought of that. I should have checked. Do you think anything might have, ... I mean, those bolts and that lock could keep an army out."

"Unless they persuade him to open the door."

"Artur needs to be wanted. All they'd have to do is tell him all is forgiven, and he can join the Central Committee."

"We'd better get over to your place right away, and make sure he's OK. Then we can deal with what he told you."

They had to walk down Viru Street to the gate, and then on to Narva Road, and finally turn the corner into Kreutzwald Street. It was beginning to snow again, and in the dark, the flakes glowed in the streetlights' aura as they fell. The traffic was heavy on Narva Road, and there were plenty of pedestrians on the pavements. A police car passed them, siren wailing, then an ambulance. Hallmets had a bad feeling.

As soon as they turned into Kreutzwald Street, they could see, through the snow, the vehicles stopped at the roadside, and a crowd of people.

"That's my block," shouted Kallas, and started to ease his way through the crowd, Hallmets behind him.

They were stopped by a uniformed policeman. "Just keep back, sir," said the officer, "Let us do our job."

"He's with me, officer," said Hallmets, showing his ID. The officer saluted, "That's all right, sir," standing aside.

"What happened?" Hallmets asked him.

"Seems some chap jumped out the window, three floors up. Killed himself."

"Who's in charge?"

"Inspector Sõnn. He's just over there, by the body."

"Thank you, officer," said Hallmets, "Come on, Jaan."

On the pavement lay the shape of a body, covered by a tarpaulin. By it stood a stout man with a bushy moustache in a raincoat and fedora.

Hallmets greeted him, "*Tere*, Hjalmar! What have you got here?"

Sõnn peered, then smiled. "Jüri! Good to see you too. Looks like he jumped out of the second floor window. It's still open up there. I'm just going up to find out who lives there."

Kallas moved out of Hallmets' shadow. "I live there, Inspector. Jaan Kallas. I was just ..."

Hallmets squeezed his arm. "Later, Jaan. Hjalmar, you know Jaan Kallas. You saved him from some bent cops a couple of years ago."

"Of course," said Sõnn, "I'll need to talk to you. Do you know who he is?"

"I think we'll all recognise him," said Hallmets, "Could we see him for a moment?"

"Certainly. I haven't seen him myself. I just got here a few minutes ago. The uniforms who were here first put the tarp over him."

Sõnn walked over and pulled the corner of tarpaulin back to reveal the head of the dead man. Then he knelt down, and produced a pocket torch, for a closer look. The man lay with the front of his body on the pavement. His head was turned to one side. Sõnn gently lifted the head with his gloved hand, and shone the torch under. "Massive crushing of the skull, consistent with a fall from a height." Hallmets knew it didn't need much of a height for a fall to kill a man. Sõnn pointed at what was visible of the face. "Gingery hair, small moustache. This guy looks vaguely

290

familiar. He's crossed our paths at some point."

"It's Artur Simm," said Hallmets. "He was involved in some trouble two years ago. Vaguely connected with the Vaher case."

"That's poor Artur all right," echoed Kallas, "He was hiding out at my place."

"Hjalmar," said Hallmets, "Can we talk up in Jaan's apartment. There are some confidential aspects to this that I need to explain to you, as the investigating officer." He mentioned this to reassure Sõnn that he wasn't going to take over his case.

A doctor had arrived to certify the body as dead, and the ambulance crew were waiting to take it to the morgue. Sõnn told the uniformed officers to fence off the area around the corpse, and one of them went off to get a van to bring over the fence panels. Then he accompanied Hallmets and Kallas into the building and up the stairs.

When they got to the door they found another uniformed officer. "We just checked there was no-one else in there, sir," he said to Sõnn. He recognised Hallmets and his eyes widened.

"Was the door open when you arrived?" Hallmets asked the officer.

"Yes, sir, I mean, no sir. Er, what I mean is, it was closed but unlocked."

"Thank you. That's exactly what I wanted to know."

"We'll have a look in now," said Sõnn. He tried the door and it opened easily. There was no obvious damage in the narrow hallway. But in the living-room, it was a different picture. Pictures had been taken from the wall and flung on the floor, and two upright chairs were lying on their sides. The window was fully open and the sounds of the street could be heard clearly. Flakes of snow were drifting into the room, and there was a wet patch on the carpet under the window.

"So that's where he jumped," commented Sõnn.

"I think you'll find he was thrown out," said Hallmets, "Look, on the lower part of the window frame. There's a nail projecting slightly, and there's a piece of material caught on it. If he'd gone voluntarily, he'd have carefully got himself onto the ledge outside before jumping. It's quite wide. He wouldn't have let a piece of his jacket get ripped off like that. But if he was being pushed through against his will, that would be a different matter. Plus there's the business of the door. Jaan here left him here earlier this afternoon, and told him to lock the door and bolt it on the inside. Jaan, do you know if Artur did that?"

"Yes, definitely. I waited until I heard the lock turn and the bolts sliding before I went down the stairs."

"So," Hallmets went on, "It looks like he was persuaded to open the door. Then he either invited his guests in, or they pushed their way in."

"They!" said Sõnn. "That suggests you know who they were."

"I'd guess they were two Finnish thugs called Antti and Matti. Perhaps they were also accompanied, or led, by ex-Inspector Lepp."

"Lepp! What the hell's going on, Jüri?"

Hallmets pointed to an armchair. "Take a seat, Hjalmar, and I'll explain. Jaan can check what other damage has been done to the place. Just look in each room. But don't touch anything. Our forensics people will have to go over the place, I'm afraid."

Hallmets explained to Sõnn what he knew from Kallas. "The problem is that, as you can see, there's a political dimension to this that will be of great interest to our friend

Colonel Reinart. So just be careful how you investigate this. Keep it as discreet as possible, and don't hurry, as I fear that at some point the colonel will want to massage the results. I'll have to tell him what I know today, as the plotters are having a meeting tomorrow, and he may wish to take action then. It all depends how he's playing it. And not a word of this to anyone, until things get a bit clearer."

"My lips are sealed, Jüri. Okay, we'll take this one slowly. Let me know anything I need to be aware of."

"Will do, Hjalmar. Now, where's Jaan got to?"

Hallmets found Kallas in what was clearly his study, a small room facing the back of the building, lined with bookshelves, and with a large steel filing cabinet in one corner. Kallas was sitting at his desk reading a book.

"I thought I should keep out of the way until the consultation between the two detectives was over. By the way, nothing's been disturbed in here. Mind you, the filing cabinet has a separate lock on each drawer, the toughest sort, and all the drawers in my desk are secure too. The worst they could have done was tipped all the books off the shelves onto the floor. My kitchen and bathroom are fine too. And the bedroom."

"Yes, it does look as if they were more interested in Artur than yourself."

"I should have come straight over to you rather than going to the paper and then thinking about it. Then Artur might still be alive."

"No-one forced him to open the door, Jaan. He chose to do it. You warned him. What happened was not your responsibility."

"So what do we do now?"

"I'm afraid you'll have to stay here this evening. This is a crime scene and you're a key witness. Inspector Sõnn will need to take you through your meetings with Artur. Then the forensics people will have to look at the living-room. And you'll have to give detailed descriptions of Antti and Matti, as they're the most likely suspects. And Sõnn will put a man at the main door, in case they come back."

"I think I'll be all right here. At least I have the sense not to open the door to any dodgy characters. But in the next day or two I might get one of those little spy-holes put in the door, so I can see who's outside. What are you going to do?"

"I'll have to talk to Colonel Reinart next, and tell him what Artur told you. It's up to him what he does with the information. But if Lepp is involved, I'd like to see him caught and punished. Keep in touch, and I'll do likewise."

Hallmets said goodbye to Sõnn and left the building. It was still snowing, as he made his way back into the Old Town, to the Interior Ministry. As he expected, Reinart was still in his office. He recounted to the colonel what Simm had told Kallas, and the fate that had befallen him.

Reinart expressed no sympathy for Simm. "That's very helpful. Tomorrow evening, in a house in Volta Street. Pity Simm didn't hear which house. Still, we'll watch the whole street, and we'll soon spot them. In fact, one of our agents had reported the meeting was tomorrow evening, but not where. By the way, do you want to come along for the ride?"

Hallmets was about to turn down the offer, but stopped himself. "Thank you, colonel, that's very kind of you." He hoped he would run into Lepp. "By the way, did the papers you found in the general's flat give you anything useful?"

"Not so far. But we've only got through a quarter of the material so far. What are your next moves regarding the general's killer?"

"We can't do much tomorrow. But I'll get down to Tartu on Monday morning. I feel sure someone at the university will tell us who this Jonsson really is. Or at least give us a trail to follow. What's noticeable is that all the people who've encountered him describe him as well-educated, intelligent and well-spoken. He's been through a university, there's no doubt about that. That's clear to me too, having seen how he's rewritten the general's memoirs. I'll have people go to the Technical Institute here too, but he sounds like the sort who's followed an arts rather than a science course."

"He might have gone to Riga or even one of the German universities. Königsberg's not that far away."

"I'll consider that if we don't find him in Tartu or here. When shall I come along tomorrow?"

"Come over here at six. I'm guessing the meeting will start at seven or half past. I'd like to wait until they're all there and the meeting's well under way. Then we can catch them red-handed."

"Do you know who's on their Central Committee?"

"Oh yes, most of them. We've been keeping them under observation for a while. I thought something like this would happen sooner or later. We let them off far too lightly last year."

"You didn't have any evidence against them. They weren't doing anything illegal. They'd have got their way through the ballot box."

"Yes, just like Hitler."

Hallmets made his way to the Baltic Station. The snow

was lying now, and he felt it compacting under his feet with every step he took. But the trains were still running, and the journey through the darkness to Nõmme, with nothing to see outside the windows, enabled him to relax.

Back home, Kirsti was pleased to see him, and had kept some stew warm on the kitchen range for him. With rye bread and butter, and a glass of beer, it restored him something like normality.

44

Sunday 8th December

On Sunday the snow lay thick again, and getting around wasn't easy. Hallmets spent the morning reading the rest of the general's memoirs. It added nothing to what he'd concluded the previous day. Apart from Lesser, who'd gone to Paide to talk to Kirik's brother, the others had been despatched to the bus and railway station, the taxi ranks, the ferry terminal and the hotels, with pictures of Kirik and Jonsson.

Not long before twelve Lesser phoned: "Hi, chief. Didn't take long for Kirik's brother to tell all. Apparently Kirik phoned him on Monday 2nd December, at about 10 am, from a public phone in Türi, and asked him to fetch him over to the farm. Kirik claimed he'd walked into Viljandi and got the first train out. He told his brother some people were after him because he owed them money, and asked if he could hide him for a few days. Which he did, rather reluctantly, I think. On Thursday 5th he got a letter, which he didn't show to his brother. But that evening, he got the brother to drive him over to Tapa, where he intended to pick up the train to Tallinn. I guess he went straight to the flat, entering after Tannberg had gone off duty. He must have already had keys."

"So the letter was probably from our killer, who either arranged to meet him at the flat, or induced him to go there by telling him we were onto his hideout at the farm."

"But how did the murderer know Kirik was at the farm?"

"If we assume the killer was Jonsson, he'd have had plenty of opportunity to find out where Kirik's next of kin were. The general may even have told him. Jonsson simply had to send an anonymous note to Kirik telling him the police knew where he was hiding. That's useful, Henno, it fills in a gap in the story. Come on back as fast as you can. We'll meet once you get back."

They met up again in the workroom at half past two. Lesser, not long back from Paide, presented the account of Kirik's movements, concluding: "So it looks as if the killer may have arrived at the flat late on the Thursday evening or early on Friday morning. The fake summons to Tannberg that morning may have been to enable his getaway. The trouble is, we don't know where he came from before the killing, or where he went afterwards."

The reports from the others did not clarify this. Jonsson had not been sighted at the railway or bus stations, or the ferry terminal. No taxi drivers remembered him. And none of the staff in the hotels. "Of course," commented Hallmets, "he could have stayed with an associate. He might have come in directly from somewhere else by car. Or he might be living in Tallinn now. We might have to search all the lodging houses here. But let's not go there till we've been to the university tomorrow. I'll go down to Tartu with Ants and Eva. Henno, can you go with Ilmar to the Technical Institute here in Tallinn. Keep an eye open for Kirik's post-mortem, which I suspect will be tomorrow sometime; can one of you get there if it's on. We'll meet up again on Tuesday morning, unless we have to stay overnight in Tartu."

Everyone seemed satisfied with this. There was a sense that they were getting closer to the killer.

"One other thing I have to tell you about," continued Hallmets, "And not a word of this must get out." He went on to tell them about Artur Simm's death, and the suspected plot. "I don't think it has much, if anything, to do with the general's death. However, the political police are planning to round up the conspirators tonight, and have invited me along, no doubt to prove they will behave like gentlemen. If there's anything that's relevant to this investigation, I'll let you know."

He made arrangements to meet Kadakas and Larsson at the railway station the following morning, then told them all to take the rest of the day off.

Hallmets spent the afternoon completing his reading of the general's book. It became more tedious as it went on, despite Jonsson's best efforts to make it sound interesting. The general's political opinions had mostly vanished. Occasionally he would express mild approval or disapproval of some political event, and that was it. At ten to five Hallmets had got to the end, and laid the manuscript aside with some relief. He walked to the *Alt-Revaler* and had a cheese and onion pie and a slice of blueberry cheesecake with some coffee. Then he walked back towards the Interior Ministry. The evening was very cold, the sky was clear, and the lying snow sparkled in the moonlight and crunched underfoot. It would get even colder before morning. He was well wrapped up, and had a fur hat on to keep his ears warm.

Colonel Reinart welcomed him to his office, then asked him to come down to the ground floor where his men were waiting. There were about thirty of them, all in plain clothes, most of them dressed as working men, who might be passing by to or from the factories in the area round

Volta Street. They were all armed, a couple of them even carrying sub-machine-guns that would have made an American gangster proud.

The briefing by the colonel was short. Hallmets guessed the men already had their instructions, and this was just a final pep-talk to fire them up. "Remember, men," the colonel concluded, "I want all these people alive. Got that!" He scanned the assembly and they nodded as his gaze passed them. "You are armed only in case there is trouble, so avoid any shooting of you can. These people are talkers, not fighters. I suspect most of them will surrender without much trouble and allow themselves to be taken away. And we'll have several wagons on hand to do that. They'll spend the night in the Patarei Prison, wondering what we're going to do with them, then we'll start the interrogations tomorrow morning. Any questions?" There were none. "Oh, by the way," the colonel concluded, "This gentleman, in case you don't know it, is Chief Inspector Hallmets of the Special Crimes Unit. He'll be observing our action, as there's a possibility of a link to a case he's pursuing. If he asks for your assistance, give it. All right, let's go."

45

Six unmarked black cars were waiting for the men in the lane between the Ministry and Police HQ. Reinart asked Hallmets to come with him in a rather more luxurious vehicle, also black and unmarked. In the car were Lieutenant Tamm, and another man, who Reinart introduced as Lieutenant Korvik. "The cars will set off at intervals of two minutes, and take different routes to our destination, so that the men can get into position without attracting any interest. We want to observe the committee members arriving, partly because we don't know which house they're meeting at, and partly to get an idea of who's there."

The car made its way down Pikk Street past the building where Kirik had been found to the former town gate by the Paks Margareeta tower. Once through the narrow gateway out of the Old Town, the vehicle turned left onto Rannavärav Street, and sped westwards. Soon Hallmets recognised the smoky odour that told him they were nearing the Volta Electrical Factory, and its neighbour, the Krull Machine Works. The car turned left and drew to a smooth halt.

"This is Kungla Street," said Tamm, "The next one along is Volta Street. Do you know it?"

"Yes," answered Hallmets, "If you walk down it, on the right there's only the walls of the factories, and on the left there are houses. Quite big ones, I think. Probably built for the factory managers, in the days when they lived nearby. Before they moved out to the suburbs."

"You know Tallinn well," commented Reinart.

"It's my job. When you're dealing with criminals, you

need to know the environments in which they live and work. So, what happens now?"

"We wait," said Reinart. "The men will report to me here as things progress. At this point all they're doing is watching, identifying the house and the people going to it."

"It could get cold just sitting here."

"This car's got an excellent heater. I've also got a bottle of brandy in case we need more warming up. Only *in extremis*, of course."

There was a tap on the window, where Korvik was sitting, and he wound it down slightly. Something was whispered from outside, then he wound it up again. "Number thirteen," he said.

"Unlucky for some," said Reinart. Tell them to stay where they are for the moment."

Korvik wound down the window a fraction and muttered the instruction, then shut it again.

Despite the heater, Hallmets was glad of the warm clothing he wore. He'd noticed earlier that Reinart still wore his immaculate uniform. However, his overcoat looked like something very expensive, and no doubt kept him warm.

At five past seven, they got another message. Korvik listened, then reported. "Looks like the meeting started at seven, in the downstairs front room. There's lights on, but they've got heavy curtains on the windows."

"We'll give them another twenty minutes," said Reinart, "That'll give time for latecomers to arrive, and for them to get well into the agenda, and forget about the outside world. Then we'll move in. Meanwhile, Korvik, tell someone to get to a phone and summon the jail vans."

Korvik whispered his instructions, and the invisible

presence outside disappeared.

"I'd like to get a bit closer, if you don't mind, colonel," said Hallmets. "But I don't want to get in the way either. The main action will be at the front, so perhaps I could join your men watching the back door of the house."

The colonel hesitated. He hadn't expected that. "Er, yes. I suppose that's OK. Provided you only observe. You understand that?"

"That's no problem, colonel. I wouldn't dream of interfering."

"Tamm," ordered Reinart, "Take the Chief Inspector to the men watching the rear door. Stick with him, and make sure he doesn't get into any trouble." He tapped the glass, and his driver leapt out and opened the door. Tamm got out, and Hallmets followed.

It was cold on the street, but he felt very relieved at getting out of the thick atmosphere in the car. He stamped his feet to get some circulation back. "Lead on, lieutenant," he whispered to Tamm.

They walked a few metres further down the street, when a man appeared suddenly from a narrow gateway. Tamm spoke quietly to him, then he and Hallmets followed the man into a garden, past the side of a house facing onto Kungla Street, and through a wider gateway into a narrow lane. A few metres down the lane, on the opposite side was another gateway – this was how vehicles accessed the houses, from the lane at the rear. Four men were waiting there, in the shadow of the high wall beside the gatepost.

After a whispered consultation, Tamm explained to Hallmets, "This is the rear access to number 13. If anyone tries to sneak out the back they've got to come this way." He glanced at his watch, which Hallmets noted had luminous hands and numbers. "The latest thing," whispered Tamm, "Apparently the stuff that makes the glow is radioactive. They reckon it'll last two thousand years before it starts to fade."

They waited in silence. Apart from a dim light, probably filtering through the kitchen from the hallway, there was no sign or movement in the house. At twenty past, after consulting his watch again, Tamm whispered again, "All right, we need to be alert now. They'll be going in the front in a few minutes. Weapons ready, but remember, we want people alive if possible."

A few minutes later they could hear heavy vehicles moving along the street at the front of the house. Then suddenly lights came on in the house. A few moments later, they could hear a door opening, and an electric torch beam passed the gateway and moved on.

"All right, men, let's go!" whispered Tamm.

Two electric torches flashed into life and were pointed at the rear door of the house. Caught in the beam were three men in the yard and one coming down the stairs from the door. Hallmets recognised three of them immediately: Antti, Matti and Lepp.

"Police!" shouted Tamm, "Hands in the air, now!"

"Watch out!" whispered Hallmets, "The big guy has a gun."

They ducked back behind the wall on either side of the gateway, as a hail of bullets smashed into the wall across the lane. "Shit, that's a Chicago piano," muttered Tamm, "Sorry, a Thompson submachine-gun. Vicious weapon."

"Matti's not very bright," said Hallmets, "He'll use up the whole magazine at one go. Just wait." By now he had his own Browning automatic out. He wasn't going to remain an observer if someone was firing a machine-gun at him.

Sure enough, after an ear-splitting cascade of bullets burying themselves in the wall, there was a sudden silence. Tamm's men sprang back into the gateway and a barrage of shots rang out. Matti was desperately trying to get the empty magazine off the gun, then dropped it, pulled out a pistol and lumbered towards the men at the gate, seemingly ignoring the fire directed straight at him. But his own shots went wide or high – he must have been seriously wounded by now, thought Hallmets – and finally he crashed over onto his face onto the gravel of the yard.

The man on the steps was kneeling, and shooting with an automatic. One of Tamm's men staggered behind the wall and collapsed. A furious volley in response toppled the man on the steps.

Meanwhile Antti and gone and Lepp was shooting from cover in the open doorway of the garage.

"Come on out, Lepp, it's all over," shouted Hallmets.

In the torchlight he saw the hate in Lepp's eyes. "Go to the devil, Hallmets. I'm not finished with you yet," Lepp shouted back, and a bullet ricocheted off the wall just above Hallmets's head.

Hallmets aimed carefully at Lepp's left knee, which was just poking out from the garage door, and fired. He heard a shout and Lepp ducked away.

Then came the sound of a car engine.

"They've gone for the car," shouted Hallmets.

A moment later the wooden doors of the garage burst open and the car, headlights blazing, shot out. The men sprang out of the way as it raced through the gateway, scraping the gatepost as it did so, turned right and roared off down the lane. They directed a volley of fire after it, as it disappeared.

"Into the house!" ordered Tamm, "We need to help

round up the rest."

But Hallmets had other ideas. He ran up the lane in the opposite direction to that in which the escaping car had gone. His thinking was that the best escape route for Antti and Lepp was to come back up Kungla Street to regain the main road, where they could head off in any direction.

He ran back through the gateway and yard of the house behind, alongside the house, and back through the gate into the street, then the few metres back to Reinart's car. Leaning his arm on the roof of the car gave him a steady firing position. "Get down!" he shouted into the vehicle.

He could see the other car racing up the street towards him. He aimed for the driver's windscreen – his best hope was to disable Antti, whom he assumed was driving the car – and fired. The windscreen shattered, and he fired again. And again. The car slewed towards Reinart's, scraped along its side with an ear-grating screech, then accelerated again toward the other side of the road, to crash into a lamp-post.

There were shouts from Reinart's car beside him. Hallmets stepped back as the driver jumped out and opened the door by the pavement. He guessed the doors at the other side had been wedged shut by the collision. Finally Korvik climbed out, gun in hand, and peering round watchfully, followed even more cautiously by Reinart.

"What the hell are you doing, Hallmets?" said the colonel, "Look at my bloody car. I ordered you not to get involved. Wasn't that clear enough?"

"Perfectly clear, colonel, but when I'm shot at, I tend to shoot back. Especially when Indrek Lepp is shooting at me. Be careful. He got away in that car over there, and may still be dangerous."

"Korvik, check out that car," ordered the colonel, "The men inside may still be dangerous."

Hallmets and Korvik crossed the road, guns at the ready, and circled the crashed car. There was no sign of movement, nor sound, apart from a hissing from somewhere in the engine.

Korvik peered in the driver's window. "Driver looks as if he's dead," he said, "Bullet hole in his forehead. Good shooting, sir."

"Lepp may be lurking in the back," said Hallmets, "You pull the door open, and I'll cover him."

Korvik grabbed the door handle and heaved the back door open, as Hallmets covered the space, ready to shoot at any movement. But there was none. And the seat was empty.

"Where did he go?" said Korvik.

Hallmets opened the boot, but there was nothing here either. "He must have got out at the bottom of the lane, and told Antti to come on up here."

"You got him though," said Korvik. He was holding a small hand torch now, rather than a gun, and pointing at the foot well in the rear of the car. "That's fresh blood. And there's more on the seat there. He's wounded all right. He can't have got far. If we take the car down, we might be able to catch him."

This was when they noticed the colonel's car had gone. Whilst they were occupied with Antti and Lepp, the colonel's vehicle had silently slipped away.

"Typical!" said Korvik, "Just when you need him, he's off. He'll have gone round to number 13 to supervise the rounding up. He likes to be in evidence when the danger's passed. Sorry, forget I said that, sir."

"Already done," replied Hallmets, "Let's walk down to

the bottom of the road. There may be some trace of Lepp."

They walked rapidly down to the bottom of Kungla Street, and round the corner at the bottom. There was no sign of anyone. But Korvik did spot a small patch of blood on the pavement. "Maybe he got out here," he commented. Then swung his torch across the road. "Ah! Then went through that old gate. Where does it lead?"

"The railway marshalling yards," said Hallmets, "We might be able to catch him there, but we'll need more men. He could have gone in any direction."

"Sorry, sir," said Korvik, "I'll need to get back to the colonel. He gave explicit orders that there was to be no pursuit of suspects who managed to get away. He didn't want this operation arousing any suspicion amongst the populace. His view was that any escapees could be rounded up later. The others would soon tell us where they were, once we applied a bit of pressure. And it would be very dangerous for you to go there on your own. Lepp could be hiding anywhere, waiting to pick you off."

Hallmets had to admit to the wisdom of this statement. He was pretty sure he'd hit Lepp's knee, so he'd be limping. But even so, the chances of finding him were slim.

There was noise from the marshalling yards, the clanking and puffing of engines, and the clatter of wagons and coaches, as they were moved into position for the morning's journeys. But even among that, they both heard the revving of a motor cycle engine starting up, and then accelerating.

"Dammit!" said Hallmets, "He must have come to the meeting on the motor-bike, and left it through there by the yards. So all he had to do was get out of the car here, get through the gate and as far as the bike. Then he's away. All right, lieutenant, I'm coming."

Colonel Reinart did not seem too worried that Lepp had got away. Hallmets knew why. Lepp had, two years earlier, been highlighted as a noble example of the capital's detective force, only to be revealed not long afterwards as a murderer and a sadist. Hallmets suspected Reinart had aided Lepp's subsequent escape from Estonia. Whilst his return would irritate the colonel, it was still better to have him out of the limelight which the trials of the plotters would attract.

The captives having been ferried off to the Patarei Prison, Reinart's men were busy searching the house for evidence. "Only one casualty," he said to Hallmets, as they stood in the big room where the meeting had taken place, "And that was Palsson, who took a shot in the shoulder at the back gate. But that big guy, what was his name?"

"Matti."

"Yes, that's him. They counted fifteen bullets in him. Fifteen shots before he went down. Well, the fifteenth was actually after he was down, I'm told. He was still alive, till someone put him out of his misery."

This kind of talk didn't interest Hallmets. He was thinking about Lepp. He could put out a general search order for him the next morning, put every policeman in the capital on the lookout. But he knew that wouldn't achieve anything. Lepp would be long gone. His best guess was that he'd got himself to the harbour area on the motor-bike, perhaps found an associate who'd bandage his leg for him, then, probably with same associate, gone to a small boat moored there, and was by now probably half way across the Gulf of Finland.

"But the main casualty was my car," went on the colonel, "The whole side will need to be fixed. And one of the wheels was damaged. Of course, it's a ministry car, so they'll pick up the tab. But how long will it take? Couldn't you have done your shooting further down the street?"

"These things happen, colonel. Best to be philosophical about it. Anyway, I'm off. It won't take me long to walk to the station. Many thanks for inviting me along. Do let me know if anything relevant to General Madrus turns up."

In fact, it took him half an hour to get to the railway station, but he felt the walk doing him good, and by the time he got to the station, he was quite relaxed, and got himself a coffee and a pie at the kiosk there while he waited for the train to Nõmme.

It was half past nine by the time he got home. "A hot bath's what you need after all that excitement," commented Kirsti, as soon as he got in, "You have a nice glass of something while I run your bath."

46

Monday 9th December

Hallmets was back at the Baltic Station the following morning, to meet up with Larsson and Kadakas for their trip to Tartu on the 8.30 am train. They had overnight bags with them, but he hoped they wouldn't be necessary.

On the electric train into Tallinn with Kirsti, he'd had a look at the morning paper. "Huge Plot Against the State Uncovered" screamed the headline on the front page. The article revealed that enemies of the state had been planning a *coup d'état*. However, the political police, ever vigilant for threats to Estonia's security and happiness, had discovered the plot and had only the previous evening arrested all the leaders. More details would be revealed once the police had completed their investigation. It was likely that trials would follow, since such actions could not be allowed to go unpunished. There would be an announcement by the president later that day on the wireless.

On the train to Tartu he explained to Larsson and Kadakas what they'd need to do. "We simply have to get round as many departments as we can, plus the administrative offices, and show that picture to anybody who'll look at it. I feel sure here is where we'll find Jonsson."

"But if we get an identification," put in Larsson, "We've still got to find the guy. And that may not be so easy. He could be miles away living under another new name."

"That's always possible. But at least we'll have filled in another part of the jigsaw."

Travelling through the snow-bound landscape gave Hallmets the impression of being in a kind of empty space, a feeling corroborated by the sky, where a thin layer of white cloud, promising neither snow nor rain nor sight of the sun, reflected the blankness of the fields.

"We're almost there, boss," he heard Larsson saying loudly, and realised he must have dozed off. Once this case was over, he'd have to take a few days off and relax.

Exiting the station, he suggested they walk down to the university. The pavements had been cleared, and in fifteen minutes they had reached the ruin, still impressive, of the great cathedral which had in the Middle Ages dominated the town, and the countryside around it. One end of the building was still in use, having been converted in the early years of the nineteenth century into the university library. It was here that Kirsti had worked, before their move to Tallinn two years previously. The cathedral stood on a low hill above the town, and it was now a short walk down to the main buildings of the university, which clustered at the foot of the hill.

Hallmets pointed out the main building, a fine neoclassical structure built in the first decade of the nineteenth century, when the university had been refounded after being defunct for over ninety years. "I studied here before the War," he explained, "When most of the teaching was in Russian. Thankfully that's all over. Now let's find a telephone, and I'll call Marta."

Rather than looking for the post office, however, he led them through the main door of the university building, and they found themselves in a long bright corridor that seemed to stretch the entire length of the building. In front of them was a hallway, with a door on the left marked 'Reception.' Hallmets identified himself and his colleagues, and explained to the middle-aged woman behind the desk that they were on an important case and needed to make an urgent call to Tallinn.

"I don't know," said the woman doubtfully, "If you had some connection with the university perhaps, but ..."

"I'm sorry," interrupted Hallmets, "I should have said that I am an alumnus of Tartu. I was a student here from 1909 until 1913. *Hic studebam quattuor annis. Historia et litterae.*"

"*Bene recordatus*," said the woman with a smile, pushing the phone over, "It's all yours."

Hallmets called Police HQ and asked to be put through to his office, then asked Marta if there was any news. All she had for him was that the post-mortem in Kirik was at ten, and Lesser had gone to it. He wasn't back yet. Hallmets thanked her, and said he'd phone again later. He rang off, thanked the receptionist profusely, and asked her to direct them to the University records office.

At the rear of the hallway was a stone staircase taking them up to another corridor. Three doors along they found the Records Office. Hallmets asked for the records of a Villem Jonsson, who'd attended the university sometime in the last eight years. It didn't take long for the file to be put in front of them. It just wasn't the one they were looking for. It was the forty-something-year-old whom Dr Roosna had already mentioned to him.

"Well," he said, as they retraced their steps to the building's entrance, "That didn't altogether surprise me. But it does confirm where our man got the name from. Now we should split up. I'll take Arts; Ants, you take Sciences; and Eva, Law, Theology, and Medicine. The receptionist down here will tell us where all the departments are located."

The ever-helpful receptionist did better, and gave each of them a printed map of the university buildings, with all the departments marked. "Are you looking for a murderer?" she asked.

A gossip alert flashed in Hallmets mind. He leaned over the counter and said, in a conspiratorial tone, "Not a word of this to anyone, do you understand. The man we seek is very dangerous. But thankfully he is not at the university any more. He left about four years ago."

47

Having sent the other two off, Hallmets headed first for the Literature Departments. He soon found Dr Roosna's office, and introduced himself. Dr Roosna, a younger man than Hallmets had expected, with fair hair that flopped over his eyes every time he inclined his head, greeted him like a long-lost friend. *"Herr Hallmets. Wie geht's? Hoffentlich, sehr gut. Bitte, eine Tasse Kaffee? Ja? Gut. Kommen Sie mit."* He led Hallmets to the Literature department's staffroom, where several of Roosna's colleagues were sitting around in armchairs chatting and sipping coffee. Hallmets realised it must be a break between lectures.

He coughed politely and asked for their attention. "My name is Hallmets. I was a student of this university from 1909 to 1913, and studied in this department then. Now I'm a Chief Inspector of Police, and I'm trying to track down somebody who may have studied in this department within the last eight years. I've a picture of him that I'll pass around. Have a good look and tell me if you recognise him." He had two copies of the sketch, which he passed around. There was silence as the academics peered at the face. But no-one jumped to his feet shouting 'Eureka!'

"He does look vaguely familiar," said one, "But then, quite a lot of the students look like him."

Dr Roosna was most apologetic that no-one had responded positively. *"Vielleicht Sie haben mehr Glück bei Geschichte,"* he suggested, pointing Hallmets in the direction of the History Department.

But here he fared no better. The same close-up peering

at the image. And the same shaking of heads. And again one of them, an older man with horn-rimmed glasses and a beard, seemed to recognise him. "Yes. I've seen him around, I think. But I can't put name to him, and I have a good memory, I can tell you. I'm pretty sure he was never a student in this department, and I've been here for almost twenty years. But he may have sat in on my lectures. You know what I mean. A student from another department, just attending the lectures out of interest. They're supposed to introduce themselves to the lecturer, but they don't always do that."

Hallmets left the History common room feeling frustrated, but not depressed. He'd not made a definite identification. But, on the other hand, two people had seemed to recognise Jonsson. That suggested he had been at the university. Or at least had attended some lectures. Perhaps he wasn't a student, but had merely come in and sat in some lectures. But no, Hallmets had read Jonsson's work on the general's memoirs. That was the work of a well-educated person, someone who had studied the art of expressing himself. And it wasn't the work of a scientist, or a lawyer, or a medical man.

Geography offered no encouragement. No-one there even thought they might have seen him. Similarly at Economics. Now he was running out of options.

A small, and rather dilapidated building housed the offices of the Department of Classics and Ancient History. Hallmets remembered the arguments in his own student days about whether Ancient History should be grouped with History or with Classics. The former shared the methods of study, but the latter shared the environment, and the atmosphere.

There was no-one in the staff common room. He went to

the departmental office, explained who he was, and asked where he might find some of the staff. The young woman who had paused her typing to answer his query thought about it. She looked at the clock. "There's a departmental seminar on now, Professor Lutyens from Zurich is presenting his interpretation of the role of the Chorus in early Greek drama. It could go on all day. You know what these academics are like. And Lutyens is only here for two days so they won't give him a minute to himself. You might come back later this afternoon, or tomorrow morning. What was it you were wanting anyway? Was it to do with Alexei?"

"What?"

She pointed to the sketch which he'd laid on her desk whilst he asked about the staff. "Yes. That's Alexei, isn't it?"

"You recognise him?"

"Yes. It's a very good sketch." She smiled at the image. "We were quite close, for a while. I hope he hasn't got himself into any trouble. He could be very sad, you know. That was understandable, after what happened."

"I'm sorry, Miss ..."

"Anvelt. Anneli Anvelt. Please, just call me Anneli. Everyone else does."

Hallmets drew a deep breath. "Anneli, you know the person whose picture I'm showing you."

"Didn't I just say so. It's Alexei."

"Thank you. What's his surname?"

"Oh, sorry. Strelkov. Alexei Strelkov. His father used to be a professor in the History department. Alexei was very interested in history. But he didn't want to take the courses here, as his father was in the department, and he didn't want people thinking he'd get any special favours because of his Dad. So he did Classics and Ancient History. He was a very good student. And a really nice boy, too. But as I said, so sad. His older brother and sister, you see. They were killed by the Reds. Trying to get out of Russia. And almost made it."

"As far as Hapsaküla?"

She gasped. "How did you know that? He only mentioned the name once, and told me he'd never told anyone the name of the place. His parents had told him he must never mention the word. They'd found it very hard, harder than he had. Losing a son and daughter must be even harder than losing a brother and sister, don't you think?"

"Look, Anneli, can you show me Alexei's record, please. We need to find him. His evidence might be crucial in an important case we're pursuing."

Anneli fetched the file. "Of course, the Records Office will have a file on him too. But we like to keep track of all our former students, so we keep a copy of the file here, and add to it anything we find out. What other studies they take, what jobs they get, books they write, and so on."

"Did Alexei write stuff. I mean, apart from his course work."

"Oh yes. Poetry and short stories. Some were published in the student magazine. He even won a prize for one poem. It was called 'Memorial for Lost Souls.' It was so sad. People cried, you know, when he read it out. In the Great Hall, after he'd been awarded the prize."

Hallmets opened the cardboard cover of the file, and scanned the contents. "So he was here from 1928 to 1932. And got a very good result. Do you know what happened to him after that?"

"The staff all wanted him to stay on, and go for his doctorate. Professor Bauer thought his translation of Aeschylus's *Agamemnon* was good enough to be published. But he wanted to go. He told me he had to get some things sorted out in his head before he decided what to do with the rest of his life. I guess it was dealing with what happened to his brother and sister. I don't know where he went. I think he just planned to travel, and that at some point he'd experience some sort of revelation, and then everything would be better. I told him he should talk to a psychiatrist. Someone who knew how these things worked, who had the expertise to help him get through it. But he wasn't for that. To be honest, I thought he was running away from his problem, not standing and facing it. He never spoke to me after that." She sniffed, and wiped her eyes with the back of her hand.

"Did you see him again, after he left?"

"No. Though Piia, that's one of the other girls on the office, she said she'd seen him a few weeks ago, in one of the bookshops in Tallinn. She said hello, but he just stared at her as if he didn't know who she was, and then made himself scarce. I really hope he's all right. But somebody must have seen him, if they drew that picture. I'm guessing it was done by a woman. She's managed to capture the sadness in his smile." She sniffed again. "Is she his girlfriend?"

"No. Just someone he worked with. But he was using a different name. That's why I came here."

"He's in deep trouble, isn't he? Using a fake name, why would he do that? It must be something bad, or you wouldn't be taking so much trouble to find him. You being so high up, too. What did he do? Please tell me. I won't share it."

"I'm sorry, Anneli, I can't give you any information. But we really do need to talk with him, to clarify some information we have. If he speaks to us voluntarily, it will help him a great deal. For what it's worth, I agree with you that he's a very talented writer. I read a book he had worked on, and it really was well-written. That sort of talent shouldn't go to waste. If you do see him, please ask him to come forward."

She nodded without speaking.

"Can you help me with something else?" Hallmets continued. "I'd like to meet up with my two colleagues, who are visiting the other departments in the university. Could you call around and see if you can track them down. Sergeant Larsson was visiting Law, Theology and Medicine, whilst Officer Kadakas was in the Sciences."

This gave Anneli something new to focus on. She phoned Theology, who told her Eva had been there and was heading for Medicine. Medicine pointed her to Dentistry, where she still was. Hallmets asked her to meet him in front of the main building. The same process tracked Kadakas down at Botany, and he also was summoned. He thanked Anneli again for her help.

"Have I got him into trouble by identifying him?" she asked, "I'm starting to think I should have kept quiet."

"We would have identified him for sure later today, as soon as the staff came out of their seminar. You helped us get there a couple of hours earlier, that's all. But you've also helped to make him more human for us, and that's very important. I think you're right about him. He needs to come to terms with his family's loss, and think about the future. One more thing, Anneli. Please don't mention this to anyone."

"Don't worry, chief inspector, I won't. I do hope it all

works out for him. And if you do see him, please tell him I, ... I'd love to see him again."

48

It was after two o'clock when Hallmets met with Kadakas and Larsson outside the university's main building. He led them back into reception and asked if he could use the phone again. This time Marta was able to pass the phone on to Lesser.

"What have you got from the PM?" he asked, "Did the dead man tell us anything?" He noticed the receptionist's eyes open wide.

"Just like it looked, chief. He was killed by a single knife thrust in the chest. Straight into the heart. Doc said the killer knew exactly where to strike. The knife was very sharp, so it wouldn't have required a lot of force, especially as most of the dead man's clothing wasn't there."

"Any other injuries? Torture? Mutilation?" Now the receptionist's mouth dropped open.

"No. No sign of anything like that. Seems he was tied up, then killed. How long between those two actions is difficult to tell, but from the rope marks on the victim's arms and legs, the doc reckoned maybe an hour, not long enough to cause serious bruising."

"Thanks, Henno. Anything else?"

"Doc told me to say they're looking at Artur Simm's body this afternoon at two. Should I go to that one too?"

"Good idea. But find Inspector Sõnn this morning, and ask if it's all right for you to sit in. I'll call later this afternoon. I assume Ilmar went to the Technical Institute."

"Yes. He's just back. No luck, I'm afraid."

"OK. I think we may be onto something here. I'll call you later."

There was a cafe opposite, and he suggested they have some lunch there.

"Who'd have thought it," said Larsson, as they finished eating, "Professor Strelkov's son."

"So it does look as if what happened at Hapsaküla is something to do with all this," added Kadakas, "But we just don't know how it connects up."

"There's one way to find out," said Hallmets, "We need to visit the professor again. I'm sure he knows more than he's been telling us. His wife's been trying to shield him from us too. Now I suggest a brisk walk to focus our energies. It should only take us about fifteen minutes to get to the professor's house. As long as no-one slips on the ice."

Hallmets rapped on the door-knocker, whilst Larsson and Kadakas stood a little way behind. After some delay the door was opened and *Proua* Strelkova peered out.

"You haven't made an appointment to see my husband, chief inspector. At the moment it is really not convenient. Please phone later. It is never a good idea to turn up out of the blue."

With that she made to shut the door, but Hallmets' foot prevented it from closing, and in seconds he was presenting his ID card. "*Proua* Strelkova, this is not a consultation. This is an official police visit. These are my colleagues Sergeant Larsson and Officer Kadakas. We wish to interview both of you in regard to your son Alexei Strelkov, also known as Villem Jonsson and Oskar Kitsnik, whom we have identified as a prime suspect in the case of the murders of Arnold Madrus and Raud Kirik. Would you like us to carry out the interview here, or at the police station?"

Proua Strelkova had paled as her son's name and his aliases were pronounced. She stared at Hallmets as she processed his words. Then seemed to come to, and looked down. "Please wait a moment. I must consult my husband." She left the door ajar and turned back down the hallway, exiting to a room on the left.

Hallmets led Larsson and Kadakas into the hallway. He didn't see why they should wait out in the cold. He shut the door behind them loudly enough for it to be heard in the house. Through the first doorway on his left, he could see the living-room where he'd previously interviewed Professor Strelkov.

A minute later *Proua* Strelkova emerged from a door further down the hallway. She scowled but quickly affected a smile. "I see you've come in. Please, take your coats off, and it's this room here, our study. I'll make some coffee for you." She made for the kitchen door, at the rear of the hallway.

They entered the room. The professor sat behind a dark wood desk. He pushed himself to his feet with some effort to shake hands with the visitors. "Please sit down," he said, indicating three upright chairs set against the wall facing the rear window. There was another chair in the opposite corner. They sat down, and Larsson and Kadakas produced notebooks and pencils. Hallmets said nothing until *Proua* Strelkova brought them coffee and home-made biscuits, then moved the other chair closer to her husband's, and sat down.

"Thank you for the coffee, *Proua* Strelkova. The biscuits look delicious too," Hallmets began, "And thank you for inviting us into your home. I don't wish to take advantage of you, so let me say first of all, that if you prefer to have this conversation down at the police station, with your lawyer present, I would be happy to arrange it."

"Thank you for making that clear, chief inspector," said the professor quietly, "My wife and I have discussed the options available to us, and would prefer to have this conversation in a relatively friendly and informal atmosphere." He paused, and glanced at his wife, who nodded back. "I would first like to make it completely clear that our son Alexei is not guilty of any murder. But, with your permission, I would like to tell the story from the beginning. Then you may ask all the questions you wish."

"I would be very interested to hear it, professor. Do go ahead."

"Thank you. You'll be aware that my wife and I came here to Tartu in 1914, just before the War, when this was still part of the Empire. My colleagues at St. Petersburg thought I was crazy, going from the imperial capital to a provincial backwater. But it was a liberating move. Tartu University, even though the teaching was mostly in Russian, was a window to the West, and a more open environment than St. Petersburg, where academics were always regarded with suspicion by the secret police. We worked hard to learn Estonian. It's not an easy language, but it enabled me to talk to my students, and Ludmilla to her patients, in their own language. And they appreciated it. We soon had many Estonian friends, and a happy and fulfilling life here.

"Our son Nicolai was in his second year at St. Petersburg, and our daughter Ilsa had just started at the Nursing College. Nicolai was twenty, and Ilsa just nineteen. Both wanted to finish their courses there. They also, I think, liked the cultural life – theatres, concerts, the ballet, and so on. So we left them there, in good lodgings, and brought only Alexei with us. He was seven at the time, a somewhat late arrival, unexpected but welcome.

"Then came the war. A game for politicians and princes and generals; everyone else was just cannon-fodder. Of course, it destroyed the Empire, a creaking relic that hadn't really changed since the seventeenth century. But what replaced it was even worse, and even more destructive. I urged Nicolai and Ilsa to come to Tartu, but they hung on in St. Petersburg. I think they were caught up in the excitement of the Revolution. At first it seemed as if democracy would replace the autocracy. But the fumbling liberals were too slow to respond to the people's mood. They even tried to continue the war. And then it was too late. Autocracy was back with a red flag.

"Nicolai and Ilsa had no doubt hoped that a newer and freer Russia would emerge. But by the end of 1918 it was clear that the university would become a target for the bolsheviks. As so-called 'bourgeois intellectuals,' most of the staff and students at the university in St. Petersburg came under suspicion. Many of my former colleagues are now in labour camps, or dead. Some got out, of course, through Finland and then Sweden, mostly. So they finally decided to make their way here. Four of their friends, fearing their own fate in the chaos, joined them. They managed to leave St. Petersburg and made their way south-westwards to Pskov, hoping to cross into free Estonia."

"I'm sorry to interrupt," put in Hallmets, "But how did you know that?"

"Nicolai sent me a telegram to say they were coming home. That was the only way. Letters simply disappeared. Everything was being read by the authorities. All he could say was, 'Coming home.' That was the last we ever heard from them. When they never came, we knew something awful had happened. I made it my business to find out. Of course, getting into Russia was impossible, even after our treaty with the Soviets in 1920. But there were many Russian exiles here in Estonia, especially in the early years, when it still seemed possible that the Soviet state would collapse. I put advertisements in the newspapers asking for information, offering a modest reward. In this way I met a man down in Petseri who'd lived in Pskov before he fled in 1920. He was related to one of the other students who'd gone with Nicolai and Ilsa, and had put them all up for a night at his house in Pskov. That was the night of the 16th January. The following day they planned to try to cross the border by a track that connected the villages at the lower end of Lake Peipus. He took them in his cart from Pskov to the village of Malaja, only a few kilometres from the border. He remembers it took him three hours to get there. He dropped them just outside the village, not far from the track they were going to follow. It was almost dark when he was overtaken on his way back by some mounted units of the Red Army. He was able to call out the right slogans as they passed, and they gave him no trouble. He never saw the six students again.

"The night of the 16th?"

"You recognise it, Chief Inspector, don't you?"

"That must have been the day before the massacre at Hapsaküla."

"Yes," said the professor, "How much do you know about it?

"We are aware of the Red atrocity which took place there," said Hallmets, "But only in general terms, from newspaper reports of the time."

"You probably already know more about it than most people, who would prefer to forget such events, and believe that our world is now a much better place. I fear they will, in the coming years, be deeply disillusioned. I came across Hapsaküla quite soon after I'd spoken to the man from Pskov. Now that I knew where they'd been last seen, I looked at what was happening on the south-eastern front in mid-January 1919. Like you, I found the newspaper accounts. I was immediately drawn to the report of the six young people killed in the house, separately from the other horrors. I feared that these could be our children and their friends. It was too much of a coincidence. I considered various theories. One was that they'd reached Hapsaküla before the Reds arrived. But in that case why not just treat them like the rest? Another possibility was that they got there after the Reds had completed their massacre. Perhaps some of the Red units had already left, but a few are left, preparing to leave. Suddenly six young people arrive. Perhaps they decide that, whoever they are, they cannot be witnesses of the atrocity, they must not be allowed to live. Or they assume they are villagers who've been out somewhere, and kill them. Or they they find out who they really are, and condemn them to death as traitors to the Soviet state.

"As a historian, and as a father, I wanted to get to the truth. An easy word, but a difficult commodity. So many people have an interest in changing it, or suppressing it. I tried to find veterans of the 19th Regiment who'd been there the next day, when our forces arrived. Perhaps they heard something which hadn't got into the papers. Most veterans, as I'm sure you know, don't want to talk about their wartime experiences. In the Patarei Prison I found a man who'd deserted from the Red Army after witnessing the events at Hapsaküla. A junior officer, he'd been sickened by the brutality, and fled as soon as he could, and gave himself up to our forces. His arrest was recorded in the official war records kept in the National Archives, and I traced him to the prison. He was one of the last to leave the village; he hoped this would give him a better chance of escaping without running into other units. And he knew nothing of the six young people. The affair was becoming more puzzling."

"May I ask why he was in prison?"

"He'd been jailed for being there at the massacre, and not stopping it. Had he tried to stop it, I suspect he'd have been shot as an 'enemy of the people.' But it made people here feel good to put someone in prison for involvement in the Hapsaküla atrocity. He had to be kept in solitary confinement, to protect him from the other prisoners. I went back to speak to him a few weeks later, and found he'd been released. They had no record of where he went.

"I continued to seek out veterans of the 19th Regiment, and spoke to perhaps a dozen. A pattern soon emerged: when I mentioned Hapsaküla, they described the Red atrocity in the briefest of terms, but claimed they'd not been there. Eventually one man admitted they'd been ordered never to speak of it in detail. He himself was willing to talk, but knew nothing of the six young people. However, he supplied the names of others he knew, who'd reached the village before he had. And with these new names, I went to work again. And only three years ago I found the man I needed.

"In fact, it was Ludmilla who found him. She was working in the hospital here in Tartu, when a man was brought in from a village near Lake Peipus. He'd been injured by a threshing machine he'd been trying to fix.

He'd been holding part of the machine steady with his foot, and the upshot was, the foot was ripped off. He'd already lost a lot of blood by the time he got to the hospital, but they did what they could. Unfortunately the wound became septic, and soon the poison spread throughout his body. He asked for a priest and said he had something to confess. But our Lutheran pastors don't do confession and absolution. They leave it all between you and God. Our man wanted a real person to hear his confession and grant him some sort of absolution. Ludmilla called me."

He glanced over at his wife, who nodded. "He needed only an ear to pour his sins into," she said, "I called Anton, just in case it was about the war."

Professor Strelkov took a folded piece of paper from the inside pocket of his jacket. "I carry this with me," he said, "to keep me focused on my task. It is the confession I wrote down as he gave it. I told him that putting it into writing would draw part of the guilt out of him and lock it into the paper. Whether he believed me, or he didn't care, I don't know. I'll read it out to you."

My name is Sulev Koppelmann. I was a soldier of the 19th regiment. I was with one of the first groups who entered Hapsaküla. This was in January 1919, I don't remember the date. I tried to forget everything about it, but it never leaves me. And this poison in my body is punishment for my sins of that day. I was with Sergeant Kirik and five others. Lieutenant-colonel Madrus was somewhere behind us, with more men. As we rode into the place, the silence told us something terrible had taken place. Soon we saw it all. The open pits full of corpses of old men and children, and the women, crucified. Not on

*crosses, like you get in bible pictures, but nailed to the
sides of wooden barns with their arms spread out, or onto
fence posts or gates. It was utterly bestial. None of us
were prepared for such obscenity. I was sick more than
once. And then the fury grew in us, the need to kill those
who had done this deed, to inflict upon them the pain and
terror they had created here.*

*As we rode on out of the village to check for stragglers
of the Red horde, we came across six people all of
military age, four men and two women, hiding in a
sheepfold. When we challenged them, they answered in
Russian. That was enough: we had caught some of the
Reds. It was known that even women fought in their army.
And what kind of women would take up arms to kill. We
escorted them back to the village, and put them in the first
house we came to, and Sergeant Kirik sent someone to
inform the lieutenant-colonel. Colonel Renner hadn't yet
reached the village at that point.*

*Lieutenant-Colonel Madrus came back with our man.
He was shaking with rage. His eyes were wild. It was
clear to us he'd been very badly affected by what he'd
seen.*

'You've caught some of those bastards?' he says.

'Yes, sir' says Kirik.

'Did they confess?' says Madrus.

*'They only speak Russian,' says Kirik, 'None of us
speaks enough to know what they're saying.'*

*'I'll speak to them,' says Madrus. He'd been in the
Russian army before the war.*

*We're in the main room of the house. He starts by asking
their names and units. I know that because they say them
clearly, one after the other. At least the names, that is.
Then he's shouting at them, I think he wants to know what*

unit they belong to. 'Ia student' and the others say 'Da, da, studenti,' or something like that.

'The bastards are pretending to be students,' screams Madrus. 'Get their fucking clothes off, and we show them what atrocity really means.'

And we're caught up in the rage too. Soon we've got them all naked. The women are weeping and the men are still shouting, 'Mi studenti. Ne soldati.'

'Fucking liars! Red scum!' shouts Madrus. He pulls out his sabre and slashes one of the men right across the chest. We all jump back. And then he swings the thing again and slashes through his neck. There's blood everywhere, and the man falls down. Madrus hacks the head right off with his sabre. 'Torture the bastards,' he screams, 'Let me hear their pain.'

'What about the women, sir?' asks Kirik, winking.

'These scum are not here for your enjoyment,' says Madrus, 'They are all Red soldiers. Make them feel pain they've never felt before. Use your bayonets. Small cuts, slices of skin cut off. Fingers, toes, whatever appendages you can find. Punish them!'

And we did. They suffered all right. In just a few minutes two more of the men were dead, they'd lost so much blood. It was everywhere, and the stink of it was filling the room. Madrus stabbed the fourth man to death, then hacked his head off. So now there are two heads rolling round the floor.

Then Madrus says, 'All right, that's enough. Finish off the women.' Kirik finishes off the two women with his bayonet. Stabs one, and cuts the other's throat. None of the rest of us could do it. But Kirik were a real sadist, I think.

'Get cleaned up. We should get out of here,' says

Madrus. Now the rage is wearing off him. 'We'd better say the Reds did this. Remember that. We just found them like this. Now, once you've had a wash, get out and look shocked.'

By the time we'd washed some of the blood off, and got out the house, Colonel Renner and the rest of the men had just come in. They'd left their horses, and were walking round, clearly shocked by what they were seeing. So we just drifted in amongst them. It was a while before Colonel Renner ordered the houses to be searched. And since the one where the bodies were was near the edge of the village, it took even longer to come across them. Naturally we rushed to see what had been discovered, and were as angry as the rest. It was presumed these were also villagers.

We were feeling pretty ashamed of ourselves by now. After all, we allowed ourselves to be as bad as the Reds, if not worse. But that wasn't the end of it. Colonel Renner soon realised something wasn't quite right. For a start, one of his staff officers noticed that the six bodies weren't as cold as they should be. He called in the regimental MO, who spent ages in the house examining them. Then it was also obvious that Lieutenant-Colonel Madrus wasn't his usual self. He was very jumpy now, snapping at everybody, and taking frequent nips from his hip flask. Kirik meanwhile told us all to deny everything, and say the Reds must just have left when we arrived.

Next thing was we were all taken to the temporary regimental HQ, a manor house near the village, and put in separate rooms. Then each of us was interrogated by the colonel and two officers. Colonel Renner didn't mess about, I'll say that for him. 'All right, laddie,' he began, and I guess he said the same thing to each of us,

'Lieutenant-Colonel Madrus has told us everything, so if you give me any bullshit I'll have you taken out and shot immediately. I know you did for those people in the house, so just give me your version of what happened. I've got better things to do with my time than fiddle about with this – we've an army of demons out there to beat – so don't waste my time, or I'll be very annoyed.'

What could you do in the face of that? I coughed up right away, told him everything, just the way it all happened. I don't know whether the others did too, I never ever saw them again. First I had to sign a confession. Then the colonel told me I must never, ever, mention this event again. If I did, my confession would be in all the newspapers, and I'd stand trial for war crimes. We weren't going to be shot, which, he added, was what we all deserved, because it would be bad for morale. But we were all transferred to other units in different parts of the country, and from the reception we got, I guess they'd been told we were cowards or thieves. I was never put in the advance guard again, so I survived the war. I never heard what happened to any of the others, barring Madrus. In a few weeks I heard he was in Supplies Division, and people said he was doing a good job there.

That's all I have to say now. Can I be forgiven?

"If I'd been a truly good man, chief inspector," said Professor Strelkov, "I'd have taken the priestly role and offered him absolution. But I couldn't bring myself to that, not after what he'd done. I told him he'd burn in Hell for all eternity, and left him to die."

49

There was silence in the room, so that the ticking of the grandfather clock in the corner of the room seemed to grow louder and louder until each tick was the crack of a rifle.

Hallmets broke the silence. "Thank you, professor, things are becoming clearer now. Hapsaküla is why Madrus and Kirik had to die."

It was the professor's wife who responded. "We talked it over, Anton and I. We had discovered the fate of Nicolai and Ilsa. Now we decided they must have justice. Alexei had just completed his four years at the university, and the classics department were expecting him to go on to his doctorate. We explained to him what we were thinking of, and made it clear that he was not to be involved. Anton had already arranged for him to study for a doctorate in Utrecht, at the other end of Europe, so that he would not be implicated in anything we might do. He refused. 'Nicolai and Ilsa are my blood too,' he said, 'I must share in the righting of things.' We should have expected it, after all that study of ancient Greek tragedy. He was like Orestes set to punish the killers of his father."

"So now the direction of my research was different," added the professor. "It was to track down and deal with Madrus and Kirik. Finding them was in fact easy. The general, as he now was, was a public figure, who lived in a castle, and Kirik his faithful creature, always lurking behind him somewhere at his public appearances."

"Excuse me a moment, professor, but why did Alexei seek work with a lawyer in Pärnu under an assumed name?"

"That was his idea. To build up a false identity, so that if he could get close to Madrus or Kirik, he could not be connected to me. It was very clever, don't you think, using first one false name, and then another, so that he'd be two steps removed from his real self. His skills as a forger were also a revelation to me. He confessed that he'd often at lectures signed in for his absent friends. But let me be clear about this, chief inspector. Yes, Ludmilla and I planned to kill Madrus and Kirik. And Alexei knew that. But he was not to be directly involved in the deaths, we made that clear to him. And he accepted that we had the prior claim, as the avengers of our children. His role was purely to obtain information and assist in setting things up. And he stuck to that, I assure you.

"Here's how it worked. I happened to meet Rist the publisher at a conference. I suggested to him that General Madrus's memoirs would be worth publishing, especially his account of his war experiences. Rist took the bait and approached the general, whose vanity would not permit him to refuse. I guessed from his speeches that the stuff he'd write would be dull as ditchwater, but I didn't realise just how awful it would be. Alexei showed me some of his stuff later. Anyway, I'd told Rist that Madrus would probably need a secretary to get the best out of him, and that I knew a few former students who could do the job. It worked out even better than planned. Rist persuaded Madrus to take on some secretarial help, but the general, being rather mean, was only willing to offer two days a week, with a smaller payment for typing up at home. That served to dissuade most potential applicants, and Alexei's good presentation, and the references he'd prepared, got him the job. Now we had someone on the inside, who could report on the general's habits, and his staff. Which included Raud Kirik. We were in no rush, and allowed time to pass, while Alexei proved himself essential to the general's literary efforts.

"By the middle of November we were ready to act. I arranged to visit the general on the afternoon of the 25th. As I explained on your previous visit, I said I was writing a book about the Supplies Division, and the wonderful work they did keeping the army fed, clothed and armed. So he spent the afternoon reminiscing about his work in that area. I have to confess, I did learn some things from talking with him. At the end I said I'd be very keen to talk with him again, and naturally he agreed. Who wouldn't like to spend an afternoon spouting to a flattering admirer, especially if he's a professor? That was the Monday. On the Thursday, that would have been the 28th, I phoned him up and said that I'd come across some information about an occurrence at a village called Hapsaküla. The information was rather sensitive, and included reference to himself, so I proposed coming over late that evening for a private chat about it. I suggested he should not tell his staff, and he readily agreed. After all, he didn't know what I might have found out."

The professor smiled. "I drove over there with Ludmilla. Thankfully the snow hadn't started, and it was nice and dark. We got there about half past ten. I parked the car just outside the courtyard wall, where it wouldn't be visible to anyone in the house. Then I tiptoed to the door and knocked. He let me in himself and ushered me into his study, offered me an armchair to sit in. He said he'd gone up to his bedroom at his usual time, and tiptoed down again later, once his maid had gone to bed. Alexei had learned from her that she took an elixir at bedtime, so we knew her sleep would be sound. I turned down the

ALLAN MARTIN

offer of a brandy. When he sat down and asked me what it
was I wanted to talk about, I simply told him I knew about
Hapsaküla, that he'd murdered six students who were
simply trying to escape from Russia to Estonia. He said
this was utter nonsense, and surely I didn't believe it. I
said my evidence was irrefutable, and I was going to
publish it. At that point he jumped to his feet. 'I've had
enough of this,' he snarled, 'You wouldn't dare. I have
very powerful friends. You'll soon be out of a job,
professor.'

"'I already am,' I said, 'But your pals can't save you
from your fate. This is for my children, whom you killed.'

"At that point he stopped and stared at me. Then he
noticed the gun, which I'd taken from my briefcase. I'd
bought it from a veteran who seemed to have got hold of a
whole cache of German weapons during the war and
made a nice living selling them on the black market. I
can't remember his name, I'm afraid. Now I could see
Madrus rewinding the film in his mind, of those moments
in that house. 'I'm sorry,' was all he said. He knew what
was going to happen next. Perhaps he too had been living
with Hapsaküla in his head since that day.

"I must admit, it was a good shot. Ludmilla had
explained to me exactly where to aim for, and I was spot
on. I had no desire to make him suffer, to torture him as
he had done our children, only to put an end to him. He
fell to the floor without a sound. I went out to the car and
Ludmilla came in, and confirmed he was dead. There was
a little blood on the polished wood floor, but Ludmilla
had brought a damp cloth and wiped it up. We got his coat
on him and dragged him out into the courtyard. We knew
to keep to one side, as Alexei had told us, so we'd not be
visible from the outbuildings. Ludmilla fetched his sabre

from his study, and she managed to push it through the wound made by the bullet. She didn't study surgery for nothing. He'd used a sabre on our son, so it was symbolic. But also a warning, to Kirik. He would understand that whoever killed Madrus would come for him too. We left him there, got back to the car, and drove home. The snow came on half way back, and it was a hellish drive after that, but we made it.

"Now we had to deal with Kirik. Alexei had found out about his family from the general, and it seemed to us his best move would be to hide out at the farm. He could hardly go to the police and say his life was in danger because he'd tortured six people to death and got away with it. I sent him there a copy of *Macbeth* with a threatening note in it, just to keep the pressure up."

"An apt choice," said Hallmets quietly, "The murderer who cannot escape his fate."

"Quite so. We knew we couldn't get him at the farm, so we had to move him on to a more exposed location. Alexei had also discovered that the general had an apartment in Tallinn. On a couple of occasions he'd met up with Madrus there to talk about the book, while he was in the capital on official business. On one of these occasions they'd discussed a couple of chapters over lunch at a restaurant, then went back to the flat so that Alexei could note the changes on the manuscript. Madrus told him to do it while he had his afternoon nap, and he'd have another look at it when he woke up. Alexei knew exactly how long Madrus would sleep, and that he was a deep sleeper too. So he took the keys to the apartment, went to a locksmith, and had them copied. He'd even forged a note from Madrus authorising the copy.

"Now we had to lure Kirik to the flat. I sent him another

anonymous letter on Wednesday, that would be the 5th, again to the farm. 'We know you're there, Raud. We're coming to get you,' was all it said. But it did the job. We knew from Alexei that Kirik had keys for the flat, and we took the chance he'd go there. That was the point where we could have lost him, but we were lucky. Alexei was watching the flat, and saw Kirik arrive late on Thursday night, after the janitor would have gone off duty. Then he phoned us to let us know. Early next morning we drove up to Tallinn, and parked near the harbour, where the car wouldn't be noticed. We'd planned to get here by six, but the roads were bad, with ice and frozen snow, so we didn't arrive till quarter to seven. Alexei gave us the keys, and Ludmilla and I went in – the janitor wasn't at his desk yet – and quietly entered the apartment. Kirik was still snoring in bed. He had a rude awakening, when I pulled the bedclothes off and put the Luger to his head. He was petrified. He was sleeping in his underclothes, so I ordered him through to the living-room, and Ludmilla tied him to the chair. 'I don't understand,' he kept saying, 'What have I done?' 'Remember Hapsaküla,' I said. 'It was Madrus,' he whined, 'He made us do it. He was the commander. We just followed his orders.' Then he began to blubber. It was pathetic."

There was a pause, and then *Proua* Strelkova spoke. "I didn't want to hear any more from him. I had the bayonet with me, in a bag. Anton had got it in a junk shop, and I'd sharpened it, so that it was almost as good as a scalpel. I just pulled it out of the bag and stabbed him. One push, straight into the heart, and he was dead. We left him there, and got out. Alexei knew the janitor was there from seven, so he'd arranged to phone him at quarter past and divert him into the flat upstairs. So we waited till we heard the footsteps upstairs, then let ourselves out, tiptoed downstairs, and got to the street."

"We went straight back to the car, where we met Alexei, and then drove home," added the professor. "And that's it, chief inspector. That's exactly what happened. That's all we have to tell. And just to make it completely clear, I, Anton Strelkov, admit to the killing of Arnold Madrus." He glanced at his wife.

"And I, Ludmilla Strelkova, admit to the killing of Raud Kirik."

The only sound in the room, apart from the ticking of the clock, was that of Larsson and Kadakas writing down the final confessions.

50

Hallmets coughed. "Thank you for your testimony. I have to give you this warning. It is not unknown for family members to confess to crimes in the hope of letting their loved ones go free. We will therefore need evidence to support your accounts. It is also absolutely vital that we interview your son. You must be aware that, until we speak to him, he must remain a suspect for both murders."

"I can assure you that we have described exactly what happened. We also anticipated that you would wish to hear from Alexei. Ludmilla, dear, I think you should call him in." *Proua* Strelkova nodded, got up and left the room.

"You mean he's been here all the time?" said Larsson.

The professor pointed to the window, its heavy curtains closed. "It's dark out there now, but were it daytime you'd be able to see a little wooden house near the bottom of the garden. I suppose in days gone by a gardener lived there. That's where Alexei has been lying low. Not idly, I'm glad to say. He's been working on his translation of *The Libation Bearers*. He wants to do the complete *Oresteia* of Aeschylus, all three parts. It will be the most up-to-date translation into Estonian. In fact, there have been very few others."

The door opened, and *Proua* Strelkova came in, followed by Alexei Strelkov. Once again, Hallmets was struck by how well Anna had captured not just his appearance, but his nature. He stood up to meet him, and they shook hands.

"I'm Alexei Strelkov. You must be Chief Inspector Hallmets. I understand you want to interview me."

"That's correct, Alexei. But it will have to be done without your parents being present. I wonder if you could go to the living-room, and Sergeant Larsson and Officer Kadakas will do the interview. The simplest thing would be for you to tell the story right from the beginning, and give as much detail as you can. Thank you for coming forward voluntarily. That will be noted."

His mother was about to protest, but Professor Strelkov put his hand on her arm, and her words remained unsaid. "This is the way they have to do it," he said to her, "We can't be seen to influence what he says. Even a look could be construed as interference."

"Don't worry, Mum," said Alexei. "We've nothing to hide now." He left the room, followed by Larsson and Kadakas. A few moments later Hallmets heard the living-room door firmly close.

"Would you like some more coffee, chief inspector?" said the professor, "And perhaps a piece of my wife's cherry and almond cake. She only baked it yesterday."

"Thank you, that would be very nice," replied Hallmets. *Proua* Strelkova got up and turned to the door.

"And remember, dear," said her husband, "No listening at the living-room door. That too could be construed as interference."

"So what happens now?" he asked Hallmets, once his wife had gone.

"In the normal course of events, I would place you and your wife under arrest for murder. If your son's account fits in with yours, I would arrest him too, as an accessory to murder. I would then call the police station here, and have a car take you to the detention cells. I would then have to discuss the case with the local examining magistrate, and he would decide what to do next. He may decide, in view of the evidence, and your confessions, to reduce the charge to one of culpable homicide, but would probably include all three of you in that charge. Lawyers would be called in for yourselves, we would assemble our evidence, and a trial date would be set, probably in the spring. But, be assured, from what I've heard today, which is backed up by much of the evidence we already have, none of you would hang. However, you would certainly get jail terms, probably around five years."

The professor sighed. "That's better than I expected. It's just a pity for Alexei. Years of his life wasted. When I first met you, it seems so long ago now, and yet it was only last Wednesday, I knew it would come to this, that you wouldn't give up, and that you weren't stupid. You're an educated man, aren't you?"

"I went to the university here, before the war. I was a teacher for a few years. Then it all changed. But let me come back to what I just said. That's what would happen in the normal course of events. But we don't live in normal times. General Madrus's death is very sensitive politically, and that's why my order to investigate it came directly from the Ministry of the Interior. I will have to consult the Ministry before taking any further steps."

"Ah. So they might decide simply to give the three of us an OGPU farewell. A bullet in the back of the neck. And keep the whole thing quiet."

"That will not happen. You have my word on that."

"Thank you, chief inspector. I respect that. Let me tell you, off the record, of another little surprise I have planned. The original of the witness deposition about Hapsaküla is with a lawyer, whom I shall not name. If I die suddenly, photographs of that deposition will be sent to newspapers in Finland, Sweden, Belgium, France and even Britain. I can see the *Times* of London putting the whole thing on the front page."

There was knock at the door, and Hallmets got up and opened it. *Proua* Strelkova came in with the coffee and cake. For a while they sipped and ate in silence. The coffee was good, the cake delicious. They could hear a distant muttering of voices from the next room.

Then the door was opened, and Larsson popped her head in. "Could I have a word with you, sir? Perhaps in the kitchen."

"Of course. *Härra* and *Proua* Strelkov, perhaps you could remain here for the moment."

He left and shut the door gently behind him, then turned to the left to enter the spacious and well-appointed kitchen. He shut the door behind him.

"OK, Eva, what have we got?"

"His story checks out with what the others say. It doesn't sound as if they cooked it up to keep him off a murder charge. He also seems on the level to me. It was clearly the parents who cooked up the whole plot. I also feel it's actually done Alexei good to get it off his chest. He became more relaxed as the interview proceeded."

"Right. I'm not going to charge them with anything yet. If I do that, it sets off the whole legal engine. And I need to talk to Reinart to find out what the options are. What I'll do now is place all three of them under precautionary house arrest."

"I've not heard of that."

"I just made it up. But they'll go for it because it's better than being in the detention cells at the police station. Then we'll have to get their statements on paper and signed. I don't want to bring in the local police yet, so we'll have to find someone else to do that. However, I need to call

Reinart first. In the meantime, let's keep Alexei and the parents apart till we've got their statements on paper."

He went back to the study, but didn't sit down. The Strelkovs looked up expectantly. *"Härra* and *Proua* Strelkov, I've discussed your son's testimony with Sergeant Larsson, and we are now able to proceed. I am therefore placing all three of you under precautionary house arrest. You will not yet be charged with any crime, but you must remain within this house, and be supervised by Special Crimes Unit personnel, until further notice."

"It's a kind of limbo, isn't it?" said the professor. "Until the powers-that-be decide what to do with us."

"That's one way of looking at it. Another is that it's better than being in jail. The only disadvantage is that it means you can't contact anybody. Not even a lawyer. Sergeant Larsson and Officer Kadakas will stay here to make sure you observe these rules. For the moment you must not communicate with your son either. Don't worry, that's only until we can get written statements from all three of you. After that you can mix freely. I'm hoping we can get the statements taken as soon as possible. Do you accept these terms?"

The professor looked to his wife, who nodded. "Yes, we do. As you say, being at home is better than being in prison."

"Thank you. Sergeant Larsson will remain with you here while I explain the situation to Alexei. After that, may I use your telephone?"

"Of course, chief inspector. It's in the hallway."

Hallmets informed Alexei of the house arrest, to which he readily agreed, asked Kadakas to stay with him, and headed for the telephone. He phoned Colonel Reinart's secure number.

"Well, Hallmets, where are we?"

"I can tell you with certainty that General Madrus was killed by Emeritus Professor Strelkov, formerly of the History Department at Tartu University."

"Are you joking? He was killed by some old professor. With a grudge over his interpretation of history, no doubt?"

"Yes, in a way you're right. General Madrus tortured and murdered two of the professor's children, at a place called Hapsaküla in January 1919."

"This is not sounding good, Hallmets, you'd better tell me the whole story."

Twenty minutes later, the story had been told.

"This is going to need some sorting out," said the colonel, "You haven't charged them yet?"

"No. I've placed all three under precautionary house arrest."

"Precautionary house arrest. I like it. That's good."

"And I'm going to take statements from them. So we have their confessions on paper and signed. I won't use the police typists. I think I can get one from the university."

"That sounds acceptable."

"Just one more thing, colonel. I have personally promised all three that they will not be subject to arrest and summary execution by any government agency. And I will stand by that promise."

"All right, I know you well enough, chief inspector. But you should also know that that's not our style here. And I've no intention of changing it."

"Thank you. One more thing. If anything sudden should happen to the professor, he has arranged for the evidence he has about Hapsaküla to be sent to the foreign press. It's just his insurance, that's all. Naturally, he wouldn't give me any more detail."

"These professors aren't stupid, are they? I guess that's why they get the job. Right. I need to talk to the minister about this now. I'll get back to you as soon as I can, at that   number."

51

Hallmets looked at his watch. Nearly five o'clock. He called Kirsti and told her he'd probably be staying in Tartu that night, and promised to call again once he knew what he was doing. Then he phoned Tallinn Police Headquarters, and asked for Inspector Lesser. He brought Lesser up to date with the solution to the case.

"That's great news, chief," commented Lesser, "We'll all have to have a drink when you get back. A couple of loose ends, by the way. Einar Sepp has confirmed the bullet we suspect killed Madrus was a 7.65 by 21 mm Parabellum, probably from a Luger pistol."

"That fits with what we know. Go on."

"And the post-mortem on Artur Simm. Scratches on his body and tears in his clothing show he was pushed through the window, rather than climbing out himself. And fingerprints the forensics people found in Kallas's apartment match with our late Finnish visitors, Antti and Matti. Inspector Sõnn sends his thanks for giving him the background there."

Hallmets' next call was to the university reception desk. He asked to be put through to the Classics department, and asked Anneli if there was an external line to the department, rather than one passing through the university reception. She gave him a number, and he called again.

Twenty minutes later a taxi drew up at the house, and the doorbell rang.

Hallmets answered it. "Ah. Come on in, Anneli. You've brought the portable typewriter. And plenty of paper, I hope. Remember to keep a note of what the taxi cost. You'll be able to claim that back, as well as the hourly rate, with 50% extra for working at night."

"Thank you for asking me, chief inspector," said Anneli, taking her coat off. "I can assure you I'll do a good job. And will not say a word to anyone. Tell me please, is Alexei here? You only mentioned his parents."

"He's in the living-room. You can say hello, but that's all." Hallmets ushered her into the living-room. Alexei gaped at her. He didn't seem to know what to say.

"Hello, Alexei," said Anneli. "It's nice to see you again."

All three Strelkovs were told to sit in the living-room. One at a time, each one was taken through to the study to give their statement. Sergeant Larsson supervised this operation, listening, asking questions, and on occasion directing Anneli what she should type. *Proua* Strelkova asked to be first, so that afterwards she could start cooking the evening meal. "I'm assuming there are going to be seven round the table. Quite a dinner party." Hallmets noted that she was beginning to relax too.

At ten to seven, Colonel Reinart phoned back. "Sorry to take so long. I finally managed to get hold of *Härra* Eenpalu, and get some direction on this business. He has the president's ear, I'm told, so we can take it this will have approval from the very top. He's happy with the house arrest. And it's good to have the statements. However, under no circumstances are you to charge them with anything. If the whole story comes out, it would be political dynamite. The policy at the moment is that nothing rocks the boat."

"So it all gets brushed under the carpet?"

"That's it in one. I'm sure in later years people will call

this period 'The Era of Silence.' But believe me, Hallmets, silence is better than labour camps and shots in the head at midnight. So here's the deal."

The statements were completed by eight o'clock. *Proua* Strelkova, now much more relaxed – Hallmets suspected assistance from a bottle of sherry in the kitchen cupboard – had prepared bedrooms for Larsson and Kadakas. She also insisted that Hallmets stay the night too. Smelling the odours of cooking from the kitchen, he could hardly refuse. Two hours in a freezing train followed by another train out to Nõmme was not an attractive alternative. He phoned Kirsti and let her know what was happening. She wasn't surprised, and was relieved that he would have a good meal and a warm bed, and a more relaxed journey back the following morning.

At quarter past, all seven of them sat round the table. Anneli had suggested she go once the statements had been done, but both Alexei and his mother had insisted she stay for dinner. The meal was excellent: roast pork and potatoes with cabbage sautéed with smoked paprika, and then a cheesecake topped with sharp-tasting orange sea buckthorn berries. And a delicate Riesling from the foothills of the Tatra Mountains in the south of Poland. The atmosphere at the meal was amiable, as if some old friends were meeting together again. Even first names were permitted to be used.

As they sipped their coffee, Hallmets cleared his throat. "May I thank our hosts Anton and Ludmilla for a most excellent meal. Each item will reported to my wife, so that she can replicate it. But now I have something important to say, before we have anything more to drink."

The amiable atmosphere evaporated, to be replaced by

the silence of apprehension.

"As you know, this case is a very sensitive one, involving the death of someone who was seen as having made a significant contribution to the War of Independence. I was asked to investigate it directly by the Ministry of the Interior. Earlier this evening I asked for guidance from the ministry as to how to proceed. Just before this meal I received an answer. It comes directly from the minister, *Härra* Eenpalu, himself. There are three main points. First, no charges will be laid against Anton, Ludmilla or Alexei Strelkov, and no further penal or other restrictive measures will be taken against them." He paused to let this sink in.

"That's fantastic!" said Alexei, smiling at his parents, and as if unconsciously, his hand gripped Anneli's, who was sitting next to him.

"I'm so happy for you, all of you," said Anneli, beaming.

Larsson and Kadakas tried to look impassive, but Hallmets could tell they were relieved.

Professor Strelkov smiled, "That's a relief. But let's hear the rest. There's bound to be a catch. That was probably the best bit."

His wife rested her hand on his arm. "Whatever it is," she said, "we can be together."

"You're right, of course," said Hallmets, "There are conditions. The second point is that you must sign an agreement never to speak of the events at Hapsaküla or the deaths of General Madrus and Raud Kirik again. If you do so, the statements you have made will be used to bring all three of you to trial for murder."

"They want Hapsaküla buried for ever," said the professor. "To rewrite history, and make Madrus a hero.

Well, I can't accept ..."

"Yes. You can," interrupted Ludmilla Strelkova, very firmly. "We have brought justice for our children. That was our objective. There are plenty of other historians besides you who can stand up for historical truth, and most of them are younger than you are. I want us to enjoy the rest of our lives together, without any more of that stress. And I want Alexei to be happy knowing that his parents are happy."

"She's right, Dad," said Alexei. "It's not our battle any more. And I want to be me again now, not Oskar Kitsnik or Villem Jonsson. We should be thinking about the future now, not the past."

"That was beautifully said, Alexei," added Anneli.

The professor stared into his coffee, then looked up again. "I guess I'm outvoted then. Very well. I bow to the will of the majority. Don't anyone say this family isn't democratic. All right, chief inspector – I'll call you Jüri again when this is over – what's the third point?"

"The third point is that all three of you must leave Estonia, and not come back until you are given specific permission. Your departure must take place within the next four weeks, and must appear to be a voluntary and natural decision."

Again Hallmets felt the professor was about to explode. How dare he be asked to leave his home and the university which was his natural habitat, even after retirement? They all waited for him to speak.

But he remained silent. Then he smiled. "Yes, of course, I can see where they're coming from. They just want us out of sight for the moment. Maybe even for ever." He cleared his throat. "There are no restrictions on where we can go?"

"None at all," answered Hallmets, "As to your immediate destination, that is. They just want you out of here within a month. I would avoid Finland and Latvia. People here might think you were just waiting for a chance to sneak back. I was told the minister would prefer you ultimately – within a few months, that is – to settle somewhere outwith Europe."

"It would have to be a place with a good university," said *Proua* Strelkova, "Alexei must study for his doctorate. There must be a good Classics department."

"There are good universities in Canada, I've heard," said Alexei tentatively, "McGill – that's in Montreal – and McMaster ..."

"Yes," said his father, "I know of it. And I believe the University of Toronto has a good reputation too."

"There's a small Estonian community in Toronto, isn't there?" said his mother.

"It's an awfully long way from here," whispered Anneli. Hallmets could see she was close to tears.

"But aren't you coming too, Anneli?" said Alexei. "Come on, I don't want to lose you again. And I'm not leaving you here in Tartu, at the mercy of every Casanova who creeps into the Classics department office." He raised her hand to his mouth and kissed it.

"I think our drinks need a top-up," said *Proua* Strelkova.

Fifteen minutes later Professor Strelkov stood up and rapped his knuckles on the table. "Ladies and gentlemen. I propose a toast to our friends from the Special Crimes Unit. To Jüri, Eva, Ants, and your colleagues back in Tallinn too. I now understand why you are regarded as the sharpest of Estonia's detectives. You've actually made it possible for us to move on with our lives. If you hadn't found us, we'd have spent the rest of our days looking over our shoulders and agonising about the past. As it is, we can now put Hapsaküla behind us. We'll never forget Nicolai and Ilsa, and their photographs will always be on the mantelpiece. We will always mourn them. And we will never forget that we took the lives of two men. Their blood will always be on our hands.

"Canada will be, I'm sure, a good home for us. Ludmilla's medical skills will find a place, and Alexei has a great future to look forward to, in a country where there's plenty of opportunity, and no dictator telling you what to think or say. Er, you didn't hear me say that, Jüri. Seriously though, I fear for the future of Europe. One day there's going to be another war, and I worry about our poor Estonia, the country that embraced us when we came here. She is like a fawn seeking to live peacefully in a forest where already the wolves are howling. We will watch her from a distance. And even if the worst happens, we will not forget her. She has made us welcome, and has been a good home to us. In fact, before we leave I think we should take up the president's offer of a more Estonian name, as a final gift from Estonia.

"Finally, I've now got something to look forward to myself. OK, I won't be able to do any more research on the Independence War. But I'm sure there are a lot of people out there who need to be informed about the Baltic states in the twentieth century. I can already feel a new book coming on. *Terviseks*!"

And they all raised their glasses.

Acknowledgements

Since our first visit to Estonia, we've grown to love the country, and I've even attempted to learn the language (not completely successfully!). So what better place to set a crime series. My wife Vivien is my First Reader and honest critic, and that makes a big difference. Thanks also to others who have read part or all of the book, and Estonian friends, especially Ülle Campbell and Maarika Teral, for valuable comments, and to Richard Foreman of Sharpe Books for deciding that books set in 1930s Estonia are worth publishing.

Historical Note

I've tried to set the story in an accurate historical background. The only real historical figures who appear, very briefly, in the book are Artur Sirk, one-time leader of the Vaps Movement, and Kaarel Eenpalu, Minister of the Interior in 1935. President Konstantin Päts, Jaan Tõnisson, and Generals Laidoner, Põdder and Larka, are real historical figures who are mentioned in the story. All other characters taking part in the action, including General Madrus, are entirely fictitious. I have visited the locations where the action takes place, and recreated Estonia in the 1930s as accurately as possible. However, I apologise for any inaccuracies or misinterpretations, which are entirely my own.

A Little Bit of Estonian

Estonian is similar to Finnish, and completely unlike the Romance or Germanic languages that have shaped English. When you see any Estonian words in the text – names of people, streets, towns, etc. – remember that every letter is pronounced. Even two vowels together are sounded separately. And unless you want to learn Estonian, don't worry about the accents.

Here are some useful words, which appear from time to time in the text. Any Estonian spoken by characters in the story is shown in italics. There isn't very much.

Tere! – Hello!
Härra – Mr.
Proua – Mrs., or, as in German, used to address any woman older than her mid-twenties.
Preili – Miss, or used to address any young woman.
Terviseks! – Cheers!
Ülemkomissar – Chief Inspector
Komissar – Inspector
Plats – Place, Square
Pealinna Uudised – Capital City News

A Brief Overview of Estonian History

Although the Estonians have been settled at the eastern end of the Baltic Sea since at least the beginning of our era, Estonia only became an independent state in 1918. Up to the late twelfth century the tribes lived more-or-less undisturbed. But at the beginning of the thirteenth century foreign domination arrived, in the shape of the Knights of the Sword, a crusading order recruited mainly in Germany. Under the guise of bringing Christianity to pagans, the knights subjugated the tribes and seized their lands. The Germanic landowning class, known as Baltic Germans, remained in place for the next 700 years.

After a serious defeat in 1236, the Knights of the Sword were incorporated into the larger and more powerful Teutonic Order. The Estonian lands were divided into a patchwork of territories, owing allegiance to the Order, the Bishop of Ösel (on the island of Saaremaa) or the Bishop of Dorpat (Tartu), and this situation persisted up to the Reformation, when the area became Lutheran, and the Teutonic Order transformed itself into the Duchy of Prussia. Ruins of several of the castles of the Teutonic Knights can still be seen, including the impressive remains at Viljandi and Põltsamaa. The ruins of the mediaeval cathedral of Tartu can also still be viewed.

A major upheaval came in the late 1500s, when Ivan the Terrible, Tsar of Russia, attempted to incorporate the eastern Baltic shores into his empire. A bloody war followed, as other powers in the area invaded the Estonian lands to resist the Russian advance westwards. Ultimately the Swedes emerged supreme in the early 1600s, and their rule in Estonia was regarded as "the good old Swedish time." Although the Baltic Germans, now swearing allegiance to the King of Sweden, retained their lands, their powers were constrained by the Swedish authorities, and peasants gained rights they were not to regain until the 19th century. During this period the University of Tartu was founded in 1632 by King Gustavus Adolphus.

By the early 18th century Swedish power was waning,

and the Russia of Peter the Great on the move, and in the Great Northern War (1700-1720) Russian armies gained control of Estonia (as well as Latvia and Lithuania), and the Baltic states were incorporated into the Russian Empire. The Baltic German landowners once again retained their lands and now swore fealty to the Russian Tsar. They weren't unhappy about this, as the protection of peasants' rights given by the Swedes was swept away, and they could treat the indigenous people as their slaves once again.

The city of Tallinn had been founded by the Danes, during a short-lived involvement in Estonia's history in the twelfth century, hence the name (from Taana Linn = "Danish town"). They built a castle on the hilltop site of a native fort, and the town grew at the foot of the hill. A cathedral was built on the hill, hence its name Toompea (= "cathedral hill"), and here the governor's office was located, and the aristocracy built their town houses.

With a good harbour, Tallinn became a major port, and during the Middle Ages was a member of the Hanseatic League. Most of the merchants who established themselves there were, like the landowners, of German extraction, and the German merchants ran the town council until well into the nineteenth century. Tallinn's trade was boosted by the incorporation of Estonia into the Russian Empire, as the port was ice-free in winter, yet not too far from the capital St. Petersburg, and much traffic now passed through its harbour.

During the nineteenth century an indigenous Estonian middle class emerged, and with it came a movement for cultural emancipation, focused on the use of the Estonian language, which had survived as the language of the peasantry. This cultural movement was met with suspicion from both the Russian rulers and the German landowners. Nevertheless books were published in Estonian, dramas were performed, and a tradition of local choirs was founded, which fed into a national Song Festival held every four or five years. Tartu University, which had ceased to exist during the Great Northern War was re-established in 1802 and the fine classical building remains the University's headquarters.

Industry also grew, and the western links of German entrepreneurs enabled some large factories to develop, producing such materials as textiles and plywood for the huge Russian market. Tallinn grew as people moved from the land into the city in search of work. The port of Tallinn also continued to prosper as the winter gateway to Russia, goods being moved directly from ship to railway wagon for shipment eastward. During this period the town of Pärnu developed as a spa and seaside resort.

The First World War and its aftermath changed everything. Russian and German armies moved through the Baltic provinces. But Russia's archaic structure could not support modern warfare, and the result was mutiny and revolution in 1917. As Russia imploded into civil war, and the soldiers came home, the Baltic states saw an unexpected opportunity to free themselves. Estonia declared its independence on 24th February 1918, a few days before invading German armies arrived. But later that year Germany surrendered to its Western opponents. This marked the start of the two-year Independence War, as Estonian armies fought against the Red army on one front, trying to bring Estonia into the new Soviet Union, and a freelance German army seeking to make the Baltic states into a German duchy, supported by most of the Baltic German landowners. Finally the Estonian Army, led by General Johan Laidoner, emerged victorious, beating off a number of Red army thrusts, and defeating the German mercenaries at Võnnu in Latvia, making possible both Latvian and Estonian independence.

The new state had much to do to build its social, economic and political infrastructure. The first task was land reform, and a radical measure confiscated most of the Baltic German-owned lands and redistributed them to Estonian farmers. Estonia was transformed from a nation of landless peasants to one of small farmers. Many of the Baltic Germans left for Germany. Those who remained were left enough land for a single farm, on which they were obliged to be resident. With the loss of the huge Russian market, industry too had to readjust itself to the comparatively tiny domestic market. But Estonians are a hard-working people, and new export markets were found, as Estonian agricultural produce, butter and bacon in particular, found ready customers in Britain and Germany. Estonians had to learn how to do politics too. The new constitution was thoroughly democratic, leading to constant coalitions, with the same politicians shuffling power between them. Leading politicians during this period were Konstantin Päts and Jaan Tõnisson.

With independence, a new police force was formed. Standards of recruitment were high and there was no shortage of applicants. Consequently, Estonia's police were held in high regard within the country. The police were formed into three divisions, the uniformed police, focused on minor crime and public order, the criminal police, focused on the solution of major crime, and the political police, focused on the identification and surveillance of individuals and groups judged to be a threat to the state. The police were under the control of the

Ministry of the Interior.

Yet the country was not isolated from what was happening in the rest of Europe. The economic crash of 1929 was not good for Estonia, but gradually the country worked its way back towards prosperity. Politically there were threats from both ends of the spectrum. Estonians knew that over its Eastern border was a Soviet state eager to reclaim the provinces of the Old Russian Empire. A Soviet-sponsored coup had failed in 1924, and there was a constant sense of threat from Stalin's empire. But there was also the rise of totalitarian movements, which happened across the whole of Europe. But the accession of Hitler to power in Germany, with his claim to protect Germans everywhere, added a new source of worry. As the 1930s progressed, Estonians tried to enjoy the life of citizens of a modern European state. But the clouds were not going to go away. The Vaps Movement, founded in 1929 as an organisation to promote measures to help veterans of the Independence War, was led towards adopting some the trappings of fascism by its leader Artur Sirk.

All three Baltic states slid into dictatorship as the years passed. In Estonia, with the prospect of the Vaps Movement's candidate, General Larka, winning the April 1934 presidential election, the Acting President, Konstantin Päts, with the active support of General Laidoner, declared a state of emergency and suspended parliament. This was the beginning of the 'era of silence' as it has been called, which lasted until the Soviet occupation of Estonia in June 1940, which marked the end of Estonia's first independence period. Russian occupation only ended with the declaration of the restoration of Estonia's sovereignty on 20th August 1991.

Further Reading

The best history of Estonia easily available in English is still *Estonia and the Estonians* by Toivo U. Raun (Stanford, California, Hoover Institution Press, 2nd edition, 2001), which includes good coverage of the first independence period. For a wider view of the Baltic states, see *A Concise History of the Baltic States* by Andrejs Plakans (Cambridge, Cambridge University Press, 2011).

About the Author

Allan Martin has worked as a teacher, teacher-trainer and university lecturer, and only turned to writing fiction after taking early retirement. His first novel, *The Peat Dead*, was shortlisted for the McIlvanney Debut Prize, and he has written two further novels, *The Dead of Jura* and *The Dead of Appin*, featuring Oban-based Detective Inspector Angus Blue. *Death in Tallinn* was the first of three novels to feature Chief Inspector Jüri Hallmets; *Winter Blood* is the second. Allan and his wife live in Glasgow, and are regular visitors to Estonia and to Scotland's islands.

His website is: www.allanmartin.scot

Printed in Great Britain
by Amazon

60115877R00211